LUCID

LUCID

LUCID
The Dreamwalker

ORAINE JOHNSON

First published in Great Britain in 2025 by Gollancz
an imprint of The Orion Publishing Group Ltd
Carmelite House, 50 Victoria Embankment
London EC4Y 0DZ

An Hachette UK Company

The authorised representative in the EEA is Hachette Ireland,
8 Castlecourt Centre, Dublin 15, D15 XTP3, Ireland
(email: info@hbgi.ie)

1 3 5 7 9 10 8 6 4 2

A CIP catalogue record for this book is available
from the British Library.

ISBN (Hardback) 978 1 3996 1015 5
ISBN (Export Trade Paperback) 978 1 3996 1016 2
ISBN (eBook) 978 1 3996 1018 6
ISBN (Audio) 978 1 3996 1019 3

Typeset by Goldust Design
Printed in Great Britain by Clays Ltd, Elcograph S.p.A

www.gollancz.co.uk

I dedicate this book to my son Oshea-rain, and all the dreamers out there. May your dreams become reality, and may your reality surpass your dreams.

CHAPTER 1

3:15

This is not real. It can't be. One moment I was sitting in my seat on the train, feeling the sensation of the wheels speeding over the rails, and then in the twinkling of an eye the sky disappears. I've seen and felt this before, but it seems to be happening more frequently, like I'm trapped in a loop. Hold it together. It'll all be over soon; it's not real! Everything around me fades, the carriage evaporates and I become weightless, as if floating in water. I look down as I hover over a labyrinthine network of luminous rivers. A great gate rumbles, unfolding before me. The sounds of battle. Flashes of light, distorting my vision. Then, just like before, it appears: a terrifying shadow, thin eyes burning with malice. It sees me and reaches up to me. I feel a tightening around my throat. I struggle to breathe and then . . . then I . . .

'*You have now arrived at Birmingham New Street.*'

I wake up.

My hand squeezes the armrest, which slightly lifts from the force of the train gliding to a halt. The half-empty carriages jerk. Beads of sweat drip down the back of my neck; nerves knot my stomach accompanied by a strange burning sensation in my palm. The engine goes quiet. I'm here, I wipe the condensed window next to me and see glowing hazed lights pulsating against the dark structures of the slumbering city, blanketed by fog. We're certainly not in the PROL anymore.

I catch myself in the reflection of the window and quickly avert my eyes. It's strange and weird to explain, but lately I feel as if someone's watching me through my own eyes.

The train doors open. A gust of cold air blows into the carriage, letting in the faint sound of civilisation as passengers disembark. I get up out of my seat and hood up, wrapped for the grim Mercian weather, clutching the broken zip of my over-packed rucksack.

The last passenger from my carriage steps off the train.

I take out my thumbtack from the front pouch of my ruck-sack; the top of it is shaped like a pineapple. This helps. I don't know why but twirling the tack back and forth between my fingers and thumb, memorising each groove, comforts me. My thoughts travel back to home.

Charlotte should've understood. I wish I wasn't doing this alone, but I tried to tell her so many times. Maybe now, with me leaving like this, she'll finally understand. I need answers and I can't run from the truth anymore.

The swirling tack rhythmically slows down in my hand. Opening my eyes, placing the tack back into its resting place, I take deep breath, refocus, and exit the train.

The train station is eerily still, bar the few night security guards, railway workers, and the faint, echoing hum of a floor buffering machine polishing in the distance. The platform ticket gates are wide open, manned by an uninterested ticket guard scrolling through his phone.

'Go through,' the guard repeats, in a slow, monophonic tone, rolling his R's and dropping his tone at the end of his sentence in a deep Brummie accent. Mum lost her Brummie accent after a while, maybe because we never stayed in one place. It's a shame. I kinda like it.

Walking closer to the gate I fix my hood, pulling the red fabric further down in front of my face, noting the facial recognition CCTV cameras peering down at me like birds of prey. Relieved at avoiding interaction — the guard didn't once raise his head from his device — I pass the gate unnoticed and proceed through to the main station floor. That was simple enough and I didn't even break Rule 1: Keep your identity safe — never draw attention to yourself.

The main waiting area of the station is huge: a wide open space with frozen escalators leading up to the retail and food courts above. At the centre of the station is a gigantic thirty foot screw-faced metal statue of a raging bull. Grand Central.

A *ping!* sounds from my coat pocket. An incoming message. He must be here. Picking up the pace, I walk, looking for a place to read the message, out of sight of the prying security lenses. The open layout of this station doesn't allow for much privacy. They've even got Identification scanners on the toilets, which is really not helpful. A holographic digital advertisement stand is ahead of me; bright images project and glitch, capturing the city's most iconic landmarks. The images present a narrative of this city's inclusive culture, boasting the slogan: 'Birmingham, the Industrial City of Dreams.'

I take shelter behind the screen, pulling out a black, palm-sized phone from my coat pocket. Can't believe I've been reduced to using an illegal burner phone. No new tech, stay off the grid! Guess he wanted me to have something easily disposable, harder to trace. Anxiously pressing the code on the small rubber keypad, the screen unlocks, revealing a new message icon.

Click! New message.
23:40 — Unknown: Victoria Inn Hotel, Station Street.

What? This can't be it. We were supposed to meet here and now! Clinging on to each word and hoping for more instructions in a follow-up message, I scroll up and down the screen, frustrated, hoping to squeeze out a few extra words, but no luck. My hand starts to tremble, but it's not me, it's the phone. Multiple vibrations; more incoming messages. Frantically skim-reading them, I realise that the network changed a while back and that these messages have been delayed, probably because of the crap reception on the train. Sticking to Rule 2, I delete the messages, repeating the words 'Victoria Inn Hotel, Station Street' to myself. Once again, I find myself alone, wondering if—

'Excuse me!' echoes around the hall. 'Excuse me!' echoes again, this time louder, closer than before. It's definitely me he's calling. My heart races. Rule 1: Keep your identity safe and never draw attention to yourself. Damn!

Loosening my hood, I peer around the display screen. I catch the eye of the ticket guard, now off his phone, undistracted, and walking towards me with another guard. What do they want.

'Yes, you!' he bellows across the station. 'Oi!'

Whipping my head swiftly around the back of the display, breaking eye-contact with the guard, a single thick dreadlock of my hair is released, swinging in front of my face. Not good. I've messed up. I repeat the address. My heart thumps rapidly, then it all goes blue . . .

Oh no not again. My eyes close, flickering rapidly. Time seems to stand still but shadows of people blur around me. Sounds of quickened whispering voices whoosh past then fade. The smell of asphalt burns my nostrils, all the muscles in my body contract . . .

FLASH!

Ughhh! The taste of coffee and cheese pasty builds, bulging my cheeks. *Splat!* I vomit, holding my stomach as my knees hit wet pavement. I gasp as cold air hits the back of my throat. This is the third time this has happened and it hasn't got any easier.

The first time it happened, I was found on the top of my student digs. It was a little hard explaining to the firefighter what I was doing up there in nightclothes at 3:00 a.m. But this is the first time it's worked by focusing on a specific point.

My strength comes back after the dizziness of the nausea. Well, at least enough to lift my head. A thin, blue, vape-like smoke dissipates around me as sounds of the city comes alive around me.

Muffled bass notes thump from a car speeding down the road, swerving from side to side, maniacally beeping its horn and spitting up water from under its wheels. Slowly getting up from my crouched position, my eyes squint from the headlight's beams, a guy leans out of the badly tinted passenger's window. Scratched into the metal of the door are the letters SOJ; above, an image of a baby sporting a green, spiked mohawk, fist-pumping, swaddled in a distressed Union Jack flag.

'Can't handle your drink, bab!' he yells, hurling a can towards my head, which misses and clatters against the steel shutter-gate behind me. 'Slag! Go back to your own country!'

Laughter trails from the other passengers in the car as the engine revs, speeding off down the road in a blanket of smoke. Steadying myself, unable to reply, I'm hit with a whiff of fish and chips, greasy kebabs, and the smell of sewage, heightened by the falling rain. So this is Birmingham, 'City of Dreams'? Yeah, right.

Harsh electric lights from the city's towering buildings cast gothic shadows against the streets. Semi-holographic advertising hoardings project from screens, glitching in the rain. As I walk, I spot a digital public city map and look for Station Street. It's only around the corner from the station. The sound of sirens intersperses with thumping beats and distant chants from drunken ravers spilling out from nearby clubs, as hydro-trams silently transport late night passengers to their destinations. As the last car tails past, I see it: Victoria Inn Hotel, Station Street.

The hotel is wedged between two buildings. Above the entrance, old scaffolding protrudes, shading the dimly lit sign. Great, another Cecil Hotel. Next to the hotel is a small, art deco-style cinema, The Old Electric.

In the window, tonight's screening is one of my favourite cult classics: *The Crow*.

'It can't rain all the time,' I quote.

A group of friends leaves the late-night viewing. I watch them joke, flicking popcorn at each other, discussing their favourite parts of the film. It's been a while since I spoke with my friends. Wonder if they miss me.

Catching sight of my reflection in the window, I run both hands over my face and hair to take off my hood. I turn slightly to look at myself in the glass. Damn girl, you look tired. Leaning closer, that feeling surfaces again, as if someone else is here, watching me from behind my eyes, like I'm the main character in my own movie.

'Hello?' I whisper tentatively.

'Hi,' the last of the group of friends responds.

Idiot, he thinks I was speaking to him! He holds the cinema entrance door open for me.

'Oh, sorry. No thanks,' I reply, fixing my damp locks neatly behind my head. 'I was just looking.' He smiles before catching up with his friends. He's cute, real cute, but I've got to stick to the rules.

The inside of the hotel is much nicer than I had pictured. The decor is a bit outdated but at least it looks clean, kinda homely.

'Yes?' the receptionist asks, dismissively.

'I'd like a room, please.'

Typing on her computer without looking up, she asks: 'Single or double?'

'Single, please. Just for the night.'

'You're new. Not many your age working tonight.'

I'm confused by the comment before I realise what she means. Words tumble out my mouth: 'Uh, pardon? Oh no, I'm not a— I'm waiting for—' I stop myself mid-speech. Rule 1.

'Just keep the noise down; we do have other guests.'

Swallowing my pride, I stick a piece of gum in my mouth, and try my best to fit the stereotypical character she has insinuated. I change my posture slightly, slouching my back, leaning forward on the desk.

'I just need a room, yeah?' I say, slamming my hand on the desk, giving my best fake smile. The receptionist quickly changes her attitude and gives me eye contact.

'You'll need to sign here and date there.' I sign the only name I could think of that would fit the role: Vivian Ward. Can't believe she's buying this; I was always rubbish at drama. I pop my gum for extra effect, rolling my eyes as I grab the keys and head into the lift.

Wow, I really just did that. As if. I congratulate myself, fighting back the laughter. Well done, Vivian. Right: sixth floor, room 36.

Made it! The door shuts behind me and now I have to contend with that uneasy sense of loneliness. What am I doing here? Maybe I should try Charlotte. I know it's against the rules but . . . screw it.

Ring-ring . . .

'C'mon, Charlotte, pick up.'

Ring-ring! Ring-ring!

'You have now reached the voicemail of . . . "Charlotte" . . . Please leave a message after the tone' . . . Beep!

'Charlotte, it's me . . . Look, I know you're probably still angry with me but I had to do this. I had to leave. Ugh, you know how much I hate talking to voicemail. Anyway, I just wanted to let you know where I've gone, in case, y'know . . . In case something happens. I'm in Birmingham: the Victoria Inn Hotel, Station Street. I'll be back home soon, then maybe we can finally put all this behind us . . . Speak soon.'

I hang up and stand in silence, feeling almost mournful as I delete the last-called number.

* * *

Before I can rest, I enact the final Rule. Rule 3: always check your surroundings. Lock the chain across the door behind you for extra security. Done. Draw the curtains to block out any unwanted attention. Also to stop the glaring light from that huge, creepy, eye-shaped screen above the train station. Done. No killer clown in the bathroom (always a bonus). Tick. I catch another glimpse of myself in the mirror. Recently, mirrors are one of the things that I've been keeping away from. Beyond the sensation that someone is John Malkovich-ing me, I've also been seeing strange white lights appear in my reflection. Maybe it's nothing, maybe it's the stress of doing all this, but one thing I know for sure: when I see them, it's terrifying.

Ping! New message.

00:02 — Unknown: Did you make it to the location?

00:02 — Sent: Yh I'm here. This place is definitely better than the last but full of prozzies WTF!!

00:03 — Sent: What happened tonight?

00:04 — Unknown: It wasn't safe. I'll meet you at the front for 7am.

00:04 — Sent: How will I know it's u?

00:05 — Unknown: Did you memorise the words I sent?

00:05 — Sent: Yh. 'First was the spark, Imādris gave birth. Infinite light formed and creation was born.'

00:06 — Sent: Who is Imādris anyway?

00:06 — Unknown: You'll know soon enough. We can't have any mistakes if this is to work.

00:06 — Unknown: Until tomorrow.

One more night and hopefully this is all over.

Lying in bed, light from the hallway bleeds through the crack under my door. My single bed lies in the middle of the room, facing a small desk with the TV on it. There's a bedside table under the window with a retro digital alarm clock, displaying the time: 00:45.

Desperately trying to calm my thoughts, I begin to twirl my thumbtack. Each turn slowly eases my mind, allowing me to doze off. The background noise of the TV begins to fade into the distance and I drift more and more . . .

* * *

Suddenly, I wake up. I spring into an upright position, with a violent gasp for air. My hands wrap around my throat. I pant, trying to catch my breath. Dripping in sweat, I turn on the bedside lamp, seeing the time: 3:15 a.m.

The room is exactly how I left it before I fell asleep. No sign of the shadowed figure that haunts my dreams, floating above my bed, gripping my throat. It's just the TV, playing re-runs of the classic Hammer Horror film *Dracula*. But it's always the same, the same shadow with burning eyes, the same recurring nightmare: a tall, thin, stalk-like posture of a man in a plague mask, piercing my thoughts, standing motionless, soundless, above my bed.

My palms feel like they're burning again. I stumble to the bathroom and splash water on my face. What's that? The sink is discoloured with a reddish dust that has washed off my face. Gross. Again, that sensation that I'm being watched creeps over me. I spin round but, of course, there's no one there.

'It's just a bad dream, it's not real,' I say out loud, dabbing my face dry with the towel. I climb back into bed and check the time again. 3:15 a.m. That's strange, why is it flashing? The clock must be broken; that's annoying. Tired and unable to fix it, I pull the socket out of the wall and roll over to face the door. A gasp escapes my lips. What the—?! The light from the door crack is slightly obscured by the shadow of two feet.

Slowly sitting up, carefully removing the duvet, not taking my eyes off the shadow, I tiptoe and put my ear against the wooden door, listening carefully.

'Hello?' I whisper, pressing my ear closer to the door, waiting for a response.

BANG! A thump on the door startles me and I recoil. Almost immediately, a black envelope slides under the door.

'Who is it?' I ask, trying not to sound panicked. Hearing nothing, I pick up the envelope, still seeing the shadows behind the door. 'If you don't get away from my door in three seconds,

I'm calling the police. ONE! . . . TWO! . . . THR—'

The shoes step away from the door and then . . . The TV starts to flicker, switching between channels, my mobile and the room phone ring, increasing in volume. Numbers begin to flash on the disconnected alarm clock, the faint sound of the rain hitting the window gets louder, resembling the sound of crows squawking and pecking the glass, each sound building up into a crescendo. I put my hands over my ears and scurry to my phone. I pick it up to stop it from ringing but it's red-hot and I drop it to the floor. The deafening sounds thicken the air.

'Somebody, help!' Overcome with panic, I grab the door-handle, only to be over-powered by two earth-shattering impacts. *BANG!* They smash against the door from the other side. *BANG!* The wood splinters, and the force sends me flying across the room.

CRASH!

'Aarrghh!'

The room is plunged into sudden darkness and silence. I crawl to the furthest side of the bed from the door, whimpering, tears rolling down my cheeks, still holding the black envelope in my hand. What is going on? Why is this happening to me? I don't know why but I peel open the envelope slowly. My tear-filled eyes widen as I see a symbol of an eye with a sword through it, etched with the letter A in its pupil. What does this mean? I desperately repeat the words 'home' to myself, hoping by some miracle that I teleport out of the room but nothing happens. The door handle clicks unlocked.

I flee, grabbing my thumbtack from the bedside table, before slamming the bathroom door behind me and locking myself inside. Something enters the bedroom. My heart pounds. Blood rushes to my head as each beat hits harder, pulsating against my chest and up into my throat.

Crack! I hear the sound of furniture being overturned and destroyed and the deep *thud* of footsteps resembling hooves shakes the walls of the bathroom. Each step brings them closer to the bathroom door. My hand flies to my mouth to stop myself from screaming. From the other side of the door, I hear raspy, violent — inhuman — breathing. It snarls and crackles, causing the hairs on my arms to stand on end. The temperature drops rapidly. Suddenly, the taps of the bath and sink squeak, unwinding, gushing out water with such force that it breaks the faucets. The lights flicker on and off; a cascade of water spills over the lip of the bath, flooding the room. Scrambling to turn the taps off, I slip, hitting my head and blacking out.

A high-pitched sound rings in my ears, followed by the sound of muffled movement in water. My throat and nose are burning, suffocating me. I feel trapped. Almost immediately, I regain consciousness, only to feel the pressure of my head being forced down under the surface of the overflowing bathwater. Precious oxygen releases from my lungs as they burst with fire and I scream: 'Help!'

My eyes glimpse the raging, discoloured water as it mixes with the blood from the open wound on my head. I kick, push, scratching and clawing at the side panel of the bath, crying out with all my might, grabbing at whatever I can in the fight for my life.

The heavy oppressive hands push my head lower into the bath. I begin to feel weightless, blacking in and out of consciousness, my life flashing before me. So this is it; this is how it ends. I take one final feel of my precious thumbtack, squeezing it in my hand to try to stay awake and then . . .

* * *

I stand, looking at myself lying on the bed in the undisturbed room. There's no sign of the chaos from the bathroom. No water creeps under the door, no sign of a flood or flickering light.

Instead, the room is clean and tidy. The TV quietly hums and I see myself, asleep, convulsing silently on the bed. In the calm of the room, water pours from my ears, eyes, and mouth. Beside the locked door lies an unopened black envelope. The time on the clock switches from 3:14 to 3:15 and I watch myself dying, as life pours away from my body. I scream at myself, but no sound comes out. I cry but no tears fall. I reach out but feel nothing. I begin to fade, vanishing, watching my physical body die alone on the bed as I silently drown in my dream.

Psssst, Joseph! Wake up!

CHAPTER 2

Welcome to CBU

'. . . *Hey, Joe! I said: wake up!*'

BANG!

My eyes snap open and I jolt upright in my seat. My bag and tablet clatter to the floor. I blink, trying to bring my eyes into focus as my head vibrates from the laughter and sniggers of students around the lecture hall. It's happened again, hasn't it? If they saw what I just woke up from they wouldn't be laughing. Still disoriented, I fumble around my pockets, feeling the outline of my inhaler.

'Joe, you okay?' whispers the same voice I heard trying to warn me. Leiyah. Pushing a pile of books aside and trying to look alert, I now realise who slammed the books down: Professor Grey. Just my luck.

As lecturers go, Grey knows his stuff; he's one of the best — if not *the* best historian — in his field. And if anyone ever doubted that . . . well, his award-winning books perched neatly on his overcrowded desk should tell them otherwise. I mean, he can be a bit stiff but he's way better than my previous lecturer, who left shortly after getting caught demonstrating the intricacies of the human anatomy on students. Or so I heard. Grey's knowledge on history is crazy. He has this rare ability of speaking as if he were actually there. Guess it helps when you're fluent in multiple ancient languages, several of which he annoyingly loves to pepper into his sentences. I mean, don't get it twisted: the guy's a genius, he is; just totally intimidating at the same time. Imagine a Black 6'4", bald-headed guy, looking like Professor X, who hardly ever blinks as his light oak-brown eyes penetrate your soul, like some sort of mythical . . . lion. Yeah, deep. And if that doesn't get you shook, the way he can turn his slight Caribbean twang into full patois when he gets annoyed will have you running to your mother.

I know I'm in for a personal 'greeting' with him at the end of this session and, to be honest, I could do without it.

Nothing new there I guess; just one of the many fails that is my life at the moment. Not that anyone would be able to read my emotions, with the constant dead-faced, dark-rings-under-the-eyes look of a sleep-deprived student. This latest crash was inevitable. My sleep's been on and off again for, like, seventy-two hours. When you reach that stage you start seeing some wavy things . . . But that wasn't my usual nightmare: no white flashes, flames, or distorted memory. This was weird. My eyes were hers and hers mine.

Grey walks down the sloped auditorium, past different tribal masks from around the globe, ancient statues of the Egyptian gods Bes and Tutu, and spears from the Kush dynasty, which I'm pretty sure are illegal. He stands in front of his lecture board, which is full of diagrams, hieroglyphics, runes and annotations. 'I want as much detail as possible about the *partum et unde*: the origins of ancestral tribes.'

See what I mean? There he goes again, switching up his languages. Show-off. Even though his lecture notes are projected and downloadable, he still insists on writing extra notes on a chalkboard. 'Being present is important' is just one of his many famous quotes, which I always found contradictory; he's a history professor.

Grey continues writing. The warmth of his low voice reverberates around the wooden, tech-fitted, Victorian-style lecture hall.

'Your assignments are due two weeks today. And don't forget . . . to include references and no AI.' Grey looks around the hall pointedly at individual students.

Before I can reach for my tablet and scrounge a few last-minute notes, Leiyah — always one step ahead — beats me to it. She slides over my tablet before pinging her lecture notes onto it. Clearing her throat, she silently mouths 'You're welcome', raising her eyebrows and pushing her black, square-framed glasses up her nose.

'Any questions?' Grey wraps up the lecture. The silence echoes. 'You may leave.'

I start packing, wanting to make a hasty exit. Leiyah hands me a mirror, gesturing for me to wipe the post-sleep drool from my mouth. She has a look on her face that says *fix up bro*, but she's kind enough to spare me the embarrassment.

'So, did Sam tell you what he's got planned for tonight?'

'Nah,' I say, picking up my skateboard to beat a hasty retreat. Leiyah hurries alongside me as I try to blend in with the other students to escape Grey's scolding.

'Okay, well . . . word of advice, I did try and stop him, but you know him. Let's just say it's going to be very "Sam".'

I don't really acknowledge her because I can see that I'm only a couple of steps from getting out of the door. I'm going to make it!

'Mr Jacobs. A word please.'

Damn. Five words I didn't want to hear. Leiyah stops talking and smirks, tapping me on the shoulder twice for good luck before leaving the hall. Grey starts wiping chalk off the board.

'Still burning the midnight oil I see, Mr Jacobs?'

Without really thinking I just start to blurt things out: 'Ahhh, I'm really sorry. It— It won't happen again, I umm . . .'

He calmly cuts in, still wiping the board: 'That's what you said last time.'

What does he want me to say? That I haven't been taking my prescription and I've been having these horrible lucid dreams, watching girls drown in their sleep? Way too much info. So I try appealing to his good nature.

'I know, this has happened before but this time I—'

'Joseph!' He cuts in again, this time his accent becomes slightly stronger. He turns towards me. 'You're a good student, Mr Jacobs. When you are awake.'

I try to avoid eye contact.

'Your essays — when on time — are outstanding, but sleeping in lectures will stop you from reaching your full potential. "For often when one is asleep, there is something in consciousness which declares that what then presents itself is but a dream."'

'Aristotle,' I quietly respond.

His eyes light up before turning back to finish wiping the board. 'Good, Mr Jacobs. Good.'

For a moment there, I thought I glimpsed a smile.

'Don't waste your life dreaming, but rather turn your dreams into reality.'

I finally look up to see him writing something on the board:

pA Khat iw pA Hwt-nTrw m-khent Ten
ikh eref sew ir pat rex Des-sen

What the hell? I stand there transfixed.

'You may leave, Mr Jacobs.' I walk backwards, still staring at the board. That's definitely ancient Egyptian but what does it mean? I open the door to leave.

'And Joseph?'

Now what?

'Happy birthday.'

I got off lightly; what Grey said wasn't wrong. I mean, it's not great being told to fix up, but it's true I have been failing for a minute. Really though, what was that? And why did my palms feel like they were burning? I've had some pretty messed-up dreams in the past. But that last one was different. I can still hear her voice, calling for help, still see her damp, bloated face, the texture of her skin gleaming, almost like black diamonds. My own personal viewing to a murder. Horrible.

I walk down the crowded corridor of students. Advertisements for freshers' week are still up, alongside upcoming events, like the Student Hallowe'en Ball. You can definitely tell who the freshers are: all that new-found freedom, out-of-towners enjoying their independence. Exciting times I guess.

Leiyah leans against the wall, reading a comic. I love that about Leiyah; she doesn't need approval from anybody. Her geek-chic nature oozes out of her, from her red Doc Martens and green bomber jacket filled with embroidered badges, down to her black dungarees. She's deffo in her own lane and possibly one of the most intelligent people I've ever met.

'So, what did he say?' she says, pulling her *Akira* pen from her hair, using it as a bookmark. I don't respond. A bit of a douche move, I know, but Leiyah knows me. I'm not really one to discuss my feelings.

'Did he give you the "reach for your dreams" speech again?' She nudges me, trying to lighten the mood, mimicking Grey's voice with uncanny accuracy. 'With great power comes great responsibility?'

'Yeah, something like that. I need to sort my life out. The last thing I need right now is to fail a module.' Leiyah grabs my skateboard to stop me from walking.

'You'll be fine, Joe! And if you need any extra notes, let me know, 'kay?' She gives me a reassuring look, which chips away at my defences. I nod reluctantly and take a deep breath.

'Thanks, Leiyah.'

'So, birthday boy, have you—?' Before Leiyah can even finish her sentence, we get interrupted. A commotion begins making its way towards us from the other end of the busy corridor. Students begin to move out the way, almost resembling a Mexican wave as they move against the wall. One voice pierces through the hubbub. Leiyah and I look at each other. We both know what's on its way.

'Sam!' we blurt out at the same time.

* * *

Samuel West, where to begin . . . Well, he's my oldest friend. He's kind of what I'd imagine having a sibling would be like. In many ways we're quite the opposite but our love for everything sci-fi is what forged our friendship. Gaming, comic books, manga, anime — especially *Dragon Ball Z*, even though he would never admit that Vegeta is better than Goku. Yeah, he's loud and yeah, he never thinks before he talks and yeah, you got it, he has a habit of getting himself into some stupid situations. But he's my bro, my oldest friend.

'Out of the way, coming through!'

I can see Sam now, legging it down the corridor, his bright yellow hoodie and a nineties Fresh Prince-style snapback bobs around on his head. Oddly enough, he's holding his phone up as he runs.

'No! You're kidding me. Is he live-streaming?' Leiyah laughs in disbelief. 'What. An. Idiot.'

Behind Sam, three guys are in hot pursuit. One of them is red in the face trying to keep up with the other two. All my instincts are telling me this is not going to end well. Sam skid-stops in front of us, grabbing my shoulder to stop himself from falling.

'Jhh . . . Joe,' he pants, barely able to get his words out. 'Hey Leiyah. Jhh— Joe, look, you've got to back me.'

My attention is quickly drawn to Sam's pursuers. The one at the front, closely followed by his two boys, turns his run into a quickstep. Each of them have definitely taken their dress sense out of the Brummie roadman starter pack: black trackies and hoodie and Air Max 90s. The leader cusses as he walks towards us, unzipping his red gilet.

'Oi, dickhead! You think that's funny?!' the head of the pack shouts as another lobs a projectile. Unaware of the UFO hurtling towards him, I shield Sam, deflecting the missile with my skateboard. Immediately a small crowd gathers and Sam is surrounded by the three guys.

'Look, Miles, hang on.' Sam switches off the live-stream on his phone, then throws up his hands in a desperate plea. 'Wait a sec, bro.' Miles looks like he's about to shot him a box but Sam's quick intervention makes him pause. 'Okay, maybe not my "bro", but look, you said you wanted something eye-catching. Something that represents your music. As an influencer I feel like I understand your target audience.'

Sam unlocks his phone and shows me the cover design, which he has already posted on his socials. I look back at Sam and hand the phone to Leiyah. She shakes her head but can't suppress her chuckles, which sends an already-heated Miles over the edge. Miles and his guys rush Sam, grabbing him.

'Woah, woah calm down!' I shout trying to fend off the many

hands grasping at Sam. Leiyah's voice can be heard amongst the scuffle trying to calm things down and I manage to pry myself in between Sam, Miles, and his cronies. 'Back off him!' I yell.

Instantly Miles squares up to me, clenching his fist. 'Are you mad, who you chatting to Doni?! You wanna get bodied?!'

He steps closer, almost chest-to-chest with me. An even bigger crowd starts to form. This is insane. I mean, really? This is how your day goes from bad to worse. I keep silent, trying to hold my nerve as he continues to eyeball me. I notice his friends move off Sam, who's looking dishevelled, hoodie all ruffled up. All three move towards me like a pack of hyenas. Miles aggressively reaches into his pocket. His hand re-emerges and I flinch as I catch a flash of silver. He laughs intimidatingly, then blows smoke from the vape pen in my face. My hand starts to shake. Damn, not now.

'You deaf, idiaat bwoy?' My chest starts to feel tight.

'Yo Miles, leave it man, please. It's my fault . . . Here, take your money back, let's call it quits . . .' Sam's voice feels distant, like I'm underwater.

I continue staring down Miles, feeling Leiyah pulling me back.

'Leave it, Joe. They're not worth it. You guys are absolutely pathetic.' Miles and his two pals laugh mockingly.

'Got your little mix-breed lighty fighting your battles for you, yeah? Wasteman. Ain't gonna touch you, pickney bwoy. Looks like you're about to keel over anyway.'

My breathing gets more and more erratic and everything starts to sound muffled.

'You okay?' Leiyah turns to me with a look of concern on her face.

I try my hardest to get a word out, putting my shaking hand on my chest.

'Ah . . . Ai . . . Airrrr.' My other hand searches my pocket for my inhaler.

Sam hands over the money: 'Take it.'

'Shut your mouth; I wasn't talking to you. I'm dealing with Django over here him and his loud mouth gyal.' Miles snatches Sam's wallet out of his hand, takes the money, and throws the wallet on the floor in front of me.

Campus security shuffles through the crowd towards us, moving students out of the way. Miles walks backwards, staring me out with his boys, taunting my breathless predicament whilst showing me his middle finger before making a hasty exit.

'Joe, my bad. I'm sor—' Before he can finish his sentence, I rush away, leaving Sam, Leiyah, and all that mess behind.

I dart down the hallway and jump — clearing the flight of steps. I need air, I need space, I need to get away. Bursting through a fire exit, I find myself behind the building. I collapse to my knees.

'My inhaler. Damn, where is it?' I rummage through my backpack for a spare. 'Come on . . .' The other one must have dropped out my pocket during the scuffle. Found it. I shake it, close my eyes, then take two huge puffs. Closing my eyes, I focus on my breathing. I begin to feel heat, hot flames warming my face, bright white flashes and I realise I'm back . . .

* * *

I open my eyes and I'm a child again, sitting at the top of a smoke-filled   case, gripping onto   banister so tightly that the brown pigmentation in my hand begins to pale. Through the bars, barely visible,   bright flashes of
   , almost like sparks, sporadically illuminating the destroyed,   room. I can hear the sound of   break-

ing, sporadic   through the thick, suffocating
smoke.   furniture and
          . At the back of the room, a single double-glazed patio
door   a shadow. From outside the glass,
     emerges from the darkness,
                    approaches the glass   a substance
                              begins to paint what
looks like a type of   on
the window. Underneath   a sequence of symbols, too
distorted   I stand there, staring
then   almost blinds me. A hand
       grabbing my shoulder. Blue police lights blaze and
     I feel someone's arm   two hands blend
simultaneously into one, bringing me back . . .

* * *

'It's alright, just breathe. It's going to be okay.' Opening my eyes,
I see the most beautiful girl standing in front of me. Crazy . .
. If I were a photographer this would be a perfect picture: the
way the sunlight beams behind her, highlighting her brown
skin and Bantu knots, its angelic. One word, peng. She rubs my
back reassuringly. 'Breathe. Concentrate on my voice.' Her face
glows. Wow . . . who is she? 'You good? You blacked out for a
second. You okay?'
    'Umm yeah, thanks. Just needed some air,' I say, trying to make
minimal fuss but honestly still feeling light-headed. Noticing me
slightly struggling to get up, she helps me back onto my feet. I
try my best to act normal, brushing myself down, trying not to
look like *that* guy. You know, the idiot that nearly got beaten up
trying to help his friend. Yeah, *that* guy.
    'That was either pretty stupid or brave, sticking up for Sam.'
I nearly choke on my tongue. 'Were those guys even students?'

'God knows. I nearly got decked.'

'Yeah, you did,' she says with a smile. I smile back at her uncomfortably. She picks up a wooden placard from the floor with the letters M.Y.V.C. sprayed across the front.

'You going to the protests?'

'Yep, me and some fellow anarchist students are gonna stick it to the system and burn the place down,' she says, showing me her placard. 'Just kidding. But seriously we're going to make our voices heard.'

'Cool . . . And you think it'll make a difference?'

'Well, we have to do something. Or at least try. We can't just sit back and let them keep forcing fake narratives down our throats. "Birmingham, the Industrial City of Dreams"— it's never been further from the truth.'

'What do you mean?'

'They say the pandemic's over but crime, poverty, pollution is worse than ever,' she says with conviction. 'And don't even get me started on the reinstatements of workhouses— It's barbaric. Being silent doesn't lead to change. If you get the chance, you should go. Make your voice count,' she adds, pointing to her placard.

'Oh, no, I— I've never been to a protest. My voice ain't going to change anything. I'm a ghost.'

She hesitates before responding. Oh man, I've completely flopped this. 'Ghost huh...Well some people believe in ghosts.'

I smile to myself. Yeah, she's dope. 'So you know Sam?'

She rolls her eyes, which means yes. 'We're on the same graphics course . . . He's a bit . . .'

'I know. We've been together for years.'

'Together?'

'Oh no, not "together". I meant— that came out wrong. Not "came out" . . . I mean . . . I meant to say I've known him since, like, forever.'

She laughs and extends her hand. 'I'm Harmony, by the way.'

'Cool ehh . . .' I drop my skateboard, brushing my hand against my jeans. 'Joseph, I mean. I'm Joseph.' I go to shake her hand.

'Yo, Joe!' sounds from across the campus courtyard. Harmony looks over and sees Sam.

'Well, Joseph, look after yourself. See you around maybe.'

Harmony leaves, looking back at me with a smile.

Sam comes over, bouncing his eyebrows up and down, looking at me impressed. 'Well, well, well and a happy birthday to you too.'

Leiyah catches up, pushing Sam out the way: 'We've been looking for you everywhere.'

Still looking in Harmony's direction, I reassure them: 'I'm good. Just needed some air.'

'Ooh, "I just needed some air",' Sam says, taking the mickey out of my voice. 'Is that what they call it? Can't believe you were talking to Harmony May. She's literally the piffest ting I know. No offence, Leiyah.'

'None taken,' Leiyah replies, kissing her teeth.

'Did she mention me?' Sam asks, now looking in Harmony's direction.

'A bit,' I shrug, pop-flipping the front of my skateboard into my hand.

'Wait, what?!' Sam shouts, putting his hands on his head in total disbelief. 'Do you know how many times I say "hello" to this ting? At least five times a day and all I get is "a bit"?!'

Leiyah brings him back down to Earth: 'The thirst is real. Sam, you're reaching and — word of advice — calling her a "ting" is giving Ick vibes and definitely not going to help either.' She clears her throat in a not-so-subtle signal.

'Oh yeah. Look bro, about what happened . . .'

Not wanting this to get all mushy and to save Sam from what is usually a drawn-out apology speech, I jump in: 'Don't worry about it. It's cool. Let's say we're even and I never need to go to another Villa game.'

Sam fist-bumps me before adopting a kung fu-type pose with his hands. 'Anyway Miles and dem man are lucky, one more second and I would have hit them with a HADOUKEN!' He unleashes a Ryu-style *kata* move from *Street Fighter*, using his hands to imitate a fire ball.

Leiyah walks away first. 'What. An. Idiot.'

She is closely followed by me, trying to avoid eye-contact with the other passing students, who are all watching Sam as he remains frozen in his pose.

* * *

We make our way to Birmingham Library. Its contemporary but now-faded architecture of interconnected, overlapping rotunda beaming down natural light, and its interweaving neon escalators, is the perfect reminder of how the city thrived before the second pandemic. Leiyah peruses the shelves, occasionally stopping to flick through some pages that catch her eye.

Sam scrolls through his socials, talking his responses out loud as he types: '*No, I wasn't scared you doughnut, Miles and his opps just misunderstood my intention, hashtag never stop for the opps hashtag thuglife hashtag West's World.*' He never learns.

'So Joe, tonight: you ready for it?' Sam probes. These two know that I'm a low-key, keep-it-to-yourself kinda guy, but every year they do their best to try to make me celebrate. Leiyah's not so bad. But Sam . . . One year we ended up in the canal after Sam told us we were going to a rave on a barge. Turns out we gate-crashed a gypsy wedding. Not cool.

'Sam, you know I'm not into—'

'Yeah, yeah. Whatever. You'll like this one. I managed to organise us a lock-in at Digbeth Comics. Food, drinks, and not to mention some comic book hotties. Courtesy of yours truly and the "West's World" admirers.'

I know there's no way I'm getting out of this so I decide to switch it up and maybe, just maybe, in the long run it might benefit me if a certain person is there too.

'Let's take a rain check on that plan,' I begin. Sam stops in his tracks, taking his attention away from his phone for the first time since we arrived in the library. 'It's Student Night, right? Let's go out.'

Sam's jaw drops. Leiyah stops book-diving and turns round in amazement.

'Wow!' Sam shouts, causing several others in the library to turn around. 'Now you decide to be sociable? It took me ages to sort this out! Leiyahhhhh, tell him!'

Leiyah continues book-diving. 'It's true, Joe; he has been working that underdeveloped muscle he calls a brain.'

Sam bows. 'Thank you.'

We make our way over to the front desk. Leiyah hands her small pile of books over to the librarian.

'I appreciate the thought, Sam; I just think it might be fun to go to Student Night, might be a vibe.'

Sam drags his feet like a big baby and goes back on his phone, typing away to cancel his plans.

The librarian scans the books and Leiyah weighs in: 'Sam, I think Joe's entitled to do what he wants today, without the guilt of your prepubescent, erotic fantasies being an issue.'

Sam fires back: 'Whatever, Leiyah, and — just for your information — no one even goes to the library anymore,' Sam says, leaning on the desk next to the librarian. 'Ever heard of the net? Seriously, how is this still even open?'

The librarian throws Sam a glance. Leiyah looks over the top of her glasses and leans in to Sam: 'I've got two words for you: your breath.'

I can't control my laughter. Even the librarian lets out a sly smile whilst scanning the last book. Several *shh*'s echo around the building. Sam turns, and checks his breath. Leiyah collects her book, receiving a wink from the librarian, and we make our way down the escalators towards the exit.

'Okay fine! Let's go to the Digbeth. Arcadian's trash and Broad Street's kinda dead, unless you like the more mature cut of meat.'

Leiyah narrows her eyes. 'Eww, Sam, you're the worst!'

Sam continues: 'And, just so you know Joe, I ordered a *Cat-woman and a Storm* for tonight. Just saying. No refunds. Facts! Dave at the comic store's gonna have a heart attack.'

Leaving the library, the city streets are heaving with people. The majority are holding banners and signs and walking towards the protest. Sam pats his stomach. 'You guys up for getting some grub?'

I prep myself onto my board, securing my bag straps a little tighter before pulling out my ear buds. 'I can't, sorry. I promised my mom we would grab a bite to eat. Birthday lunch. But we'll catch up later, yeah?'

'Looks like it's just you and mwah, Leiyah.'

'Actually Sam . . .'

'What! Don't tell me you got D&D group or something, even for me that's a whole nother level of—'

'Actually D&D's on a Monday, I'm running the annual EyeSpy group meeting.'

'Oh great more weirdos spouting out delusional conspiracies, how riveting.'

Leiyah shows Sam the finger.

'Supernatural beings are amongst us, Sam, you can't deny it forever.'

I secure the buds in my ears, selecting my 'ride or die' playlist from the app — one of my favourite genres of music: Clash Wave. I push off hard on my board, leaving Sam and Leiyah to bicker, and blaze down the city streets.

CHAPTER 3

PLayLIST

Track 1: 'Dre@mer'
Loading . . .

♫ *It's like I'm lost up in this dream world.*
I'm dream talking, purple swirls
And Afro curls with Afro girls.
Cloud surfing, chasing girls and chasing worlds,
Heaven cruising, leaving all my problems snoozing.
It's in the past, can I pass it back to the future,
The power of love.'

Cssssssshhhhhhhhh!
The trucks on the bottom of my board squeal as I manual into a grind against the rail of the mini ramp. Here I feel like I belong; this is where I feel free and listening to some Clash Wave has got me pumped. The sun warms the back of my neck as I skate the park. It's empty today, which is a first, but I'm not gonna complain. Sometimes my best company is my own.

I pick up my speed, popping the tail of the board, first ollie-ing, then doing a varial flip over the bench but I mistime my landing. Need a little more control with that trick. I never manage to land it on the first attempt. Before I try again and reset for another attempt, I call my mom.

'*You've reached the voicemail of Elizabeth Jacobs. Please leave a message after the beep.*' *BEEEEEEEP!*

Typical; she's always busy. 'Hey Mom, hope you're good. Just checking in to see if you still want to meet up for lunch at two? I'm gonna make my way over in the next hour. So yeah, errr, see you in a bit.'

Nothing new there. I mean, I would've been cool just jamming on my own but she insisted that we meet for a birthday lunch. Think she's worried about me — you know, the not-being-able-to-sleep and constant lethargic look.

Many times I've tried to soldier on through and keep stuff to myself but she's always been able to tell if I'm hiding something. I guess her natural instinct as a police officer is still there. She'd never admit it but I think she misses that life: all the action, chasing criminals, being on the front line. Her current job with the PSD still keeps her on her toes, but it's different. Instead of locking up criminals, she now investigates and locks up corrupt officers; not the most popular occupation amongst her peers.

♪ '*Mario jumping, powering up, this ain't a cheat code.*
Sometimes I'm up see, even been down see
Punch with the left see, so I can right see.

Switching the track, I skate over to the graffitied half-pipe, swerving into a tre flip, then doing a front smith. Landed it. I love when that happens: a perfect run. Any skater would tell you there's more falls than successes but it's all about the getting up, trying again.

I ride fakie, twisting the back-end of the board to the front and crouching lower to readjust my balance. Reaching the lip of the half-pipe, I prepare myself for the drop, wiping the sweat from under my Afro curls.

Squinting, the sun blurs my view of the congested city in front of me. 808 percussive beats from my headphones smack hard against my eardrums, charging me for the drop.

'You got this,' I whisper to myself, before plunging off the edge in a rapid descent. I speed back and forth, up and down the half-pipe, building momentum. The wind blows against my face as I attempt a backside air. Just need to hit maximum air. My board leaves the half-pipe; I'm in mid-air at the apex of my jump, shifting my weight, turning to execute the move. Everything slows down and — for a split-second — I see her face, pouring out water in front of me, before she evaporates into thin air.

'Help!'

My board flies from under my feet. I hit the deck hard *boof!* I slide into the middle of the pipe. Shit, that hurt. I take out my ear buds and lie there, looking up at the sky. Damn. I must be crashing again. I've had wavy dreams before but this one seems to be haunting me.

'What's this?! You're short . . . Where's the rest?'

'That's all I've got, I swear.'

Raised voices catch my attention. I get myself together, looking over, putting faces to the voices.

A shifty-looking guy is man-handling another, roughly throwing him to the floor.

'If you try play me like that again, I'll cut ya, got it?'

'Oouhffffff!'

He boots and lays into the man on the ground; then leaves. Cars continue to drive on, with no one stopping to help.

I skate over, pulling out my phone, ready to call the emergency services. I don't take my eyes off him.

'Are you okay?'

He crawls to pick up a half-empty bag of multicoloured pills off the pavement, clenching his fist, trying to keep it out of sight. Great. Joseph, you, my friend, have stumbled across a sted-head. Hyper-sted addicts are the worst. Mom says they're as addictive as heroine, give you the erratic behaviour of someone on meth, but with the energy as if you're on molly. Worst of all they're cheap to buy.

'Do you need me to call the police? You hurt?'

Across his right cheek a huge red mark where he got hit. The man stinks of burnt coal. He looks at me, grinning, which creeps me out as most of his teeth are gone.

'*Dol'khrāb!*' he growls.

'Pardon?' Then, suddenly, he grabs at my ankle, almost tripping me up. His face contorts and his eyes turn bright white, then roll to the back of his head as his whole body convulses.

He begins mumbling what sounds like gibberish. Before I can call the police, he stands up like a ravaged zombie from a grave and sprints across the dual carriageway, shouting at the top of his voice: 'We ArE WAtcHiNq YoU!'

Cars screech, trying to avoid hitting him, skidding and swerving along the road. One car mounts the pavement, crashing into the back of another. More cars collide and an ensemble of horns crescendos. I see the chaos and skate away in a panic.

What in the world was that? I'm not sticking around to try to explain this to the police. A black student — in the wrong place — at the wrong time — around a sted-head that's one coincidence I wish not to explain.

Next track: 'Gotch@!'

I try to put some distance between myself and the main roads, taking some side streets towards New Street.

* * *

That was crazy. There was at least a four-car pile-up back there. What was in that stuff? He went from homeless to bloodlust in a second. That was some next level high; I'm talking face-eating, bath-salts crazy. He was definitely on hyper-steds. His proclamation, 'We are watching you', sends a shiver down my spine just thinking about it. So I try not to, dismissing all thought of him to the back of my head. What an absolute nutter.

I head towards Peace Gardens Park, holding on to the side of random hydro-trams that are heading in my direction, to cut towards New Street. This park was created to commemorate those from the city who lost their lives in the wars. But, in true Brum style, the memorial statue has been tagged and defaced. People have lost connection with their past; the things they held dear aren't so dear to them anymore. I always thought this park was randomly placed — homeless tents tucked away in the corners, over-shadowed by a mountain range of tall buildings and the facade of a high society lifestyle at the nearby Mailbox — the park almost invisible amongst the congested roads and fine-dining chain restaurants of the commercialised inner-city.

Brum definitely has two faces. The one, in the day: bright, congested, hopeful. And then there's its nocturnal brother, as the city changes faces like the moon. The fallout of the second pandemic unearthed a colossal gap within our society; the poorest suffering the most. Same old story, I guess. If this were a computer game, this place would be *Midgar* in *Final Fantasy Seven*, but with no hero to save the day. If the second pandemic showed us anything, it's that suffering is an inherent part of the human condition.

* * *

Peace Gardens is heaving with protesters, but, if I'm honest, I don't think it will change anything. Protests have been popping up all over the city. But those at the top have moved way past listening.

It's been two weeks of demonstrations; people are fed up. Allegations and rumours of the Lord Mayor's dealings with organised crime have really got people riled. All types of diverse groups are here, all wanting their say, calling for change:

'Down with the system!'
'The end is nigh!'
'We will not be silenced!'
'Take our city back!'

Anti-social groups in the corner add a bit of mayhem, letting off fireworks to disturb the peace. Amongst the madness, a weird religious fanatical group called Nox Lumina prowl these rallies, looking to indoctrinate anyone that gives them eye-contact. All in all, a regular circus.

Jamaican Maroon drums start playing a repetitive rhythm. The crowd cheers. I hear a familiar voice through a megaphone. Is that . . . Harmony?

'We are more!
More than charts, more than numbers, more than graphs,
More than government statistics and
Compassionless linguistics
For our collective epitaphs.

We are more
Than students, workers, fathers, mothers
Even in the darkness you've created

I still recognise my brothers
As we fight
Screaming for justice, truth, peace, and light.
A city on the brink, breathing life!
Know thyself!

We are more than your corruption, more than your lies
And each time you cocoon us we break free
Immortalised
Like butterflies
Still we rise
Know thyself!
We are
Voices to be feared, lights to be shone
Plentiful like stars, blazing hotter than the sun.
Know thyself!

Our circumstances don't define us,
In unity you'll find us
We are one!
Love yourself, know thyself!
Now we know that they can hear us
They try to commandeer us
The truth is that they fear us
When we come together.
That's where our strength is
Smash through their defences
And together
We are more.
Know thyself!'

The crowd roars again and Harmony walks off the platform.

I'm stunned. That was amazing.

I stick to the outside of the crowd, not daring to venture too deep, as others take the platform. Leaders of the groups continue to cheer and shout through megaphones.

I need to get moving. I switch track on my playlist to 'An@ rchistic L*o*v*e' to drown out the noise and continue skating, weaving through individuals.

* * *

I wait outside Yoshi sushi bar. It's 2:00 p.m. Can't see Mom anywhere. I'll give her five; she's probably just running late.

Harmony's words still echo around my head; she really struck a chord with me. And for some reason my mind goes back to Grey's writing on the board. Even though I didn't fully understand what it all meant, something about the symbols and phrasing meant that they, too, resonated deep within me. Maybe I'm just reaching, looking for answers.

Ever since I was diagnosed with psychic trauma, my anxiety made sense, and I'm cool with working through my problems . . . But it can't be all that I am.

Better try Mom again . . . Nothing. Still no answer. Better try her office.

'Hi, I'm trying to get in touch with Elizabeth Jacobs. I can't seem to get her on her mobile.'

'May I ask who's speaking?'

'Joseph, her son.'

'Hi Joseph. Yep, she's been called out this morning. She last checked in thirty minutes ago and was headed towards the city morgue. Do you want me to pass on a message?'

'No thanks, I'm good.'

* * *

The city morgue. I can skate there in fifteen minutes if I cut under the Queensway bridge, past the food court. There's a strong police presence on the steps of the station, just waiting. They must be on standby in case the protest actually makes a difference. I head towards the morgue, Grand Central station on my left. Then I see it, right there, held together by scaffolding as it towers above the streets.

I hop off my board, my chest tightens. I take two deep puffs of my inhaler and walk closer.

The Victoria Inn Hotel, Station Street.

Yellow police-tape is stretched across the front of the entrance. Instantly my mind flashes back to my dream and I stop in my tracks. I can see the girl entering the hotel and my mind flashes back to her struggling violently to breathe under the water as she shouts for help. This must be just a coincidence, maybe it was a robbery or someone set off an alarm.

I can't stop myself from inching closer to the hotel, as if it's pulling me into its arms. An officer stands in front of the entrance, another is trying to speak with annoyed guests, some of them holding their belongings.

A woman sobs by the side of the street with a blanket around her, speaking to another officer, who is taking notes. One of the guests near the entrance tries to force her way back into the hotel. The officer rushes over to stop her. I walk over to the crying woman.

'Um, excuse me. What happened?'

She wipes her face, eyes glazed red with tears.

'I . . . I— I found someone . . .'

My heart begins to race. 'Are they okay?'

'No . . .' She starts sobbing again. 'She's dead!'

I gulp, feeling my eyes widen. Dead . . . Okay Joseph, calm down; there could be a million and one people that could have died many different ways in a dodgy hotel. What you dreamed was just a dream. Calm down and just leave it there. Don't ask any more questions.

'Dead? A Black girl?'

The woman stops crying, startled at my question.

'Yes, lying on the bed.'

My heart misses a beat and I back away, gripping my inhaler. I take two, three puffs in quick succession.

'How did you know that?' she gasps, gradually getting louder. 'How did you know that?!'

Before she can make a scene, I run. Finding a small side road, I jump on my skateboard trying to get away as fast as possible. Her bloated face flashes in front of mine and I fall off my board, grabbing some service bins to stop myself from hitting the pavement hard.

It was a dream, it can't be real, it can't be! I'm going mad. That's it, I'm crashing. Yeah, crashing, that's all. I take three hard puffs from my inhaler again. And then freeze. My stomach bubbles.

'Uuuuuuhhhhkkkk!'

I fall to my knees and throw up down the side of the bins. What does this mean? What— Did I—?

Did I just dream a murder?

CHAPTER 4

The Maiden's Name

'I'm here.'

                                        'First was the Spark.'

'Imādris gave birth.'

                                      'Infinite light formed.'

'And creation was born.'

                                             ' . . . '

'Mr X?'

                                    'Have . . . body?'

'You're breaking up.'

                            'Have you viewed the body yet?'

'No, I've just arrived. Sorry; signal's not great.'

                   'You need to make sure the description matches
                                up with what I told you.'

'I'll keep you informed. If it's anything like you said, then I need to see this for myself. Hold on, I'm at the front desk.'

                                          'Okay.'

'Hi, my office should have called ahead? Name should be under Jacobs, PDS.'

The security guard checks the computer. Things have changed a lot round here. She looks up from her screen.

'Yes, I've got you on the system. Straight down the corridor, third—'

'I know where I'm going, thank you . . . That was weird.'

'What is it?'

The cameras behind the desk were off and her cup of coffee was untouched; looked cold. Maybe I'm over-analysing.'

'Stay vigilant.'

'What if the body doesn't match? The fatality rate in the city is starting to peak again.'

'We will know soon enough. We have to be sure, we can't take any chances. Trust your instincts and look for the unseen.'

'Before I go in, is there anything else I should know? They're not going to like me just showing up like this. PDS are not welcome at the best of times.'

'You remember the description of the symbol?'

'I remember.'

'If I'm correct, then this is just beginning. The pieces on the board are moving. Tread carefully, Elizabeth. They're watching.'

I put the phone down, wondering if I'll ever get an explanation on the weird code words he has me say before we converse. What does it all mean?! My phone vibrates in my hand. Two missed calls? Ahhh, shoot; I'm late. I made plans with Joseph! I'll text him.

14:02 — Sent:
Hey son, I'm so sorry.
Caught up at work, will call you as soon as I'm free.
Hope everything is good. Mom x

I feel terrible but I'll call him back later.

Never thought I would have to visit this place again. Clinical white tiles reflecting harsh white light in this cold and empty space. My heels clatter against the floor, the sound carrying up to the broken, discoloured slabs in the ceiling. Weirdly enough, I find a comfort in this place: the silence.

I remember my first visit here like it was yesterday. The city was in recovery from the second pandemic. In what became known as 'The Great Divide', the country split, reassigning old regions and reverting to their former kingdom names: Wessex, Northumbria, Mercia. A desperate attempt to try to remind us of our 'glorious past'. At least it stopped talks of a civil war and another War of the Roses. The United Kingdom divided.

The poor suffered the most. People were desperate, and crime rose to a new high: murder, extortion, drugs, human trafficking, you name it. Backdoor deals infiltrated positions of justice like never before. Gang wars erupted, with many innocent bystanders paying the ultimate price. A section of the city called the Industrial — an area of old iron mills, factories and coal mines that had closed down in the sixties — had been carved out and is now run by Birmingham's underworld boss: Kaine Nelson, also known as the Dragon. A mid-level, disgraced politician, who preferred the company of under-age children. A real piece of work. He strong-armed his way to the top of the criminal underworld and created what we now know in the city as the Industrial Crime Loop, an organised system controlling the majority of the illegal action.

It felt at that time as if our society was imploding. So, I answered the call. Law and order was needed and, with the few officers that remained on the force, it was hard to find one that wasn't on the take.

The Loop was a hard system to crack, built to keep the ones at the top on top. In a city where you could lose your life for a fiver, where title and rank won't save you, Kaine Nelson created an illusion for the petty crooks and gangs to level up. A great illusion to solidify his power. At the bottom is the Third Loop, open for any gang to grab a spot. There are only two positions available in the Third Loop and each street gang wants that spot. This affords them better opportunities to make more money. But there's a catch. They have to keep their place, making them a target for all the other gangs. However, the longer they hold their title, the more likely they are to move up to the Second Loop. Gaining Second Loop status comes with more perks and allows the criminals access to working more closely with the Upper Loop. All feeding the Dragon. The Dragon sleeps soundly, knowing that his agendas won't be disturbed, whilst all those below are busy making money, fighting, killing each other to get on the bottom rung of the ladder. In this Loop system, there's no space for any random, bloodthirsty idealist to make a move to the top.

It was by Kaine's hands that I came to the morgue for the first time as a rookie officer. That sight will stay with me for the rest of my days. Twins. A girl and a boy. They were just children . . .

Nelson's been behind bars for some time now, but his system has been adopted and embedded, now run by the Three Heads, known as Cerberus. His legacy still guts the city even to this day.

* * *

I push through a double set of stainless steel doors and enter the examination room. It's freezing; you feel the temperature change as soon as you walk in the room. The faint, distinctive essence of death lingers like a fog. Lying before me on the cold metal slab is a young Black female, lifeless, pale. Her long dreads hang down off the edge of the table, almost touching the floor. Faint blue lights reflect against her grey skin. The coroner scratches his head, mulling over his folder, then switches attention to his notes whilst typing on his laptop.

Two officers are on guard duty. They must have been first on the scene. They're clearly keeping their distance; not everybody's cut out for this job.

The male officer looks preoccupied, almost unfazed. He towers at around 6'4", stocky build, early forties. He's definitely seen his fair share of action. The female officer is definitely a rookie: her uniform and equipment are pristine, by the book. You can always tell when they've just come from the Academy. I wasn't much different. She's not much older than the young girl lying in front of her. She's putting on a brave face, trying her hardest to stay professional, fixating her eyes downwards to avoid glimpsing the corpse again. Like I said before, not everybody is cut out for this.

The unshaven South Asian man pacing back and forth, wearing a black windbreaker, slightly crumpled greyish trousers, and looking pissed off, is Detective Kukadia. He hasn't noticed me yet, but whoever is on the receiving end of that phone conversation is getting a serious earful.

'Are you taking the piss?! Who authorised that? How am I supposed to do my job if . . . Ahhh, come off it, you know as much as I do . . .' He looks more annoyed than usual, which is saying something, and seeing me here is going to piss him off even further. He puts his phone away, looks up at the porcelain ceiling-tiles, and breathes out, frustrated.

Turning, he sees me; a surprised-but-slightly-confused-slash-what-the-hell-are-you-doing-here look is written across his face. He begins to walk over, clenching his fist before sliding something into his pocket.

'Elizabeth, long time. To what do I owe the pleasure?' His forced half-smile only underscores his passive-aggressive tone. I walk towards him, meeting him halfway, beside the body.

'Detective,' I say, nodding my head in response. No handshake from either of us. Some things never change.

He gives me some courteous but half-arsed introductions to the officers in the room: 'That's Officer Scott and the new blood over there is Officer Lace.' I nod again to acknowledge them before looking back at Kukadia. He looks a lot older. Permanent frown lines are indented above his eyebrows, grey patches of stubble pepper his beard, accompanied by the strong smell of Scotch and cigars. Never was one to look after himself. The job's taken its toll.

'They're getting younger every time, ay?' He moves around the post-mortem table, slowly examining the body. He puts on another set of gloves, whispering to himself, making countless deductions about the victim in his head.

'Detective, the reason I'm—'

He cuts me off mid-sentence. 'Hotel cleaners found her this morning.' He leans over, staring at the victim's face with a blank expression. I'm not gonna let it rile me; he's trying to get a reaction. He was aways good at getting into people's heads to provoke a response. I proceed to my next question.

'Suicide?'

'Looks that way.' He keeps his head down, continuing to stare at the body. 'We're waiting on results. She signed in under the name of Vivian Ward. Obviously fake, but you know these Loop-fronted hotels, they're not going to ask any questions. Whoever she was, she didn't want anyone to know.'

The coroner stands up from the desk. 'Detective, a word please.' Kukadia goes over to the coroner, who's looking discombobulated.

I move closer to the body, taking a mental picture of her face and anything else I can notice at first glance. I've got to be careful not to over step boundaries or look as if I'm investigating.

So far her description matches up with what I've been told. I spot a distinctive mark on her hand: small pin marks indented, almost punctured, in her right palm. I lean in a little closer, then stop when I notice Officer Scott watching me.

'Do we have any leads on her real identification?'

Kukadia ignores me, looking more and more confused as the conversation between him and the coroner continues.

'Not yet,' a softer voice replies. It's Officer Lace. 'She's from out of town, probably a PROL—'

'A Londoner,' I correct. I've always disliked that pejorative for those from the People's Republic of London, even if some of them have reappropriated the acronym to refer to themselves lately.

'Right. Sorry. She paid the hotel in cash. She had a couple of fake IDs: Anna Hudson being another. She had a burner phone on her. They're checking her phone to try and establish an identity. But so far, nothing.'

'Cause of death?'

'It's too soon to tell but the thought is—'

'Asphyxiation!' Kukadia answers triumphantly, cutting in over Officer Lace. He marches back, holding the coroner's folder in his hand. 'She drowned. Which explains why her body was soaked.'

'Any physical trauma to the body?'

'No, nothing. Ay, are you going to tell me why you're here, Elizabeth?'

'Just doing my job. Making sure procedures are being properly kept. Do you have any further information?'

Ooh, he didn't like that. Not one bit. He slowly opens the folder, trying to hold in his frustration in front of his colleagues. 'Well, there's no sign of foul play, marks, or physical bruising to indicate a homicide . . . Hang on . . . Red substance? What's this then?' Kukadia asks the coroner.

'At the moment we don't know, the sample looks to be contaminated. These are just early findings. We'll need to do further examinations, more time and tests, but . . .' The detective expresses a moment of realisation and looks back in the folder. I know that look.

'What is it?'

Kukadia turns the pages back and forth, cross-examining the notes. 'She was found on the bed, drenched. There was no water residue on the floor; the bathroom was spotless. So unless she drowned herself and floated into bed, this doesn't make any sense.' He turns to Officer Scott: 'Radio the forensics team for an update now.' He directs his annoyance towards the coroner: 'Mate! You sure these are the right results?'

Seeing Officer Scott on his radio and Kukadia speaking with the coroner, I take my chance to move closer to the body, transfixed on the victim's face. Her closed eyes are slightly bloated, with dried lines from water-trails from her nostrils and mouth visible.

Leaning in closer, I focus on her face, and the conversation between Kukadia and the coroner begins to muffle. The crackle and voices from the police radio also become distant and slowly fade out. The room temperature drops and everything around us dims. It slowly gets darker and darker, like oxygen being sucked out of a room. A muffled but audible whisper seeps through into my consciousness. It gets harsher with each dull phrase . . . What is that? The sound bounces around the darkness, getting louder. We're now lit by a single white spotlight. I try to make out the source of the sound. The more I look, the more I realise that the sound is coming from the body. I press my ear against her frozen, lifeless lips. Suddenly her eyes snap open, piercing bright white lights blare from her, blurring my vision.

'Dol'khrāb!' A strange word spits out of her lips in a choked

voice. I stumble back in horror, furiously rubbing my eyes.

'Are you alright?' Officer Lace stares at me. My eyes start to correct themselves.

'I'm fine,' I reply, trying to deflect her concern. I look back at the body. Her eyes are closed, the lights are normal and the temperature not as cold. What the hell was that? I must have been daydreaming. No one else looks as though anything happened. If I'm going to get the answers, I need to be more direct. 'Was there anything else in the room, officer?'

'There was an envelope . . . I think we're having it analysed.'

Kukadia spins around, glaring at Officer Lace, and abruptly interjects: 'Who gave you permission to divulge sensitive information? One more peep out of you, rookie, and you'll be pushing paper for Community Support Officers. Do I make myself clear?!'

I can't help but feel guilty, but I can't get involved. He's her superior officer and I've seen him in this mood before. I walk towards the door to make a call.

'Elizabeth, what's going on?' Kukadia shouts across the room, stopping me before I can get to the door.

'Like I said before, just making sure proper procedures are being kept.'

'Oh, come off it!' Everyone senses the tension in the room. 'Don't try to take me for a fool! So PDS sends the famous Elizabeth Jacobs — the hero behind locking up Kaine Nelson — to watch over a random suicide investigation?' He lowers his voice, his eyes pleading earnestly. 'Please.'

'Look, it's better we speak in private.'

As frustrating as this is, I need to know what's in that envelope. If that means giving a little information to get some cooperation, then I'm going to have to do just that. He's stubborn, but he's not stupid and — most of the time — he's trustworthy.

Kukadia follows me into the hallway.

'So, are you going to be honest and tell me why you're really here?'

'The envelope your officer mentioned, what was in it?'

'Why are you so interested? I knew that you showing up here was not a coincidence. I'm getting blocked at both ends. You're not the only one interested in what happened.'

'What do you mean?'

Kukadia hesitates for a second. 'It's above my pay grade but I know the chief's under pressure. Someone's blowing smoke and I want to know what's going on. Come on. One officer to another.'

Ex-officer, I think to myself. We stand there in silence. Kukadia puts his hands in his pockets. Some things are best not said. But his help could be useful. I lower my voice: 'This isn't just another random case. There have been six incidents. All with the same outcome: missing pieces that make the cases unsolvable.'

'Why wasn't I briefed on this?'

'PDS is investigating people on the force. They think . . . ' I choose my words wisely. 'They think someone's tampering with evidence.'

'And you?'

'Me what?'

'What do you think?'

'Could be. Mercia Police Department hasn't got the greatest reputation. Just last month I investigated four officers on the take in your station alone. It's a possibility that it could be someone from the force. Or it could be . . . It could be something else.'

'Like what?'

'Not sure. But I do know an unusual symbol has been mentioned that link the incidents together. The symbols usually disappear from evidence before they can be analysed.'

Kukadia pulls out a piece of crushed parchment from his pocket. I look down at it: a symbol of an eye with a sword through it, etched with the letter A in its pupil, stares back at me.

'I was told to hand that black envelope in to my superior. They left before you arrived. It didn't sound right to me, so I kept what was inside. What do you think it means?'

I don't look up from the image. It's exactly like what Mr X described. An uneasy feeling starts to gnaw at my brain, which is working overtime to analyse the symbol.

'Elizabeth?' Kukadia breaks my train of thought.

'I'm not sure what it is. Do you mind if I take a picture?'

'Go ahead, but you owe me one.'

The coroner comes hurtling into the hallway. 'Detective, I've found something.'

A high-pitched whizzing sound shoots past me, followed by a guttural noise, breaking my concentration.

'Ouff!'

I turn to see the coroner holding his chest. He looks down at his hand — blood is seeping through his fingers — then back up at us, shock drawn across his face. Calmly and collectedly walking up the hallway, brandishing a black pistol with a suppressor attached, is the security guard I passed at reception earlier. She raises her pistol and fires. Two more shots hiss, hitting the coroner, who falls back, bursting through the double doors. Kukadia and I dart through the doors to find cover.

'Get down!' he shouts to the officers in the examination room. Three more shots fire, the last one ricocheting off the metal doors, which are being partially held open by the coroner's prostrate body.

'You okay?' Kukadia yells, crouching behind cover to the left of me.

'I'm fine! Are you hit?' I shout back.

'The bastard grazed my shoulder. Scott, radio for a medic and back up now!'

Another barrage of bullets propels our way, breaking beakers, test tubes, and spreading glass everywhere. I pull out my phone and turn on the selfie camera, quickly taking as many pictures as I can to see the position and identity of the shooter behind me. The picture's slightly blurred, but she's definitely still there. The blurry image — or it could be lens flare — makes it look like there's a ghostly red aura around the shooter. Shit, I must have landed on my phone and broken the display. Except the bright glow is also emanating from her eyes. It's similar to what I thought I saw coming from the victim's body . . .

Bang!

Kukadia shoots, sending off blind shots down the hallway. *Bang! Bang!* The sound of his revolver echoes loudly. I hear sirens in the distance.

We sit amongst the broken glass as the sirens get closer and closer, until they are directly outside the building. The coroner lies dead. Poor guy didn't stand a chance; two in the chest and one in the head. Smoke is still rising from his body. The woman posing as the security guard was definitely a professional. Judging by the positioning of the bullets — centre mass and head — this was an execution. That was not your run-of-the-mill pistol either; it looked like a Kimber 1911, special forces model. Those are expensive and rare. Thank God I'm still alive. The thought of not being able to see Joseph . . . It's the reason I'm no longer an officer in the first place. In these situations, the slightest hesitancy or wrong footing and it's your life. That was a warning.

'Mercia PD! Is anyone there? Identify yourself!'

'It's Kukadia, I have three officers with me and a man down. We need a medic!'

The corridor is suddenly full of Armed Response officers, masked-up, in two-by-two tactical formation. They secure the area and walk into the bullet-riddled room. I had had my doubts but Mr X was right; the chess game has started. I had made my move by looking for the truth and now the pieces on the board are moving. Kukadia holds his arm. Medics rush in, attending to him and the coroner on the floor. I check on my former colleague: 'How's the arm?'

'It's fine; looks worse than it is. That was close. Felt like old times, ay?' He deliberates. 'Look, Liz, maybe we can help each other out here. You're clearly onto something dangerous, but you're not a officer anymore. If you insist on stirring up the hornets' nest, you're definitely going to need my help.'

'Look, Paul . . .'

'Liz,' he cuts me off again. 'Send me the picture of the shooter and I'll try and run an ID.'

Reluctantly, I send him the pictures. He's right; we need to identify the assassin. 'I'll be in touch to give my statement later. Right now, I just need to call my son.'

'Mom?'

'Joseph, can you hear me? Signal's rubbish here. Sorry I missed your calls; it's been a crazy morning.'

'Mom, I'm outside the morgue, the place is crawling with police. Is everything—?'

'Wait, what?! You're here?!'

'Yeah, I called your office when I couldn't reach you. They told me where I could find you. I'll meet you by your car.'

'*No! Don't do that. Stay near the crowded area. I'm coming out.*
Meet me by the side street and I'll pick you up, okay?'
'Okay yeah, see you in a sec.'

* * *

Man, there's police all over the place, looks crazy. Barricades
have been put up in front of the building. Search drones occupy
the sky, their propellers twirling as they hover effortlessly. A few
police officers try to contain a small crowd of onlookers, who
have their phones out pointed at the commotion.

Directly in front of the entrance stand armed officers, holding
machine guns. One has his face screwed up tightly in concentration, his hand on his headset, listening intently under his tinted
visor. An ambulance is parked right in front of the building, its
back doors wide open. A medic stands waiting as the vehicle's
blue lights flash noiselessly. Kinda looks like a scene from a film.
What are the odds of turning up to two different places and
seeing them both swarming with police?

In amongst all the movement I take out my phone and snap a
couple of pics. Sam and Leiyah have to see this, especially Sam.

Beep beep!

I turn my head to see Mom's silver convertible drive down
the exit ramp of the morgue's car park. I put my skateboard in
the boot and hop in.

'Mom, you okay?'

She drives towards the road block, checking her rear-view
mirror multiple times.

'I'm okay, Joe.'

We get to the police barrier. Mom winds down her window
and shows her badge. The officer inspects it and then looks at
me. I quickly avert my eyes and stare directly in front of me, at
nothing in particular. Smooth, Joe, way to not look dodgy. Mom

winds up her window. They move the wooden barriers and she drives us through, once again looking through her rear-view mirror.

'What are you doing here?' We both say it at the same time. We usually laugh when that happens, but not on this occasion.

'We made plans to meet, remember? I didn't hear from you, so I made my way here. I didn't see your text until I arrived.'

I look over at her. She's still checking the mirrors, which makes me look too.

'You've got broken glass on your jacket, Mom.' I pick a chunk off her shoulder, brushing the others off with my hand. She checks her jacket, then brushes some dust off her leg. We slow down at a junction as the lights turn red.

'There was a shoot-out at the morgue.' She grips her hands tighter on the leather steering wheel.

'What?!' I gasp. 'Are you hurt?'

She calmly puts the car in first gear and continues driving. 'One person was killed.'

'Wh . . . why?' It's probably a daft question to ask in the circumstances, but words tumble out of my mouth. Mom's told me stories of her time on the force. Some of the grim realities she faced as an officer . . . Being raised by a single parent, you hear a lot. 'Was anyone arrested?'

'No, the shooter got away.' This explains why she keeps checking her mirror. She looks over at me to reassure me. 'Joe, I'm good. I promise.'

I sit looking at her, sort of lost for words. Mom's kind of badass. My own woes pale in comparison right now. Just doesn't seem right to burden her with more problems, which — let's face it — could all just be some sort of random cosmic coincidence. If only I believed that to be true . . . It's a hard thing to try to deceive yourself. But now's not the time.

'So what happens now?'

'Right now, we're going to celebrate your birthday.'

* * *

We go to a sports bar called Sizzle & Score. Signed jerseys and retro pictures of football teams hang on the walls. Bright neon lights glow with vaguely sports-related slogans, like 'eye of the tiger' and 'GOAL!' Pop music plays throughout the restaurant and bar area. Replica trophies sit on display in glass cabinets; great for selfie opportunities, if you like that kind of thing. Adorning the walls above the bar are loads of TVs, each one displaying a different sport. A couple of the screens show the news coverage of the current protest in the city centre.

We grab a table in one of the booths. Mom sends a quick text, so I take the opportunity to get my phone out and check the group chat:

14:44 — Sam 🕹: Yoooooo @Joseph 😌 my G. Those pics of the police you sent were Mazza!! I'ma come round urs before we go out 2nite. I'll pull up bout 9. Make sure u r bro! 2nite we're getting lit 🍻 🔥 🔥 😂 👊.

I've never got why Sam uses so many emojis in his messages. Starting to regret agreeing to go out.

14:46 — Leiyah レイヤ 👹 🍃: I'll meet you guys in town. Digbeth near the square by the custard factory at 2200h.

14:46 — Leiyah レイヤ 👹 🍃: Don't be late 😫 ✌

15:20 — Sent: We won't b late @Leiyah

55

レイヤ🐵🗡X

15:20 — Sent: Yh that's kl @Sam ⚓ c u guys l8er

A waitress comes over to take our order. Mom's still texting, oblivious to everything else. I order myself a soft drink and a tea for Mom. She puts her phone on the table and takes off her jacket.

'Right, I'm all yours. How's your day been?' If only she knew. I want to say 'Yeah great! I dreamt about a girl being murdered by some sort of masked bestial spectre. Went to the hotel where I dreamt it happened, only to find out that a girl actually did drown there . . .'

'It's been an interesting day,' I reply.

'Meaning . . . ?' She raises her eyebrows and gestures for more.

Should I tell her about the crazy homeless guy at the skatepark, who was clearly on drugs — whose eyes rolled back into his head, shouting some demonic crazy lingo? Maybe not. But I do need to give her something before she does that Mom-cop thing and starts asking questions until she gets the information she wants.

'Today's been alright, I guess. Haven't failed my course. Yet. Still jobless. Social status still very much defined as awkward, so . . . yeah, my student life is . . . average, I think. Oh, before I forget, my lecturer Professor Grey hates me.'

Mom gives me The Look. I sigh, pulling my hand through one of my many curls, detangling one in frustration. She can always tell when I'm hiding something.

'To be honest, I just feel like I'm letting myself down some-times. I should be doing better. But . . . it's happening again.'

The waitress comes back over with the drinks and takes our food orders.

Mom leans forwards conspiratorially, but the waitress is

already halfway to the kitchen and out of earshot. 'Have you been taking your prescription?'

'Sometimes,' I shrug.

'You need to take them, Joe. We've been through this before, worse even, and we've always come through. You'll be fine, I promise. Do you need to book more sessions with Doctor Sia?'

I take a sip. 'Probably. I was hoping I wouldn't have to see her again.'

'Or you could try yoga?' She says it with a straight face but she has got to be taking the mick.

'I'm not doing yoga.'

'Why not? I do it.'

'Exactly! Look, Mom, falling asleep isn't just the problem. It sounds stupid but . . . when I'm sleeping, I feel like I'm awake.'

'You always did have a vivid imagination. I remember when I used to find you in the middle of the night, sleepwalking in the hallway by the stairs. Scared me to death. Never understood how you didn't fall down.'

The waitress brings our orders to the table. Mom looks at the waitress, then wags her eyebrow at me as she pours tea into her cup. I take another sip of my drink.

'So, have you met anyone yet?'

I almost choke on my fizzy drink. 'Mom!' I'm not sure if my red cheeks are from choking or embarrassment.

The waitress is trying her hardest not to laugh. Mom winks at her. She's not funny. 'Just asking, I remember being a student. What about that girl on your course? Errr . . . '

'Leiyah's a close friend,' I reply swiftly.

'If you say so. She's nice. What about . . . ?' she continues to reel off some random names that I don't even know. A family of five takes the booth area across from us. I can't help but stare. The youngest child is playing, jumping on the seat, wearing a superhero costume. Reminds me of that time when I went to my first Hallowe'en party with my mom. All the kids thought it weird when they saw us together.

'Mom, can I ask you a question?'

'Sure.'

I hesitate, focusing on my glass, watching the droplets of condensation run down the side onto the table. I glance at the family again.

'It's about my biological parents.'

Mom shuffles in her seat, looking slightly uncomfortable, and sees the Black family in the booth across from us.

'Oh. Okay?'

'I've never really asked before, and I know you've always encouraged me to ask any questions and always been open and honest about my adoption . . . I don't know why now, I just . . . But . . . Nah, forget it, um, don't worry about it, stupid question.'

My chest starts to tighten up. I rush food into my mouth to stop myself from speaking, taking a huge gulp from my drink. Mom grabs my hand, which has suddenly become very clammy.

'Joseph Jacobs, look at me. I can't imagine the things that you've gone through and . . . I see the brave face you show every day. I want you to know: you can ask me whatever you want when you're ready. I'm here. I'll always be here to help you: whatever, wherever.'

I start to feel calm again. 'Maybe more sessions with Doctor Sia would help.' She's always said that the beginning of reclaiming my past would be a door that I would have to open. Then, and only then, will I start to find some sort of peace. I can agree that there's some truth in that, even if I would never admit it openly. Mom's face changes, from gentle into a concerned frown.

'What's up?'

I follow her eyeline to one of the screens above the bar. Other customers also divert their attention to the TV, mumbling amongst themselves. The volume is off, but there's a man outside a police station giving a statement. His right arm is bandaged, held up in a medical support sling. *Detective Kukadia, Central Mercia Police.* A caption scrawls along the bottom in bright red: *Suspected Serial Killer.*

'Bastard!' Mom grits her teeth and curses under her breath. Her phone vibrates on the table. Caller ID: 'X'? Who's that? She quickly grabs her phone, puts her coat on and places money on the table to pay for the meal.

'Everything good, Mom?'

She throws her bag over her shoulder, rushing to find her keys.

'I'm so sorry, I've got to run; it's an emergency. I'll make it up to you, I promise. Enjoy your night out; be safe.' She starts to walk away. 'Oh, I almost forgot!' She pulls out a small wrapped present from her bag and places it on the table, then kisses me on the forehead and leaves. 'Happy Birthday! See you at home.'

I sit there alone, unwrapping my present. Opening it, a huge smile spreads across my face. A small photo frame with a picture of me, aged eight, holding my mom's hand, dressed in a superhero costume that Mom put together herself. It took a lot of counselling to help me to smile again, but I remember this day. Both of us dressed up. It was my first Hallowe'en party and I remember being so excited. I felt like a real superhero.

CHAPTER 5

Happy 🎉 Birthday!

Ahhh. No place like home. What a day. As birthdays go, this has probably been the craziest, considering I try not to celebrate them. The truth is, with each year that passes I feel more hollow and, while I'm being honest with myself, maybe it's the fact that I still can't bring myself to follow through and speak to my mom about what happened to my biological parents.

I hang my jacket in the pantry under the stairs and head into the kitchen. A small, red velvet birthday cake with chocolate icing is left on the worktop. Mom must have put this out after I left this morning. I take a slice and connect my phone to the surround sound speakers that we've got hooked up in the open-plan kitchen and dining area. I like spending time in here; there's loads of natural light from that spread from one side of the room to the other. It's a great panoramic view of the sky and, also, you're never too far from the food. It's 5:30 p.m., which means I've got a couple of hours to chill before Sam gets here. So, what to do . . . ? I could catch up on some anime or jump on some online gaming . . .

Ding dong!

I check the doorbell interface app on my phone. It's a delivery guy holding a package.

'Hello, can I help you?' I say through the app.

'Delivery for a Mr Jacobs?'

Snap, it's for me. 'Yep, one sec.'

I go to the front door. A delivery guy in a bright orange vest stands there, holding a brown package covered in old stamps. 'Mr Jacobs?' he enquires.

'Yeah, that's me.'

'Sign here, please.' I sign electronically and take the small box. 'Have a great evening.'

'Thanks.'

I close the door, looking at the square parcel. The brown paper it's wrapped in looks old and crinkled. It's tied together with string, knotted neatly at the top. Must be another birthday present from Mom.

I head back into the kitchen, take another small slice of cake, and fall back onto the couch next to the huge glass doors. The sun's starting to set, violet streaks washing against the oncoming clouds in the dimming sky. Looks like it's going to rain. I turn the package over in my hands, rotating from the corners, looking at all the different stamps. Some of these stamps don't even look like they're British. Curiosity's killing me and I sit up and start to untie the knot. I release the string and the paper unfolds like a flower bud. Inside is a small, carved, old-looking mahogany jewellery case. What is this? Looks expensive; cool. I lift open the lid and, resting on a bed of soft purple satin, is a small, bronze, antique necklace. The design resembles a dreamcatcher: circular and intricately designed. Wow, amazing; it looks handmade.

Carefully picking the necklace up by its reddish bronze chain links, I check the box for any notes or an address to try to figure out where this came from. Maybe it's a mistake and it's for another Mr Jacobs. There's nothing! That doesn't stop me from inspecting. The design on the full moon centrepiece has a spiral, interwoven, web-like design. On the right side of the main circle is a black outlined triangle, which houses strange symbols. Hanging directly beneath the moon centrepiece are three small industrial looking cogged circles. The top circle resembles the image of the sun and the other two are accompanied beside three small, black, dangling feathers which are jewelled with wooden beads. I'm totally entranced by it; it's exquisite, truly beautiful, it and has a strange pull about it.

I feel my palm start to vibrate where the bronzed necklace is touching my hand. Why is my heart racing? I need my inhaler. Feel out of breath. Why do I know that pattern . . . ? I begin to feel heat, hot flames warming my face, bright white flashes and I realise . . . I'm back.

* * *

I open my eyes and I'm a child again, sitting at the top of a smoke-filled   case, gripping onto the bars of the banister so tightly that the brown pigmentation in my hand begins to turn pale. Through the bars, barely visible,   bright flashes of   , almost like sparks, sporadically illuminating the destroyed,   engulfed   room. I can hear the sound of   breaking, sporadic pops and crunches through the thick, suffocating smoke. I glimpse scorched furniture and

. At the back of the room, a single double-glazed patio door reveals a shadow. From outside the glass, a   emerges from the darkness,   eyes

    hair   approaches the glass then, in a substance that looks like   diamonds, begins to paint what looks like a type of circle-and-triangle patterned insignia on the window. Underneath   writes a sequence of symbols, too distorted   I stand there, staring   then the   shadow points at me, and with one bony finger taps on the glass where the insignia is. The taps turn into a knock, getting louder and louder, matching my racing heart-beat.

Knock knock, knock knock.

I feel myself fading, sinking, as the image from the necklace imprints on my mind. Everything turns blue. My stomach flutters with that sensation you get when you're lying in bed, falling in your sleep.

I snap back to reality.

I find myself on the floor, sweaty, still gripping the necklace in my left hand. I lie there for a moment, while my breathing normalises.

It's dark outside. How long was I out for?

Knock knock, knock knock.

The knocking is coming from the lounge window. Rubbing my eyes, I walk into the front room. A hand hits against the window, jumping out of the dark, scaring the hell out of me.

'Yo, Joe! Open up man, it's cold out here!'

Phew, it's just Sam. I open the front door. Sam's blowing into his hands to keep himself warm.

''Bout time,' he says, pushing past me to get into the warm. 'I've been out there for ages. I could've been that serial killer's next victim,' he says, miming a pretend noose. 'Don't your doorbell work or something? How are you not dressed yet? It's 9:30,' he says. 'Leiyah's gonna kill us if we're late, you know what she's like.'

I go to get ready.

'Wait, what's that?' Sam notices a piece of the bronze chain from the necklace in my hand.

'Oh, it's nothing.' Pushing the chain into my pocket, I try to change the subject. 'Drinks are in the fridge. I won't be long, yeah?'

'Whatever. Quick-time, Snorlax. You know them hydros are

bare long and we've got 'nuff partying to do. You might even catch a wine if you're lucky.'

The blinds in my room haven't been opened for the last couple of days due to my inconsistent sleeping patterns. LED lights run across the corners of my ceiling, glowing in multiple colours. My Nebula projector beams onto the ceiling above my bed, near the skateboard collection on my wall. A collection of masquerade-themed masks look down on my bed. Mom hates those masks; she thinks they're weird. I think it's kinda arty. Makes me feel like someone's watching over me. I imagine that they're the faces of my long-forgotten ancestors, checking in on me to make sure I'm alright. Next to my wardrobe are my collectibles. An assortment of retro consoles ranging from Atari, Mega Drive and Saturn to Nintendos and my PS1. My comics and first issues are neatly stacked on the shelves amongst the special edition Funko Pop models above my laptop. Wish I could say the same about my history books being neatly stacked; they're all over the place in preparation for my next assignment.

Okay, what to wear? I haven't got much time so, after a quick shower, I throw on my black, distressed jeans with my black Doc Martens boots, my black bullet-hole-ridden-style longline top and black distressed denim jacket. Denim on denim — is that a no-no? Not sure; looks kinda fire! Ain't got time. One thing I do know is you can't go wrong with black!

* * *

Sam and I hit the streets of Brum. It's Student Night and, tonight especially, the city feels alive. Sam's buzzing with excitement! He's got his phone out, updating his social media followers. He says it's audience engagement; I think of it as social enslavement. I've got to rate him though: 122k-plus followers on West's World, plus endorsements, is quite an achievement.

Leiyah stands alone by the wall in the Digbeth courtyard, exactly where she said she would meet us. She's rocking a black-and-white-flowered biker jacket, meshed black dress, black Docs and she's wearing her hair (which is really long) partly down, with two Pikachu buns at the top of her head.

She spots us and gives us a look of relief mixed with frustration.

'It's about time! You're always late!' she chides us whilst walking over, holding a blue gift bag.

'It wasn't me, swear down. It was Joe.' Wow, cheers for that Sam. Snitches get stitches.

'My bad, Leiyah. It was my fault. I lost track of time. You look . . . different. No glasses tonight?'

'Contacts. I forgive you. You're lucky it's your birthday. First round's on Sam, yeah?'

'Agreed.'

Sam sticks out his bottom lip, confused as to how we came to that conclusion.

Leiyah hands me the blue gift bag. 'Happy birthday!' I pull out a limited edition comic book and a strange ornament that kinda has the head of a tusked elephant mixed with the body of a tiger.

'Cool.' I say examining the model.

'It's Baku.' Leiyah says proudly. 'Its a Japanese mythical creature — it's suppose to protect against bad dreams. Hope you like it. Thought it might help you sleep.'

Holding both gifts, I give Leiyah a hug. 'This is amazing, thank you.' Sam peeks over and tries to join in the hug.

'Yeah — that present was from me too, Joe.'

'Uhhh, no it wasn't.' Leiyah shoves Sam, breaking up the hug.

'Yeah, yeah, whatever. It's the thought that counts. Can we stop with the sentiments and get hammered now?'

We all laugh, nodding in agreement, and head off to the first bar on Sam's list.

* * *

'THREE, TWO, ONE, SHOTS!'

Ughhhh, that burns! Chilli shots are deffo not my favourite but as long as Sam's buying we continue to knock back whatever he puts in front of us. We hit a retro arcade and VR venue first. We play a co-op survival game on a Zombie VR simulator. Leiyah's out first after running out of ammo, getting cornered and mauled to death by loads of zombies. Sam drops out, complaining about motion sickness. Yeah, right.

* * *

'THREE, TWO, ONE, SHOTS!'

'Ughhh!' That one got me good.

Leiyah's face scrunches up like she's just bitten into the sourest lemon she's ever tasted in her life. We burst out laughing. This bar's themed like we're in Hawaii, with palm trees and tiki torches in the outside area.

Sam's being held up as he gulps from a funnel, being poured from a keg by a group chanting: 'Sam! Sam! Sam!' They say they're followers of West's World. That's definitely gonna get messy. My eye lands on two older women sitting across the bar from us. One of them blows me a kiss. Leiyah catches the mortified look on my face and looks over in time to see the older lady bite her lip, as well as do something interesting with her straw, before calling me over. I snatch Leiyah's drink from her, down it, and make a swift exit.

* * *

'THREE, TWO, ONE, SHOTS!'

'Yakkk! I'm done, no more, tapping out!' I use the back of my hand to wipe my mouth. Sambuca is where I draw the line. After playing a very tipsy game of indoor golf, we grab some tacos from one of the many food stalls surrounding the area. We mess around, snapping selfie after selfie. Anime pose: *SNAP!* Serious face, middle finger, Brum pose: *SNAP!* The obligatory corny rabbit ears pose: *SNAP!* Sam attempts a fourth picture, mooning the camera. Leiyah shuts that down quickly, before he gets the chance to loosen his belt. As nights go, I'm having a fantastic time and — dare I say — I'm actually enjoying my birthday night out. What more could I possibly ask for? I've got my two best friends and the city is buzzing with excitement.

We head towards a club called The Night Owl. Sam said he can get us in free, one of his followers tagged him in a vid as the place to be tonight. The surrounding buildings are covered in huge, impressive graffiti. The industrial structure of the old Custard Factory against the illuminated neon signs hanging from building to building, all the way up the road, is the perfect mix of urban-meets-industrial. The queue for the club stretches around the corner, with bouncers checking IDs and searching students as they wait anxiously to get in.

'Follow me,' Sam says confidently, walking up to the bouncer and showing him a QR code, which the bouncer scans. We pass straight through with no issues. Leiyah and I look at each other. Nice. Walking into the main area, you can feel the body heat from the crowd dancing and vibing to the music. It's rammed. My head nods to the Clash Wave beats, the thump of the bass shakes my chest with each hit. Leiyah starts to dance, blending in with the rest of the crowd, who are singing along, drinking and throwing their hands towards the material-covered, Aladdin's cave-style ceiling. Screens above us project old

1920s Prohibition Era dance films onto the exposed brick wall. Sam turns, putting drinks in mine and Leiyah's hand looking impressed with himself. 'Not bad guys, if I don't say so myself. Not bad at all.' He's got a point; it looks amazing. Although Sam is unable to keep his eye from wandering, checking out the various groups of ladies en route to the dance floor.

Leiyah nudges both of us, signalling us to look forwards into the crowd. Miles pushes through the busy crowd, bouncing people dancing out the way, with full-on black Air Force 1 energy. Sam turns towards us, shielding his face. He probably doesn't want a repeat of what happened to us earlier. Miles doesn't see us and heads up the stairs towards the canopy bar.

'Hold this, will ya? Back in a sec, just going toilet.' Sam gives his drink to Leiyah and disappears before we can say anything. We stand there, listening to the music.

'You enjoying your night?' Leiyah shouts, holding two drinks and swaying to the music.

'Yeah, I'm having a great time! Way better than this morning!' The DJ pulls up a rewind, stops the track, and grabs the mic.

'Testing one, two. Birmingham, make some NOISE!' The crowd goes wild. 'I'm giving you what you've been waiting for. Make some noise for the 0121 Kings and Queens of the mics!' He double-scratches the track, sending the crowd into a frenzy, dropping the beat as a horde of local artists take the stage. They begin to cypher and spit over the beat with crazy bars.

'Tune! Sooooo good!' Leiyah holds up both drinks, wining to the beat. 'You wanna dance?'

'I'm good. I'll wait for Sam.' Leiyah continues to dance, joining in with some of the MCs' lyrics as they spit lyrical fire over the tunes. I wonder what's taking Sam so long? Just as I'm about to go and find him, I feel a light tap on my shoulder.

'Hello again.' I turn to see Harmony, accompanied by two

Amazonian-looking, Black identical twins. Not going to lie, she looks incredible. Her Afro's out and her outfit's dotted with small, sparkling, golden rhinestones. Looks fire.

'Hey, Harmony, hi.' I wave awkwardly. Fix up Joe! Who waves when someone's right in front of them? Stay cool, you wasteman. 'Hey,' I repeat clearing my throat.

Harmony chuckles, as do the twins. She nudges one to stop them laughing. 'These are my friends: Omanah and Omaru. It's nice to see you again. You here with friends?'

'Yeah. Actually . . . It's my birthday. I'm just out celebrating.'

'Aww no way, happy birthday!' She raises her drink, I raise mine and we both drink. We awkwardly stand there, looking at each other. Leiyah takes a noisy slurp from her empty glass through a straw.

One of the twins is dancing. The other is standing next to Harmony and whispers something into her ear, which makes her smile. A dazzling, heart-stopping smile. Another track comes on; the crowd roar their approval.

'We're gonna go and dance, did you wanna maybe . . . ?'

I look over at Leiyah, not wanting to leave her on her own.

'I can't, I was just—'

Harmony looks at me and Leiyah. 'Oh. Right. I'm so sorry, are you two . . . ?'

'No!' we both blurt out at the same time.

'This is my friend, Leiyah. Sam's here too, somewhere.'

Leiyah waves at Harmony, then pushes me forward. 'I'll wait for Sam. You should definitely go, Joe.' Leiyah gives me a soft smirk, then a wide-eyed look. 'GO!'

Harmony grabs my arm, leading us into the thick of the crowd. I look back at Leiyah as she disappears from view. The swamp of the dance floor closes in around us.

The music switches, mellowing out to Afrobeats and slow

dancehall music. Smoke and bubbles from the DJ booth blow over the crowd. Green lasers twist and turn slowly to the rhythm of the music as some students raise lighters in the air. Harmony moves closer, dancing to the slow beat. She puts my hands on her hips. Not gonna lie, the alcohol's got me all in my feelings, but I'm trying to keep it cool, two-stepping to her rhythm. Nothing too fancy. No room to mess up. She smiles and moves even closer. I guess that's a good sign. I can feel her soft breath on my neck. If I'd asked myself earlier if I'd be out celebrating with my friends, enjoying myself like this, dancing in a club with Harmony, I would never have believed it. 'Perfect,' I say to myself. I don't often use that word, but it fits here, believe me. Three more songs go by but it feels like a second. Time really does fly.

Rushing down the stairs, I see Sam, on his phone, leaping down the last two steps and disappearing into the crowd. Moments later, Miles is at the top of the stairs, almost frothing at the mouth with anger. He cusses, gesturing wildly with his arms. People lined up on the stairs hold their noses as Miles makes his way down, scanning the club, peering over the railings. Sam, what have you done now?

Parting the crowd like the red sea, two huge bouncers grab Miles, dragging him out through the crowd. He gets closer to where Harmony and I are, almost lifted off his feet, skidding and pulling as the bouncers drag him out. As he passes me I see that he's completely soaked; others around him, including the bouncers, hold their noses as they remove him from the dance floor. The DJ reloads the track and everyone carries on raving. After a couple more songs, Leiyah comes over. 'Joe, Sam's drunk. I'm gonna get him back before he makes a fool of himself.'

'Cool, I'm coming. Wait for me by the entrance.' I really don't want to leave but it's not fair to leave Leiyah to deal with Sam. We came out together, we leave together.

* * *

We exit the club. Harmony and I sit on the side of the wall underneath a huge graffitied pharaoh. Omanah and Omaru walk slowly towards their taxi. Leiyah tries to prop up a drunken Sam, who attempts to rizz up the twins as they pass in front of him.

Slap!

'Aww, the sweetest sting I've ever felt.' Sam holds his cheek, then blows a kiss to Omaru. Omanah is not impressed.

'He's gonna feel that in the morning,' I say, watching Sam. I signal with my hand to an annoyed Leiyah: two minutes. I catch Harmony smiling to herself.

'What's up?' I ask.

'Nothing. I just really enjoyed myself. It's nice to meet someone a bit different.'

'Different . . . ?'

'Yeah, different. It's a good thing.'

'Meaning?'

She gets up and walks slowly towards her friends. I follow waiting for an answer. She stops and turns suddenly.

'There's definitely something about you, Joseph,' she squints, as if peering deep into my soul. 'Can't quite put my finger on it but there's something.' I've always had a problem with eye contact — makes me uncomfortable — but this is one moment that I never want to look away from. There's a moment of silence, in which it feels like we're speaking beyond words, beyond what words could ever convey. If I didn't know it before, I'm definitely in my feelings now.

Harmony catches herself. 'Well, your birthday's nearly officially over. Time to make a wish.' Before I can protest, she places her hand over my eyes.

'What are you do—?'

71

'Shhhhhhhh. Come on, one wish until your next birthday. Ready?' I play her game and start to think. Guess a cool wish would have been to have a deeper understanding of who I am and where I come from by this time next year, but deep down I'm wishing that this night would never end.

'Done it?' Harmony asks quietly.

'Yeah.'

Harmony removes her hands from my eyes.

'Wasn't so bad, was it?'

'I guess not.'

We start walking again, over to our friends. I pluck up the courage. 'Maybe we could do this again sometime?'

'You mean like a "date" date?' she asks, giving nothing away.

'Oh . . . No, well, if—'

'I would love that. You got a phone?' I pull out my phone and unlock the screen. Harmony types in her number, switches on my camera to selfie mode and leans in.

'Say cheese!' She takes a pic. 'There.' She hands me back my phone. 'No DMs: call me.'

'Will do.'

'Yooo, Joe! The ground's spinning, bro. I can see the Tesseract! Mad ting. Mighty Odin, Allfather, come hither!'

Leiyah's getting more and more annoyed, almost hitting Sam to get him to keep still.

'I better get him back,' I say to Harmony.

'Yep, I think you should.' The twins call over and jump in the taxi. 'See you soon, Joseph.'

'Night.'

I go over and help Leiyah with Sam, who's now starting to complain about feeling ill.

* * *

72

We cut through one of the many backstreets in Digbeth, heading into an alley behind the club, which is over-shadowed by a train bridge. It's pretty grimy; open bin bags and rubbish carpet the pavement. Spray-painted tags and graffitied logos like 'G3' stain the walls and the bottom half of the huge pillars supporting the bridge. I'm pretty sure there are rats here too, which is not cool. It's dim. A single light from a backdoor exit sign and a darkened window above it help to give a little visibility. It's a quick shortcut to get three roads over to where we've booked our ride. Just want to get through here as quick as possible.

It starts to rain.

'Guys, hold up a sec!' Sam runs over to the wall with his cheeks puffed out and hands over his mouth. 'Awrrrrrr!'

'Joe, Sam's being sick!' Leiyah calls out, going over to Sam and slapping him on the back, in a part-helpful-part-harmful kind of way. I walk a few paces on, thinking I hear something ahead. Can't really see anything; it's a bit too dark. And the distant sound from the clubs is making it impossible to listen carefully.

Crunch!

What was that? I definitely heard something. I stop and squint down the alleyway.

'Joe, a bit of help here please? Your superstar best friend really can't hold his booze.' I rush over to Leiyah urgently.

'We need to get going now,' I say, sharply but quietly, using my voice and eyes to alert Leiyah. She cautiously leans to look behind me. She looks back at me and nods in agreement. We swiftly try to help Sam up on to his feet, heading back the way we came. I hear multiple footsteps behind us, getting closer with each step we take.

'What do we have here?' A low, menacing voice cuts through the darkness.

We turn. I see a flash of silver and silhouettes of bodies. We

73

freeze and look at one another, holding each other a little tighter, as bodies ghoulishly emerge from the darkened alley.

There are about five of them.

'We're good thanks, just going on our way.' I position myself in front of Leiyah to shield her and Sam as best I can from the ten piercing eyes that are peering at us from the shadows. Another flash of silver. The furthest forward takes another step towards us, removing something from his mouth with a hand bedecked in huge silver skull rings. Between his knuckles are the tattooed letters: 'TIN' He walks slowly towards us, kicking litter out of his way with combat boots capped with steel. His long black trench coat billows behind him. He looks at us with cold, green, unblinking eyes.

'Rough night,' he says, looking down at Sam's vomit, revealing more of his face. His gaze snaps back to us with a twisted, emotionless grin. Under his right eye is the number 88 inked with an arrow pointing towards his bald head. I feel my chest start to tighten.

'Look, we don't want any trouble.' I back up, slowly stepping back. Leiyah and Sam follow suit. Sam has lifted his head and is alert, fully aware of what's going on. Stepping backwards, we hit against something. A huge guy blocks our path.

'Yo man, dafuq is this, move out the way!' Sam blares. The big guy grabs Sam by the neck and throws him, sending him crashing into the wall.

'Sam!' Leiyah screams, stepping back in the direction of the bald guy, who seems to be in charge. Sam holds his arm and stumbles to get to his feet. I rush to help him.

Click!

Fingers snap. I'm dragged backwards and slammed against the wall.

'*Ooouff!*'

The air is knocked out of my lungs. I start hyperventilating, trying my hardest to control my breath. Sam is dragged to his feet and pinned by his attacker against the adjacent fence, facing me, his eyes wide in pure terror.

'Evening,' the bald-headed guy says, sniffing around Leiyah, stroking her hair.

'Don't touch me!' Leiyah slaps his hand away.

'Ouch, ain't you fiery? But then, mongrels usually are,' he says, circling her like a predator.

'Leave us, please! We don't have any money!' Sam yells. The thug pinning Sam gets a signal from the leader and furiously punches Sam in the stomach with such force that it lifts him off the ground. Sam crumples to his knees.

'Sam! Someone, please help!' I shout, trying to wriggle and force myself out of my aggressor's grip.

Sssshhhhhinnnggg!

A blinding flash of cold metal swings from the shadow, pushing me back against the wall. I blink. As my eyes focus, I see a huge machete blade, centimetres from my throat.

'Move again, I dare you,' whispers the guy holding the blade to my neck. He takes deep, enraged breaths from behind his blue surgical mask, his bleached-blonde golden plaits hang over his hooded face. My hand starts to shake and I drop my gift bag from Leiyah, scattering the items across the floor. My Baku ornament rolls to a stop at the boss's feet.

'Happy birthday,' he laughs, before sadistically trampling on my presents. The thugs press me and Sam further into the wall and take our wallets and phones. The leader circles Leiyah, all alone in the middle of the alley. He licks his lips, the look of a crazed predator in his eyes.

'Stop this, please! What do you want?!'

He advances.

'Please, don't!'

The sound of a roaring train screams past on the tracks above. My breathing gets thinner and thinner. Sam rolls on the floor, holding his belly and groaning in pain. The bald guy saunters up to Leiyah, forcing her back against the fence. A flash of silver glints as he pulls out a set of silver grills from a case and pushes them into his mouth. He rolls his lips around the grills in his mouth, like a boxer. Finally, he smiles.

'Dark is the night for ghouls and ghosts. For the heartless streets are full of monsters that kill and boast.'

Suddenly, he grabs Leiyah, who screams. She tries to flee but he grabs her by her long hair, pushing her viciously against the fence.

'Now, how is that fruitful vine? Are we feeling more . . . open?' he whispers softly, tearing parts of her dress. He kicks her legs apart from a standing position. He unzips.

'Joe . . . Joseph, p— p— please help!' She looks at me, pleadingly, tears rolling down her cheeks.

'Get away from her, you bastard!' I shout.

The blade near my neck twitches. I gasp, panicking, fighting for gulps of air. Leiyah continues to cry out.

I put one foot against the wall and push as hard as I can, sending my attacker flying backwards.

Slash!

I feel a sharp pain in my side, burning, stinging. I fall to the floor. Leiyah screams. The metal-toed boots move away from Leiyah's Docs.

'Charley, you slash him?'

Leiyah drops to her knees, crying. She crawls towards me. A tattooed hand covered in skull rings, the letters 'MAN' on the knuckles, grabs Leiyah again, yanking her head back.

'Guess time's up, beautiful. Careful out there; dangerous folk about.' He lets go of her and she falls to the floor. The sound of footsteps fade.

'Sam! Help! Joseph, oh my God! Help, someone call an ambulance!' My eyes blur in and out, flashing blue lights and the sound of sirens swirl around me.

'TIN MAN,' I mutter under my breath before my vision blurs again.

* * *

'Hands up! Mercia PD! Nobody move!'

'We need help! My friend's been stabbed!'

'I said hands up!'

'We need an ambulance for a young Black male. Possible gang-related incident.'

'Joseph!'

'We need oxygen now.'

'Vitals are dropping.'

'Joseph? Can you hear me?'

Joseph, can you hear me? You're going to be alright.'

'Going to be . . . Joseph? You're going to be . . .'

'Alright.'

* * *

'TIN MAN!' I awaken with a start.

My eyes roll open to see an oxygen mask on my face. Beeping noises intermittently ping from the machine to the side of my bed; wires are connected to my arm.

'Sam? Leiyah?'

I'm alone. I sit up, glancing down at my left rib. *Slash!* My mind flashes back to the blade. I touch the area, now wrapped up and taped with a blood-stained bandage. It's tender; feels sore. All the other beds are empty; I'm the only one in the room. To my right, my black top and denim jacket are draped over a chair, rippling from the breeze blowing in from the open window.

I pull the oxygen mask from my face, shuffling to get comfortable. Something crunches in my back pocket. I reach around to see what it is. Oh no! My dreamcatcher necklace. It's broken in two. I don't even remember putting this in my pocket. Holding it in my hand I can't help but feel completely crushed. My eyes begin to well up. All the feelings of guilt and helplessness hit me like a wave. I couldn't help my friends. I see flashes of Sam being attacked and Leiyah . . . Tin Man trying to force himself on her . . . '*Joseph, help!*' Their cries echo in my head, as I relive the moment all over again.

I break down, sobbing, squeezing the necklace in my hand. When I release it, I feel something protruding from the broken moon centrepiece. A tiny, tightly rolled ribbon is tucked into the disconnected part of the ring. I pull it out and begin to unravel it. It's miniscule. My eyes widen as I read the words embroidered in gold onto the purple fabric:

Dear Joseph,
Happy Birthday. We are such stuff as dreams are made on.
Love, Mum and Dad

My heart pounds. The ribbon drops from my hands and I fall back. It's like an out-of-body experience; I can see myself convulsing on the bed. I begin to feel heat, hot flames warming my face, bright white flashes. I open my eyes and I'm a child again.

Only this time . . . I remember everything, unbroken. I can see clearly.

* * *

I'm sitting at the top of a smoke-filled staircase, gripping onto the bars of the banister so tightly that the brown pigmentation in my hand begins to turn pale. Through the bars, barely visible, I can see bright flashes of white light, almost like sparks, sporadically illuminating the destroyed, fire-engulfed living room. Horrific, nightmarish spectres roam the downstairs area. I can hear the sound of glass breaking, sporadic pops and crunches through the thick, suffocating smoke. I glimpse scorched furniture and blood trailing across the floor. At the back of the room, a single double-glazed patio door reveals a shadow. From outside the glass, a young Black girl emerges from the darkness, her eyes closed and her hair in pigtails. She approaches the glass, then, in a substance that looks like black, crystallised diamonds, begins to paint the same circle and triangle patterned insignia on the window as on my parents' note. She stops and looks up at me. She points. Suddenly, she evaporates in a black mist, then re-appears in front of me, her eyes closed. Strange embroidered glowing marks decorate her face. She puts a bony finger on the centre of my forehead and presses, uttering words in a language I've never heard before. All my hurt and pain resurfaces, bringing the thugs that attacked us to the forefront of my mind. The memories replay over and over again. How I wish I could have done something to stop them. If only . . . I wish I had fought back. I start to feel light, powerful, as my dream starts to unlock itself. A high-pitched screech cascades from deep within me and the girl stops speaking in the unknown language. Silence commands the room.

'Joseph. Time to Awaken,' she whispers with power.

The intense feeling of falling comes over me again, the same feeling I get in my dreams. This time I don't try to catch myself.

I let go.

CHAPTER 6

Blackout

'Patrol 40219, do you read? Over?'
'This is Officer Scott, copy. Over.'
'Traffic collision reported on the Queensway.
The driver has requested assistance. Over.'
'Upload exact location and we'll head there now.'
'Sending location. Out.'

'Bloody 'ell, I'm knackered. I'm getting too old for this; give me a desk job any day.'
'. . .'
'Not much of a talker, are you? Hey? Hey, Lace. Officer Lace!'
'Huh! Sorry, I was—'
'Daydreaming on the job?'
'No, I was just —'
'Looks like the morgue really got you rattled. Unfortunately, sweetheart, it's part of the job. You'll learn to put that stuff to the back of your mind soon enough.'
'All officers be advised: black smoke has been reported
across multiple building rooftops across the city centre.
Fire teams notified. Over.'

' . . . Does it get easier?'

'What?! Seeing someone die? Get blown away? No, no it doesn't . . . but you'll become numb to it. If anything, you'll lose more hope in humanity and your ability to help.'

'Is that why you signed up? To help?'

'Isn't that why we all joined the force, Lace? Naïve, really, to think what we're doing can make a difference.'

'You don't think what we do counts?'

'Just look out the window sweetheart. Look at these for example, in the other lane.'

'That fleet of SUVs?'

'Definitely up to no good. Heading to the Industrial, most likely. And you can bet your pretty head that they're making more in a day than we make in a year. But we prioritise. We can't solve everything all the time. It's an impossible job.'

'So we just don't try?'

'Lace, you're not hearing me. No matter how heavy the rain falls, this city still reeks; it's filthy, decadent, chaotic. This is one place where it doesn't need to be Hallowe'en for you to wear a mask. It's a place for the lost. That young lass in the morgue was probably just another runaway that this godforsaken place loves to welcome in and swallow up.'

'But surely—?'

'I know what you're going to say: why continue to serve? Why not just leave the force? Believe me, sweetheart, it's a question I ask myself all the time.'

'Officer Lace is sufficient, thank you. Also, we're not supposed to call ourselves "the force" anymore. Higher-ups said it sounds too aggressive. We "uphold the right".'

'Look, you're new to the job and I'm sure you've got great ambition. But word of advice, *rookie:* Being right usually involves a fat wad of cash. There's enmity on both sides of the playing field. Power and corruption go hand in hand in this city. It's not just the countless gangs gunning for you, it's your own: the ones with the numbered brass badges. You'll do well to remember that. Flashing hazard lights up ahead, we're here. Log it in and let's go.'

'Dispatch, this is Officer Lace, patrol 40219. Over.'

'Copy that. Over'

'We have reached the collision location. Over.'

'Location logged, Officer Lace. Out.'

'Excuse me, Sir, are you the one who called for assist—?'

'You're here! Thank God. It wasn't my fault, you've got to believe me. It all happened so fast, I— I—'

'Okay, keep calm. My name is Officer Lace and this is Officer Scott, we're here to he—'

'Officers, I tried to stop. There was so much rain, then black smoke, it came out of nowhere . . . I couldn't see him until it was too late. Oh God!'

'Dispatch, Officer Lace here. Send an ambulance immediately to our location. Over.'

'Copy that. Over.'

'I didn't see him! He just appeared, walked out of nowhere into the middle of the road! I slammed my foot on the brakes but—'

'Lace, stay with the driver. I'm gonna check the road.'

'Oh God! He's dead, isn't he? I killed him! I drove head-on straight into him! No one could survive that. Let me help, please.'

'Sir, we're here now. Let us do our job. Are you injured?'

'No, I don't think so. Just shaking.'

'Okay. the paramedics will be here shortly.'

'He . . . was covered in black smoke, almost like he was on fire, walking slowly, stumbling forwards, his eyes were closed . . . Just before I — My headlights bounced off him, shining so brightly I couldn't see!'

'Officer Scott! Anything?'

'No, nothing. I can't see a thing and this bloody weather isn't helping. There's no cracks on the front window or dent marks on the bonnet. Search unit's on its way, ETA two minutes. Victim is possibly inebriated, almost certainly severely injured. I've retrieved the driver's dash-cam, but there's little else we can do here. Our best bet is to let them check the driver over and log the report once the footage has been viewed.'

'He just appeared . . . Out of thin air. Where did he go?'

'Patrol 40129, report of vandalism and possible gang activity outside of New Street. Over.'

* * *

'The 2:33 a.m. has now arrived. Welcome to Birmingham New Street.'

At first I thought I was losing my mind but the more I saw her, the more I knew I had to follow. And now I'm here, back to where it all started. So this is Brum? What a toilet! To think this is where we were born. Cringe. I've not even been out of the station for two minutes and I've already seen someone tweaking on hyper-steds and a gang rushing a ticket officer. Now all I have to deal with is this bad weather and the piercing sound of sirens which—

It's happening again! I instantly freeze. My palms begin to tingle and burn and, amidst the noise of the incoming sirens and flashing police lights, everything around me slows down and she appears: Cara. She stands, almost obscured by the rain. I race down the steps onto the streets to get to her. But she's vanished. Then, the overwhelming feeling of déjà vu hits me.

Weeow! Weeow! Weeow! Weeow!

Splash!

'Neanderthals!' I shout as a police car speeds past.

Great, just great, I'm soaked! A giggle from behind me catches my ear. I turn to cuss out whoever is laughing at my misfortune but stop myself when I see a young child, no older than eleven, quickly hiding a can of spray paint behind her back. Her big bright brown eyes apprehensively track the now-distant police car from under her yellow-hooded rain mac.

'Aren't you a little young to be Birmingham's most wanted?' I say, rubbing the dirty road water off my face.

'Aren't you a little old to be taking a bath outside?' she retorts.

Wow, violation! Before I can think of something witty to respond, she walks off, cutting into a nearby alley.

'Hey!'

I follow her, shouting after her, wondering why someone so young is out so late: 'Wait up! You really shouldn't be—'

My words stop as I turn into the alley.

'Did . . . you paint that?' I ask.

'Maybe, who's asking?' the young girl replies as she collects her spray can.

'It's incredible.'

The walls are covered in scribbled graffiti. Words and quotes like 'Sons Of Jack', 'Obeah Kings' and 'Death to the machine!' are jotted around the walls erratically. But, in the midst of the chaos, stands an imposingly beautiful, graffitied tree.

'Really, it's beautiful. How old are you?'

'Old enough!' she snaps, spraying small letters under the tree.

'Isn't there someone worried that you're out so late?'

Suddenly, sirens swirl past again and I whip around, on high alert. The noise fades.

'It's okay, I think they've gone,' I say, turning back. 'Huh! Where did she . . . ?'

She's gone! I take a closer look at the tree and spot her freshly sprayed tag: SK✕.

What does that mean? SKX . . . 'Sketch?'

'Hey, you! Freeze!' a voice shouts from behind a blinding flashlight, startling me. That feeling washes over me again, and, as I look up, through the glare of the light, I see the unmistakable outline of Cara running past me, away from the police.

'Mercia PD! Don't m—'

Before the owner of that booming voice can finish their sentence, I leg it. I hear the officer call out random numbers on their radio as I run.

'This is patrol 40219, do you read? Over!'

'Stop!' the officer shouts as I dart out of the alleyway onto a busy road. This is crazy; what the hell am I doing, running from the law? But all I see through the busy traffic is Cara on the other side of the road. She's the reason I'm here, I've got to catch up with her. My eyes are still adjusting from the beam of light from the officer's torch; as she moves she leaves an iridescent trail behind her . . .

'Oi, you! I said: STOP!' the officer shouts.

I hightail it over some active hydro-tram tracks and through a jigsaw of gridlocked taxis. Their beeping horns drown out any more demands from the voice behind me. I keep sprinting as fast as my legs will go, straight into the middle of a crowded square. Once again, she fades from my sight. The cacophony of pubs and clubs around me adds further panic and I become a bit disorientated by the flashing neon signs and glitching holographic ads.

'Where now?' I say to myself. I check behind me to see if I'm still being followed. The rowdy crowd of late-night clubbers obstructs my view so I take the opportunity for a breather. I slow down to blend in with the crowd. C'mon, Charlotte, just keep walking and keep your head down. You got this.

Every yelp and cheer from passers-by causes me to flinch. Eventually I wade my way through the crowd, finding a rest spot behind a large eroded statue of a sphinx opposite a badly graffitied statue of a woman bathing in a fountain bath. I peek around the statue scanning the area to make sure the coast is clear. I breathe a sigh of relief. I'm safe and I'm one step closer. Cara has definitely got some serious explaining to do. Why the hell would she come to a place like this? Being vex with me for not listening to her is one thing, but travelling halfway across the country is a step too far.

Beep beep!

Car horns blare as people dodge out the way of a convoy of blacked-out 4x4's racing by.

I can't believe I'm here. I should've answered her call. All I have is this voice message, and now her line's down and I can't get back in touch. Something feels off. Maybe that's why I've been seeing her face everywhere I look: guilt. I need to apologise and tell her that she was right. You were right all along, Cara, and I can no longer bury my head. I too have seen it, what you described: a shadow haunting me when I sleep.

C'mon, no time to get all up in your feelings. Pulling out my phone I bring up my locations app. Victoria Square. Great, okay, now all I need to do is find where I'm . . . There! Station Street, Victoria Inn Hotel.

* * *

'Central, patrol 40219. Officer Scott speaking.'

'Go ahead, 40219.'

'Suspect got away on foot. Lost 'em in an alleyway somewhere near Victoria Square. Over.'

'Copy. Out.'

86

'Pff. Like I said, Lace, I'm getting too old for this. If they ain't protesting, they're vandalising and then trying to pull me up for using excessive force. People like us need to stick together. A lot of the problems started with immigrants; they bring violence and drugs. Bet you that red sand muck is bloody foreign too.'

'Have you ever seen anything like that on the streets before?'

'No, but the gangs and pushers in this city are always coming up with new "business ventures". First hyper-steds, then I-die, which we're still trying to clamp down on. Something's telling me it's not the last we're going to see of that red stuff either.'

All units, reports of a UFO across rooftops have been confirmed as a prank. Please ignore.'

'Storm's getting worse. Looks like it's gonna be one of those nights.'

' . . . '

'So, Lace, either you're really good at listening or at making people spill their beans. What's your story? Why did you join the force?'

'My story's nothing special. For me it's in my blood. I come from a long line of law enforcement. My mum sadly passed on the job. I was raised by my dad.'

'Bloody hell, kidda, tough score. What station were your parents at?'

'Old Riga central.'

'Never heard of it.'

'It's in Latvia.'

' . . . '

'My family migrated here when I was fourteen.'

'Oh . . . Look, I meant no harm about, y'know. You lot are alright. It's the PROLs, the Tynesiders, all those who think they've got some God-given right to come over after the Divide and make themselves at home, you know?'

'All units, a convoy of black SUVs has been reported
heading into the Industrial. Do not respond;
armoured teams have been notified. Over.'

'Pfft. Like I said earlier, Lace: priorities. It's definitely going to be one of those bloody nights.'

* * *

Clink sslinch, clink sslinch!

'Go do your rounds,' I say, flicking my lighter. Can't believe out of all the places in the Industrial, I'm stuck outside this rat-infested mechanics' garage while it's pissing it down, babysitting these other newly recruited sods. It stinks. Could be worse; could be like those two blungers on the roof doing lookout for the last twenty-four hours or that prick I just sent off on patrol. Still, orders are orders.

The Boss has got us all on high alert. We're expecting a drop from the Upper Loop, which means no screw-ups or it's night-night.

Two guys patrol the courtyard, their torches shining, guiding one of their vicious-looking, frothy-mouthed, stubby-faced dogs. Another two stand watching the front gate, holding some serious fire-power.

Clink sslinch, clink sslinch!

All this feels like over kill. No one's gonna try it down here tonight. Them bluebottle pigs definitely won't; they avoid this place like the plague, unless they're dirty themselves. They wouldn't dare; this is the Industrial. From the less grimier Southside — with its gambling halls, bare-knuckle fights, and 'coffee houses' filled with Night Flowers — to the Eastside — where products cross the border from Wessex using the old canal systems — the Loop controls the action in the city. And there ain't nothing anyone can do about it.

'Hey, Red!' one of the guards shouts.

'What?' I yell back into the darkness.

'Look alive, we've got incoming. Let the Boss know.'

''Kay.'

Boof, boof! I kick the metal door behind me twice with the back of my boot. Security's tight.

Ssshhhrrenkk! The viewing hatch slides open.

'What do you want?'

'I need to speak with the Boss. Pick-up's on its way.'

The muffled sound of metallic locks clank behind the door; chains clang and chime as they are released and hit the floor. The door slowly grinds open. I walk past the door guard, who's eyeballing me and holding a twelve-gauge, and I head towards the workshop. With all the money we've made, you'd think we'd be doing business and operations in a more cushy place, like the guys on the Southside. Even in the criminal world, the ones at the bottom still get treated like crap, slugging it out in this dark, dank wasteland. But I ain't gonna gas. I already got cracked in the face by the Boss for setting fire to parts of a shop we were collecting from today. The owner got brave; he's lucky I didn't Blackbeard him. Tin Man thought it was bad business, so he made an example of me.

Those three he set upon earlier tonight in the alley for sport were lucky. Once those silver mouth-guards go in, not many live to tell the tale. I've seen people get worse for just looking our way funny. They're lucky the pigs were close. Even amongst the grimiest, Tin Man's known as being one of the cruellest.

That 'dark is the night' speech he says before attacking is another example. I used to think that was his edge, something he did to freak people. I've got my blood-red dyed hair and skull mask, but it's not an act, that's him. In Mandarin, we'd say he's 神经病 — shénjīng bìng: mentally unhinged.

89

After we earned our third tier position in the Loop by wiping out the Wretch Crew, one of our guys made the stupid mistake of laughing at one of Tin Man's poems. Slim, who was the opposite of what his name would suggest and actually the biggest guy among the G3 gang, wasn't the smartest guy. Tin Man was in the middle of toying with the remaining Wretches, when Slim interrupted his speech.

Crack! Before we could even blink, Slim's head had snapped back from the fastest, most vicious uppercut I've ever witnessed, breaking his chin, his bottom row of teeth exploding everywhere.

Tin Man stood in a boxer's stance, bouncing. I'd never seen anything like that ever. He popped in his silver grills and adjusted the many huge, weathered silver and brass skull rings on his bloodied hand. Slim's knocked out cold, sprawled on the ground. Whistling, Tin Man walked over to him, rested his knees on his fallen opponent's chest and spewed out some mad jargon that sounded kinda like some Shakespearean mess. He then repeatedly punched Slim's unconscious face, not missing a breath, splitting his flesh, cracking bone, turning his face into mush against the floor. *Thack . . . Thack . . . Splack!* None of us dared look away. Golden Charley didn't even blink, his I-died lamps dead, unshaken behind his surgical mask.

After satisfying his bloodlust, Tin Man picked himself up and said: 'Now, where were we?' He then pulled out a silver strap and blew the brains out of the three Wretches that he had been toying with earlier. I knew then: shénjīng bìng. There's only one way out of this life: eat or be eaten. It's just the way things are.

I enter the workshop. G3 members pack cash into black duffel bags, watched closely by armed Upper Loop guards. Custom-built, souped-up cars sit on ramps above, exposing their inner workings. Old tyres pile up in the corners. Tools hang from the rails, covering the walls. It looks more like a slaughterhouse than a garage. Cob, our 'fix it' guy, uses the blue flame from his blow-torch to light his cigarette, then goes to town on Charley's machete. Sparks fly everywhere as he welds a new handle onto the blade. It's all systems go; one huge, illegal band and we're the musicians.

Clink, sslinch!

I walk towards Tin Man, who's leaning back in his chair, watching the live feed from the security cameras outside on the big screen. News plays through the tinny-sounding radio, reporting on a suspected serial killer. Sicko. Probably some old Anglo getting his rocks off because he's got too much power. Alongside the radio chatter is the low hum of the tattooist, drilling a new piece onto Golden Charley's upper torso. I've got several myself; Charley's covered in 'em. It's mandatory after initiation into the Golden Glove Gang to get inked, so everybody knows who you're repping. Some, like me, have G3 above the brow; others on the hands or under the eye. We thought we'd get a new addition when we joined the Loop — circular chain links on the neck, the higher up you are the more links get added — but it takes time to rank up and there's no ranking up without blood. And, as Third Loopers, you never know when your time's up.

Clink sslinch, clink sslinch!

'You got something to tell me, Zachary?'

Tin Man slowly turns his chair to face me. His gaze fixes on my bloodied eye. 'Tut . . . tut . . . tut. Not still upset, are we?' he asks, rolling the rings around his tattooed fingers.

Before I can speak, Trizz knocks one of the bags of cash onto the floor. Tin Man stands up and walks over.

'Careful, dear! Wouldn't want to short-change the three-headed dog upstairs now, would we?' Trizz goes to pick up the bag quickly, but Tin Man grab his face firmly and shakes it left and right in a 'no' motion, like a puppet. 'There's a good lad. Now sort it! Or do you want to look like Red Zack?'

He releases Trizz's face, whose cheeks have gone blood-red, and walks back to his seat.

'So, Zachary, what news from the gate?'

'Pick-up should be arriving any minute.'

'Good! Charley, you added your takings to the pile?'

Golden Charley slightly pulls his surgical mask down to take a draw of his cigarette. 'It's all there: seventy for the Top, twenty for the mids, and ten for G3.'

Horns beep from outside. The surveillance monitor shows bright headlights as a convoy of blacked-out SUVs pulls up to the guarded courtyard gate. *Click!* Tin Man snaps his fingers: 'Showtime, my lovelies.' The crew finish packing the bags as the convoy enters the yard, forming a semi-circle with their headlights trained towards the workshop shutters.

*　＊　＊　＊*

3:00 a.m. Victoria Inn Hotel. Well, as far as hotels go, this is definitely giving off creepy, old-fashioned killer vibes. Especially with the torn police tape lying on the street near the entrance. Not a good look. Okay, there's no need to draw this out, just find out what room Cara's in and then we can get out of here.

I walk towards the receptionist, who glances up from her desk, then double-takes. As I approach, she stares with an odd look of either suspicion or confusion.

'Hi, I wondered if I could—'

'All rooms are currently unavailable,' the receptionist inter-rupts.

'No, I don't want a room. I'm looking for—'

'We're not allowed to give out guest information.'

'Please, it's urgent. It would just take a sec, her name might be in the guest book,' I say, pointing to the book. 'Cara James? She has long dreadlocks.'

My eyes catch something on the page: 'Vivian Ward?' I swear that's from a film. The handwriting looks familiar too; only Cara would draw a small star above the letter I.

I get another strong feeling of déjà vu but quickly snap out of it as the receptionist slams the guest book shut, narrowing her eyes at me. Her hand hovers over the phone. 'You need to leave now.'

I throw her a standoffish stare.

'Listen-er-bab, this hotel is owned by some not so nice people, if you don't get out, I'll be forced to make a call.'

'Okay, I'll leave.'

I back away from the front desk slowly, but in my mind there is no way I'm leaving without finding Cara, especially not in a place like this.

Ding!

The lift doors to the right of me open, letting out a dodgy-looking guy who keeps his head down, trying not to be recognised, rubbing smeared red lipstick off his neck. The ghostly outline of Cara appears once again, entering the lift and pressing a button. The ground floor icon turns to a six. The receptionist looks over, momentarily distracted by the man leaving, and — without any hesitation — I dash into the stationary lift. The shimmering mirage of Cara fades as I press the button for the sixth floor.

'Wait! You can't—'

The doors close and the lift begins to ascend.

* * *

Clink sslinch, clink sslinch!

The blacked-out car right in the middle of the convoy begins to wind down its tinted window. A hand with a gold dog-headed sovereign on its index finger points at Golden Charley and beckons him. I follow but keep a few steps back.

'Hello, Charley boy,' a voice says from inside the shaded vehicle. 'How's this pisshole of a place keeping ya? Busy, I hope.' The dim overhead light falls across the face that the voice belongs to. That must be Karl Vagus, one of the Three Heads of Cerberus. I've never met him, just heard rumours. He's also Golden Charley's uncle; he pretty much raised him. Charley doesn't say much, but there's bad blood. I can barely see his face but I've been told he has a red glass eye and that Charley had something to do with that. How else did the heir of Cerberus get kicked into the gutter to slum it down here with the rest of us?

'Is it all there this time?' I hear Mr Vagus say. Charley nods his head. 'Good boy, Charley. That's a good boy.' Vagus knocks the partition screen in front of him. 'Mr Punch, get him the bag please.'

The car suspension jolts as a broad-shouldered Goliath in a full three-piece suit steps out from the driver's seat, opening an umbrella to shield himself from the downpour. How the hell did he fit in that car — he's huge, at least 6'8"? He grabs a bag from the boot and drops it at Charley's feet. The suspension bounces again as he retakes his seat.

'Your boss is expecting that. Be a good golden boy and take it to him.' Charley stands there without answering. His hand slowly moves to the inside of his long desert-sand camo rain mac. Just say the word, Charley, and we'll burn him. Everyone bleeds; that's G3's tag. We've got you. G3 for life. Charley's hands fall back to his side. Vagus's window winds back up. I pick up the bag from by his feet and head towards the workshop. Charley stands there sharking his uncle as the car pulls away.

'Oi, that's crazy,' one of the newbies says, walking over to Charley. 'That was one of the Three Heads, right?! It was, wasn't it? Yo, I heard he's your unc—'

Slash!

Before the grunt can finish his sentence, Charley shifts his weight and, with a single swing of his machete, cuts the recruit down in silence. Everyone outside stops and watches as the body hits the floor, his mouth wide-open in shock.

Clink, sshlink!

Hm. Prick. These newbies trying to flex; now just another body for the rats. What a waste. We walk back inside as the last bags get packed into the vehicles.

'Trouble in paradise?' Tin Man smirks, as Charley sits back down with his bloodied surgical mask to finish off his tattoo. '"Conscience wakes despair that slumber'd; wakes the bitter memory of what he was, what is, and what must be worse; of worse deeds worse sufferings must ensue." Good things come to those who take.'

Charley drips more I-die into his lamps, turning his pupils jet-black, semi-acknowledging Tin Man's words.

'Now then Zachary, what do you have for me?' The Boss snatches the bag and unzips it. Looks like red sand.

'Don't worry your mind with the secret endeavours of fallen men,' Tin Man says, slapping my cheek as he turns his back to me to inspect the contents. Just as well; knowing too much can get you burnt, my Oriental friend. Sometimes ignorance is bliss.

Huh! Something grabs my attention on the security screen. What was that? Swear I just saw . . . Scanning the screen I see the two guards on patrol with the dog, searching with their torches. The mutt pulls away, its front legs raised, barking like crazy as the guards walk out of view. Wonder what they're looking at. I must be seeing things; it's been a long night.

'What the—?!' A torch rolls across the wet floor from the direction of the two guards. I stare intently at the screen as the torch rocks to a stop. The beam on the ground from the torchlight shows the shadow of the dog for a split-second as it darts away, unmanned, dragging its heavy chained leash across the floor. Where're the guards? Before I can turn to call the Boss, I spot movement. One of the guards slowly crawls out of the darkness on his belly, pulling himself along, clawing at the ground with his hands, looking back like he's trying to escape from something.

'Boss, you need to see this,' I say, still eyeing the screen. Tin Man looks up; Trizz and Cob also gather.

'Hey, hey, look! There! What's he doing?' Trizz points, as the guard is rapidly pulled back, enveloped by the darkness.

'You see that?!'

'Where'd he go?!'

Tin Man stands, his lamps still fixated on the screen. 'Alert the men outside. Seems we've got an intruder.'

BOOFF!

'What was that?!'

'Sounded like a bomb.'

'Someone's up there!'

'Go check it out, will ya?'

'Shhh! Pipe down!' Tin Man hisses.

'Someone's on the roof.'

Suddenly everyone's attention is snatched away as the radio goes crazy.

'*Fsshhhhh . . . zzzz . . . ssszzz Help! ZZZZ hel . . . zzz Fsshh-hhzzzzz!*'

It crackles loudly with mad static noises, sounding almost like a voice calling out from the speakers.

BANG!

A single shot goes off outside. The power goes out: the lights shut off and all the electrics in the workshop go down. Drenched in total darkness, confusion hits the air.

Tattatattatatatata! Bang! bang! Tattattaatttta!

A barrage of machine gun and pistol fire echoes around the courtyard. We hear shouting and yelling from all directions.

'On the rooftop!'

'Aarrghh! HELP!'

'Behind you! Whoa, aarrghh . . . '

'There! THERE! Behind the car!'

'Shoot it! Shoot it!'

It's chaos; sounds like a full-on turf war out there. Shots fire in all directions, ripping holes through the huge metal shutter, letting in strobes of light from the cars and muzzle flashes.

'What are they shooting at?!' Trizz shouts.

'Must be some sort of ambush for a takeover,' Cob yells back. 'Who'd dare come down here? This is the Industrial, this is our turf!'

Between the manic sounds of shouting and gunfire, I hear something that shakes me to my core. It doesn't sound human, more feral, like a wraith screaming. It's horrific. After each screech, cries of terror and screams of pain can be heard. The gunfire gets more sporadic, the voices get quieter, eventually stopping dead. The emergency service light snaps on in the workshop, covering us in a hellish, dim red glow. It goes silent. Something ain't right. You can sense the fear amongst us.

Tin Man readies himself, fixing his rings, then slides back the silver barrel on his pistol. 'Right then, you fairies. Time to dance with the reaper. Arm up! Open the shutters.' The crew tools up, pulling out baseball bats, shanks, chains, whatever we can get our hands on. I top up the petrol in my flask, ready for an encounter, ready to Blackbeard anything moving. Golden Charley wraps a damp cloth around his hand and picks up the heated handle on his newly welded machete, sporting one in each hand. We're twelve deep. This is what we do; everybody bleeds.

From behind me, somebody whispers: 'Go time.'

* * *

'All units: Multiple callers reporting loud disturbances from high-rises Eastbound of the Industrial, please be on the lookout for any suspicious activity. Over.'

'Wait, so . . . your name, Lace?'

'What about it?'

'It's Latvian?'

'It's pronounced Lah-see'.

' . . . Why didn't you say?'

'Why didn't you ask?'

'I didn't want to come across rude, did I?'

'Really.'

'All units: More reports of black smoke on rooftops have been spotted. Stand by for updates. Ov—.'

'There, that's better.'

'Scott? What are you doing? I don't think you should switch off the radio. What if—?'

'Just a second; it's doing my head in! There'll be plenty more criminals to catch when I switch it back on — that you can be sure of.'

'So . . . you really think we have a serial killer on our hands?'

'Kukadia seems to think so, but I don't know. There's plenty of wackos in this city; gangs go on killing sprees all the time.'

'You've got to admit the circumstances of her death don't add up.'

'True. Kukadia wasn't happy about that, was he?! Especially with that bird Elizabeth breathing down his neck.'

'She did seem more clued in than him.'

'She always has been. Drives him mad. Anyway, some of

us have real police work to do, without chasing supernatural, hocus-pocus, serial killer theories. That said, I better turn the radio back on . . .'

* * *

Ding!
    'Sixth floor.'
    Right then, Cara's got be in one of these rooms. I need to find her before the receptionist makes good on her threats. I walk down the seedy, shadily-lit hallway, hearing questionable noises from behind some of the doors. What the hell are you doing in a place like this, Cara? I stop suddenly, out of the corner of my eye glimpsing something moving to the left at the end of the corridor.
    'Hello?' I call out.
    I walk with a little more urgency as I hear the lift behind me begin to operate again. I turn the corner. Room 36 is covered with police tape around the doorframe. Déjà vu hits me again.
    'In here.'
    'Cara? Cara!'
    I knock on the door in a panic.
    'Cara? Cara! It's Charlotte.'
    As I continue to strike the door maniacally, the mechanised handle beeps and unlocks.

* * *

Cla-cla-cla-clank-clank.
    The workshop shutters go up.
    We step into the courtyard. Bodies lie everywhere. There were at least twenty men deep out here; now they're all down. Who — or what — could have done this? We cautiously step out, eyeing our surroundings. A fire blazes from one of the

cars. Tonnes of cash crackle and smoke in the heat. This isn't a normal turf takeover. Money's power; you don't just leave it to burn. This is something else.

'What's that?!' I shout, jolting back as I hear a sound. Some of the guys immediately let off shots in the direction of the noise.

'Hold your fire!' Tin Man orders. The shooting stops. We all look tensely in the direction we just targeted. The sound is heard again, this time surrounding the courtyard like a murder of crows, sharper than the wind, somehow coming from every direction at once.

'What the hell is that noise?!' Cob yells.

'You see that?!' Trizz swivels to look behind him.

A blurred shadow emerges, casting itself from wall to wall as the sound moves from one side of the courtyard to the other.

'What's going on?' Trizz whispers. We all scan around in the dark. The surrounding noise swells.

'Nah man, no way! This ain't right! This ain't natural!' One of the guys freaks, dropping his baseball bat, and starts to leg it.

Bang!

Tin Man stands with his arm stretched, smoke dancing from his gun. 'That's enough of that. We'll have no cowards in this outfit. Time to earn your keep, boys! Spread out; they're still here. Go find 'em.'

We spread out in twos, leaving Tin Man, Golden Charley and the door guard with his twelve-gauge in front of the shutters. Can't help but feel like we've been sent to our deaths. Trizz and I go left, using my phone as a torch. Trizz walks behind me watching my back.

'Can you hear that? It's stopped,' I whisper. The surrounding wraith noise has finally died down.

'Red, who do you think moved on us? Thought being part of the Loop gave us protection. Did you see them just lying

there . . . ? Bullet, 9ine, Smashely, 40or, all down for the count.'
By the sounds of Trizz's voice he's starting to panic.

Crash! A metal drum falls down in front of us.

'Shit!' I blurt out, readying my hatchet for what ever awaits
us. I scan my phone torch ahead looking movement. Nothing.
'Trizz, you good? Lets move forward. Trizz . . . ?'

As I turn to check on Trizz, something suddenly grips my
wrist and twists it, smashing my phone from my hand and then
knocking my hatchet to the floor. I snap my hands back to
me, and throw a chain of punches into the dark, trying to hit
something, anything. Uuuff! I fly backwards, crashing into the
fallen barrel, holding my chest in agony. Can't see a damn thing.
Quickly shoving my hand in my jacket, I pull out my flask and
pour petrol into my mouth.

Clink sshlink! With a flick of my lighter, I spray fire, trying to
burn whatever's attacking me. Nothing, just that black-purplish
smoke. I grab my chest, feeling it pound from the impact. Guns
go off, followed by yelling in the distance. Echoes of that horrific
wailing sound rise again. I drag myself to my feet and limp back
towards the workshop shutter gate. This isn't a turf war. We're
being hunted.

* * *

*All units. Multiple gunfire has been reported from the Industrial,
armed response is en route. Requests immediate back up.*

'Told you it was going to be one of those nights. Lace, hit
the siren.'

'Do you reckon we're gonna have to go in? I mean down into
the Industrial?'

'No idea. This sounds bad! There hasn't been a grab for power
down there since the Dragon got nicked. They'll more than
likely have us make a perimeter on the outskirts. Damn animals,

don't know why we don't just leave them to off themselves.'

* * *

Clink sshlink!

I make it back to the courtyard. Tin Man and Charley stand ready with weapons out on the far side. My body trembles as I see only three of us are left standing. I prop myself up against one of the cars. Out of nowhere something shoots through the air, knocking me off my feet. I smash into the side of the car. My head whacks the wet floor. My vision blurs. I pull my skull balaclava off over my hellish red hair, wiping the rain water from my eyes to see better. It's Trizz. His leg's broken, snapped at the shin.

He lifts his head. Before slumping unconscious, he manages to mumble: 'It's here . . . Black . . . Ghost . . .'

Shaking with fear, I grab Trizz's phone from his jeans then crawl under the car, hoping not to be seen. The footsteps tread closer and closer. I try to keep as still as I can, listening, looking. Out of the darkness, silhouetted amongst the blazing wreckage and covered by the night, a figure emerges. Its movement is slow, almost stumbling, dragging its unlaced black boots against the rubble on the ground. The figure stands motionless in the rain. It stands there frozen, head hanging slightly, down towards its chest.

I press record on Trizz's phone and zoom in.

'Aarrghh!' Sprinting from the right side of the courtyard, Cob and two other men charge forward, swinging bats and whipping chains. They try to attack the figure, which quickly raises its head and dodges back into the shadow in a cloud of black smoke.

'Hāakgwái,' I breathe out in horror, Cantonese cuss words escaping my lips. Black ghost! Between flashes of movement, I hear the thud of punches, screams, bodies hitting the floor. In no time at all, the sounds cease; the last chain crashes to the ground. Cob's face pushes out of the black mist, terror written all over it. His hand reaches for help before he is snatched back into the dark. The figure stands there, emitting that same black-purplish smog, which twirls and wraps around him like a dense, vaporised cloak, concealing his identity.

'This can't be real,' I whisper to myself. The phone's battery icon flashes. I quickly press send.

'Who are you?!' Tin Man shouts from across the courtyard.

Laughter echoes from the shadow, resembling Tin Man's voice. The figure re-emerges, dispersing the black mist. I can see him more clearly: he's in all black: torn jeans, black boots and a black, bullet-riddled top. His hair's covering most of his face, drenched from the rain, which streams down his chin like tears. He opens his mouth.

'WHO. ARE. YOU!' he responds, replicating Tin Man's voice. Tin Man and Golden Charley take a step backwards, looking at each other in bewilderment.

The guard steps forward, unleashing his twelve-gauge, yelling 'Die! Die! Die!' Each shot misses as the target acrobatically moves from shadow to shadow, then swiftly springs forward. The guard crumbles as the figure brings its knee down onto his head.

Golden Charley springs out from behind the target, cutting through the rain with both machetes, swiping and slashing with each strike, aiming for a kill. Strike after swipe misses, slicing through raindrops. For every strike he misses, he receives a flurry of blows knocking him back. A kick to the face rips his surgical mask off. Charley staggers, a look of disbelief on his face as he loses his balance.

Blam! Blam! Blam!

Tin Man shoots at Charley's attacker. In the blink of an eye, the ghost morphs into black vapour and shoots up towards the night sky:

Screeeeeeeeeeeeeeeeeeeeeeeeeeeeeeeeeeeeeeeeeccccchhhhh!!

'Aarrghh!' The ground rumbles. My hands shoot to my ears, trying to block out the intense high-pitched screech. Windows vibrate, glass shattering everywhere. The unconscious guys on the floor wake up, cupping their ears in pain. 'What's happening?!'

A strange current rushes through my veins. I'm burning, heating up from the inside. It's unbearable. 'Aarrghh!'

The black vapour boosts higher and higher into the sky, forming a massive invisible sphere, temporarily outlined by the rain. It pulses, disrupting the weather. The rain stops for an instant. A huge flash explodes into the atmosphere, opening the sky and, for a split-second, I see what looks like a thousand mirrors looking down on me . . .

VOOOOOOOOMMM!

* * *

Screeeeeeeeeeeeeeeeeeeeeeeeeeeeeeeeeeeeeeeeeccccchhhhh!

'What the bloody hell is that in the sky?! Shit! Lace, turn! Watch it!'

'It's not me; there's something wrong with the engine. The ground's shaking. Why are all the street lights popping everywhere?!'

'Look out!'
BANG! CRASH!

* * *

'tālò dō–ëri!'

'Aarrghh! Lace, help! Get back! Get away from me! What do you want with me?!'

'iri mī–ëdri . . . ido#ri–ëdri . . . '

'No, you can't, I won't let you! Noooo!'

                          'dīto mírod–ëdri . . . '

' . . . '

'Scott! Scott, wake up! Central, come in, over—'

fzzzzzzzz shhhhhh!

'Central, do you read? I need assistance, over!'

                          fzzzzzzzz! cccsssssshhhh!

* * *

Screeeeeeeeeeeeeeeeeeeeeeeeeeeeeeeeeeeeeeeeeeeecccccchhhhh!

The lights go out and the building shakes. The door to room 36 swings open.

'Aarrghh! What's that noise?!'

I crumble to the floor holding my ears tightly. Screaming guests stampede from their rooms, trampling me. My body begins to pulsate with a fiery heat as the high-pitched noise pulses through me, vibrating right into my inner core. A strange sensation swirls around the centre of my forehead. I crawl and place my hand on the door handle to pull myself up and I hear the faint echoes of Cara's voice, as if in the room:

'Get away from me!'

                    'Rule three.'

                              'Who's there?'

'Cara?' I call out. 'It's me, Charlotte! Where are you?'

The whispers start to form into images, swirling spectral apparitions, just like I saw before. Then I see it: standing over her, tall and terrible in the darkened corner of the room with burning red eyes, as she chokes on the bed.

'No! Get away from her!'

It turns slowly towards me before vanishing. I run over to the bed, now empty — nothing but small, yellow, numbered evidence markers.

'Cara!'

* **

The screech stops. My ears ring. Struggling to raise my head, I spot Tin Man stumbling to his feet, still holding his ears. Black smoke begins to rise, circling around him. He pushes his silver grills into his mouth whilst emptying his clip into the smoke.

'Come on then, let's have it. COME ON! YOU WANT SOME?! Let's dance, come on!' His gun runs empty. He dashes to pick up one of Charley's machetes and starts to furiously stab at the growing mist, swinging and slashing like a wild animal. 'Where are you? What you waiting for?!'

A hand snaps out of the mist and grabs Tin Man by the neck, lifting him off his feet with ease. The machete clangs to the floor, as Tin Man gasps for air, struggling to free himself. His eyes widen with immense fear.

'Wait, wait . . . I've seen you before,' he chokes. It's as if he's seen a ghost. 'What are you?'

The black smoke twirls and grows. Tin Man grinds his silver grills together and grins. 'Dark . . . is the night for . . . ghouls . . . and gho—'

A blue beam flashes from the attacker's face as they're both consumed by the darkness. Tin Man screams and gargles as the darkness spits him back out onto the floor, holding his face in agony. The walker stands over him, black as the night. It turns towards me and walks in my direction. Charley rolls over onto all fours. For a sec I thought he might come and help me but, terrified, he sprints off. The vapour around the figure starts to flicker as if angry.

'Please . . . please!' With nothing but my lighter in my hand, I hold it up, cowering backwards.

Click ssh—

* * *

'... Lace? Wha— What happened?'

'Scott, take it easy. I think we just got hit with an earthquake. We're in a massive pileup.'

'An earthquake? In Mercia?'

'Power's out everywhere, the whole city's been plunged into darkness. It's a complete blackout.'

'And that ... thing that got through?'

'What thing? What are you talking about?'

'That beast, like ... that ... white shadowy ...'

'White shadowy? You must have a concussion. You were mumbling gibberish when you started to come back around. Here, take this, apply pressure to the wound.'

'Something in the sky ... flashed ... like gates.'

'Look, try and sit tight. Comms are down but I'm going to try and get help.'

'In the boot. There's an old-school analogue transmitter. See if you can get anything on there.'

'Will do.'

Flick tick tick! Whmmmmmmm!

'All units—'

fzzzzzzzz! Cccsssssshhhh!

'Almost got it ...'

Cccsssssshhhh!

Click! Tick! Tick!

'Got it!'

'ALL UNITS, THIS IS A CODE RED. PLEASE RETURN TO CENTRAL. I REPEAT: ALL UNITS, THIS IS A CODE RED, PLEASE RETURN TO CENTRAL.'

CHAPTER 7

Because of the Internet

'Joseph . . . ?'

Knock! knock!

'You up? You're gonna be late.'

'Huh . . .' I wake, raising my hand to my eyes to keep out the daylight, which seeps through the slats of my blinds. Man, I'm hungry. Wait . . . What? That's Mom's voice. I'm home? How did I get back in my room? I mean, how did I . . . ?

Knock! Knock!

'Joe . . . ? Joseph?'

'I'm up, I'm up.'

'It's 9:15. I'm making breakfast, okay?'

'Thanks! I'll be down in a bit.'

* * *

Okay, okay, don't freak out. There's got to be a perfectly good explanation for how you got from the hospital bed to waking up on the floor of your room. Think! Ahh, I can't remember a thing. Maybe I was in shock. Yeah, that's it, makes sense. I must have been in shock after last night and somehow got myself back home; that's why I can't remember. Perfect, yeah; that's what happened. I take a puff of my inhaler, not buying any of the explanation I just thought up. None of it makes any sense. I take another puff, purely out of habit, thinking my chest might be tightening up but, weirdly enough, I'm okay. No breathing difficulties and — for once — I don't feel tired. In fact, I feel kinda good.

The blinds rattle as the wind blows cold air through my window. Getting up to close it, I spot myself in the mirror. 'Man, you're a mess, looks like you've been through the wars.' Definitely the opposite of Tobey Maguire's mirror scene in *Spider-Man*. I look like crap. I look out the window to see some of my neighbours gathered across the road. Weird. All of their car bonnets are open; looks like something's up with their engines. That's pretty random. I mean, what are the odds of that happening at the same time? Parts of the road and pavement are flooded with huge puddles; a huge tree has fallen over down the road, wrecking someone's fence. Looks like there must have been a storm or something. First things first, I need to get out of these clothes, which are completely caked in mud. I've also ended up sleeping in my Docs, which look like they've been on their own adventure. Kicking them off, I see bits of glass, burn-marks on the side, and what looks like a tooth sticking out from the rubber-gummed sole. 'The hell?'

Throwing my boots to the side of the room, a dull pain shoots around my left wrist. 'Ouch.' Must've hurt it when I fell. I reach towards my side where I was cut, patting it softly to see if it hurts. Can't really feel anything. Must be the painkillers they pumped into me, probably still haven't worn off yet. As if that happened last night; it happened so fast. One moment I was having the best night of my life then boom, out of nowhere ... I keep trying to remember what I dreamt last night. I recall only feelings: pain, anger, and wanting to find those that attacked us and, somehow — in a fantastical way — to get even, a raging

tempest of vengeance. I can still see their faces in the alley —
cold, merciless — and Tin Man's grin as he touches Leiyah.
The one that attacked me didn't even blink behind his surgical
mask. Ruthless. I wonder how Sam and Leiyah are doing. I feel
naked without my phone; can't even check in on them. Hope
they're okay. Knowing them, I bet they've been worried sick. The
hospital's still a blur, but I do remember seeing a tall, young girl
appear in my dream-memory-vision-thing. It was weird, she was
disappearing into vapour at will, like she had the mutant X-gene
or something. Her face was decorated with distinctive marks, she
looked right at me and she said . . . something. What did she
say? I can't remember. But it felt so real. I've had that flashback
loads of times and never seen her before. Could it have been
the drugs they gave me? Must have been the drugs, making me
hallucinate, right? The crazy thing is, everything was clearer. I
had more of a complete view. That part of my past didn't feel
as broken.

'Breakfast will be ready in five minutes,' Mom calls from
downstairs. She never makes breakfast; she's usually out the
door first thing.

Peeling myself out of my clothes, I see the blood-soaked hospital bandages wrapped around my torso, covering my ribs. I'm
not the biggest fan of blood, especially my own, but I guess it
looks worse than it feels. We could have lost our lives last night,
for no reason. Brum's got gangs, Brum's always had crime, but
you never think you'll be the victim. I really should tell Mom.
I don't think a patient's disappearance from a hospital is going
to stay quiet for long. I just don't want the barrage of questions
that I know is going to follow. Can't deal with any more drama
right now. I need to get my head straight, make sure my friends
are good, then I'll tell her.

I throw my dirty clothes into a pile in the corner and hear

something hard hit the floor. 'What was that?' Rummaging through, I pull out my broken dreamcatcher and a red hospital wrist-tag. Holding the dreamcatcher, I lay back on my bed, reading over the ribboned note that I found inside its broken shell: 'Dear Joseph, Happy Birthday. We are such stuff as dreams are made on. Love, Mum and Dad.' I repeat the words over and over, quietly comforting myself, tracing my finger across each indented golden letter, memorising it. I look up at the masks on my ceiling, which stare back at me, lifeless, soulless, void of emotion. I don't even know how to feel. Is this even legit? My parents are dead, right? That's what I was told. But deep down — if I'm being honest with myself — a part of me hopes . . . No! I *want* this to be real. Inspecting the symbols on the broken dreamcatcher, I realise the main pattern when put together is the same pattern the young girl was drawing on the glass.

'Breakfast is ready.'

'Yep, coming. Won't be long!'

Downstairs in the kitchen, Mom's put together a whole spread: crumpets, blueberry muffins, granola with yoghurt, an assortment of fruits and juices, all set out neatly while she scrambles eggs in the frying pan.

'Morning,' she says, kissing me on the cheek before going back to the stove.

'Morning. Wow, this looks amazing. What's the special occasion?' I ask, pulling up to sit at the breakfast island.

'Well, I felt guilty about having to run out on you yesterday. Work's just been crazy of late. Anyway, I thought I could surprise you with breakfast. Ta-dah!'

'This is amazing, but . . . I kinda gotta go or I'm gonna be late. The trams aren't always on time.' Great work Joe, polite way of being an absolute killjoy.

'I can drop you off? That should save you some time.'

'Okay,' I nod, taking no time to bite into a blueberry muffin — one of my favourites. Mom puts the eggs onto the plates, sprinkling chopped spring onions on top, then sits beside me to eat.

'Did you manage to get any sleep? I didn't hear you come in.'

Not wanting to lie, I choose my words carefully.

'You didn't hear me come in? Oh, I guess I umm . . . Must've been quiet, you know? Trying not to wake you.'

'How was last night?'

I take another bite of my breakfast, slightly stalling. 'Most of the night was good, I enjoyed it. Got caught in the rain though, weather was horrible.'

'The weather was all over the place last night. At one stage the wind sounded like a banshee screaming, it was awful. Probably why I didn't hear you come in. Some of our electric was knocked out this morning and the signal on my phone and the telly's playing up.' Mom sips her tea, watching me as I go in for more food. I'm not gonna lie, it's really tasty and I'm really hungry.

'This is nice, isn't it?' Mom says, holding her mug up under her mouth. 'Breakfast together in the morning. Reminds me of when you were smaller. "Frosties please,"' Mom mimics, sounding like a cartoon mouse. 'Remember? You were obsessed. "Frosties please, Mom."'

'Wow, was that an impression of me? I never sounded like that at all. Also, Frosties still bang.'

'Yeah, if you want a sugar rush.' We both laugh, reminiscing. 'This is nice. It's nice to see you smiling and looking like you've slept. Your face looks fresh.'

'I'm gr-r-reat!' I do my best impression of Tony the Tiger, making Mom laugh again. Pouring a glass of freshly squeezed orange juice, I feel that dull pain again, travelling down my left forearm.

'What's wrong with your hand?' Mom asks, concerned, as I rotate my wrist and rub my arm.

'Eh, nothing, think I hurt it when I fell off my board at the skatepark. It's alright, I'll get a support bandage on it.'

'Make sure you do, there's one in the medical drawer. Oh shoot, before I forget, do you have your phone on you? What time is it?'

'Uhhh . . .' Before I can get words out to make an excuse, Mom picks up her phone. 'It's doing that thing again, screen keeps going blank.' Mum taps her phone. 'There it is: 9:56. Great, it should be here any minute. Let's go to the front, come on.'

I grab another muffin and stuff it in my face whilst being shooed to the front door. We go outside. The sun's breaking through the grey clouds. It doesn't feel too cold considering the bad weather we've had. You can smell the freshly cut grass, wet from the day before. That smell reminds me of playing football with Sam in the summer holidays. I hated it. All I wanted to do was play Tekken and read comics, but, looking back they were fun times. Mom looks at her phone, then looks up at the sky.

'What are you doing?' I join her, staring up at the clouds as they drift past.

She looks at her phone again mumbling to herself: 'It's late; where is it?'

Bzzzzzzzmmmmmmm!

A faint buzz hums in the sky, getting closer. Mom's phone pings: a notification. 'Brilliant, it's here. Happy belated birthday present, Joseph!' she says excitedly.

From above a drone starts to descend onto the driveway, carrying a bag and a box. '*Keep Clear. Keep Clear. Preparing to land,*' the drone repeats in a robotic rhythmic tone. I see drones flying across the city airways all the time; people order gifts and get deliveries this way, but I've never done it myself. Mom's cool like that, she's always trying new things. The city even has a commercial drone taxi service that can fly you to other counties of the former Kingdom. It's really cool, kind of bougie. Mom's gone all out; this is epic. The drone lands. Mom enters a code into her phone to release the packages from its domed holding chambers.

'*Thank you for choosing Air-U. Happy birthday, Joseph Jacobs. Have a lovely U-day. Goodbye.*' The propellers begin to rotate again. The drone hovers over the ground, swaying slightly from left to right, before buzzing off high into the air and flying away.

'That was epic. Thanks, Mom.' I carry the packages back inside the house.

Mom takes a seat with a huge smile on her face. 'Go on then, open them!'

Wasting no time, I open up the bag. Inside are chocolates, champagne, aftershave (which — not gonna lie — was needed. Definitely a lifesaver) and also, neatly wrapped and compacted in bubble wrap, is a book of Basquiat's art work. 'This is awesome, you're the best!'

I move onto my other packaged item, picking it up and ripping off the protective plastic. 'No way! As if! How did you even get these? These are like limited edition.'

Mom playfully brushes off her shoulders like she's got style. 'I have my sources,' she says, feeling proud of herself. Opening the minimalistic stencilled box and removing the light tracing wrapping paper, I smell the distinctive scent of new creps. 'Yo!' Inside are the limited edition Nike SB REMs. These are super rare. I pick them up, marvelling at the next-level colourway. The bottom sole is transparent and within the rubber sole there's a cool Da Vinci-esque diagram of the moon cycle. At the front toe bumper, the sole blends from transparent into spacesuit-white, separated by teal and wolf-grey fixing stripes. The main shoe is covered in a reflective silver-chrome, holographic texture, topped off by the 'Swoosh' logo on the side, which glows neon blue. Also, did I mention? They self-lace. Absolutely flames.

'Mom, THESE ARE FRESH! I can't thank you enough.' I throw a massive hug around her.

'You're welcome,' she says, hugging me back. 'Maybe this will help you stay on your board.'

'Wow, touché.' Mom's got jokes.

She grabs her keys. 'Right then, I think we need to hit the road.'

'Cool, ready.' I carefully put on the new kicks, stopping to admire them before heading to the car.

Ekkk chchchchch! . . . Ecchhhhchch!

Ah man, as if. The car's not starting. Mom twists the key again, pressing down on the pedal, trying to pump the accelerator. 'Think it's dead.'

'Just my luck. Sorry, Joseph. I'm going to have to call you a taxi. Sounds like the battery's packed in.'

'No probs. If I shoot now I can probably make it to class on time. You sure you don't need any help?'

'No no, I'll be fine. I'm just going to ring breakdown services. Get going before you're late. Have a good day. Love you.'

'Love you too,' I say as I jump on my skateboard and roll away. 'And thanks again for the gifts!'

* * *

I rocket down the street, hoping to catch the next hydro-tram. The city feels strange. It's hard to explain. I mean, it's still Brum but I'm clocking all sorts of things on my journey that register as weird. For instance the high number of fire engines on the road, or shops that I pass every day that are suddenly closed. Some buildings — mostly high-rises — have shattered windows on the higher floors and most of the traffic lights aren't working.

The four-way junction ahead is rammed. Horns beep like it's carnival; nice to see that some cars are still working. Yellow-vested construction engineers are busy setting up temporary traffic lights. Further up the road, police surround a car, making traffic worse. Nearby motorists stick their heads out the windows in frustration. No time to be nosy; your hydro's pulling in straight ahead of you. Pushing off harder to gain more speed I zoom onto the platform, nearly colliding with a pedestrian.

'Oi! watch where you're bloody going!'

'Sorry!' I shout back, flicking my board into my hands, just managing to squeeze myself through the closing doors.

I find a set of empty seats and place my board on the seat next to me. Yeah, I'm one of those guys. The hydro sets off and I sit day dreaming. Sometimes I wonder what it would be like to actually meet a blood relative, or if I have ever unknowingly walked past one on one of my many journeys. Learning about historical tribes and genealogy this term made me realise just how interconnected we are as humans — you know, the whole six degrees of separation theory. I'm sure it's probably like four degrees nowadays but anyway. It's opened a deeper longing for me to find out my ancestral history. Sam said I should do one of those 'Who Are You' genetic tests but, to be honest, I'm split, almost afraid to get the answers I desperately want. Mom's always been enough, growing up: a constant nurturer, a source of good. She sacrificed a lot to raise me by herself, even to the detriment of her own happiness. It can't have been easy, especially with us humans still unable to get a grip on racial equality — so old but still raw. It's tiring. I'm forever grateful for her and always will be but, lately, I want more, almost like — I don't know — I need that connection, to find out who I am. What's my ancestry? Whose eyes, hair, and nose are these when

I stare at myself in the mirror? For the longest time I brushed it away. But if there's a chance that the visions in my dreams and the symbol from this mysterious gift hold the answers, I'm going to find out what they are.

'You have now arrived in Newtown. Next stop: Millennium Point.'

Great, one more stop until CBU; should still be able to make it on time. Different groups of students flood the hydro-tram. One of them grabs the last Metro from the holder by the door. As if physical newspapers are still a thing. I sit there, looking out of the window, minding my business, but I can't help but overhear their conversations:

'Did you hear it, though? I didn't. We were in the middle of a session, then our building just blacked out, definitely something to do with the government.'

'Nah fam, it's a conspiracy.'

'The city's getting more dangerous.'

'It was tipping with rain. We got caught in it. Then the place shook.'

'Sounded like an air-raid siren.'

'How many got arrested?'

'My whole area blacked out, internet an' all.'

Sounds like it was a crazy night all over the city. Must have been something in the water. CBU's up ahead, time to get ready. The tram slows down to let us out.

'You have now arrived at Millennium Point. Next stop: The Bullring.'

As I leave the hydro, I glimpse the headlines on the Metros left behind on the seats:

GANG WARS ERUPT

MULTIPLE ARRESTS

WORST STORM IN 14 YEARS!

Mad; as if. Here's hoping they caught the guys that attacked us.

Walking through the campus grounds towards the main building, temporary blue waterproof shielding covers some of the windows and doors. Looks like this place wasn't immune from the storm ether. There's a huge number of students, more than usual, hanging around outside, huddling in groups, conversing in corners, avoiding the water-logged grass. Others walk fast, heads down, glued to their phones like they're awaiting some big news. I spot Sam sitting on a wall near the entrance, reading a newspaper. He sees me, double-taking as he looks up.

'Yo, Joe! Joe!' Sam signals, jumping off the wall and rushing over to me. 'Bro, what you saying, you good?! I've been worried sick.' He hugs me with one arm. He flinches and hops back, rubbing his stomach. 'Still sore. What you doing here? I went back to the hospital this morning to check in on you and they said you'd already left.'

'I'm okay,' I try to reassure him. 'A little achy, but I'm good. Promise. Have you seen or heard from Leiyah?'

'No. I was hoping to bump into her at the hospital. Thought she might have checked in on you this morning too. Those dickheads stole our phones, man. I'm lost without it; haven't been able to call anyone. Tried to send her a message from my laptop, but my connection's been playing up all morning. I last saw her at the hospital, when we were getting checked over. She was pretty shaken up, bro; it was really bad. I think she was more worried about you than herself though. We both were. She was trying to soldier it but she just kept crying. They dropped her home first. Haven't seen her since. It's crazy how courteous the police were trying to be after the hospital. When they arrived at the alley they were goin' on-a-way. They tried to arrest me like I was the criminal, roughed me up, pulled a taser and everything, not even gassing. Ridiculous.' Sam finishes his monologue and leans back against the wall, rubbing his stomach.

'Oh yeah, word of mouth is all lectures have been cancelled. Must be something to do with the torrential weather last night. I couldn't sleep, so I got up early. Thought I'd try my luck here. Been waiting at the front, thinking Leiyah might turn up.'

Leiyah's face flashes before me, as I lay on the floor helpless, in a pool of my own blood, as Tin Man's hands stroke her face. My hand squeezes into a fist in anger. 'Sam . . . I . . . I . . . I'm sorry, I couldn't do . . .'

'Bro, I know,' Sam cuts in, as if afraid of awkward silence. 'Don't, man; there's nothing any of us could've done. It was just a messed-up situation. You had a flipping machete to your throat, bruv. On a real one though, how are you even standing? You went down hard; they cut you.' Sam points to where the machete sliced me. Wish I could tell him that I don't even know how I'm here.

'Just lucky. I guess it looked worse than it was. They patched me up good, can't really feel it,' I half-smile to curb any suspicions.

'I'm just happy you're here and we're good. Hundred.' Sam firms me with a fist bump. 'Also, don't think I haven't noticed the grails on your feet. Those are serious. Are they the REM's?! How the hell did you get a pair of those?!'

'Mom hooked me up for my b-day. It was a huge surprise. Apart from the stomach, you're good though, yeah?'

'Yeah, you know me. Takes more than that to keep me down.' Sam shadow-boxes, throwing air-punches like he's Ali, then screws up his face, first holding his stomach and then his head. 'Tell you the truth, not sure what's worse: the punch I took to the gut or this mad hangover banging out my head.' He rubs his temples again, shaking his head comically as if he's dizzy.

'Just promise me if we ever go out again, remind me never to drink any cocktails called "Rum and Daggah" no matter how piff I think a gyal is. Also anything that has any sort of chilli in it: chilli shot, chilli jam, the Red Hot Chili Peppers, nothing bro, I'm not on it. Man's batty been running like the River Rea out 'ere. It's killing me. Anyway I'm doing way better than some people, that's for sure.'

I shake my head slightly in confusion: 'What you talking about?'

Sam unfurls the paper he was reading. 'Haven't you heard the news?! Last night the city was on a mad one. A whole load of craziness went down. All I'm gonna say, is karma's for real for real.' Sam hands me the newspaper. Unable to contain what he's read, he narrates the articles as I skim-read through the story.

'See what I mean? It's a madness.'

'No way,' I say, staring blankly at the column.

Sam takes his paper back, rolls it up and places it under his arm. 'Told you. Crazy, innit?! They think it was some sort of turf war. I wonder if any of the guys that attacked us was involved.'

* * *

The computer lounge is populated with students. Connections seem to be fully up and running in here. The room is divided into three sections, bold signs hang from the ceiling to point to specific areas. The furthest of the three is the noise-restricted rooms, which are always booked out. The section in front of that is decked with single-cubicle work stations for independent studying. Before that is the communal study section, where a small crowd of students is now huddled around one of the computer screens. Sam taps me and signals at me to look ahead.

'Leiyah!' Sam calls over. She turns towards us, an apprehensive smile on her face. She drops what she's doing and meets us halfway. Sam goes in to hug her; Leiyah visibly tenses. I nudge Sam playfully so as not to make a scene, and he stops. Leiyah quietly breathes a sigh of relief. 'Hey . . .' we all say simultaneously. We look at each other, then down at the ground in awkward silence.

'I'm fine, guys,' Leiyah blurts out, unprompted. She doesn't look fine. Understandable. Behind her glasses, her eyes are slightly puffy, which she has been trying to hide, to put on a brave face. A part of me can't help but feel like I let her down. Can't imagine how she's feeling.

'Joe, what are you doing out of the hospital?' Leiyah enquires. 'I called to check in on you this morning but they said you'd disappeared. Oh, before I forget: these were dropped off to me this morning. Here.' Leiyah hands over our stolen phones and wallets.

'Sweet!' Sam immediately tries to turn on his phone. 'Ahh man, battery's done.'

'Thanks, and I'm okay.' Leiyah gives me a dubious look, not buying what I'm saying. 'How did you get these?' I try to change the subject, brushing the dirt off my screen and checking through my wallet.

'Police dropped them to my digs before I left out. They said they recovered them in the early hours of the morning but don't get too excited, networks are still struggling. They also want us to come into the station today to go through stuff.'

'No way! For what?!' Sam sharply responds, as he pulls his charger out of his bag. 'So they can arrest me and taser me for real this time? I ain't going there, what more do they want?'

'I don't know, Sam!' Leiyah snaps. 'Maybe they want us to finish off our statements. Don't shoot the messenger. It could be to do with the guys that atta—' Leiyah stops in her tracks and takes a sharp breath in. 'Look. Maybe we could all head up there together and get it out of the way. I'd rather be doing that — or anything else — than sitting at my place alone. It was driving me crazy.'

'Sure, Leiyah, yeah, that sounds like a plan. Whatever you need,' I respond, trying to reassure her but unable to give her eye-contact. There's a small commotion from the crowd gathered on the other side of the room where Leiyah was when we arrived.

'Hey Leiyah, I've found something!' calls the guy sitting in front of the computer. Leiyah acknowledges with a head nod.

'Have you guys seen the news?' Leiyah asks as we make our way over.

Sam pulls out his newspaper: 'Yeah, it's crazy. I was showing Joe earlier.'

'Wow, reading? Well done; you've changed. Also a newspaper? Very retro.'

'There she is,' Sam jokes, trying to lighten the mood. 'Actually for your information, Leiyah, I'm an honorary member and avid reader and subscriber to *Lubes and Boobs*. And I still like newspapers. They're good for wiping your batty with.'

Leiyah slaps Sam around the back of the head. 'It's so nice to see you haven't lost your sensitivity meter, considering what we've just been through.' Sam gives us a slightly embarrassed *oops* look, zipping his mouth with a hand motion.

Before we reach the group, Leiyah stops us and leans in conspiratorially: 'No, but seriously. Whilst mainstream news outlets are preoccupied with reporting the effects of the freak storm or the gang war, I'm not so sure the two are unrelated. We've managed to get one computer up and running and we've been following the story all morning. There's been numerous reports from credited, independent sites and eye-witnesses on social media of a weird deafening screech around the entire city at the same time as the reported "turf war". A black, smoke-like vapour was also seen rising from the area of the incident.'

Sam butts in: 'Okay, yeah but couldn't that just have been a fire? The Industrial's like the Wild West. Who knows what the hell was going on down there?'

'True, but some people are also reporting seeing this black smoke trailing up into the sky, as if attached to a missile. Some believe that's where the screech came from and that's caused the city-wide blackout. The dark net's flooding with conspiracies: "hashtag Blackout". Some swear they saw a shooting star falling from the sky; others think it was some sort of sonic missile weapon testing and that's what's actually caused the diverse weather. It's all government-controlled.'

'Oh please, that's ridiculous,' Sam interjects, flicking his eyebrows up as if to say *nonsense*. 'What's next? The Earth's flat and run by reptilians? You can't believe everything on the 'net, Leiyah.'

'Says the influencer that didn't know *The Da Vinci Code* was fiction,' Leiyah retorts.

Leiyah turns her back and carries on walking towards the crowd. We follow her. 'I admit a lot of this sounds wild and highly unlikely,' she continues. 'But whatever happened, more's going on than is being reported. Just look at the Blackout. The city's connected on many different grids. Individual buildings own their own back up generators: hospitals, etc. Yet at a single point — 3:27 a.m. — the whole city blacked out. Windows shattered, signals were disrupted and countless vehicles, building structures, and roads were damaged. No earthquake or seismic activity has been mentioned, but the epicentre of the incident is — you guessed it — the Industrial. Turf war or not, you got to admit, guys: it's a bit booky.'

Sam slow-claps. 'Good work, Sherlock. Your powers of deduction are impressive. Better be careful that the tinfoil hat brigade don't try to recruit you.'

Leiyah wrinkles her nose and kisses her teeth.

We join the crowd. The plumpish, green-haired guy with dangly earrings sitting at the computer clicks multiple links, redirecting him to a private page with a video link.

'What you got for me?' Leiyah asks.

He raises one finger: *one sec.*

'Just a min, hun. Think I might just have an answer to our questions,' he says without diverting his eyes from the screen.

Leiyah gestures to us: 'Before I forget, this fabulous tech nerd-slash-rival is Aaron. Aaron, Joseph and Sam; guys, Aaron.'

'Hi boys,' Aaron says with a wave of his hand, as Sam and I say hello to the back of his head. 'And I prefer "tech bird" hun, not "tech nerd",' Aaron clicks his fingers but still doesn't turn around, completely engrossed in the task at hand. 'You guys are just in time for the show, online security's an absolute mare — it's pretty much crumbled, which is allowing us to grab a lot of information that would usually be flagged and pulled down.'

He ostentatiously taps the keyboard to open the link. 'There, found you!'

A video plays on the screen. It looks like footage from a camera phone. The lens is cracked, so the image is unclear, the footage is shaky and visibility's not great at all. Leiyah squints and leans forward onto the desk as everyone else bundles closer together, trying to get a better view. The screen remains blank for almost ten seconds.

'What am I even looking at? This is a waste of time. Someone's just put this up as click bait,' Sam belts out.

Leiyah shushes him. 'Aaron, turn the volume up please,' she asks.

The camera pans around slowly, zooming in. The sound of shouting is heard and also what sounds like some sort of a chain clashing about. *Clang!* I prick up my ears at the sound and suddenly I see a chain swinging towards me. I jolt backwards.

The sharp movement brings me back to reality.

'Joe, you good?' I hear Sam ask.

'Yeah, I think so.' I shake it off, disorientated. I refocus my attention on the computer screen. Raindrops hit the lens, distorting the footage even further.

Aaron points at some fuzzy blobs towards the bottom of the screen. 'No way, is that people on the floor?' I can just about make out bodies lying bloodied, unconscious on the ground.

Thud! I blink again and I see my fist pummelling a guy's face into the wet ground, like a first-person point-of-view shot in a video game. A kick curls towards me. I grab the leg. I grip it tightly then raise my own knee, driving it into the thigh, feeling the resisting bone *snap!*

I snap out again. My breathing starts to get heavier, my chest lifts up and down quickly. I feel clammy, confused. What's going on?! What am I envisioning? Come on, Joe, hold it together.

'Look, there's a car on fire,' Aaron exclaims. The camera zooms in to the smoke. It's too dark to see anything.

'Doesn't this camera guy know about night mode or flash?' Sam comments irritatedly. Faint screams continue to be heard within the dark.

Crickkk! Thwack! Huh. I'm back in the rain, moving between attackers. My fists let loose with freedom, grabbing and punching at will, with devastating speed and ferocity. I feel light, unstoppable. Bullets fly through the air and appear to me in slow motion. I dodge them acrobatically, moving as fluently as smoke.

'Pause it!' Leiyah voice brings me back to reality. I put my hands over my eyes to wipe the sweat from my forehead. *Blam!* For a split-second I see gunfire flying towards me and I duck.

'Bro, you sure you're okay?'

'Yeah, yeah, I . . . Uh . . . I'm good, Sam.' No I'm not, I think, far from it. I think I'm losing my mind.

Leiyah leans forwards and starts to mess around with the video settings. 'Let me try and lighten the footage.' The image brightens, allowing us to make out more of the picture. 'Now rewind it a bit. Keep going . . . Keep going . . . There! Play.'

'What's that?!' Aaron points at something in the middle of the screen. 'Looks like one, two, maybe three people in the smoke. Are they . . . fighting?' We glimpse flashes of punches and outlined movement, still very vague. The camera jerks, trying to zoom in closer. The pixilated picture slightly improves. A face and hand shoot out of the black smoke reaching to get away, calling 'Help!' The hairs on my arms stand on end, as I feel the night air blow against my skin and there, in front of me, crawling beneath my feet, trying to get away in fear is . . . I snap back like a sheet has been pulled away from my eyes.

'WOAH!' Everybody jumps back simultaneously in shock as the man in the footage is sucked back into the black smoke like a vortex and disappears. A short raging screech crackles and distorts the camera sound. This is unbelievable. I blink my eyes and try to catch my breath, struggling to orientate myself and differentiate what is real.

'Look, there's movement! Something's coming out of the shadow!' Sam shouts, now mesmerised. 'Yo, what is that?' The outline of a shadowed figure stands still, silhouetted in front of a burning vehicle. Mumbles starts to ripple through the crowd as excitement hits the air.

'Oh snap, is this real?!'

'What did I just watch?'

'That was AI, can't be real.'

'Did you see that?'

'Shhhhhhhh!' Leiyah hushes the crowd. 'Quiet down; listen.' The camera starts to fumble. Deep, panicked breaths are heard from behind the camera, muffling the words: 'It's just one man.' The voice whispers and shakes with fear. The video ends. Everyone stares at the screen, lost for words.

'OH MY DAYZ!' Sam pops out. 'Did you just see that?!'

'Aaron, download that asap before it gets pulled down,' Leiyah orders.

The room's ecstatic. I stand in shock, dazed, trying to gather my thoughts as Aaron downloads the footage. Everybody fusses in manic excitement, trying to type on their phones, asking Aaron for a copy of the footage. My mind's doing overtime. It felt so real, like I was there. I was moving in and out of shadows, stalking, like a vampiric nightmare from the darkness. I took every hit and felt the resistance and impact of every shadowed, blurred blow I dished out.

'Looks like it's been pulled down now,' Aaron informs us. 'That can't have been legit though, right? Like, how's that even possible?'

Sam star-jumps in front of the crowd in pure excitement like a football fan celebrating a goal. 'I'll tell you how, because this guy's a frickin' real-life vigilante like Batman or Blade, or Kick Ass even— Well, maybe not like Kick Ass, but you know what I mean. Oh my days, this is cray! Joe, it's what we've always dreamed of.' Sam puts his hands on top of his head in disbelief and celebration. Even though I'm hearing Sam talk, my mind is a hollow box right now; his words are going in through one ear and out the other. Sam continues to talk: 'Can you believe this? Come on, this is epic. Come On!'

'*COME ON! YOU WANT SOME?!*' Sam's words morph from his voice into Tin Man's voice, which freaks me out.

'Joseph?' I hear Leiyah voice calling me back to the here-and-now. My stomach turns and I begin to tremble. No way. 'Do you think it's real?' Leiyah asks.

I try to calm myself but words fail to come out. Sam jumps in, still hypothesising. 'It's got to be real, right? Why else would it have been pulled down like that, huh?'

'This coming from the guy that told me not to trust what you see on the 'net?' Leiyah raises a sceptical eyebrow, but Sam continues talking to himself.

'I wonder who he is. Who's the richest playboy in the city? Yo, we need to keep an eye on any blind lawyers. I need to coin a name fast before other influencers do . . . Brummie Man, Black Shadow, The Nightstalker . . . Nah, can't use that; swear he was a serial killer.' Sam leans his hand on my shoulder trying to think of more names.

'Ow!' I flinch.

'What's wrong, Joe?' Leiyah asks.

'Not sure,' I say, as I reach my hand round to my shoulder and see blood on my fingers.

'Bro, you're bleeding.' Sam says.

A stinging pain shoots down my shoulder and both my hands start to burn. 'I'll be back in a sec, yeah; just need to go to the toilet.'

* * *

I rush out of the room, hyperventilating. How is this even possible? I'm a nobody; I'm just a student. The more I try to convince myself that this isn't real and that I'm probably having a mental breakdown, the more the footage plays over in my head, matching with the flashbacks.

'Ahh!' My hands are burning; why are they hurting so much? I rush down the corridor, looking down towards my palms.

Ouuufff!

'Ow, that hurt!' My head hits what feels like a brick wall, followed by the sound of a pile of books falling onto the floor.

I'm flat on my back from the collision. What did I hit?

'Busy night, Mr Jacobs?' I know that voice, that deep, low voice with a slight Jamaican accent. Professor Grey must be hitting the gym hard; feels like I crashed into a tree trunk.

'Sorry about that, professor. I should've looked where I was going.'

'Not to worry. It is not all the time we can see what is in plain sight. I've heard it say that the only thing worse than being blind is having sight but no vision. Here, let me help you onto your feet and back onto your path.' Grey extends his hand, springing me up onto my feet. 'There you go. Much better now, Mr Jacobs.' Grey straightens his blazer. 'A firm root must be planted firmly.'

Grey starts to pick up his books.

More and more visions of violence haunt me, flashing sporadically in front of my eyes.

'Mr Jacobs, are you alright?'

'I'm sorry, professor . . . I gotta go!' I leg it away, waving my arms erratically, scaring students as I peg it down the corridor. Bruised faces wrapped with golden bandanas, hellish red spiked hair, inked skin, bodies indented into car windows and the sounds of machine gun-fire reverberate around me.

* * *

I burst through the bathroom door, leaning slightly against it, blocking out the noise from the corridor. I check my shoulder again. 'Ahh, it stings!' Okay, okay, it's probably just a scratch. I check the two cubicles: no one's there. Right Joe, it's quiet. You're safe and you're alone. I take a moment to compose myself and go over to the sinks, throw my bag on the floor, and stand in front of the mirror. Why do I feel like I'm having déjà vu?

I slowly lift my top to check my back and the bandage around my torso.

Swish! Slash! Shing!

The sound of knives tears through the air. Suddenly, all over my body, thin lacerations appear. I fall to my knees in harrowing pain, cushioning my fall with my hands. 'What's happening to me?!' More wounds and bruises appear on my forearms, slicing, drawing fresh cuts along my skin, almost as if inflicted by a pinned hex doll. I spread my palms, the lines and fingerprints in my hand swirl like an optical illusion. The deep impression lines seem to rearrange themselves to form a faint circle. The pain is excruciating.

'Aarrghh!'

I pull myself back up to my feet and see my carved-up, bruised body in the mirror, my reflection ambushed by a ghostly complexion. I struggle through the pain to turn on the cold tap, dousing my hands under the water. I splash my face, covering my eyes with my hands and — all at once — the pain stops.

Water splashes from the running tap. I split the wet fingers covering my face apart and peek between them. I see myself in the bathroom mirror. It's all gone. The cuts over my body, hands, and palms — they've disappeared. Removing the bandage from my torso, there's no sign of any slash marks or stitching. Nothing.

'Yo, Joe!' I hear Sam calling. 'You in here?' Sam bursts through the door, catching me with my hands against my face, frozen in front of the mirror in a New Zealand rugby-style haka pose.

'Okayyyyy,' Sam raises his eyebrow like the Rock, looking at me like, *what are you doing?*

'That's kinda weird, Joe. Did not expect that but whatever floats your boat.'

I throw my top back on quickly. 'I, uh, I . . .'

'How's the shoulder?' Sam asks, using the urinal.

'Yeah, it was nothing; just a scratch.' Which has now remarkably healed, as well as all my imaginary knife-wounds. I pick my bag up. Sam finishes up and washes his hands.

We come out of the toilets. Leiyah stands waiting by the main doors leading out of the building, talking on her phone.

'Okay yes, I'm with them now so I'll let them know. Okay, sure. We'll make our way over now.' She puts down the phone and sighs, looking worried, the colour drained from her face. 'That was the police.'

CHAPTER 8

UPHOLD The RIGHT

'Well, spank me and call me Murphy,' says Sam as he takes off his snapback. 'Guys, I hate to say it but I told you we shouldn't have come here,' he reiterates, looking around at the chaotic setting of the police station, where officers in riot gear congregate near the side entrance.

'Looks like they're getting ready for a huge operation or something, doesn't it?' I comment. More and more armed officers move casually through lines of people, all waiting with varying amounts of patience to be seen.

'Yeah, for real.' Sam sounds unimpressed. 'What's the actual point though? Facts: the city's got its own real life superhero pummelling mans left right and centre. "Hashtag Brum's avenger" is deffo gonna go viral. Not gonna lie bro, I'm for it. Soon places like this will be obsolete and, in my opinion, it can't come soon enough. It's just another extension of the man's corrupt system. Brap, brap!' Sam does his own sound effects while saluting himself with gun-fingers, which probably isn't the cleverest thing to do given our current surroundings. Leiyah hears him and turns, but keeps silent and puts in her headphones.

Dd! Dd! Wummmmm!

Loud feedback sings through the station's tannoy, grabbing everyone's attention.

'*We are currently delayed due to a technical malfunction. All non-essential reports please be advised to reschedule.*'

Sam kisses his teeth and jumps back on his phone, trying to find a signal whilst reeling off more made-up superhero names to himself. Leiyah stands patiently in the queue, almost oblivious to the constant movement of bodies around her. She's noticeably quieter than usual. I guess we're all still processing last night in our own ways. Thankfully, the inside of my hands don't feel like they're burning anymore, so I can at least focus on our present situation for now.

'NEXT!' shouts one of the officers from the front desk. The queue moves along. The station looks kinda old, like a Victorian mausoleum. Even though the place feels like you're stepping back in time, state-of-the-art security cameras, scanners and tracking beams are posted at every entrance.

'Damn!' Sam cusses. 'This is looooong. The network is acting janky. Leiyah, you got any bars? Hellooo, Leiyah?'

Leiyah doesn't hear Sam with her headphones in. Sam taps her and silently mouths, over-exaggerating his words and pointing at his phone. She shakes her head. 'No!' she replies loudly, unaware of her own volume, before turning back to face the direction of the queue.

'What about you, Joe? Any luck?'

'Same. My signal's on and off.'

Sam raises his hands, still trying to get a decent signal. 'I am vex. You know how many influencers are scheming right now, putting their twopence in and naming our night-fighting superhero whilst I'm stuck here in Babylon?' Sam calls Leiyah impatiently and taps her again as the queue slowly moves closer to the front desk. 'Are you sure they didn't mention anything at all about why we've been called down here so urgently?'

Leiyah, really not impressed, turns again, breaking her silence: 'Like I told you before, they asked about you and Joe. I told them we were all together at uni and then the officer on the phone said that we needed to make our way immediately to this station. Now if you could please stop talking to me, I'm just trying to have a moment.'

Sam throws his hands hopelessly into the air. 'This place is the worst. How is it covered in mad futuristic security tech and they can't even sort out the reception? I bet they're jamming it or something like that. Gots to be.'

'Maybe it's a good thing. Sometimes it's good to keep a bit of distance between you and people.'

Sam reacts like he doesn't understand English, a *what-are-you-on-about* look plastered on his face. 'You mean like you and Harmony?'

'What you talking about?'

'You telling me you didn't see her?'

'See who? What? No. Where? What are you on about?'

'Bro,' Sam says, shaking his head in comical disappointment. 'Harmony. I ran into her minutes before I got you from the toilets at uni. She said she called and waved at you to get your attention and you ran straight past her, straight-up blanked her.' Sam stares at me in silence, blinking, which is really irritating. 'Yeahhhhh broooo . . .' He elongates his words whilst dropping his bottom lip, putting his hand on my shoulder, making a stupid, insincere, caring face. 'Even for a baller like me, who plays hard to get, that's cold. Who are you, Pepé Le Pew? One night Mr Romance, the next Mr Freeze? Risky tactics, bro. I like it — not gonna lie — treat 'em mean, keep 'em keen - but it's risky.'

I pull out my phone and walk from the reception queue.

Opening my messaging app, I quickly scroll through my contacts to type a message to Harmony. I hope I haven't blown it.

Hey Harmony, hope you're good. I had a great time last night. Soooo, Sam mentioned that I may of walked past you today at uni. Random as it sounds, I didn't see you . . . weird I know lol—

Delete . . .

What are you thinking? You sound like an idiot. But then, what am I supposed to say? *Hey Harmony, sorry I didn't see you, my body was being fatly wounded by imaginary slash-wounds, so anyway what's good?* Sounds so stupid. Just keep it simple. Don't mention any weird crap or not seeing her . . . which would then make me sound like an arrogant tool. I can't win. Why is sending a message so hard? Right, look: just send something simple.

Hey ☺

Not with a smile emoji, that's soft. Delete. Delete. Just send:

Hey

That should be cool, right?
    Sending . . .

14:44 — Message failed.
No service.
Press to resend.

Wow! You're kidding me. No bars, what the f—
    'Hey! No filming allowed,' an officer shouts at Sam, who's trying to film a commotion taking place in the corner of the station.
    'Back off, let us do our jobs. Back up, get back!' another man

yells. Officers rush through the lines of people towards the noise, past Leiyah, knocking her glasses slightly askew on her face. Leiyah tenses and exhales sharply, fixing her glasses. Outside of the side entrance door, media crews and news teams gather. Cameras and mics are pushed into the face of a rough-looking, unshaven Indian guy wearing a slightly crumpled suit.

'Is there any further news from the Industrial?'

'Detective, first a serial killer, then a shootout at the city morgue, now a turf war and a rumoured vigilante. Are the police losing control of the city?'

'Any comments on the video from last night?'

'Is it connected with last night's unrest?'

'Why are authorities actively trying to block the footage?'

I avert my eyes as, one by one, exhausted-looking police lead detained individuals through reporters and their flashing cameras into the building towards the restricted area. The queue parts as the onlookers watch prisoners go past.

'Oi mutton-shunter, get your stinking hands off me!' shouts a handcuffed detainee, enjoying the attention of the crowd as he's hauled through the lines. 'I cook pork like you for breakfast. We run this city. You hear me, you tosser?!' He spits in the officer's face and laughs: 'Oink, oink!'

Extra officers race to grab the prisoner and drag him faster to his destination. As he passes me, he meets my gaze. He smiles at me, which rattles me.

'SeE YOu SoOn,' he says, still smiling weirdly at me, almost breaking his neck to maintain eye-contact as he is led away. I look away again, but keep watching him from the corner of my eye. His eyes catch a weird reflection of light or something, because, for a split-second, I swear they were glowing white.

'Wow, you sure know how to attract the weirdos, don't you Joe?' Sam says.

'You just saw that, right?' I say to Sam, who's now looking in another direction.

'See what?'

'He's real, I swear it!' Two officers manhandle and drag another prisoner, who's skidding his feet across the floor, yelling at the top of his voice: 'You gotta believe me. Black as night, smoking, like a phantom! He just kept walking! You got to believe me, I swear!'

'Quiet down, you!' The officer escorting him bundles him away from the crowds. '"Black ghost" — I've never heard anything so ridiculous in my life.'

Sam jumps in front of me and Leiyah. 'Oh snap, did you guys just hear what that crazy future prison bae just said?!' Sam tries to lower his voice, which brings his volume to a regular speaking voice: '"The Black Ghost!" Did you hear him? He's got to be taking about what we saw, right?! I got to admit it's a pretty dope name: "Black Ghost." Guys, that's got to be further proof that the footage was real.'

'NEXT!' The desk officer summons us towards the protective screen guarding the desk. We walk over. 'Case number?'

Leiyah takes out her headphones and pulls out her phone. 'Oh sorry, yes. Here.' Her hand rattles nervously as she reads out the numbers on the screen. The officer types it into the computer, turning the dial down on her radio that's spurting out numerical codes. Leiyah jams her hands into the front pouch of her dungarees, waiting anxiously. 'We were called by an officer and asked to come down to the station,' Leiyah cuts through the silence.

The officer looks up. 'If you could wait over there, an officer will come and collect you shortly.'

I approach the barrier. 'Could you tell us what we've been called in for?'

The officer scans the screen. 'Statements need completing and also it looks like you've been called in to identify suspects in a line-up.' We all look at each other. Leiyah steps away from the glass and walks over to the designated waiting area.

'NEXT!' The officer calls as we walk away.

* * *

Leiyah sits, cleaning her glasses lenses. Her face looks perplexed and her leg rocks anxiously up and down.

'Hey Leiyah, if you ever—' Leiyah grabs my hand, clenching tightly, to stop me from speaking. It sinks in. The possibility of seeing and pointing out the people who attacked us is daunting enough, scary even. From what I know of Leiyah, she's not a person that likes to lose control. As long as I've known her she's always been calculated, precise in her decisions — basically, the total opposite of Sam — which I've always admired. She keeps it together even when we don't, especially me. It can't be easy moving across county lines to study alone in a strange city, with no family or childhood friends nearby.

'You guys want to hear something funny?' Sam says sitting beside us, trying to lighten the mood.

Leiyah lets go of my hand. 'Do we have a choice?' Leiyah sighs.

'No you don't, but it'll cheer you up, promise.' Sam playfully smirks. 'So, did you guys catch Miles Brown's eye-dropping, roadman, meme-worthy exit at the Night Owl yesterday?'

'I did see him looking angrier than his usual self,' Leiyah responds.

'Yeah, I spotted him when I was dancing with Harmony. People were holding their noses as he went past.'

Sam chuckles to himself, amused. I look at Leiyah with a sarcastic apprehension.

'Sam please tell me you didn't—'

Sam shushes me, putting his fingers on my lip. 'I hope you washed your hands bro,' I ask as I flick his hand away.

Sam jumps up and repositions himself, wedging in between me and Leiyah with no regard for spatial awareness. He proudly prepares himself, rolling up his sleeves theatrically like a magician. Leiyah raises her eyebrows, looking wide-eyed at me as if to say: *here we go.*

'So, after I left you guys at the bar skanking and knocking back a few to go to the loo, let's just say the visit wasn't what I expected at all. The toilets were rammed. It was a complete sausage-fest; mans weren't adhering to the two-space rule at all. So I'm standing there, desperate, waiting in line. Then, out of nowhere, busting through doors like a velociraptor from *Jurassic Park*, I hear the unmistakable voice of Miles Brown entering the men's room. He's chatting bare, gassing loud on his phone, chatting about how he's got bare rizz, telling out all his business, flaunting in some Brummie roadman-pirate dialect like he's hopped up on hyper-steds. What a knob. Anyway, so he's bunksin' guys out the way, completely ignoring the queue. Luckily, he doesn't see me and pushes his way to commandeer one of the only two cubicles, which, if I may be so bold to say, was a dick move. No pun intended. I'm waiting and the toilets get more empty and the distinctive smell of the herb starts to permeate. Finally, I get to a urinal but one of the guys leaves the cubicle next to Miles's so I go in there to beat having to sword-fight and dodge guys with no control at the watering hole.'

'Not cool Sam! Way too much info,' I say as Leiyah screws up her lip and puts her hands on her head in disgust at Sam's over-descriptive tour of the men's lavatory.

Sam continues without missing a beat: 'I'm in the cubicle. It stinks so bad, I had to hold my nose, the person that was just in deffo left his mark, merkin' out the toilet. He really should've flushed twice. Anyway, so I'm in the toilet, bursting, but there, right in front of me, on top of the toilet box flush-thingy is — not the three seashells — but an empty bottle. All the humiliation of that morning floods back and I just think about how Miles went on bad with us, throwing his weight around with his mandem like he's some top boy. Then the penny of sweet revenge drops. Cue *Mission Impossible* theme song. I grab the bottle and relieve myself, filling it to the top.'

'Uggghhh!' Leiyah and I exclaim simultaneously.

'Sam, you didn't.' I cringe at the thought of what's going to come out of his mouth next.

'Quiet guys, let me finish the story; this is the best part. So, as I was saying, there I was filling the bottle and remember I'm kinda faded, so I'm trying not to hit my hand, which is a real skill. I finish up then stand on the toilet seat, peeking over to Miles's cubicle like I'm in some American teen high school movie scene. Miles is on the other side, just sitting there, chilling on the lid of the toilet seat, burning it down and rolling the next one with his head phones on. I know what you're thinking — who brings headphones into a club? Stupid, right?'

'Really, Sam, that's not what we're thinking,' Leiyah mutters.

'Ssshhh! I'm nearly finished. So, I'm holding the pee-filled bottle, taking my time to position myself, thinking about pure payback. I slowly place the—'

'Leiyah McGregor!' calls an officer, cutting Sam's story short. We all turn our heads to see a young female officer coming to collect us. Leiyah lifts her hand and stands up to make herself known.

'Hello, Leiyah, I'm Officer Lace. Sorry for keeping you waiting. I take it these two were also involved in the altercation?' Leiyah nods and gestures me and Sam to our feet. The officer points at us to guess our names: 'Joseph Jacobs and you must be Samuel Gles—'

Sam interrupts her by clearing his throat loudly. 'Uh-hmm, Sam's fine, officer. Or Sam West, if you want to get official. Either way.'

Officer Lace signs us in on her tablet then we follow her through the secure doors.

* * *

We get to a two-way corridor and follow Officer Lace to the left. The walls are covered with leaflets and WANTED posters, stuck to green felt display boards. Technicians stand on ladders checking wires in ceilings, which must have been affected by the storm.

'You guys hear that noise?' Leiyah whispers, looking back at me and Sam.

'Don't worry, it's just the processing area,' Officer Lace responds, continuing to walk ahead.

The noise starts to get louder as we get closer. We hear a military voice yelling instructions with authority: 'Stop!', 'Turn!', and 'Cough!' We pass the area the noise is coming from. Handcuffed individuals are lined up like live stock at a cattle market. Some of the guys jeer at us through the thick security window as we walk past, swearing at officers, trying to get a rise out of them. One guy tries to escape but is swiftly tackled onto the ground. Officer Lace ushers us along quickly to prevent us from seeing any further disturbance. Leiyah looks at us wide-eyed in shock.

Click, ping!

Officer Lace uses a key-fob on her belt to open a secured door. Inside, another officer stands picking his teeth. He's a lot older than Officer Lace: taller, dense, his right ear shaped like a cauliflower. Just like one of those cage fighters. He has a bandage wrapped around his head. Like every other officer we've seen in this place, he looks exhausted. It's quiet in here, almost too quiet. The one-way viewing window he's leaning against separates us from the room on the other side — well, at least I hope it's one-way.

'This is my senior officer: Officer Scott. He'll be joining us for the line-up today.' Officer Scott nods his head with little acknowledgment and continues picking his teeth, a blank expression across his face. Officer Lace continues, looking slightly embarrassed at his behaviour: 'So there'll be three separate line-ups coming in, which you'll be able to see through the glass.' Sam puts his hand up to cut in but Officer Lace continues to speak without missing a beat: 'And yes, it's a one-way glass, if that's what you're asking. You'll be completely safe; no one will be able to see or hear you. If you recognise anyone in the line-up, or if anyone looks familiar, just say the number which will be projected onto their chest and we'll make a note. Please do not touch the glass. Any questions? Anything you're unclear about?' The room stays silent. 'Great, let's begin.'

Bzzzggggrrrr!

A harsh noise clangs around the room as Officer Scott hits a grey button on the wall and the mechanised door in the line-up room unlocks and begins to slide open slowly. The jingling sound of chains — rattling, pulling, scraping — transmits through the speakers above our heads. Sam switches his hat from backwards to forwards and Leiyah takes a controlled deep breath.

'You good?' I ask, not taking my eyes off the sliding door. They both respond with thumbs up, gazing through the window, focused, calm and collected. Five men wobble into the room in a line, wearing blue-and-black striped jumpsuits, chained and cuffed at the feet and hands. They face forward, a green laser beam projecting a number onto each of their chests. They stand there, staring dead ahead. A pre-recorded voice gives instructions: turn left, then right, eventually making them do a three-sixty to face back towards the glass. The men vary in size, each of them covered in tats: G3, circular loops, numbered symbols and artwork, which bulge on their bruised foreheads and scrapes. Number Three has a slight smirk on his face as he over-exaggerates his yawn to show his boredom, then sticks his middle finger up. Number Five looks like he can barely stand, let alone see. I'm not sure what's more alarming, his swollen, bloodshot, bruised eye or his red, fire-coloured hair. He looks like he's had one hell of a night.

'Do any of these men look familiar to you?' Officer Lace queries.

'No,' I shake my head. Leiyah follows suit. Sam moves closer to the glass, then turns, giving his answer: 'No, I don't recognise any of them. It's hard when their faces look like they've been hit by a truck.' Sam taps on the glass then throws his hand over his mouth, realising what he's just done. All the prisoners' heads snap towards the direction of the sound.

'Don't piss around, sunshine,' Officer Scott says, standing assertively. Sam backs away from the glass, embarrassed. The suspects begin to get worked up.

'I know you're watching us,' the guy with the red hair says, slurring his words. 'You think you've got it all worked out. But you have no idea.'

'Get back in line!' An officers yell, entering the room. 'Oi, keep quiet!' The suspects rattle their chains and start to get more rowdy.

THUD!

The guy with the red hair hits the glass with his fist, his one good, almond-shaped eye looking intensely, almost gazing through the glass and into our souls.

For an instant, his spiked red hair seems to glow and flicker like a flame. In my mind's eye, I see a fist — my fist — fly out of darkness and into his face.

'You're not listening!' I am pulled back to reality as officers clear the room and pull the guy away from the window. 'Pricks! There's something worse than us out there: Hāakgwái!'

'What's my man babbling about, Leiyah?'

'How am I supposed to know? It sounds like Cantonese.' Sam looks at her. 'I'm Jamaican and Japanese, dumbass,' she says, rolling her eyes.

'You've got to believe me! The Black Ghost! A WALKING SHADOW OF DEATHHHH!'

The officers drag him away and close the door. The room is empty once more.

Sam raises his shoulders. 'Uhh . . . My bad, guys.'

Bzzzgggggrrrrr!

The buzzer sounds again. More men are led through the door, dragging their chains against the floor, repeating the same routine. Again we stare through the glass and again nothing.

'Psst,' Sam side-mouths to me and Leiyah as the line files out. 'Did you hear my man call me "sunshine"? The disrespect. Why is he standing there like a weirdo staring at the glass like that? No one's there.'

We look at the officer, who is standing stone-still in front of the window, looking at his own reflection. He mumbles something inaudible under his breath.

'Officer Scott?' the other calls. He snaps out of his trance-like state.

'Huh? What was that?' he says.

'Are we okay to carry on?' Lace asks.

'Y— Yes, of course,' the officer says, looking at me with a strange, intense glare.

The last line-up enters. I cross my fingers nervously, hoping that Tin Man and his surgical masked crony would be part of them, and hopefully put an end to this whole process. They march in . . . Again, nothing. A small part of me feels kinda relieved to not see their faces again but, in the back of my mind, the thought that they're still out there, ready to pounce on and attack whoever they wish is unsettling.

'Him! There!'

Sam walks purposefully up to the glass but this time manages to stop himself from touching it. 'Number Four. That's the guy who almost punched my stomach through my throat.'

'Are you sure?' Officer Lace asks.

'Yeah, I'm sure. I remember his face; he was all up in my morning with his fire-breath. That's definitely him!'

Officer Scott leans over to speak with Officer Lace in a low voice. The prisoners are led out of the room. Sam walks back over to us: 'At least we got one.'

Leiyah kicks her Docs into the floor. 'Yeah, great news,' she responds unenthusiastically.

Officer Lace joins us.

'Before we can let you go, we need to finish off your statements and show some pictures that might further help identify your attackers.'

Sam and Leiyah are asked to follow Officer Lace to sign off on their statements and, as I haven't given mine yet, I follow Officer Scott to start mine. It definitely feels like I've drawn the short straw.

We move into a tiny side-room. It's stuffy inside and feels really claustrophobic, which I imagine must be the intention when grilling suspects. Two chairs face each other on opposite sides of a small table that has a lock loop for securing handcuffs attached to the side. Orange LED strip lights line the ceiling, reflecting and gleaming against the wall-sized mirror behind the officer, causing me to squint.

'State your name for the record.'

The officer sits across from me and rests his hands on what looks like a screen-topped table. He's got one of those proper strong Brummie accents, almost borderline Black Country or, as Sam likes to call them, 'yam yams'. I go to speak but my throat feels dry. I clear it.

'Joseph Jacobs,' I state, which activates the tabletop screen. A huge grid appears on it with a sound wave that spikes and falls as it maps my recorded speech.

The officer leans back in his chair which creaks. The sound wave spikes.

'Right then. Start at the top. What happened last night?'

I proceed to tell the officer what happened in the alley. He listens as I describe the attack in as much detail as possible, but every so often he checks behind him as if hearing something coming from the direction of the mirror. After I finish, the officer switches off the recording.

'I just have a couple of questions for you, if that's okay?'

'Sure,' I reply as the officer loads images onto the screen.

'Have you ever been in trouble with the police before?'

'No.'

'Have you ever been affiliated—' The officer stops. He turns again to look behind him. 'Did you hear that?'

'Hear what?' I respond.

'Sounded like glass being scratched.' The officer looks at me with confusion. He rubs the wound on his head and composes himself.

'Have you ever been affiliated to any gangs or crimes in the past?'

'No.'

The officer looks up from the images and concentrates on me. 'Are you sure?'

I clam up, diverting my eyes up towards the green light on the security camera in the corner of the room. Not sure how to respond to his calm insinuation.

'No need to take offence, I'm only asking.' The officer looks at me as if I've said something wrong or am somehow guilty of being a victim. His silver-shielded police badge engraved with the words 'Protect the right' stares me in right the face.

'*What* exactly are you asking?' My words come out a bit more abruptly than I had intended.

'Settle down, sunshine. I'm just doing my job. I have to ask questions.'

Wow, again with the 'sunshine'. The officer begins to scroll through images of men on stretchers. They're all battered, beaten and bloodied, some with broken bones.

'Your friend pointed out an individual in the line-up who is known to us: Markus Small. He's connected to wanted organised criminals with a number of felonies.' The officer continues, flicking through some truly graphic images.

'Him.' I point to the screen. 'That's one of them.' The officer zooms in on the picture. My breathing starts to go erratic and my hands become clammy. 'He's the one who pinned me up against the wall.'

SNAP!

'Aarrghh!' I flash back to the night before and hear shouts of pain, accompanied by the sound of the rain clattering against the ground. Gripping me tightly are the arms of the guy in the picture.

'Hey! I'm talking to you. Are you positive?' Officer Scott asks, bringing me back to reality.

'Positive.'

'Well, unfortunately for him he won't be pinning anybody up for a long time. Both his arms are broken in three different places.' The officer ticks the photo, adding it to a digital list and continues to scroll. I point out another from the alley who's pictured with his jaw dislocated. This can't all just be a coincidence, can it? Since I've woken up, my dreams of vengeance have been vividly flooding back to me, like a disjointed jigsaw puzzle.

'What . . . happened to them?' I ask.

'Just animals fighting animals. I'd rather they wiped each other out; makes my job a lot easier.'

'What about that footage that's gone viral? Did that have something to do with this?'

'It's not real. Can't be. One person couldn't take these guys out. Believe me, some of us have been on the front-line for years. Don't believe everything you see, it's definitely a hoax, sunshi—'

'It's Joseph,' I interject. The officer dead-eyes me, insulted at the correction. He repositions himself in his chair, once again rubbing his head. Sweat drips from his forehead.

'You mentioned a specific description in your statement: the letters T-I-N-M-A-N tattooed onto someone's knuckles. Is this the guy you're on about?' A picture of Tin Man in a prisoner's jumpsuit appears on the screen. It startles me. I sit back in my chair and move away from the table. Seeing his face again — those eyes staring at me with malice — sends cold chills through my body. Officer Scott stands up to stretch. 'His real name is . . .' The officer's voice begins to muffle and fade out. My eyes are fixed on the picture and I hear Tin Man's voice.

'*COME ON! YOU WANT SOME?!*' The hairs on the back of my neck stand up. The officer's muffled voice morphs into Tin Man's. My elusive dream solidifies into a memory and flashes me back into the night, back into the rain . . .

'Come on!' Tin Man shouts. I circle around him like a tornado, seeing him in 360° vision. He viciously swipes and slashes his machete. All my anger, tears and pent-up fear charges. My hand snaps at his throat, lifting him off his feet. He tries to utter words, choking as I squeeze tighter. I allow him to see me, looking into his eyes as they widen with terror. I absorb all the pain, misery, humiliation and suffering that he's inflicted on others and unleash it back upon him all at once like a terrible reckoning. His mouth opens in horror, a purplish glow reflecting off his metallic grills, which start to bur—

Spishh!

The sound of breaking glass brings me back. The big mirror behind Officer Scott cracks and continues to slowly split across the surface like thin ice, warping the reflection of the room. The strip lights flash like a strobe

'No, no, not again!' Officer Scott hysterically shouts, jumping up from the desk. 'Can't you see it?!' he says, pointing at the mirror.

'See what?'

'They're clawing closer! You've got to help me get away!'

'I'm going to get some help.'

'Huhhhhhhhhhhhhhhhh!'

The officer makes a sharp exhalation noise, as if the air is being sucked out of his body. He stands still, slumped, soulless.

'Officer? Is everything okay?' I ask.

His head is down, he's gently swaying back and forth. I slowly lean forward in my chair to get a better view of his face in the mirror.

'Officer?' I cautiously move to stand up, noticing that the green light on the CCTV camera has gone off. This isn't right. A weird hissing, like a whisper, rises to an audible volume around the room, then stops.

'Officer? Offi—'

Spishhh!

The tabletop screen in front of me explodes, spitting glass shards everywhere, causing me to fall back and over my chair, tumbling backwards onto the floor. Before I can collect my thoughts, I hear a low grumbling, an almost animalistic growl. It sounds like multiple voices being squeezed through a single, tortured voice box all at once. I immediately sit up on the floor, wiping bits of glass and wooden shards off me. Quick crunching sounds signal footsteps on glass stomping towards me.

Szzwoom! The remains of the table-frame is tossed aside. It smashes into the wall and there, standing above me, face contorted with pieces of glass sticking out of his neck, is Officer Scott. He growls, lunging across the broken shards at me. In a single motion, I roll over on my side and grab the chair. Placing it between me and him to use as a shield, I scuttle away on my back across the glass-strewn floor. The officer, eyes rolled back into his head until I can see the blazing white of his eyes, swipes viciously at my throat.

'Get off me! Help! He's gone crazy! Help!'

His mouth snaps like a rabid beast, chomping, grinding his teeth, crunching, frothing at the mouth. His fingers scratch at the air as he reaches for my throat, getting closer with each try. I push the chair with all my might to hold him back, but I can feel my arms starting to shake under his weight. Out of the corner or my eye, I glimpse the reflection of Officer Scott, trapped inside the cracked mirror, pushing against the glass, shouting at the top of his lungs, intermittently looking behind him with his fear-stricken face. His physical body takes no notice and continues to lurch towards me. If that's Officer Scott in the mirror, then who — or what — is in his body?

Before my mind can even fathom the thought, the attacking officer raises his head, thrusts it forward and smashes face first into the wooden seat of the chair that separates us. It splinters into pieces and the officer sprawls onto the floor, out cold. I kick him away and pick up one of the loose chair legs, ready to defend myself in case he gets back up. I run to the door, making sure to keep one eye on him as he lies there. The officer in the mirror mouths a desperate 'help!' before turning his back swiftly, as a weird fog rises around him. Astonished by what I'm seeing, I knock on the mirror to get his attention, but the officer doesn't even flinch, peering transfixed into the thickening oncoming fog.

Duff! Duff! Duff!

I pull and bang at the locked door in the hope someone on the other side might hear me.

'Hey! Anyone?! In here!'

Crunch!

Movement. I inhale sharply and turn to look behind me. Nothing. Where's he gone? A trail of saliva drips in front of my face from above.

'WE . . . SalD . . . We . . . wOuLD . . . SeE . . . yOu!'

Crouched on all fours upside down on the celling like a Xenomorph, his hands squeezing broken glass into his own flesh and his head twisted all the way round like an owl, nearly to breaking point, is the officer. His mouth opens and he stares at me like a predator, ready to pounce. A weird, whispering language seeps from his lips: 'iri mī-ëdri . . . ari drēla-ëdri!'

Suddenly, he freezes like a contorted statue. He looks down at me, watching, waiting, completely still. He grumbles again: 'wE . . . SeE . . . yOu!'

His voice sounds likes he's speaking in multiple tones, as if his vocal cords have been split and painfully trebled, tortured from within:

'WE . . . KnOw . . . You.

'We . . . HAve . . . HeArD . . . Your . . . ScrEam . . .

EcHo . . . tHroUgh thE AGES . . . oF TiMe!

    'YOur . . . POWeR wILL nOt . . . SaVE yOU!

    'YoUR . . . AWakEniNG . . . WIlL NOt suCCeeD.

    'We . . . Are . . . MaNY!'

I press my back harder against the door, trying to keep what little space I have between us. I grip the chair leg tighter as I look up at the gravity-defying officer.

Duff! Duff! Duff!

The door shakes behind me from the other side.

'Officer Scott! Can you hear me? Open the door.'

'Help! He's gone crazy,' I shout. 'Hurry!'

The doors behind me booms again with more voices fussing to open it.

'Quickly!' I yell.

The officer drops down and ferociously leaps towards me before I can even raise the chair leg to clobber him. He swipes the object out of my hand and grabs me by the neck. The choking force lifts me off the floor and pins me against the door. His eyes glow bright, streaming white, clouded with tears. He moves closer to my face, close enough to feel his warm breath growling. I turn my head away towards the mirror and see Officer Scott in the mirror, watching himself attack me. He strikes the mirror with his fists to assist me, shouting and banging away.

'FoOliSh HuMaN!' the officer grunts.

And then I see it, in the distance: eyes, behind the officer's reflection, moving towards him. Outlines of a bright and terrible form, an almost invisible — nearly inexplicable — horde of white shadows. Officer Scott freezes and stops in mid-action. Suddenly, a huge talon rips at his leg, pulling him down. Within seconds, more of these horrific pincers claw at him as the officer disappears into the now-retracting white mist.

Again, the officer in the room whispers that strange language at me: 'iri mī-ëdri . . . tīrifākh dō-ëri,' spitting as he inflects with intention. I refocus on the officer's physical body, trying to loosen his grip, but his arms are ice-cold and as stiff as rock.

'YOU . . . aRe . . . AlOnE!
' . . . YOU . . . aRe . . . AlOnE!
'YOuR . . . DREAMS . . . arE DEaD
' . . . DREAMSsss

                                         ' . . . Deaaaaad!

'wE wiLl HuNT yOu
'WE SeE yOu
' . . . WE SeE yOu
'WE arE WaTChinG YoU
' . . . WaTChinG
'JOSEPH, Son of Imādris!'

Son of who? Before I can register anything else, I hear the police begin to break down the door from the other side. The officer grins at me, then the mirror collapses and shatters into a million pieces. The officer screams and convulses rapidly, releasing me from his vice-like grip. I hit the floor like a sack of potatoes and lie there, rubbing my throat as I try to catch my breath.

The officers break through the door. They pause for a split-second as they take in the chaos of the room. They see me and the wooden chair leg in front of me, then Officer Scott's unconscious body on the floor. Before I can take another breath, the officers flick out their batons and rush into the room.

'Don't move!'

'Stay right there!'

'Hands above your head!'

'Wait! Please, I can explain,' I plead.

'Do it now!'

'Above your head!'

'Oi! I said keep them where I can see them.'

'We have a pulse, he's still alive.'

'Urgent medical assistant needed in Interview Three. Over.'

'I didn't do anything!' I insist, my own voice drowned out by the noise of the officers swarming the room, as my head is pushed down and pinned against the floor, facing the now-empty mirror frame.

'Move again and you'll wish you hadn't. You hear me?'

My arms are forcefully pulled backwards, almost popping my shoulder from the socket. Cold metal wraps around my hands as the cuffs click and squeeze tightly against my skin. I continue to mouth my innocence but my voice goes unheard amongst the cacophony of stomping, black leather boots on the broken shrapnel near my head. I block out the noise and just stare blankly at the mirror frame. How . . . Who or what were those things? Glowing bright. It's all real, what I've been seeing, dreaming, envisioning. It said my . . . It called me Joseph, Son of Imādris . . .

'Where is he?!'

'He's fine, Elizabeth. Just calm down.'

'Don't tell me to calm down, Paul. My son was just arrested and detained in your station. What was he even doing here?! If anything has happened to him, I will bring this place down brick by brick. Now tell me where Joseph is.'

Kukadia backs off, rubbing his shoulder. He pops a pill to

nurse the wound from the bullet that grazed his shoulder at the morgue. He signals to an accompanying officer who precedes to escort us down the arched corridors.

'What exactly are you charging him with?'

'Attacking an officer, assault and battery,' Kukadia responds.

'And what proof do you have?'

'The officer was lying on the floor unconscious. Joseph was the only the other person in the room.'

I stop walking and turn to the detective. 'And this officer has accused Joseph of attacking him, has he?'

' . . . '

'Well?'

' . . . No, not exac—'

'No?! What do you mean, no?!'

'He's still unconscious but we have reason to belie—'

'I want the CCTV footage from the interview room.'

The detective rubs his temples again, breaking eye-contact with me.

'We . . . can't.'

'Why not?!'

'We're still having power problems from last night's storm and there's a possibility that . . . that the cameras could've been down during the incident.'

'I beg your pardon?!'

' . . . '

'Did I just hear you correctly? You're telling me that you have detained my son with no eyewitnesses, or knowledge, or any proof of what actually happened? This is a complete abuse of power. I wonder if there could possibly have been another factor in how you and your brood came to this conclusion?!'

The detective raises his hands, unable to fire a comeback. I continue walking at a more urgent pace.

'No, no! Don't! You're not listening to me! They were in the mirror!'

That's Joseph's voice. I can hear him from down the hallway, which is completely out of character for him. Why is he shouting?

'Joseph!' I shout, walking in the direction of his voice.

'Elizabeth, wait!' Kukadia calls following.

'Sharp claws! They've got him! You've got to believe me: white shadows!'

Joseph's friends, Sam and Leiyah, are sitting on chairs outside the room. Leiyah looks up at me with tears in her eyes, lost for words, and Sam shoots me a look of overwhelming worry, before quickly staring back down at the floor. They both sit in silence like two school kids waiting outside the headteacher's office.

'Elizabeth, hold on a second. Before you go in this might not be—'

'Get out of my way, Paul!'

The detective immediately steps aside. Joseph's voice quietens and, just before I reach to grab the door-handle, the door opens and a nurse steps out. She closes the door softly behind her.

'Can I help you?' the nurse asks with a broad Scottish accent.

'Yes,' I reply abruptly. 'I'm Ms Jacobs, I need to see my son.'

The nurse blocks my hand as I reach for the handle again.

'Ms Jacobs, I'm not sure that's wise. It's best we speak for a moment.'

'No, I need to see my son now!' I say impatiently.

'Your son is quite unwell. He seems to be experiencing delusional episodes and will need further examination.' The nurse continues to block my way. I step closer to her.

'Either move or I will move you.'

The nurse looks shocked and glances at Kukadia, who nods his head, ushering the nurse out of the way.

'Elizabeth—'

I raise my hand to stop the detective talking. I don't want to hear another word from anybody. I open the door. I see my son bruised, ruffled, and handcuffed. He sits silently, still, staring blankly forward, pale-faced and disorientated. A medic on the other side of the room is filling in assessment papers.

'Joe . . . Joseph,' I say softy, kneeling down in front of him, reaching for his hand. 'It's me: Mom.' He responds by slowly raising his big brown eyes up at me. My heart breaks.

'What have you given him?' I ask the medic forcefully.

'The nurse administered a sedative,' the medic responds sheepishly. 'He was becoming quite aggressive; we felt he would be a danger to us and himself.'

'A danger?!' I say, lifting part of the handcuffs that they have chained him to the chair with. I rub his hands. Joseph stares at me. I've seen that look on him before; that look that went straight through me and woke me up when I first met him, a long time ago on a night that lasted forever. Joseph opens his mouth slightly to speak, his eyes looking through me like glass.

'They . . . took him,' he says, a spaced-out look across his face.

'Took who? Joseph, it's me: Mom,' I probe.

'White . . . Body snatched . . . Parasite.'

'What do you mean?'

'Mirror . . . Claws . . . They were in there . . . Attacked.'

'Joseph, I need you to try really hard. What happened? Did the officer attack you?'

'Officer?' Josephs furrows his brow and momentarily locks his hazy gaze onto mine and whispers: 'That's not the officer.'

'Joseph, I'm trying to understand.' I desperately try to get him to focus on me and to make sense out of what he is saying. 'Help me—'

The paramedic walks over to check him and shines a light into his pupils.

'NO! Glowing, bright eyes, glowing!' Joseph starts to raise his voice and pulls at his handcuffs, lashing out manically and knocking the torch from the medic's hands. 'WHITE SHADOWS, GLOWING EYES IN THE MIRROR!'

'Joseph, try to stay calm!' I plead.

'They killed him, took him in the mirror! HE'S DEAD!'

Officers burst into the room to assist the medic in restraining him, followed by the nurse. I walk back, unable to do anything but watch as they restrain and sedate my son. Kukadia escorts me out of the room and I see Sam and Leiyah looking on in disbelief. The door shuts.

Kukadia sits me in a chair outside the room. I'm shaking. I look at my hands and hear the muffled voices on the other side of the door. I instantly spring back to my feet and pace up and down.

'Elizabeth.'

The detective calls me away and we walk a few steps down the corridor away from Sam and Leiyah. 'Elizabeth, I'm not sure if you're aware but Joseph was admitted to hospital last night after suffering minor slash wounds.'

'. . .'

Kukadia hands me some papers and I skim over the report, raising my eyebrows as I spot some of the information he just told me.

'He ran out last night without being cleared, through the ward window.'

'My god, how did he—' The detective's words catch me off-guard, leaving me speechless, feeling like the worst person in the world.

'Look, I know you're probably feeling shit right now. I understand but—'

'No, you don't understand. You never did understand.'

Kukadia quietens down, unable to respond, and looks at the door. Officers walk past us in the corridor, making sure to keep a respectful distance.

'Look, I'll try my best to get to the bottom of exactly what happened. You'll just have to trust me.'

'Trust you?! You mean like telling you sensitive and privileged information, only for you to blare it out on the six o'clock news? Do you know how that looks? The position that puts me in?'

The detective lowers his voice: 'I did what I thought was right. This thing that you and other higher-ups have been keeping close to your chests will eventually get out of hand. At least this way we get to control the narrative.'

'Detective, there's someone here to see you,' an officer inter-rupts.

'Not now!' the detective barks back.

'Here's one for you, *Detective*. Did you ever stop to think that anonymity was our greatest tool and that the idea of a serial killer at large might be giving the criminal the exposure that they want? As well as pushing anyone working on the inside deeper under cover?'

The detective frowns. He typically hates being challenged. I should have known better; he's always been brash.

'I would like to remind you that this is a police matter! You put your badge down, remember?'

'Detective!' the junior officer insists.

'What is i—?'

The detective stops speaking abruptly, his mouth wide open. I turn in the direction that he's staring.

'. . .'

To my surprise and shock, a hooded figure walks down the corridor towards us, almost in slow-motion. As she removes her red hood, we both gasp in disbelief as a familiar face confronts us.

Because there, in front of us, water tracks tracing down her face, is the girl we examined in the morgue.

With each step she takes towards us, the image of her greyish, bloated corpse lying on the cold metal coroner's slab flashes before my eyes. The uneasy sound of whispers from the morgue echo around my head.

Kukadia turns to me.

'Bloody hell. Are you seeing this?'

I continue to stare, dumbfounded.

'How is she . . . alive?!'

Her mouth opens in a half-sob.

'Detective Kukadia?' she asks in a strangulated whisper.

'Ye— Yes?'

'What happened to Cara? Where's my sister?'

CHAPTER 9

TWI

'A sailor went to sea, sea, sea
To see what he could see, see, see!'

'Tig! You're it!'

Where am I?

'wE . . . wiLl . . . HuNT yOu!'

'Nooooo!'

I wake up in an unfamiliar setting. As I ungracefully try to sit up, I am surrounded by unidentifiable individuals, all in white uniforms, all rushing to restrain me.

'They're coming for me! Please help me, help! Bright eyes, glowing! You've got to believe—'
Pick!
A sharp scratch pricks my arm and it all goes black . . .

'Firecracker, Firecracker, Boom, Boom, Boom!'

'Pass! Pass the ball!'

Why am I dreaming this?

'We . . . wILl . . . FInD YoU!

'YOuR . . . DREAMS . . . arE DEaD.'

'Stop! Get away from me!'

My eyes shoot open and I spring up in confusion, drenched in sweat. The same white-uniformed individuals grab me and pin me down. As I desperately scuffle to get loose, I see a man with circular glasses watching me and writing on a clipboard.

'Why are you doing this?!' I scream. 'Why is no one listening to me?! They're getting closer! White shadows, they'll kill us, they'll kill us all just like the—'

Pick!

'Officerrrrrr . . . ' My words slur as another needle penetrates my veins. Everything fades . . .

'One, two, three, four, hide away for us to find
'Five, six, seven, eight, seeking you is on our mind!'

* * *

I'm a child again, eight years old, sitting alone on the bench at the far end of the playground, reading my comic book. Children run around, careless and free, singing songs and chanting, playing hide-and-seek. I sit minding my own business — in my own little world — when, out of nowhere, a football spins through the air, tearing through my comic, and hitting me square in the face. I crash backwards off the bench.

'Ooohhh! What a shot!' a smug, self-congratulatory voice says.

'Right in the chops! Looks like he's about to cry.'

The two voices laugh, egging each other on, as I fumble around holding my nose, trying to control the hot liquid escaping into my hand. My face prickles with pain. I look up to see two older boys coming towards me.

'Oi, workhouse!' says one. 'Fetch my ball.'

'Yeah, go fetch the ball,' his mate annoyingly repeats, treading my comic into the dirt and snorting like a pig as he laughs.

'You deaf, workhouse?'

'Yeah, you deaf?' the other bully reiterates.

'I said: fetch!' the older pupil demands, using his foot to keep me on the ground.

'Oi! Tweedledee and Tweedledumb, why don't you try picking on someone your own size?' shouts a voice from within the small crowd that has started to form around us.

'Ooohh!' the crowd jeers in unison.

'Who said that?' the bully says, removing his foot from my back and looking around.

'I said it, you cog!'

The crowd parts to reveal the pupil responsible. The two bullies switch their attention from me to him.

'What did you say, you little squirt?!'

They tower over the younger pupil.

'Maybe you never heard me correctly. It's probably 'cause your mum forgot to clean out your ears! She was probably too busy still wiping your batty!'

The crowd bursts into a rapturous laugh. The bullies' faces turn bright red. The smaller pupil, seeing the reaction and attention from the crowd, continues to barrage the bullies with further mocking insults.

'I don't mean to be rude, but you guys need some mouthwash. Not a sip or a swallow; you lot need to down the whole flipping bottle!' The jokes continue. I want to laugh too, but that won't end well. One of the bullies grabs the cheeky, smack-talking pupil.

'Fight, fight, fight, fight!' The obligatory chanting starts.

'You're dead meat!' the bully growls.

'Yeah, dead meat!'

The bully balls his fist and pulls it back, readying himself to punch the younger pupil, who scrunches up his face and closes his eyes, preparing for impact.

'Fight, fight, fight, fight!' The crowd of school kids gets louder as the anticipation grows.

'Errr, what seems to be the problem?!' a dinner lady shouts from across the playground, causing the bullies to hightail it. The crowd disperses.

The boy who nearly got his lights punched out at my expense breathes, fixes his school tie in relief, puts his cap back on, and helps me up.

'Thanks,' I say, still pinching my nose, which makes my voice sound like a Dalek.

'No worries. Those two meatheads are always trying to pick on the new kids. They're lucky, one more second and I would've hit them with a TIGER UPPERCUT!' he yells, mimicking the voice and move from *Street Fighter*.

We both chuckle. He hands me my now badly ripped and dirt-smudged comic book.

'That's a good issue,' he says, pointing to the front cover. 'If you want to know the ending you can read mine. Spoiler alert: Nightwing returns.'

'. . . Thanks,' I reply, slightly annoyed that he's told me what happens.

'No probs. Uh-oh, here comes the dinner lady.'

'What on earth has happened here?!' She doesn't give us a chance to answer. 'Right, both of you inside. Look at the state of your nose, have you been fighting?! Right! Straight to the school nurse,' she instructs whilst marching us both across the playground by our shoulders.

'Hey, I'm Sam. What's your name?'

'I'm Jos—'

Ding, ding, ding, ding, ding, ding, ding!

The school bell rings. Instantly all the noise and play comes to a dead stop. I look around and see all the school kids are staring at me, silent, frozen like statues.

Behind me I hear a growl, then feel the grip of the dinner lady's hand digging into my shoulder like daggers or claws.

'A sailor went to sea, sea, sea

To see what he could see, see, see!' the children sing.

'We've found the patient!'

'Don't move!'

'Wait a minute! He . . . he looks like he's sleeping.'

I hear three children shouting. I turn to see them running aggressively towards me. As they run, for a split-second, they morph into men in white suits and suddenly — as if I've teleported from the playground — I'm in the middle of a field. It's night, rain pours down from the sky, and spotlights beam down from somewhere over me.

A huge rumble shakes the ground and I'm transported back into the school playground. The children around the playground are still frozen to the spot, but the three that were running towards me have gone.

'A sailor went to sea, sea, sea

To see what he could see, see, see!'

The sky cracks, unfolding like a scroll of parchment being rolled back, turning from night to day. The stars move around in the sky to form an enormous sign resembling my dreamcatcher. It appears just momentarily, then shatters like glass, turning into black diamonds. All around me, the singing schoolchildren's voices get louder and warp. I see their faces as they begin to contort and twist into a fearful sight.

They stop singing all at once, then suddenly their eyes simultaneously start to light up, glaring brightly. In unison, they chant:

'wE . . . KnOW . . . wHo yOu Are!

'YoU CaNNoT HIdE.

'We . . . aRe . . . MaNY!'

I desperately try to free myself from the dinner lady's grip, turning towards Sam. He smiles his child-like grin, then violently opens his mouth, which snaps open and elongates to the length of my child-sized body. Through his mouth a sort of gateway emerges, like a black hole. The dinner lady twists me back around to face her. Her face has now become a mirror, which reflects my adult face back at me. My reflection screams at me as a purple light flashes from its eyes, blinding me and sending me backwards. I tumble through Sam's mouthed gateway . . .

* * *

I wake. Panting furiously for air, I touch my face and inspect my hands, which are no longer childlike. I inhale deeply. I'm alone in some sort of medical room, with no staff to restrain or pin me down, just a large viewing window in front of my bed and a broken clock whose hands repeatedly twitch over twelve and five. I try to clear my mind from that horrible nightmare. 'I'm back, I'm back,' I repeat softly to myself. 'You're okay, it was just a dream.'

'Or wAs IT?!

'JoSePH . . . Son oF ImĀDrIS.'

My eyes pop wide open and, before I have a chance to react, multiple white shadow hands shoot up from under my bed, gripping me onto the mattress with their claws.

Vrooom!

The whole room revolves and rotates, twisting upside down. My head droops as gravity pulls it down. The ceiling below me cracks and bubbles with heat. The surface melts away like a vol-canic chasm, revealing below me a bottomless void. My mouth opens but no words come out, as my eyes witness the countless beastly white shadows scaling up towards me, snarling and hissing like carnivorous monsters. Their grotesque, nightmarish, not-quite-human forms have broad, armour plating strapped to them, which clatters as they clamber and bang against one another. Amidst the horde, ascending slowly, through the centre of the void, I see a bright, terrifying being. Flowing weightlessly around its form, like white pythons, its long, dreaded hair glows. I scream out in fear as it climbs closer to the surface.

'This way, quickly!' I hear a young voice calling. The door to my upside-down room opens, emitting a tremendous blue, calming light, and a young girl's silhouette.

'Free yourself. You have power,' she says. Her familiar voice resonates with me, exactly like on the night of the Blackout and I manage to pry myself away from the grip of the claws. Defying gravity, I float above the void as it begins to close in on itself. The dominating, powerful voice and the dreadful screams of those nightmarish beings muffle. I exit through the door.

Flash!

* * *

I'm awake.

'Good morning, Joseph.'

'Huh?! Whe— Where am I? Is this real?'

In a state of panic, I wriggle up and down but am unable to move my arms, which have been strapped to the bed.

'Firstly, I need you to stay calm. I assure you that all this is real. My name is Doctor Roth. I hope you are feeling much better today.'

I look round the room, half-expecting something to jump out, but nothing happens. The room's the right way up, the floor's normal, and the clock's ticking away fine. The room looks exactly the same as the one I was just in but it feels different, perfectly normal.

'It seems you had quite an eventful evening last night,' the doctor continues, removing the tight straps from around my arms.

'. . . Wha—? What are you talking about? Where am I?'

'You are in our infirmary. It is Thursday the ninth of October, approximately 9:27 a.m.'

'What am I doing in here?' I ask sitting up. 'You can't keep me here. My mom, I need to speak with—'

'Your mother is well aware of your whereabouts; in fact, she was the one who signed and granted us permission to help you.'

'You're lying, she wouldn't do that! She—'

'On the contrary, Joseph.' The doctor shows me a document with Mom's signature. I slump back onto the bed, feeling deflated, empty inside, no longer thinking about freedom. Mom, how could you? She was the one person I thought would believe me. For the first time in a long time I feel truly alone, exactly how I felt before I was adopted: abandoned.

'I thought it best for you to be kept under close supervision. We wouldn't want you . . . wandering again.'

I shake my head and flex my face. My eyes still feel a bit heavy and hazy. The doctor looks at me.

'That will be the sedatives wearing off. You'll be quite alright.'

'What happened last night?'

'You mean to say you have no memory at all?'

I shake my head.

'You assaulted three of our staff members trying to escape, one of whom has a broken nose and a serious concussion.' I look at the doctor blankly. 'Yes, you were found in the pouring rain in the middle of the field outside.' Suddenly, the distant voices of children in a school playground start to echo and swirl around my head:

'*We've found the patient!*'

'*Don't move!*'

'*Wait a minute! He . . . he looks like he's sleeping.*'

'How—? Is . . . I don't . . . ' I mumble in confusion, peering down at my bare feet, which are caked in mud. I flex my hand and see dirt smudged around it. I close my eyes, trying hard to remember . . .

Flood-lights, rain, sensation of the cold night air, men in white outfits . . . They tackle me onto the damp muddy grass.

'I . . . shouldn't be in here, I shouldn't be here!' I jump out of the bed onto my feet, completely freaking out. It happened again!

Bip!

At once, the door to the room electronically unlocks and a security porter rushes in. I back away into the corner. Just before the porter steps towards me, Doctor Roth raises his hand to stop him.

'Okay, Joseph, okay. Stay calm,' the doctor says lightly. 'Take a deep breath. No one's going to hurt you. You're quite alright.' I look at both the doctor and the staff member in his white uniform, ready to pounce. I curl up into a foetal position, trembling from the disjointed flashes of memory that have just resurfaced.

'You are going to be fine; we are going to put everything right,' the doctor reassures me, signalling the porter to leave as he helps me back to the bed. 'That's it. Take your time.' He pours water from a plastic jug into a brown disposable paper cup. 'Here you go, have some water. That will make you feel much better.'

He hands the cup over to me and I cautiously grab the cup, holding it tightly below my mouth with both hands. My hands are still visibly shaking, along with my left leg that nervously bounces up and down. I take a huge gulp, keeping my eyes fixed on the doctor, then another. I catch my breath and down the whole cup. An intoxicating feeling of calm crawls over me, reducing my anxious fidgeting.

'Good,' Doctor Roth says. He produces a brown folder with a black leather clipboard. He fixes his circular specs on the edge of his pointed nose, then pulls out an old-fashioned fountain pen from his pristine white shirt pocket that has his name tag attached: Doctor Otto Roth, Senior Psychiatrist TWI. He unscrews the pen lid and begins to write on the clipboard.

'I know this may all still seem a bit strange, but I promise you we are here to help. Try and think of this place as a bit of a retreat if you can, a little break from the pressures of the outside world. This is a safe space where you can trust us to give you the help that you need.'

'What about the staff I hurt?'

'I am sure they'll mend in time. The only long-term damage will be their egos,' the doctor says humorously. 'Now, Joseph, I would like us to have a little chat if that's okay with you?'

I nod my head in agreement. The doctor starts penning notes onto the piece paper in front of him, whilst examining me over the top of his glasses.

'You think I'm crazy, right?'

'I am not here to say if I believe you or not.' The doctor adds a full stop to his notes, before lifting his head up to engage with me. 'I am here to help you to understand why you might be seeing the things you say you are seeing and, in doing so, to help you to heal. Right, let us get started. Do you know why you have been admitted to stay with us?'

'Yeah. I'm here because I've been wrongly accused of attacking a police officer.'

'That incident is why you were arrested but not what brought you here. Come now, Joseph. You told the police that you were innocent and then stated on record that Officer Scott was taken by . . .'

As the doctor glances down at his notes again, my mind flashes back to seeing the officer being clawed at and dragged away in the mirror.

'He was taken by these . . .'

'Yes, "white shadows" you say,' the doctor finishes my sentence. 'But Officer Scott is still alive, Joseph. He is recovering in hospital.'

'That's not Officer Scott!'

'What do you mean?' the doctor asks, making more notes.

'It's . . . it's something else, something evil that attacked me and took over his body.'

'And you are sure he attacked you?'

'Yes, of course I'm sure!' I say, raising my voice in frustration. 'How could I forget a thing like th—?' I stop myself from speaking, as the doctor looks over his glasses at me. I've just snookered myself.

'But you didn't remember what happened last night, did you? I wonder how many times has that happened before; how many times, Joseph, have you gone blank and unknowingly done things that you weren't aware of?'

I freeze. 'What are you talking about?'

'Over the last few days, Joseph, we have been observing you. You have been displaying mania and paranoia, which have fed into violent delusions. On multiple occasions you claimed you were responsible for the city-wide blackout, that you attacked the gang that mugged you.'

I say nothing. Doctor Roth puts his pen away and neatly folds his papers on the clipboard.

'Sometimes, Joseph, to help deal with trauma it's not uncommon for the mind to create and believe grand stories. I read in your file that in the past you have undergone extensive counselling sessions with a Doctor Sia Leland and that you recently stopped attending sessions, even though you were advised not to. You were being treated for psychic trauma, which had brought on insomnia and crippling anxiety attacks. Correct?'

I continue to stay silent. The doctor gets to his feet and pushes his glasses further up his nose.

'Okay, Joseph. You're clearly overwhelmed, which is understandable. A member of staff will be along to escort you to your room. We can reconvene tomorrow.'

The doctor turns and swipes his ID card over the scanner, opens the white door, and leaves.

I look down at the plain, simple, off-white monotone clothes that I've been placed in; they resemble Tetsuo's facility outfit from *Akira*. I try to breathe and envision a way in which this whole situation resolves into a good ending, but I can't see it.

The door opens and a male porter in one of those stereotypical *One Flew Over the Cuckoo's Nest* uniforms collects me from the room. I follow him down the hallway, seeing other patients as I pass. Most walk silently with their heads down in a zombie-like manner. Some of the patients have had their heads shaved. The place feels like a huge contradiction: on the surface everything is so clean and pristine. The walls are painted perfectly white with not a scratch, scuff, or dent along their surfaces or corners. This place looks better than pretty much any other place in Brum. But, on other hand, there's a lingering, oppressive feeling that I can't quite put my finger on.

'Wait here, please. I'm going to check that your room is ready,' the porter says, leaving me in the communal area. I scan the room and see other patients scattered around the open, circular space. The noise fizzles down until you can almost hear a pin drop. The majority stare at me as if I've just walked into a saloon. Some of the patients are huddled in groups of two and three, with the odd person keeping to themselves. In one of the chairs a young lady folds her arms, sobbing and rocking herself back and forth inconsolably. One of the patients, who was leaning against one of the four huge white pillars symmetrically placed around the room, walks in my direction with a bop in his step. He's short, stocky, and slightly resembles a bulldog.

'They got to you too, yeah?' the patient says, moving shiftily on his feet. 'Aiyo, my bad, where's my manners? I'm Armin but my people call me Mini.'

Armin puts his fist out to bump me, but I ignore it. I'm not looking to make friends; the faster I can get out of this place the better.

'Not the sociable type, yeah,' he responds. 'That's cool, I get it. Most of us in this room are freshies too, brought in after the Blackout and it don't look like they're letting us go any time soon. You from Brum?'

'Yeah.'

'Oh, so you do speak,' Armin says in a mocking manner. He puts his hand slightly over his mouth to cover it. 'You affiliated'?' he asks, staring suspiciously.

'No.'

Armin smirks, looks left and right, before pulling the sleeve up on his arm to reveal the inked initials: SO. The letter S has a crown over it in black with golden jewels.

'You see that?' he says, showing his mark with pride. 'Smethwick Outlaws born and bred. That's what I'm about.' A porter walks past us and Armin rolls his sleeves back down. 'I've been prepared to go pen for longest if needed. For me, it would be a reunion to see some of the comrades that've already been locked. But here, this is just . . .' Armin stops speaking, shifting his weight in mid-sentence and looks around him. 'Let's just say I never thought I'd be in a place like this, not at all. So, what's your deal, why they got you in this loony bin?'

'Long story,' I say, trying to stop the conversation dead.

'Mannnn. Look at this place.' Armin doesn't get the hint and carries on talking. 'This isn't your average mental hospital, is it? They're obviously pulling in serious peas. A place like this, in a city that's been swimming in its own shit for the longest, doesn't look this nice without getting dirty, my G. I may be hood, but I'm not stupid. If things look too nice, that's when we need to be mindful.' Armin makes himself laugh and repeats the word 'mindful' with a gesture to his surroundings.

'So everyone's here because of the Blackout?'

'Yeah, mostly. They say different, but most of us all saw something in the sky that night, even though these supposed "experts" are trying to palm it off with one of their theories — what did they say it was called again . . . ?' Armin mumbles to himself. He snaps his fingers as he remembers: 'Collective consciousness! Yeah, that was it. I bet they got you in here for that too, yeah?'

'Something like that,' I respond.

Suddenly we hear a raised voice: 'I know my rights! I'm not crazy, you can't just keep me here. This is abduction; it's against the law!'

Security wardens in white uniforms push a patient strapped onto a gurney from one entrance of the open area through to another exit. 'My father will hear about this!' The patient continues ranting at the top of his voice, which slowly fades into the distance. Armin chuckles to himself.

'What's so funny?'

'That's the second time he's tried to escape since I've been here. He's lucky they don't take him to the doc's lab and give him one of them dreams — them alien probe things — start messing with his mind. Least that's what I heard. Don't know why he doesn't just get his connections to pay off the guards.'

'Who is he?'

'That's Gecko,' Armin stage-whispers, looking at me as if I should know the name. I look at him blankly.

'Matthew "The Gecko" Nelson? As in the son of Kaine Nelson? Granted, he was before our time but everyone knows about the Dragon and the town hall massacre! The guy ran the city like it was his own personal playground. He's doing life in a max prison in Winson Green. I heard on the road that he was trying to get an insanity plea to move here, but it got blocked. Good riddance. I hope they've thrown away the key.'

'So there's criminals here too?'

'Yeah, 'course. Criminals, nut jobs, crazies, sane. Like I said, it's not a typical nut house. Those that have a bit of political power — i.e. connected to the Loop — get the judge to rule them as insane. Most of them are over on the left wing of the facility I think.'

'So why isn't the Dragon here?'

'He unbalanced the order of things; too much power. Those that are running this place don't want him here. That's my guess anyway. They keep a pretty tight schedule here, rotating each wing, so we never really see each other.'

'How are you hearing all this stuff?'

'I knows what I knows,' Armin says, smugly tapping his nose with his finger.

To my left, a nurse enters the circular room, and I double-take as I see she is holding the hand of a young girl. My mind flashes back to the silhouette of the girl that called me from the door as I escaped that dark void. I gasp. Could it be the same child? The young Black girl is also being followed closely behind by a woman in grey. She's wearing a high-neck pin collar jacket, matching pencil skirt, and sharp black stiletto heels, which clatter against the chequered resin floor.

'Crap, there she is,' Armin mutters reservedly under his breath. The child suddenly stops walking, as if she's heard him, causing her entourage to stop. Her eyes are heavily bandaged, like she's just had some sort of surgery. She's young; can't be any older than eleven. The child turns her head, which rattles her thick, long, black, braided, messy pigtails. She turns in my direction, almost as if she can see me through the bandages. I look at Armin, whose shoulders are hunched up tightly towards his neck, like he's trying to make himself smaller. His eyes are glued to the floor.

'Don't pay her any attention,' Armin says quietly out of the corner of his mouth.

The young girl snatches her hand away from the nurse and turns her body to fully face me. She then strangely places her hands over her bandaged eyes for a couple of seconds — like she's playing peek-a-boo — then nods her head at me and repeats the action. The lady in grey looks over at me inquisitively. She bends down to whisper something in the child's ear, who abruptly stops. The nurse grabs her hand and — although the child never stops looking in my direction — they continue their journey out of the area, leaving me wondering what just happened.

'What was all that about?' Armin questions.

'No idea.'

'Freaky. That tall mistress, she runs this place. She's the head honcho. Never met her personally but she looks like she should be in these patients' clothes with us.'

'I didn't think they would keep children here.'

'Like I said before, there's many sections to this place. Who knows what else they have in this place? Welcome to the Thelema Wellbeing Institute,' Armin says sarcastically. He looks over my shoulder. 'Aiyo, looks like you're being summoned.'

I turn to see the male porter that escorted me here returning. Armin quickly steps closer. 'Word of advice, my G: this place changes after lights out, so beware.'

I follow the porter down the bleached-white corridor, passing a slew of locked doors with silver Roman numerals stencilled onto them. The porter stops outside my room: Door VII. He uses his key-card and lets me in.

The porter leaves and I stand in my bright white, single-bedded, plain box room. The walls smell freshly painted so I go over to the small frosted window to let some air in. The window bucks within a few centimetres of me sliding it open, revealing metal bars on the other side. No escape. There's a small desk with no drawers, an open shelving unit connected to the wall, and a rug, which adds a slight colour change to the monotonous colour theme: it's off-white.

I lie on the bed and stare up at the blank ceiling.

Bip!

Suddenly the sound of a key-card beeps and my door opens. 'Joseph Jacobs, you have a visitor,' a nurse announces.

The door opens and I stop pacing up and down. Joseph steps into the room and I just stand there staring. My eyes well up. I hold it together, wanting to keep positive and strong for him. He looks pale, gaunt, skinny, more tired than usual. This is the first time I've seen him since he's been taken away and it has felt like forever. He stands looking at me, in his institutionalised clothing, and my heart breaks. The door closes and I rush over and hug him tightly, pinning his arms to the side. I can't help but notice that he feels different, almost hollow. He doesn't fully hug back but taps me gently twice on the back. I reluctantly release him and compose myself, trying my hardest to put on a hopeful face and warm smile. We both sit down.

'How are you, son?' I ask. Joseph gives no response.

'I am so sorry that I couldn't see you sooner. They wouldn't allow me to visit you until now, not even a phone call. I've been trying every day. How have they been treating you?'

'I'm . . . still alive.'

'I . . .' I hold back my words, reluctant to speak, unsure how Joseph might respond in his vulnerable state. 'So . . . I have some good news—'

'They've given you my release date?' he says unemotionally, looking down at the ground. I pause for a second before answering.

'No . . . not exactly.'

'Then what?'

'Officer Scott is going to make a full recovery.'

'That's not Officer Scott,' he says under his breath.

'Officer Scott,' I reiterate gently, trying to ignore his previous statement, 'has kindly agreed to drop all the charges . . . if you admit to the attack and agree to stay here for a while and get help.'

Joseph sighs. 'What am I supposed to say to that? It's not like I agreed to come here in the first place. You saw to that when you signed me in here.'

' . . . '

'You signed me over to this place because — just like everyone else — you don't believe me. You think I'm dangerous, you think I did what they said, that I'm completely nuts!'

'Joseph, I know it's hard but this is the best deal we are going to get.'

'"We"?! I'm the one in here, Mom. Me!' he says, standing up and slightly raising his voice in frustration.

'Joseph, listen to me: if the charges are dropped they can't keep you here. Choosing to be here — voluntarily — will help you; you could be out in a couple of weeks, maybe sooner. Your record would be clean and you will be able to put all this whole . . . mishap behind you. The officer is willing to go on record, taking into account what you have been through . . . that you were in a state of shock. I know what happened to you in the alleyway. Think about your future. If you don't take this deal you will end up—'

'Like what, Mom? Hm? Another adopted orphan that couldn't get over his childhood trauma and is ready to get revenge on the world?'

Joseph's words throw me off-guard. 'No, no, not at all.'

'To these people I'm just another statistic. Do you even care about the truth, Mom?'

'Yes, of course I do but, right now, all I care about is you.'

'So you believe me?'

I don't know how to answer his question. Joseph looks at me with tears in his eyes.

'I didn't attack the officer, Mom. Scott is dead! You've got to believe me. Those white shadows in the mirror — whatever they are—'

'Joseph—'

'They killed him and took over his body. I'm not lying to you. I'm not making it up. I'm not losing my mind!'

'Joseph, please stop.'

'They know who I am, Mom! They said they were watching me!'

'Joseph.'

'Please, you've got to believe me. They—'

'Enough!' I cut him off. 'Please, just stop.'

Joseph sits back on the chair and grabs his head, sobbing and shaking.

I sit back beside him and hold his hand firmly to let him know that I am here.

'Joseph . . . I think . . . I think it's best that you let the nurses and doctors help you.'

He is silent for a second, then he slowly pulls his hand away from mine and turns to me with an expression of distrust that I have never seen before. 'You're just like the rest of them,' he says under his breath. 'I really thought you would be the one person that would have my back and believe me.'

'I do have your back. I will always have your back.'

He gets up and walks towards the door, knocking on it to signal that he is ready to leave the room.

'Mom, I'm innocent,' he states. 'You always told me to be truthful, even if I'm afraid. That's what heroes do, remember?'

He knocks on the door again. It opens.

'Joseph . . .'

Joseph leaves without looking back. My heart shatters.

I leave the institution and walk through the rain to my car. I get in and sit in the car park, holding on tightly to the steering wheel. The rain begins to fall a little harder. I snap. I hit the leather face of the steering wheel with my fist. I strike it multiple times, harder and harder, which triggers the car alarm. Then I let out a huge scream and tears form behind my eyes. I rest my head on the wheel as the tears roll down my cheek. What am I supposed to do now?

Vrrrr! Vrrrr! Vrrrr!

My phone vibrates in my pocket. I let it ring out as I cry for my son. I wipe my face, grab my keys, and press the button to turn off the alarm. Pulling out my phone, I swallow my tears and call the number back.

'Elizabeth?!'

'Yes, I'm here. Sorry I missed your call, what is it?'

'It's happened again!'

CHAPTER 10

Troubled Waters

I pull up the handbrake and turn off my engine. Rain tap-dances lightly across the roof of my car and faint steam rises from the bonnet as droplets hit the hot metal. Ever since the Blackout the heavens have been opening up, crying over the city like a mother grieving for their child.

Emergency service vehicles and ambulances congest the wet road in front of the Meadow Brooke Elderly Residential building. Sirens flash and spin, streets are cordoned off with blue tape, which keeps the reporters at bay as they wait for their next juicy story. Business as usual: another day, another crime. Watching the chaotic scenes outside my windscreen, I hesitate. I gave up this type of work years ago. So why now — with everything that's going on in my personal life — why continue to run after this serial killer? There's an easy answer. If I don't focus on this, I am going to come undone. It's only been a week since they took Joseph away and the feeling that somehow this is my fault presses against my chest like a concrete slab. I keep thinking about what he said, his brash unapologetic conviction, which is infectious and also really dangerous. He believes his story so much that at times he's made me question my own rationality too. I am well aware of the age-old statistic of the over-institutionalising of Black people in this country. But, as a mother — a nurturer, someone who cares for him — I've got to believe that he is in the right place. And that this will be over soon. But I still can't help feeling conflicted. I have always leaned on my gut instincts and — funnily enough — I taught Joseph to do the same thing: 'Speak the truth, do what's right, even if you are afraid . . .'

Ping!

1 new message.
16.06 - You nearly here yet?
Paul.

'Right, come on, Elizabeth Jacobs. Pick yourself up. Life's tough — crap sometimes — but we keep walking, even when it throws punches.' I take my seat belt off and half-smile at my words. They remind me of my old man: 'Get your act together, girl. You have a job to do and a case to crack.'

I exit my car and the noise that had been partially muffled comes alive around me. Police drones circle the skies. Multiple paramedics rush to assist individuals with oxygen masks on their faces; a stream of beds and wheelchairs weaves past me, through emergency workers, onto ambulances; a staff member in a dark blue uniform is tended to, sitting on the damp step in front of the building. Rain water drips down his face, but he doesn't flinch, move, or blink. In fact, he has no expression at all: just blank, zombified, almost like he has been erased. What is going on?

When I received the call from Kukadia to meet him here regarding another questionable death, I never imagined this. Especially here: a residential retirement centre for the elderly.

Usually I would have been notified by my informant Mr X but he's been radio-silent for some time. Unnerving. The previous murders were all isolated, private and intimate, no potential witnesses, all carried out at night. This is different. The killer is either evolving or this is a move of frustration. Enacting a crime here would only grab unwanted attention. But why here and why now?

After the surprise appearance of the deceased victim's identical twin sister Charlotte at the police station, we thought we might at least be able to get more answers about our victim. Who was she? What was her real name? What was she running from? Who could have wanted to harm her? This would have been a useful start, but she was in no state to answer any questions. I can't say I blame her.

Hopefully whatever's going on here will help shed more light on the murders.

As I enter the building, I feel a cold chill on the back of my neck and flick my collar up. The humming noise above me is the reason why: the air con vents are blowing out cold air at full pelt. Odd for this time of year, especially considering the weather. Music plays gently in the reception area from the overhead speakers that are dotted throughout the building.

Huh. Haven't heard that song in years: 'All I Have to Do is Dream' by the Everly Brothers. A real oldie. I button up the rest of my coat and continue walking through the home as the song continues to play. My eyes flick from side to side, clocking possible entry points that could have been used without being detected.

The building's not particularly big. From the outside, I noticed it only has three floors, with debris chutes snaking out of some of the windows, the top floor evidently undergoing some sort of construction.

That's strange. The song keeps skipping. The song is fairly repetitive anyway, but this is definitely the same verse . . .

I rub my tongue against my teeth. Ever since I stepped into the building my mouth has felt gritty and chalky, as if exposed to too much dust. There's also a faint smell in the air, but I can't make out what it is.

I make my way through the home. It looks exactly how I expected: paisley runner rugs lie on top of grey, Polysafe vinyl flooring; the walls are painted in a warm pale magenta colour, all tied together with greeting cards from the staff and pictures of carers and residents on day trips. More staff and patients are ushered past me out of the building, all in that zombie-like state of paralysis. Up ahead, a janitor stands, facing the window, broom in hand, sweeping the floor. I try to catch his eye and give him a little smile, but he ignores me. As I get a little closer, his erratic movements become more obvious: standing in one place, continuing to sweep the same spot left to right like an animatronic robot. An ambulance worker in a bright high-vis jacket comes over and puts a comforting arm around him, which seems to awaken him slightly from his stupor, and leads him away. This is getting weird.

'After this, I'm asking for a transfer.'

'We both know you're not going to leave.'

'I tell you this: this city's gone to hell. How many more incidents can happen in the space of a week? First that Blackout and all that vigilante trash, then all those shoppers in that store in Bullring wiped out like that — just one survivor. Nah, you can't pay me enough to stay.'

'Excuse me,' I say approaching the two conversing officers who are patrolling the magenta, paisley-carpeted corridor. 'I am looking for Detective Kukadia, do you know where I can find him?'

'You got any ID?' one of the officers asks. I flash my PDS badge and the officers look at each other like they are sharing an inside joke.

'Down the hall, turn left. You'll see some forensics outside one of the rooms. He'll be around there somewhere.'

'Cheers.'

I walk on, hearing the two officers mumble quietly under their breath behind me: 'That's her, right?'

'Yeah, that's her alright. Her adopted son's that savage that attacked Scott; got 'im real good too. Heard he's locked up nice and tight in the loony bin. They're all the same, ain't they? He's lucky I wasn't in that room— there'd be nothing left of 'im to lock up.'

I stop walking and the two officers immediately stop their conversation. I fight everything in my body to not turn around and give them a piece of my mind. But now is not the time, so I continue walking. The force has a tightly knit community between its officers and its units. I remember how easy it was for news and rumours to spread like wildfire. That is one of the main reasons I managed to track down corrupt officers on the take and their associates. People talk and someone's always watching. If there is a mole working within Kukadia's department — as I suspect — I will find them. They will slip up soon enough.

I follow the hallway to the left as instructed and see flashes of light from the inside of a room. In the distance, forensic officers wearing white jumpsuits, goggles, gloves, and face masks step in and out of the doorway. I spot a familiar face: Officer Lace. She is kneeling beside a middle-aged woman, who has a blanket placed over her shoulder, looking visibly distressed. The officer hands her a tissue, whilst consoling the trembling lady. She sees me and steps away to meet me, jumping to attention as if she were in the army.

'Ms Jacobs.'

'Elizabeth is just fine,' I say, trying to put the rookie more at ease. 'Is he here?' I ask.

'Yes, he's down there. In the room,' the young officer says, walking a few steps with me.

'Is it the same as before?'

'Very similar. We got a distressing call from the lady back there. She knew the victim. Apparently she was doing her weekly visit to check in on him and she found the body and . . . here we are.' Officer Lace stops, keeping her distance from the room. 'I was the first here and . . .' Her eyes widen. She can't even look in the direction of the room.

'Maybe you should check back in on the lady, officer — make sure she is okay,' I say.

'Ye— Yes, of course,' she agrees, quickly sneaking a glance at the room's open doorway. 'Thank you, I'll do that.' She gives me a brave smile then returns to the lady she was attending to.

I approach the room and wait outside the door. There's another *flash* as a forensic investigator aims their camera at the side of the room that is out of my view. Kukadia sounds stressed — as usual — as he tactlessly voices his frustrations, thoughts, and findings out loud. Typical.

Knock knock!

'One second!' the detective barks.

Kukadia steps round the door. He looks like he slept in his car all night. He greets me with an expression of surprise, annoyance, and relief. Maybe he thought I wouldn't show up. This is the first time we have seen each other since the 'incident' at the police station. We did not leave on good terms but, in all fairness, Kukadia has kept to his word and instigated the proposed deal between Joseph and the officer. This must be his way of trying to rebuild some trust in our relationship, which has been on the ropes for a long time.

'You made it then?'

'Detective,' I respond curtly.

'Oi, you!' the detective grabs the attention of one of the forensics, who points at themselves questioningly. 'Yes, you! Hand her some gloves and shoe covers, will ya?'

They hand me the items and I put them on.

'Right, guys, going to need the space for a moment. Get yourself warm, grab a cuppa, or whatever you do . . . take five!'

The room clears and the detective invites me in. It has been a while since I stepped into an actual crime scene. There is something harrowing about being in a space where someone's life has been snatched away, especially in an environment like this, where people come to retire. This is a place that is supposed to be for enjoying the winter years of your life in safety and comfort.

Stepping into the room, my mind switches into analysis mode, taking in every detail, from the broken mirror to the scattered fruits on the carpet to the backdated newspaper clippings on the desk, fluttering gently in the breeze from the tiny air vent in the ceiling.

The shards from the smashed mirror crunch under my feet as I approach the bed.

'And here he is,' the detective gestures to the body of a Caucasian man roughly in his late sixties, early seventies, lying lifelessly half-on-half-off the bed. 'His name is John Mitchell.'

Kukadia cups and blows into his hands for warmth. The victim's head is hanging off the bed towards the floor. One of his eyes is opened and the sclera around his pupil is red with blood. The opened eye is accompanied by a fresh laceration running through it from above his brow down to his cheek. The victim's mouth is open and his hands are frozen, gripping the under-sheet with his fingers: a picture of torment, of a struggle.

His body is still soaking wet, as is the mattress and carpet underneath his bed. The skin around his exposed torso area has become pale, almost translucent. But what surprises me the most is, burnt into his chest, the word: GUILTY.

'Poor bastard, what a way to go,' the detective says, popping the lid on his medication pot and downing a tablet.

'That shoulder still giving you trouble?'

'Just a bit. The cold ain't helping.'

'Any sign of a black envelope?'

'No, none at all. No symbol this time,' he adds. 'When the cleaner found the body in the hotel room, she said there was an envelope near the foot of the door. But Officer Lace swears she saw nothing like that here. We bagged a book for evidence from the floor by the side of the bed: *Classic Poetry*. His reading glasses were neatly placed on the bedside table, which tells me he went for a siesta and never woke up ... Well, not in this life. Once again, both victims were drenched in water as if baptised ... But this one's a little different.'

'Elaborate?' I ask, kneeling to take a closer look at the inscription branded on the body. The detective clears his throat.

'Well, for starters he's male, so our killer is not biased towards a particular gender. You said all the other victims were young females, right? The mirror in this room's been broken, whereas in the hotel, both the bathroom mirror and bedroom mirror were covered with towels and intact. And then there's the inscription: "GUILTY." That's new. It's obvious the killer had a vendetta and acted upon it.'

I stand back to my feet. 'The killer's trying to get our attention. He or she is trying to point us to something.' I close my eyes and my mind starts to tick: 'There's a link that we are missing, something personal ... Letters ... water ...

purification . . . cleansing, washing . . . Bed, resting . . . comfort
. . . peace. At peace. All the victims were lying in their beds
sleeping, untouched. But this victim's body is half on and half
off, which feels intentional, almost like he's falling, unable to
rest, like when a tomb or burial ground is unsettled or defaced
. . . Deface!' My eyes snap open and I take another look at the
victim's face. I pull out my phone in a hurry.

'What is it?' asks the detective as I scroll through my pictures.
I pull up the symbol of the eye. I place the screen near the
victim's face. 'See it? It's the symbol. The mark cutting through
one eye like the sword in the image.'

Kukadia tilts his head, inspecting the image and comparing
the two from every angle. Finally, he nods.

'Okay, it's definitely our killer. But why this old sod and why
the other young girls?'

I stand, rubbing my tongue again against my teeth, trying to
get rid of that chalky feeling in my mouth. 'The other residents
that have been evacuated, has anyone been able to speak? Maybe
they saw something?'

'No, we haven't done that yet. I was going to speak to the lady
outside with Lace and see if she might have been able to tell us
anything else. We'll get the body tested for cause of death and
get the whole room bagged up as evidence by the book.'

The detective and I exit the room. We remove our rubber
gloves and shoe covers and make our way over to Officer Lace.
Kukadia calls the rookie officer over. 'Officer, we need to have
a quick word with . . .'

'Her name's Jill,' Lace informs.

'Do you reckon she would speak with us?'

'Well . . . she's a bit shaken up, so I wouldn't push her too hard
but I guess you can try before I escort her out.'

We rejoin the officer and Jill.

'Jill, this is Elizabeth and Detective Kukadia. They were wondering if they could have a quick word?'

Jill looks up at me, holding a tissue in her hand. Her eyeshadow is smudged on her cheeks from her tears.

'We know it's a difficult time, but any information you can give could help us find out what happened to John.'

Jill swallows her tears and dabs her eyes. She nods in agreement.

'Hi Jill, how you holding up?' I begin.

'I've been better,' Jill replies with a shaky voice.

'We're extremely sorry for your loss. Officer Lace tells me that you were the one who found John and called the police. Is that correct?'

Jill nods yes.

'I am sorry you had to go through that. We're going to do everything in our power to find out what happened, okay?'

''Kay,' Jill responds with a whimper.

''Was Mr Mitchell a relative? A close friend?'

Jill takes a breath. 'No. I don't think John had any relatives. He certainly didn't have many friends.' She wipes around her eyes. 'I'm sorry, excuse me.'

'No, it's okay,' I soothe. 'Take your time. Maybe it's best to do this at a later date?' I say, with a glance up at Kukadia.

'No, I'm fine,' Jill insists. 'I'll be okay. I don't think John had any relatives. He lived alone in the flat below mine. It wasn't a big complex, only three apartments to the building, so we all saw each other. Quiet man. Always watered his flowers on his veranda, very meticulous. He had green fingers. I used to say "hello" every now and then.'

'So he never had any visitors?' Kukadia barely looks up from his notepad, his brow furrowed.

'No. It was sad really, with him getting on in age. I used to check in on him from time to time, bring him some biscuits that I had baked, y'know, to be neighbourly? He reminded me of my grandad. If you knocked on his door he would never open it without the latch on until he saw it was you. Can't say I blame him really, with the things that happen in this city.'

'Do you know any reason why someone would want to hurt Mr Mitchell?'

'Oh no, not John; he was a quiet old man. I can't see why anyone would ever want to hurt him. He used to help people, you know.'

'Help people?' Kukadia intervenes.

'Yeah, he worked at that place before it burnt down, errr . . . What was it called again? You know, that place that had that huge fire some years back . . . ?'

'I can't rem—'

'Actually, detective,' Jill gasps. 'Now that you mention it, I do remember something: about a month after John moved here, I was suddenly woken up by raised voices coming from his flat. I thought it quite odd, as it was so late and all and, like I said, John didn't really get visitors. I went out into the hallway to see what the commotion was but, by the time I got there, all I saw were the backs of two bald guys leaving. I never mentioned it to John; didn't want him to think I'd been a nosy-parker.'

As Jill recounts this to Kukadia, I scroll through the internet browser on my phone. Finally, I find what I'm looking for.

'Is this the place you meant?' I ask, holding the phone up to Jill. 'I can't find much information about it.'

'That's it! Saint Mordred's,' Jill says triumphantly. 'John said he used to be a doctor there or something like that.'

I glance at Kukadia but he's lost in thought, his brow furrowed. I decide to press on.

'Okay, thanks, Jill. One last thing: can you explain in your own words what happened when you visited today?'

'Well, it was very strange.'

'Strange in what way?' the detective butts in. Officer Lace joins me in throwing him a look, which causes him to quickly shut his mouth again in embarrassment.

'Well, usually the staff here create such a great atmosphere for the residents and guests; they're usually so friendly. The residents must have all been down for their afternoon nap or something, because it was much quieter than usual. I came in and went to the front desk to sign in. The receptionist was on the phone and she was taking notes on some paper. As I say, normally people greet you or wave at you as you come through the entrance. But she didn't look up, it must have been a very important or serious call. Anyway, I said hello and asked if Sue was in — Sue's a member of staff and the main carer for John — but I got no reply.'

'She said nothing at all?'

'No, nothing. She must have been concentrating very hard on the person at the other end of the call. So I let myself through and went up the hallway.'

'Did you see anyone else?'

'Just the cleaner, who was minding his own business. He didn't turn round when I walked past.'

My mind instantly flashes back to seeing the cleaner I saw in the corridor being led away, and the other sitting on the wet step outside the building as I entered. They'd both looked stunned, blank, in shock.

'I could hear the odd TV playing from the nearby rooms, but other than that it was very calm and peaceful. Then I saw Sue at the far end of the hallway. I called out to her multiple times but I thought maybe she couldn't hear me. As I got closer, I . . .' Jill's voice starts to tense and waver. 'I . . . noticed her

hear the cooing of a bird as it rampantly flaps around.

'Shit. It's just a pigeon,' I chuckle to myself. How stupid I must have looked, trying to bludgeon a bird. I free myself from the frosted separators and the pigeon flies away onto the top of a nearby ladder. I place the spanner on the ground and make my way over to the maintenance room.

Inside, a low noise buzzes. Across the ceiling, a network of foil-coated pipes spread towards extraction shafts on the walls. Right then, Elizabeth: time to see if this theory of yours is right. Seeing the staff members and residents in a state of near-paralysis, coupled with Jill's remarkable testimony and these vents blowing this horrible taste in my mouth . . . Has the killer somehow managed to intoxicate the entire building with some sort of substance dispersed through the ventilation system to get to his victim? Not taking any chances, I wrap my scarf around the lower part of my face for protection.

I walk under the silver pipes to see if I can spot anything unusual.

'There you are!'

Three metal extraction boxes are connected to the wall, but the middle one has bolts missing from its protective casing. I grab the ladder, place it against the vent, and press the override button. The power to the room cuts out. In the cloak of darkness I hear the fans creak to a slow and gradual stop. I use the light from my phone's torch and climb the ladder.

I lift up the extraction flap and shine the light down the dark tunnel. Large propellor blades partly obscure my view so I push myself further into the vent, all the way up to my waist. My light catches something beyond the blades. What is that? It looks like a small vial. I crawl further in the tight, suffocating space and reach, stretching my fingertips, to grab the object.

'C'mon, almost got it!' I say, kicking my legs. 'Just a little closer . . .' My kick hits the ladder hard, sending it crashing to the floor. 'Almost there!' I strain to reach the small glass object. I touch it with my index finger, and manage to roll it back towards me and then grab it. I breathe a sigh of relief, although I am still stranded, half-suspended off the floor in the vent, my legs hanging down. Desperate to get a look at what I have discovered, I shine my phone at the small glass tube. On first inspection it looks empty but, as I take a closer look, I see a few red sand-like particles lying dormant at the bottom.

Slam!

I flinch. Someone's just entered the room.

'Hello? Who's there?' I shout. 'Hello?! Paul, is that you?'

I hear the ladder scrape along the floor as it is placed back into position under my feet. I shuffle backwards and plant my feet firmly onto the top rung. I slowly back out of the shaft and descend the ladder, still in the dark.

'Hello?' I ask again, shining the torch from my phone as I climb. The ladder wobbles and suddenly a pair of hands grabs my legs, causing me to jump off the last three steps. I ball my fist and spin around.

'We found you!'

'Officer Scott?' I say in surprise. The light illuminates the plaster on the officer's cheek.

'Steady on, I was just trying to help,' the officer looks straight at me, unaffected by the bright light shining in his eyes. I lower my phone.

'The detective's looking for you. He sent me to get you.' Scott looks up at the vent and I use the opportunity to slip the vial into my pocket. 'Find what you were looking for?'

'Maybe,' I respond. I decide to keep my findings on a need-to-know basis.

'Well then, this way.'

We exit the ventilation room towards the stairs. The officer walks behind me, sending an uneasy feeling running over my body.

'So, how long have you been back on duty?' I ask.

'A couple of days now. Still getting the odd headache, but the doc said that's to be expected.'

I don't reply so we walk in silence down the stairwell towards the main reception. As I put my hand on the door handle, the officer plants his hand against the door, keeping it shut.

'What are you doing?' I keep my hand on the handle and continue to pull.

'I just wanted to make sure we're all good, you know, no hard feelings?' the officer says, effortlessly keeping the door shut with his arm fully extended by my head.

'Why should there be any hard feelings? You're the one who allegedly got attacked.'

The officer tilts his head and stares at me.

'I know he's your adopted son and I didn't want there to be any bad blood between us. It seems you have enough on your plate already.'

'How kind,' I respond in a fake-apologetic tone. 'My *son* is going to be just fine.'

He steps slightly closer into my personal space.

'As I mentioned to the detective, I'm happy to sweep this under the rug if he agrees to get help. He's clearly been through a lot.' The officer stares at me again. 'Seems he's a very troubled young man,' he continues with an insincere half-smile on his face.

'Thank you for your concern, officer. Now, if you don't mind, you found me to speak with your superior, correct?'

I pull on the door handle and the officer removes his hand. Before I leave I fire one more question at him: 'Just a thought, officer: how did an untrained student manage to get the upper hand on you, knock you unconscious, *and* destroy your body cam?'

The officer's eye twitches. He glares at me with deadly intensity. He catches himself and quickly softens his face.

'Beginner's luck I guess or . . . Must have been the way he was raised. The kid has a BURNING temper, very fiery.'

He looks at me, waiting for a response and — believe me — every part in my body wants to tear him to shreds. But one battle at a time. At least now he's on my watch list. I close the door and find Kukadia by the reception speaking with a paramedic.

'Elizabeth! There you are.'

'Detective, I found something—'

'So have I.'

The detective ushers me towards one of the ambulances parked near the entrance. 'We need to hurry.'

'What's going on?'

'Sue, the carer that Jill found near the victim's door, she's started speaking.'

The detective jumps into the back of the ambulance and helps me up. Sue is sitting up, her face placid and her eyes wide open, glazed over, as unresponsive as the other patients. A paramedic checks her blood pressure, then nods at the detective.

'Sue, Sue . . .' Kukadia calmly tries to get her attention. She doesn't respond. 'Could you tell us what you told the paramedic?'

She says nothing.

'Sue?'

The paramedic shakes his head, signalling to the detective and me that it's no use. We get up to leave.

'Pointed face . . .' whispers a husky voice from behind us. 'Pointed face, razor sharp beak.'

We turn and see Sue gazing at us, stretching forward and reaching out.

'Eyes red as fire, hooves for feet!' Sue gets more and more hysterical and the blood pressure machines around her start to beep. 'Burning eyes, a demon! A shadowy nightmare!'

'She's going to blow a gasket, we need to get her to a hospital now!' the paramedic yells.

'Who, Sue?' the detective asks in desperation. 'The killer?'

'He's a masked devil!'

Sue passes out. The paramedic shoos us out of the ambulance. The vehicle's siren pierces the air.

The detective rubs his head in frustration, kicking up water from the road into the air as he watches the ambulance leave.

'What am I supposed to do with that?! None of that made any bloody sense. I hope *you* found something more useful, Elizabeth, because right now I'm at my wits' end!'

I reach into my pocket and pull out the glass vial.

'I found this in the main ventilation shaft. I think our killer placed it in there to spread some sort of drug or toxin through the building, rendering everyone . . . well, like we just saw.'

The detective grabs the vial and inspects it. He shakes it and spots the red sandy substance in the tube.

'Great work! We're going to need hazmat in there and get everyone tested, including ourselves.'

'Agreed. But I don't think it's lethal; it seems more like some sort of highly concentrated psychotropic or hallucinogenic drug. If we were infected, we would be feeling the effects now and looking like everybody else.'

'I'm still not going to take any chances. Did you have any luck with the symbol?' he asks.

'Still waiting on the response. Hopefully any day now.'

'Let me know the minute you hear anything. Please.'

'Will do. What about the shooter?'

'I haven't been able to run a possible match yet. The Blackout left us completely in the dark. Literally. I hate being out of the loop in my own city. However, what you've discovered here might help us nail this psychopath.' Kukadia looks down at the vial again. 'I wonder what it is?'

He whistles at another poor forensic, like he's calling a dog: 'Yeah, you. Bag that and get it tested at the lab. I want to know where it is at all times, make it top priority. Understood?' The forensic investigator takes the vial and scuttles off.

I glance over to see Officer Scott exiting the building with Officer Lace. Kukadia notices my look of disdain.

'Listen, sorry I forgot to tell you that Scott's back on duty. The doctors cleared him a couple of days ago. He and Lace were first on the scene.'

'Thanks for letting me know,' I respond sarcastically.

'Liz! Look . . . I hope Joseph's okay. Getting that deal on the table was the best I could do.'

'No, I know. I appreciate it,' I say, watching the two officers walk along the pavement. Suddenly Scott stops in his tracks, and brings his palm to his forehead, as if he's forgotten something. He gestures to his colleague to wait for him by the patrol car and he heads back inside the building.

'I know we've got history,' Kukadia continues, 'and we're not always going to see eye-to-eye . . . But you did a great job today. Listen, when I get a chance to interview Charlotte.'

'The sister?'

'That's right. If you're not too busy, maybe you want to sit in? at the station. Or not; up to you. Just thought she might have more info regarding all this mess.'

I take a moment, leaving the detective in suspense. I'm pleased for the invite. I guess this is Paul's way of trying make amends.

'Sure. I'll be there.'

I walk back to my car through the rain and start the engine. My moment of pride in achieving what might be a breakthrough in this case soon dissipates as I think about my son locked up in a strange place. Joseph may be delusional but there is something seriously off with Officer Scott and I'm going to find out what it is. Something's nagging at me and, when I see Officer Lace standing outside the building, I take my chance.

'Officer, can I have a word?'

She looks around nervously, then crosses over to my car and gets in the passenger seat.

'Something wrong, Elizabeth?'

I scan her young, innocent face for a moment.

'You told me you were first on the scene.'

'I was.'

'You made it sound like you were alone.'

I pause, and allow my soft gaze and the silence to do the rest of the talking, to get her to confirm what I already know. After a few seconds, the rookie officer cracks.

'I wanted to tell you earlier.' Again, she looks over her shoulder and each window at her surroundings, as if hiding something.

'What is it?'

'I'm sorry . . . I wanted to say something earlier, but I didn't know who was listening. It sounds stupid but I thought you should know.'

'Know what?'

'Officer Scott was with me. Actually, he went into the room before me. I tended to Jill first and called in the paramedics . . .'

I have a feeling there's something else she's still not telling me.

'And?' I inquire with as much patience as I can muster.

'I heard some glass breaking. So I looked in the room quickly and I swear I thought I saw Officer Scott put something in his pocket. Maybe, I don't know. I probably shouldn't have said anything.' The officer looks over her shoulder again. 'I . . . I gotta go.'

'No, wait!'

She runs off through the rain towards her patrol car. Officer Scott stands there, still, his eyes fixed on me like a hawk as the rain gets heavier, beating against his body. Officer Lace catches up with him and he slowly gets in the car.

As they drive off, that gut feeling becomes more real and intense than ever. What did he take from the room? And why did he break the mirror?

CHAPTER 11

Whispering Walls

'Joseph . . . ? Joseph . . . ? There you are. Why are you sitting in the corner crying?! Come on, up! Let's wipe those tears away, shall we? We don't want to keep Mrs Jacobs waiting. Come on, this way.'

I'm a child. Seven years old and about to be adopted. A small rucksack full of essentials that have been given to me bounces on my back as I walk down a long, dusty blue corridor decorated with vinyl posters of cartoon characters along its walls. I hold on to a lady's hand, taking three extra steps to keep up with her fast-paced waking.

'Hello, Mrs Jacobs.'

'Oh, it's not Mrs, it's Ms. But Elizabeth is just fine.'

'Elizabeth, here he is: all packed and ready to go,' the lady says, pushing me forward. 'He was a little upset earlier but I'm sure he'll be fine. If you could both wait here, I'm just going to fill out the final release forms.' The lady leaves.

'Hello, Joseph.'

' . . . Hello,' I respond shyly. She looks different without her police uniform. She kneels down to my level and tries to hug me. I hesitantly take a step back.

'Oh, I'm sorry,' she says, instantly withdrawing her hug. She smiles at me and I see a kindness in her blue eyes.

'Joseph, I have a little present for you.' She kneels down and hands me a small comic book and matching action figure. 'I thought you might like a new superhero figure.' I look at the package. 'Do you like it?' she asks.

'He's not a superhero, he's a baddie,' I reply.

'Hmm,' she playfully contemplates. 'A baddie, huh? Is that so? Well then, we're just going to have to get another one. Maybe you can choose which hero you want to fight this villain. How does that sound?' I nod my head and, for a moment, I feel a small smile creep across my face. Then, a nervous realisation.

'Is everything okay, Joseph?' she asks affectionately, noticing the sudden change in my mood. I look at her but I'm unsure how to express what I'm feeling. She lowers herself to sit cross-legged on the floor, which brings us to eye-level.

'You're probably feeling a little nervous about coming to stay with me, yes?'

I don't answer and lower my eyes.

'That's okay, Joseph. Sometimes, change and new things can feel scary and confusing; it's okay to have mixed feelings.'

' . . . Do you ever get scared?'

'Me? All the time. I'll let you in on a little secret: when I was joining up to be a police officer, I was really scared and nervous. I was unsure about a lot of things: would I like it? What's going to happen to me? Is this the right thing for me? But then, there was something inside that made me realise, even though I was frightened, that it just felt right to do it.'

'You mean like your heart?'

'Yes, my heart. You see, even though I was a little unsure, there was a feeling in my heart that told me I was making the right choice and that I always wanted to help people who were in trouble. So, sometimes, when you feel like this, always remember to be truthful to yourself even if it's scary, like the heroes in your comics.'

'So, do I have to call you Mom?'

'You can call me whatever you need me to be but how about Elizabeth for now? How does that sound?'

'Okay.' I open the toy and start flicking through the comic pages.

'You hungry?'

I nod my head: 'I'm starving.'

'What would you like to eat?'

'Mmmm . . . pancakes, blueberry muffins, and juice.'

Elizabeth laughs out loud.

'Wow! All that just for you?!' Elizabeth playfully responds with a smile. 'My favourite food is . . .'

As Elizabeth reels off a list of her favourite foods, I see through the glass door the lady returning, walking down the hallway towards us, papers in her hand. She stops abruptly, like she's forgotten something, then holds the paper up, covering her face as if she's reading something.

' . . . I also like marmite,' Elizabeth concludes. 'What is your favourite cartoon?'

Before I can answer, there's a sudden movement. I turn and I grab Elizabeth's arm, as I see the lady darting towards us, across the ceiling, upside down. Her eyes blare white, leaving a light stream trailing behind her:

'ThERe . . . Is . . . NO EsCaPE!

'We . . . aRe . . . CoMInG!'

I tug on Elizabeth's arm, fearing the dreaded lady, whose strides bring her rapidly closer towards us.

'I'm scared!' I whimper, hiding under Elizabeth's arm. 'Please do something! She's getting closer.'

Suddenly, Elizabeth twists towards me. Her face has become

a mirror, reflecting my adult face back at me. My reflection screams, emitting a purple light flash from my eyes, blinding me and . . .

* * *

I wake up. I sit up in my bed, clenching my sheet, trying to get a grip on my reality. This time there's no staff members around to restrain or drug me; I'm alone in the darkness of my confinement with only the illuminating light from the moon casting against my frosted window for company. I take a moment before slumping my head into my knees and I hold myself, exhausted and tired, wondering: when will this all end?

Bip!

The electronic mechanised lock sounds from beyond my door; the light in the hallway blinks on. Multiple footsteps — five, maybe six individuals — walk gradually towards my room and the red light in my door begins to flash green.

Bip!

My door cracks slightly open and then abruptly stops.

'Not this one!' a woman's voice instructs. I lie there, pretending to sleep, but ready to fight whoever or whatever if need be. I watch the door intensely, not knowing what to expect. Then my door shuts and the light turns from green to red as it locks. I breathe a sigh of relief as the footsteps carry on up the hallway and unlock another door.

Bip!

My mattress quietly creaks as I leave my bed and make my way over to my door to listen:

Bip!

'*Umm-mmm-mm-mmmmmmmmm!*'

Suddenly I hear the mumbled, muted sound of someone struggling. I hear them being gagged and taken away. As the noise crosses past my doorway, I scramble back into bed. The sound travels past my room and up the hallway quickly, ending with another electronic door unlocking then closing. The lights in the hallway blink off.

Was this what Armin was talking about when he said this place changes at night? Who did they take, and will they come for me?

Beep, beep, beep, beep!
'The time is seven a.m.! All patients please prepare for your morning inspection and activities. Have a positive day.'

The square lighting panel on my ceiling switches on and the sound of staff members unlocking doors ensues. I've been sitting up all night, watching and waiting, on guard, paranoid of any and every sound. The monotonous vibe of this place at times has a way of making you lose hope and feel forgotten and abandoned. Throughout the night I've contemplated my own sanity, questioning what I experienced: from my unexplainable encounter with Tin Man and his crew to the attack at the police station and the haunting dreams that chase and rearrange my memory.

Bip!

A staff member enters my room.

'Morning,' she greets me robotically. 'Join the line in the hallway. You will be escorted to the shower rooms and then to the breakfast hall while we inspect your rooms.'

I go out into the hallway and see everybody stood outside to the left of their doors. No one talks; most keep their eyes pinned to the floor, showing no emotion, hollow and hopeless. Just like me. The mood reminds me of those soldiers' training camp videos, where individuals wait outside their rooms as their captain inspects their cleanliness. Ahead of me in the queue to my left, I spot the back of Armin's head. He stands there fidgeting. To my right, three more patients stand waiting, but room II — three doors down from me — is still closed with no patient in sight. One of the porters clocks me looking at the door and I quickly avert my eyes.

'Please follow the line!' the porter instructs.

We're taken to the shower area — a small private wet room with cubicles displaying our room numbers on the doors. Inside the cubicle is a sink, a small mirror, a disposable rubber toothbrush, a wall-mounted gel dispenser and an overhead shower.

Sqkishhhhh!

Warm water spits out of the shower head onto my Afro and gradually gets more powerful as I increase the pressure on the dial. For a split-second, if I close my eyes, I can feel like I'm back at home. That feeling soon trickles down the drain as the conversation with my mom replays in my head. Steam rises around the cubicle and — to my surprise — faint words start to form and appear on the mirror as condensation makes the invisible visible:

YOU ARE NOT CRAZY!

I trace my fingers against the letters as droplets roll down the glass, distorting the message.

Knock, knock, knock!

'Time up, get dressed!' the porter demands.

The words on the mirror fade and, with them, my moment of clarity.

After getting dressed, we're led into the eating hall and I am given a tray, bowl and plate, but I have no appetite. Tables of four scatter across the hall as patients line up to choose their food from the food bay. Armin spots me from across the hall and hails me over to sit next to him.

'Aiyo! Joseph, you ain't looking so good, my G. Maybe you should eat something, keep your strength up.' Armin places his green apple on my tray.

'I'm not hungry.'

'That's how they get you in these places,' Armin says, speaking with his mouth full of food. 'They wear you down, get you weak and, before you know it, you're doubting everything you believed. I know what I saw that night and nobody gonna pull no BS over my eyes. Don't let them get you, my G,' Armin encourages, slurping down his juice.

'You said this place changes at night. What did you—?'

A porter passes our table and I stop speaking. He looks at us. Armin waves sarcastically, chomping down on a piece of toast in a semi-antagonistic way. The porter walks on.

'You're talking about last night, right?' Armin says lowering his voice.

'Yeah, I heard something.'

'It won't be the last time. You're lucky it was your first night in the dorms; that shit happens on a regs.'

'What happens to them? You know, the ones that get taken in the night?'

'Some disappear. Others return, if they're lucky, but they come back changed.'

'How?'

'You've seen some of the patients with their heads shaved bald, looking all zombified, right? No lights on at home? Empty, like a blank page.' Armin takes another sip of his juice. 'It's only certain patients that they do this to — I'm still not sure how they pick.'

'So why doesn't someone say something or contact the police?'

'You're funny! We've been sectioned, we're officially on the nut list. Ain't no one gonna believe us. We're expendable. See no evil, hear no evil, right? Keep schtum.' Armin peels a banana. 'Just don't let them break you! That's how they win.'

Armin's right. Who would even believe us? My own mother thinks this is the best place for me. I guess that's what that message in the shower was alluding to: believe in yourself when nobody else does.

'Eat up, bro,' Armin says, placing the apple in my hand. I take a bite and the sour taste hits my tongue, making me hungrier. I look around the hall at the different patients. Once again I see the young woman I saw yesterday in the recreational room sitting alone and still weeping.

'She's still crying. Why has no one helped her?' I ask.

'Because she's a lost cause. She's the only survivor from that blood bath in the Bullring.' I look at Armin with no clue what he's referring to.

'Eleven customers and staff members crushed to death. You need to keep up with current affairs, my G. You do know the city's got like a superhero running wild now, right?! But we'll talk about that another time.'

'But why is she in here?'

'Look at her, G; she's cracked.'

I pour some juice into a glass and get up to take it over to her.

'Aiyo, where you going?' Armin asks.

I head over to the crying woman's table. The closer I get, the more I can hear her whispering to herself:

'You did it, it's your fault! I didn't mean to do it! I'm so sorry. *You're the one to blame!'*

She repeats these words over and over again to herself. I place the glass down. She stops repeating herself and looks up at me, her red eyes swollen from all the tears, almost as if shocked at being approached.

'I thought you might like something to drink.'

She hesitantly grabs the glass and begins to drink.

'Mind if I sit?'

She continues to drink but kicks the chair out from under the table for me to sit.

'You're going to hurt him, you shouldn't let him sit, you can't control it!'

'Control . . . what?' I ask tentatively as I sit down.

She stops mumbling to herself and stares at me, caution in her eyes.

'I'm Joseph.'

'Engozi,' she replies eventually.

'I saw you were upset and—'

'It's not safe . . . for you to be near me.'

'I don't think anywhere's safe in this place.'

'You . . . you hear them too?' Engozi stammers.

'Yeah . . .'

Engozi looks across the room at the staff members and then quickly looks away again.

'She was in the room next to me. I thought it was a dream or something. *Stop talking! You'll kill him like the others.*'

'Hmm? I thought . . . you said you didn't hurt the others, it was an accident?' I ask, hearing her other voice contradict her.

'It was an accident! *No it wasn't — tell the truth!* I was having a bad day, I never meant it to happen.'

Engozi looks like she's about to well up again but she has no more tears to shed.

'What happened?'

'*Don't tell him, you can't trust him, he's like the rest of them, he won't believe you.* I'm sorry, ever since the . . . incident I've had to say my thoughts out loud to try and control them.'

I stay silently engaged, allowing Engozi to speak in her own time.

'It . . . it all started the night the city had that storm, the power cut.'

'The Blackout?'

She nods.

'I was walking home from a friend's house, we'd had a busy day and stayed up drinking and chatting about random stuff until the early hours. Now I wish I had just gone home straight away. I only lived twenty minutes away so I decided to walk home but I got caught in the rain. For some reason, my taxi app had stopped working on my phone. In fact, my phone had cut out all together and that's when I heard it: this piercing, high-pitched howl, a scream that cut through every sound and brought me to my knees. I was so scared; it sounded like nothing I had ever heard before. I tried covering my ears but it did nothing. Seconds later, I saw something shoot into the night sky: a huge pulsating, like, ball of energy. It exploded across the sky, shutting off all the power and its energy pulsated through me.

'I felt a burning sensation in my whole body, like my insides were being rearranged; it was excruciating. For a moment a strange but familiar feeling came over me — I felt like I was falling asleep. As I drifted, I saw the most beautiful, devastating vision, like a world beyond our own. *You've said too much, you're going to get both of you killed!*' Engozi stops speaking and just looks at me, checking for a reaction. I listen, transfixed.

'Seconds after seeing that, I woke up and I felt . . . different. The sound of people gathering in the street became extremely loud, it was like I could hear other people talking in my head. I ran as fast as I could down the street, panicking. Somehow I made it home.

'I woke up late for work the next day and I remember just

having this splitting headache and ringing in my ears. My boss was being unhelpful as usual, blaming everybody else for him trying to save pennies. As usual, he hadn't put enough staff members on the rota. Typical. It all got too much and that strange feeling I felt the night before kept coming back. It was like I could hear my boss and the customers — loudly, in my head — blaming me.

'I remember just thinking I wish they would all just go away and die. *You should never have thought any of that.* I'm a good person. *You're wrong.* I was just having a bad day. Then, just like that, they all started attacking each other. It was vicious, awful. I can still hear them in my head every time I close my eyes. *That's your curse, your guilt, your reward for making them kill each other.*

'When the police came, they told me I was the only survivor. *Of course you were the only survivor, it's your fault they're dead! You did it! You killed them all!'*

Engozi plants her head into her hands and continues whispering those same words over to herself. She starts crying again, lost in some sort of perpetual loop of guilt.

Before I can say anything to console her, a nurse bursts through the doors, covered in blood, screaming hysterically. The hall rumbles and escalates into uproar. An alarm goes off and the patients that are not heavily medicated dart towards the double exit doors, almost crushing the security porter who's trying to make his way to assist the bloodstained nurse.

'Stay calm and get back! All of you!' the security porter shouts, radioing for assistance. In the chaotic stampede of pushing and shoving, someone grabs on to my shoulder. It's Armin.

'Aiyo, now's our chance; let's bounce.' Armin sneakily flashes a key-card and with no time for questions I follow him through one of the side doors and down a corridor, looking behind us. We travel quickly but silently, trying not to be seen.

Bip!

Three access doors deep, we stop and crouch, pressing our backs against a wall that has an exposed viewing window above it. Armin takes a quick look through it, then drops back down swiftly, breathing heavily with a slight smile across his face. He points up towards the window and silently mouths that someone's in there. We stay crouched and sneak all the way to another door leading us to another hallway. The alarm still blurts above us as the lights flash red against the white walls. My heart beats furiously. I'm surprised that we've made it this far without being picked up by a camera.

'Do you even know where we are going?' I whisper.

Armin raises his hand as if he's heard something, then cautiously relaxes. 'No idea, my G. But it won't be long 'til that porter realised someone's lifted his card.'

'Great,' I whisper sarcastically, but I'm worried. I should have just stayed put.

The alarm shuts off and the emergency lights reset to normal. Just as we're about to move again, we hear voices spilling our way down the corridor.

'Shit!' Armin mutters. He crawls to the edge of the wall and peers around the corner. He flinches back almost instantly. He scurries back over and uses the key-card to open the door to the room next to us. It doesn't work. Armin desperately tries again. 'C'mon!' he whispers, holding the key-card over the door lock. It flashes green then back to red. It's not opening. He tries again but panics and drops the card on the floor as the voices travel closer.

'Geez, what a mess!' the incoming voice says.

'Tell me about it.'

I grab the key-card off the floor and hold it over the lock, hoping by some miracle it'll open. Nothing.

'He would've had a better chance holing up in jail with his pops,' the incoming voice says from around the corner.

Armin readies himself to scrap and my palms start to sweat. I try one last time to prevent us from getting caught. 'Please work, please work!' I calm myself and hold it over the lock, longer this time, only seconds from being discovered. The lock flashes green and we both scuttle in, almost falling over one another.

'Well, he's a thing of the past now.'

'One thing's for sure, the Dragon is going to be pissed off!'

The door softly closes with a small click as the voices reach our previous position.

'You hear that?' one of the dampened voices says from the other side of the door. Armin and I look at each other, holding our breath. At any second they could burst through the door and our little impromptu escape plan will be over.

'I didn't hear nothing. Your ears must be playing up after them alarms stopped.' The voices disappear into nothing and we both sit on the floor relieved.

Armin starts quietly laughing.

'What's so funny?'

'Man, that was a rush and a half! We were this close to being nabbed. My G Joseph is calm under pressure,' he says, still laughing to himself.

'Someone's been killed?' I whisper to Armin.

'Yeah, sounds like Gecko got bodied! Ever since that Walker superhero tore through those Loop members in the Industrial, the streets have been unsettled. Must have started a mad power struggle. Only needs to be one drop of blood in the water in this city for the sharks to start circling. My guess is someone's sending a message to the Three Heads.'

'Three Heads?'

'You really don't know nothing, do you? Three Heads: Cerberus, the three that run the Loop. They control basically all of the organised crime in the city and initiate new crews into the Loop system.'

'Are the SOs part of the Loop?'

'Hell no! We don't want no part of that; it's just another business model to keep those at the top at the top and us at the bottom, killing each other for scraps. What we do is for us. We learnt long ago poverty won't stop with a pen.'

Armin checks to see if the coast is clear. He signals that it's safe.

'We should keep moving. Someone's bound to notice that we're missing,' he says.

Bip!

We head in the opposite direction to where the voices went. We enter an area where we hear light classical music playing from one of the rooms close by. We shuffle closer, planting ourselves against the wall underneath its viewing window. Armin lifts himself up to inspect. He slowly stands up, straight out of cover, as if transfixed by something.

'Armin!' I whisper, grabbing at his leg. 'What are you doing?!' Armin continues to stare through the glass. 'Armin!'

'Aiyo,' he replies, mesmerised. 'You've got to see this!'

I get up to join him, unsure what to expect. I see what has grabbed his attention.

'Incredible,' I utter, momentarily forgetting where I am.

Through the glass window my eyes witness something truly astonishing. The room's dimensions resemble every other we've passed, but, instead of the monotone colour which seems to coat this whole facility, this room has been completely transformed and decorated with beautiful images of life and light. On one wall is a rolling meadow with green grass kissed by the wind and bowing daffodils, which almost tricks your mind into believing that you can smell their refreshingly sweet scent. A golden sunset glistens in the skyline, coating the near-perfect clouds in an orange-purplish hue. It's truly breathtaking and reminds me of the time Mom took me to the ruins of the Sistine Chapel.

On the opposite wall, a collage of images integrate into one another like a large mural, laid out as if forming a linear timeline. In contrast to the idyllic scene on the other wall, these images are strikingly black, the texture like rough diamonds. One image in particular — the centre piece — stands out. My eyes widen as they recognise what they behold: a silhouette of a young man engulfed in smoke. He is sporting a hooded rucksack that helps hide his identity. Both hands cover his eyes, touching at the finger tips to form a pyramid shape. Multiple letter Zs swerve around his head. Around his neck, lying perfectly on his chest, dangles a necklace . . . my necklace, my dreamcatcher. It glows a neon-electric purple. In the midst of all this artwork on the wall and mounds of illustrated paper on the floor sits the skinny, unassuming, blindfolded child that was gesturing playing peek-a-boo across the room at me. Her paint-covered hands are wrapped around her knees and tucked tightly into her chest. Her head is on her knees, causing her thick, long, black messy pigtails to fall forwards and free. I'm lost for words. I stand there solemnly, stunned, beside Armin.

The young girl lifts her head, as if sensing our presence, displaying her bandage-wrapped eyes. Somehow, she looks and points straight at me. She covers her eyes with her hands, mimicking the mural.

'What's she doing?' Armin whispers. 'Aiyo, doesn't that picture kind of look like—'

Suddenly the girl stops mid-action, quickly turning her head as if she's heard something. She waits; we freeze. She turns her head back in our direction.

'Run!' her young voice shouts.

Bip!

The door at the end of the corridor unlocks. Bursting though are two security porters, accompanied by the stiff-necked woman in grey.

'There they are! Grab them!' she orders.

We run, shooting off down the corridor, and dash through another set of doors.

'Next left!' Armin pants. 'Straight ahead! Quickly! More doors ahead!'

As we hightail it towards another set of doors, we see more aggrieved security staff members in our path up ahead. We change direction and see a lift at the far end of the route; the doors have been left open. The four guards give chase. We pick up the pace, sprinting as fast as we can, aiming for the unoccupied lift . . .

WHAM!

'Ouff!'

Out of nowhere — almost in slow motion — a member of staff jumps out of one of the rooms and tackles Armin to the floor. Still running, I turn and see him toss the key-card towards me in one motion before he hits the ground. My reflexes send me hurtling through the air to catch it before it falls.

Boof!

I land hard on the lift floor; the whole thing bounces. Armin laughs as they wrestle to sedate him on the ground.

'Touchdown! Don't let them break you, my G!' he shouts, scrapping and throwing fists like a wild bulldog to try to free himself. As I scramble to my feet, ready to go back and help him, the doors abruptly close and I lose sight of Armin and our pursuers. The lift starts to descend automatically and I slump to the floor again to catch my breath. I realise I have no idea where

I'm going or what to do next.

The lift stops. I stand back to the left of the doors, out of sight.

Pssshhhhhttt!

The doors open and a cold draft prickles my skin. Through the lift doors I see a dimly lit, fully equipped, unmanned laboratory. It has been divided into small glass cubicles. Within each cubicle are neatly made-up medical beds, trolleys with empty test tubes and other apparatus that in any other setting wouldn't feel so sinister.

Pssshhhhhttt!

The lift doors begin to close and I make the decision to step out, not wanting to be greeted by whoever's calling it back up. As I move, the dim lights on the ceiling trigger like dominos. As it gets brighter, more of the lab reveals itself. I walk through carefully and see an area with what looks like huge cryogenic freezers; serious Umbrella Corporation, T-virus vibes. Why would a mental health facility need a fully equipped laboratory like this? I don't particularly want to know the answer, but I'm too deep down the rabbit hole at this point not to look. I open one of the freezers.

Thick, icy smoke at a sub-zero temperature rolls out and dissipates onto the floor. I step back, feeling its cold chill. Through the frosty mist, lined up on shelves, I make out dozens of coded test tubes. Each one has a random set a of numbers printed onto its glass shell and — weirdly — a different zodiac sign stamped onto each tube cap. I reach for one to inspect it but I am startled by a strange echoey noise. What was that? I keep still for a second, not wanting to make any sudden movements, then slowly close the cryo freezer, listening intently.

Huh! There it is again: an echoed mumble. I know I should just go, but where?! I cautiously follow the sound . . .

Here! I say to myself, standing in front of another huge cryo freezer. This one looks slightly different to the others and doesn't even seem to be switched on. I pull on the handle. Instead of opening, the handle moves down and sucks into the door, disappearing from view. There's a slow hissing suction sound, then — out of the blue — the whole freezer shifts to the right and it opens automatically like a space shuttle airlock.

'Woah!'

Peering into the abyss of the doorway, I see a steep winding stone passageway. The sound that I originally heard becomes more evident; muffled chants in low, sombre voices echo up the long passage:

'We see all. We are all. We watch all.
As Twilight rises and Daylight falls,
We are subjects to the First
And First is all.
We are the Watchers!'

'Gotcha!' a voice sharply barks from behind me. Before I can turn or run, multiple hands grab me, secure my arms, and lift me off my feet.

I wriggle, wrestle, try to fight or move my arms in any way. I shout through the hand over my mouth that is partly gagging and suffocating me: 'Get off me! You won't get away with this!' But the mumble that comes out is barely audible.

Pick!

A sharp scratch invades my arm. I feel my limbs flop and I sink to the floor. I lie on the cold tiled surface and hear the airlock sound of the door as it closes. The chanting is silenced.

I black in and out of consciousness, seeing only blurs and shadows of faces.

'What do you want to do with this one, ma'am?' a warped-sounding voice asks.

Another face looks down on me as my eyes roll back into my head.

'Well, assuming he has seen something he shouldn't have, that needs to be rectified, doesn't it?' another warped voice replies. 'Take him!'

'Yes ma'am!'

I fade out again . . .

CHAPTER 12

Card Trick

'A sailor went to sea, sea, sea
To see what he could see, see, see!'

'That's a good issue . . . Hey, I'm Sam. What's your name?'

'Tig! You're it!'

'Bring him back around!'

I'm a child again. Seven years old and about to be adopted.

'What's taking you so long?'

'Firecracker, Firecracker, Boom, Boom, Boom!'

'So, do I have to call you Mum?'
'You can call me whatever you need me to be but how about Elizabeth for now? How does that sound?'
'Sure.'

I'm sitting at the top of a smoke-filled staircase, gripping onto the bars of the banister so tightly that the brown pigmentation in my hand begins to turn pale.

'Wake him up!'

Pick!

I jolt back to reality, breathing rapidly, as adrenaline courses through my body. My eyes squint into a bright light that's beaming down directly onto my face.

'Wha— what's going on? Where am I?'

Disorientated, panicking, I struggle to free myself from the straps that tie me to some sort of operating table and the wires hooking me up to a monitor. The sound of heels slow-clicking against the floor grabs my attention.

'You didn't think you would get away that easily, did you?' a voice says in a calm and collected tone. 'Your dreams are not a safe haven. If you tell me what you saw and heard, your stay here will be much more comfortable.'

'I'm not saying anything, let me go! What did you do with Armin?' A head appears in front of the light, blocking out its glare. My vision readjusts. 'You!' I say to the woman in grey.

'I don't believe we've been formally introduced. I am—'

'I don't care what your name is! Let me go, I'm not supposed to be here! What you're doing is illegal! Just wait till I tell—' I stop myself from speaking about my mom, not wanting her to be on their radar.

The woman in grey looks at me with a hawkish, unsettling stare.

'Who would you tell, I wonder? And, furthermore, who would believe you?' The woman picks up a clipboard and reads aloud: 'Manic delusional paranoia, violent tendencies, psychic trauma . . . The list goes on.'

She places the clipboard on my stomach and leans in. 'Now,

you listen to me: I'm going to give you one more chance to tell me what you were doing in our laboratory.'

I stay silent.

'Very well,' she says, stepping away and signalling to someone else behind me. 'Doctor Roth, please administer a dose of TR-13.'

An oxygen mask is forced over my face and I jerk my head from side to side to try to evade it. 'What are you doing ?!' My ears pick up the distinctive sound of gas being released. 'What's that?! What are doing to me? Stop, please stop, don't!' I plead.

A few seconds later, I'm unable to speak. My eyes are still open but my body goes cold and a chalky sensation revolves around my mouth. I feel like I'm neither sleeping nor awake, neither conscious nor unconscious.

'Process dream wave pattern three,' the woman's warped voice demands.

I'm sitting at the top of a smoke-filled staircase, gripping onto the bars of the banister so tightly that the brown pigmentation in my hand begins to turn pale.

                    'Now set it to loop. After a couple of days
                                that should loosen his tongue!'

I'm sitting at the top of a smoke-filled staircase, gripping onto the bars of the banister so tightly that the brown pigmentation in my hand begins to turn pale.

I'm sitting at the top of a smoke-filled staircase, gripping onto the bars of the banister so tightly that the brown pigmentation in my hand begins to turn pale.

Wh . . . why does it keep repeating? No, no, please! Not this; anything but this!

I'm sitting at the top of a smoke-filled staircase, gripping onto the bars of the banister so tightly that the brown pigmentation in my hand begins to turn pale.

Beep, beep, beep, beep!
'The time is seven a.m.! All patients please prepare for your morning inspection and activities. Have a positive day.'

No please! Stop! Let me out!

I'm sitting at the top of a smoke-filled staircase, gripping onto the bars of the banister so tightly that the brown pigmentation in my hand begins to turn pale.

Beep, beep, beep, beep!
'The time is seven a.m.! All patients please prepare for your morning inspection and activities. Have a positive day.'

No, no, please!
After days of torture, I now know why other patients, the unsleeping ones, look the way they do. Drained, weak, barely able to walk; I'm not sure how much longer I can take this without losing my mind. Like me, they too have undergone the 'recurring' process, as they call it. How have they managed to harness and control your dreams, able to induce a single memory over and over again? Although my head hasn't yet been shaved, I fear it's only a matter of time before I succumb to the experiment.

It's clear to me they no longer care about what I saw. The

priority is for me never to leave this place or speak of the laboratory and the ritualistic chanting that I heard from below. I need help! I need to somehow reinitiate what I did the night of the Blackout and get myself out of here. I believe the symbol from my dreamcatcher is the key and I know who might understand what it means and be able to help me . . .

Bip!

My room door opens. I hear the distinctive sound of heels. I shakily sit up.

'It seems you have a visitor,' she says, with a pitiful insincerity, completely unaffected by my suffering. 'Remember, our hands read beyond this wall. We will be watching you. Clean him up!' She orders to one of the staff as she exits the room.

* * *

Bip!

'Joseph!'

'L...Leiyah . . . ?' I mumble, as my legs shake and give way underneath me.

Leiyah quickly throws her arms around me, catching and hugging me at the same time.

'It's really you,' I whisper through her long, curly, black hair that has fallen across my face. I hold on to her tight not wanting to let go, hoping this is real and not another induced dream. Leiyah keeps her arms wrapped around me and helps me over to the seat. She sits next to me with a look of worry on her face.

'Leiyah . . . what are you doing here?'

'I saw your mom. She mentioned that you were allowed visitors and asked if I wouldn't mind checking in on you.'

I stay silent, still feeling the hurt of betrayal.

'She told me that she tried visiting a couple of times but you denied her access.'

Leiyah's wrong. I didn't stop her; I didn't even know she'd tried to visit again.

'Well, if you see her tell her I'm doing fine,' I say in a resentful manner.

'But you're not though, are you? You're not doing fine, you don't look yourself. What have they been doing to—?'

'Shhh,' I silence her, remembering the woman's threats. What if someone's listening in? I look behind me, paranoid that any minute I'm going to get dragged away and subjected to another 'recurring' process. I shake my head. Leiyah looks me dead in the eyes and gently nods, understanding.

'Sam . . . sends his love,' she says, playing along. 'He was going to come, up until the last minute, and then decided not to. You know Sam. He's not taking it so well. He's dyed his hair blonder than Super Saiyan Goku. Some sort of cry for help, maybe? Not sure if it's him being selfish or if it would just be too much for him to see you like this. He misses you. We both do. Your mom mentioned that you might be coming out soon and that you should rethink . . . the offer?'

'Is that why you came? To persuade me to agree?'

'No, not at all,' Leiyah hastily refutes. 'I don't even know what she's referring to. I came because you're my friend and I'm worried about you. You would've done the same for me!'

'You mean the way I helped you out in the alley . . . ?'

Leiyah goes quiet and looks down at her hands. She picks at her glossy green nail polish.

'That wasn't your fault; it wasn't any of our faults. You got injured too. Those guys got what they put into the universe, they got what was coming to them . . . Whoever that vigilante is . . .' Leiyah looks up at me. 'He got them and they won't be doing that to anybody else anytime soon. So I just hope he knows how appreciative I am.'

Bip!

The door opens and I flinch in fear. Leiyah clocks my reaction.

'Five minutes!' one of the porters shouts into the room.

'Joe . . . did I ever tell you about when I moved to the city?'

I shake my head.

'Well, it wasn't under the best of circumstances. At the time, I thought I knew best and I pushed everybody that cared for me away. Growing up in Japan until the age of eleven had its challenges, especially when you're different; a Hāfu: some would call me. When we moved here my parents, especially my father, were very protective of me, sometimes to a fault. After they divorced, I just felt angry, betrayed, like I didn't belong anywhere, that I had no one who understood me. They both tried to over-compensate by micromanaging my life, my choices, and my career towards the family business. It was suffocating. Needless to say, I left. It wasn't easy moving to the city, but then where in this broken land is easy? My father threatened to cut me off so I changed my last name to my mother's maiden name to get my own back and, after a couple of toxic relationships, I slugged it out for a year or so before finally enrolling at CBU. When I met you and Sam at Freshers' Week you guys made me feel like I belonged, like it was okay to be myself. You made my choice worthwhile and I began to get my voice and confidence back. Seeing how close you were with your mom inspired me to mend bridges with some — not all — of my family. What I'm really trying to say is, sometimes we think we know best and we want to do things on our own, but there are people in our lives who are there for a reason. I don't know what offer your mom was talking about but—'

'They want me to admit that I attacked the officer, Leiyah! They want me to lie and be here on a voluntary basis to "get help." And I'd never get out.'

She stares at me.

'I didn't do it, Leiyah; it wasn't me! Something else took the officer, something evil. If I admit to doing that I'm going to lose my grip on the last bit of myself that knows what's real from what's not.'

'I believe you.'

Leiyah's three simple words stun me.

'Wh— what did you say?'

'I believe you, Joseph.'

I feel myself starting to choke up but I haven't the energy to shed tears.

'Look, I may not be "bench and batty" junior school best friends like you and Sam, but I know something's been up with you. I've known that ever since we saw that footage at uni.'

'Leiyah . . . I—'

'Don't worry, you don't have to explain. I never pried because I didn't want you to have to lie to me. Besides, I gather you don't even have all the answers yourself . . . I just need to know one thing,' Leiyah says, staring intensely. 'What do you need me to do?'

I take a moment to weigh up her proposal and whether I want to risk getting her involved in all of this. But then her words about trusting others sink in. I look back up at her.

'Get me Grey. I need to speak with the professor.'

Leiyah looks at me, slightly confused.

'Grey? Why?'

The buzzer sounds and the door begins to unlock. No time for me to explain.

'Time's up!' a voice says from the other side.

Leiyah looks at me trustingly and places her hand on mine. She nods.

'Okay, I'm on it,' she says fired up.

The door opens.

'Visiting time is up! Say your goodbyes.'

Leiyah hugs me again and whispers: 'Stay strong!'

* * *

En route to my room, I hold on to Leiyah's words. If she can deliver on her promise to bring Professor Grey to me, then maybe I can get one step closer to understanding that symbol and getting out of here. Walking through the white hallways I keep an eye out for Armin amongst the other patients. I hope he's been treated better than me. Passing a number of patients along the way, to my dismay, I see a familiar face. It's Engozi. She is standing in line, waiting alongside three other patients. Their heads have been shaved, blank expressions across their faces, just like the other unsleeping, zombie-like patients.

'Engozi!' I shout, mustering up the strength to break away from my chaperone and go over to her. I wave my hands in front of her face. 'Engozi! It's me, Joseph!'

I grab her by the shoulders and try to shake her out of her trance. The guard grabs me and pulls me back.

'Snap out of it! Engozi!' I yell.

The guard continues to drag me away and, as I look at her expressionless face, I'm angry; angry that this has been allowed to happen; angry that the voiceless and vulnerable who have been entrusted into a system of care have been used as guinea pigs and lab monkeys. I conjure up what strength I have and lash out at the security porter.

'You bastards!' I shout. 'What have you done? You're killing us!' My voice travels like a pebble in a still pool.

The porter calls for assistance. Other cognisant patients start to act out, pushing and shoving wildly. Before long I am man-handled onto the floor by a number of staff.

Pick!

Another needle, another sedation, another . . .

234

Beep, beep, beep, beep!

'The time is seven a.m.! All patients please prepare for your morning inspection and activities. Have a positive day.'

* * *

The days roll by and there is still no word from Leiyah or any sign of Grey. If I'm not being kept in my room then I'm being taken into Doctor Roth's medical area, where more of that TR-13 stuff is administered, slowly destroying the small flame of hope that I was holding on to.

Bip!

'You have a visitor,' the porter says, entering the room with two other staff members.

'What are you doing?' I ask feebly, backing away into the corner.

'Ma'am says it's for your own good. We don't want you causing any more trouble like last time.'

They hold me down and ply me with more unknown drugs. Once again, I start to feel numb, weak, passive . . .

Bip!

I enter the visitors' room. There, sitting calmly at the table, legs crossed, playing chess against himself, is Professor Grey.

'All that we see or seem is but a dream within a dream, Mr Jacobs,' he says, moving his rook, then counteracting it with a black knight from the other side.

'P . . . Poe?' I whisper weakly, using all my energy to fight off the heavy, numbing, debilitating, suffocating sensation from the meds.

'Good, Mr Jacobs. It is pleasing to hear your voice. I am happy that they have not been able to take that away from you. Death and life is in the power of the tongue.' Grey stands and walks over to me. His lion-like, oak-brown eyes look sternly at the porter and, without delay, the door closes. My eyes start to lose focus and flicker. My balance starts to wane, leaving me more and more unsteady. The professor inspects me as beads of cold sweat roll from my forehead. He guides me to my seat, then opens his weathered brown leather satchel. He places a small old wooden candle-holder on the table in front of me then, from his bag, he retrieves what looks like an assortment of herbs, dried leaves and other vegetation that have been tightly bunched together. The room gets increasingly dim and I start to lose the feeling in my hands and legs. I'm drifting . . .

He strikes a match and lights the assortment of herbs. The burnt shrubbery glows like hot ash — red then white — and small streams of smoke start to rise.

'Be still, Mr Jacobs, this will only take a minute. Concentrate on my voice.' Grey begins to speak: '*Nire kheke.*' I focus on his words, despite not understanding the language: '*Ma ghowa.*' His tone rumbles, deepening to an almost unnatural bass vibration, like distant drums or crashing waves that reverberate into my core. His words have a comforting and authoritative sound as he ritualistically circles the burning leaves around me. He instructs me to inhale. Within seconds, I start to feel strength returning to my body.

Bip!

The door opens. Grey places the smoking herb on the wooden stand like it's incense and goes over to the door.

'What's going—?'

Before the security porter can raise his voice, Grey whispers something inaudible. The door closes and the porter leaves. Grey fixes his tweed, patched blazer casually and takes a seat. Whatever he did has worked; like poison being extracted from a wound, I feel almost like me again, fully alert, with all my senses returning to normal.

'What did you say to him?' I ask.

The professor unwraps a small block of dark chocolate and hands it to me.

'Here, eat this.'

I break off a segment.

'And to answer your question, I made him an offer he can't refuse.'

'Did . . . you just reference *The Godfather*?' I ask, impressed and also a little taken aback that he actually used a pop culture quote rather than a historical one.

'Godfather?' he replies. Then, after two years of sitting in his lectures, I finally see Professor Grey crack a small smile. The smoking shrub starts to die down and the professor moves another piece on the chess board, once again countering it from the opposite side.

'What's in that stuff?' I ask with a motion to the charred leaves. I get no response. 'Professor, the dialect you were speaking in sounded . . . well, it sounded sort of familiar, like I had heard it before.'

Professor Grey continues to focus on the chess board. 'The burning of plants and herbs is one of many ancient remedies that have been used throughout history. There are still those of us who know how to cultivate their natural elements to help clear the mind, body, and soul.' Grey lifts his gaze towards me. 'And then there are also others that abuse and pervert creation's gift for power and control. "If the Sun said it had power over the Moon, then let it come and shine at night." African proverb.'

I smile. Grey reverts to moving his pieces on the board.

'There must always be balance, Mr Jacobs. One does not exist without the other. When out of balance it can throw us off course and corrupt our vision. When left unchecked, discord and chaos run riot and we forget who we are. We all have the ability of choice and to centre oneself. Or, to put it in terms I believe you would like: to become one with the force.'

'Did you just quote *Star Wars*?'

'If you are talking about that old classic that was inspired by another old Japanese classic, then . . . yes.'

Grey's cool meter just hit ten. For the first time in a long, long time, just sitting there and speaking with him, all my worries and troubles momentarily melt away.

'And . . . the words you spoke? That language?'

'That, Mr Jacobs, was one of many ancient languages that I have had the pleasure of learning whilst walking the Earth.'

The professor examines me again and checks the palms of my hands. 'Hmm. You are looking much better already.'

'Thank you, professor. Thanks for coming.'

'My pleasure, Mr Jacobs. Miss McGregor was adamant that I come to see you; she would not take no for an answer. She is a good friend. It is friends like that you will need in the time to . . .'

The professor holds his words back and then completes a series of chess moves which ends his game in a stalemate.

'So tell me, Mr Jacobs: how can I be of further assistance to you?'

The time for subtlety is out the window.

'Professor, I asked you here because there's a symbol that I was hoping you could look at.'

Grey looks at me inquisitively.

'Do you have a pen and paper?'

He folds his portable chess set away to make room on the table and retrieves a pen and a small notepad from his satchel. He tears out a fresh page and I begin to draw the symbol in detail from memory, taking my time, trying to be as accurate as possible. I slide the paper over. Grey's brows knit closer together as he scrutinises the image. He glances back and forth multiple times between me and the image. Finally, he stands, deep in contemplation.

'What is it?' I ask. Grey gives me strange look.

'How did you discover this sign, Mr Jacobs?'

'Well . . . I . . .'

'Quickly now!' Grey insists with a sudden urgency. 'Time is of the essence!'

'I received it as a gift on my birthday.'

'From whom?'

'It was a necklace, back dated, it had a note attached . . .' I take a small breath. 'The note was signed by my mum and dad. My real parents. They both passed away when I was a child. I don't really have any memory of them.'

Grey looks at me, unsettled.

'And where is this . . . trinket now?'

'I'm not sure. After I was attacked at the police station it went missing and . . .'

'Speak, Mr Jacobs! What is it?'

'Ever since I received that gift . . . other things, strange things, have been happening to me . . .' I hold my words apprehensively. What if someone's listening in? The professor leans in, noticing my discomfort. He clocks the small camera in the corner of the room. Grey walks over to it and, without missing a beat in his step, he rips the wire from the device.

'That should allow us more privacy. I gather that we don't have much time before they notice.'

'Professor, I've been seeing this symbol in my sleep.'

'As in, your dreams?'

I nod. 'And on one of the nights that I dreamt it . . . something strange happened.'

'Like what?' the Professor asks, leaning over to me again. Seeing me hesitate, he backs off.

'Joseph, I want you to look at this for me.'

The professor pulls out some blank, black, shiny playing cards from his bag and holds one up to my face.

'What do you see, Mr Jacobs?'

'Professor, I hardly think this is the time to play—'

'Tell me what you see, Joseph!' the professor insists, slightly raising his voice, which accentuates his Jamaican accent.

'Just a blank black card,' I reply confused. The professor swaps the cards one at a time behind each other.

'What do you see now?'

'The same as the others. Why, what am I supposed to see?'

'I need you to close your eyes.'

I look at him, unsure.

'Joseph, you asked me here for my help, correct?'

' . . . Yes.'

'Then I need you to close your eyes.'

I hesitate but comply.

'Tell me what you see, Joseph.'

'I don't see any— Wait . . . Hold on . . .'

I see the black card, floating in my mind as clear as day. Its blank face is now moving, morphing into different shapes, its particles undulating and turning like a moving Rorschach. An image starts to appear.

'I see something. I see three monolithic stone pillars with rivers flowing through and an illuminated blue sky. Each structure has a . . . hang on . . . there, I see it now. Each stone has a different sign or patterned engraving on its surface, with the middle stone displaying that symbol. Professor, how is this—'

'Concentrate, Mr Jacobs. Tell me what you see.'

Another card floats into my mind's eye. The particles start to gather then the image forms.

'I see . . . an eye? It has what looks like a sword through it. In

240

the pupil there's a round table, it's revolving, and there's a red crown hovering above the centre of the circle.'

'You're doing well, Mr Jacobs! What do you see now?' A new image starts to appear and then I see myself, sleeping.

'Anything?' the professor asks.

'It's . . . it's me. I can see my face. My head's down, it looks like I'm . . . sleeping.' The image of me starts to pulsate and stir. With a sudden flash, like lightning, the image of me rapidly snaps its head up and morphs into Officer Scott. He screams out viciously and reaches forward to grab my neck.

'No, stop! No! Get away! Stop!'

I open my eyes and see the black card that the professor is holding curling up and melting like camera negatives exposed to fire. My hands grip the table, my palms burn with the sensation that I felt once before. Grey grabs my hands and turns them over, inspecting them like a palm reader. For a split-second I swear I see the grooves and lines in my hand move.

'I must be leaving at once,' Grey stands up hastily, grabbing his satchel.

'Wait, what? Professor, where are you going?'

He continues to move quickly towards the door.

'I don't understand. You never answered my question about the symbol! And what were those black cards?'

Knock! Knock!

The professor bangs on the door to be let out. I try to follow, try to get answers.

'Please, professor, what's going on? I need to get out of here. Please help me. They think I'm crazy.'

Professor Grey turns and looks at me sympathetically. He lays his hand on my shoulder.

'Joseph, there is more to this symbol than meets the eye. I will return shortly with answers, I promise.'

The professor sees me deflate.

"'Are not the sane and the insane equal at night as the sane lie a-dreaming? Are not all of us outside this hospital, who dream, more or less in the condition of those inside it, every night of our lives?' I know being in the hornet's nest is not easy. Keep hopeful; you are the master of your own mind. Do you remember the conversation we had in your last lecture? The words I wrote on the board?' Grey begins to speak in another language I don't understand: "*pA Khat iw pA Hwt-nTrw m-khent Ten ikh eref sew ir pat rex Des-sen.*" Translated it means: "the body is the temple of gods within you. Therefore it is said: Man, know thyself." *You* are in control. One last request before I go: tonight I want you to place your hands over your eyes and count to ten. Try to empty your mind and release yourself from your surroundings. You are not alone.'

Bip!

The door opens and Grey exits the room, leaving me with only his word that he will be back.

* * *

Another night rolls in. The lights go out and silence takes up residence. I sit on my bed with my legs crossed, not really sure why he's asked me to do this but ready to try.

'Okay, hands over eyes like this he said. Empty your mind and count to ten. One, two, three, four, five, six, seven, eight, nine . . . *ten!*' I whisper, exaggerating the last number, expecting something to happen. Nothing.

I couldn't see very much before with the lights out and I can see even less now, with my hands over my eyes. I go over his instructions again: Place your hands over your eyes, clear your mind, free yourself from your surroundings, you're not alone . . . ? Feel like I'm missing something . . .

The locking mechanism sounds in the hallway and another muffled patient is taken away.

'Mmmmm . . . mmmm! Aiyo, get off me!'

That's Armin!

'You lot don't know who you're screwing with!'

I rush to my door and bang on it, shouting: 'Armin! What's happening?!'

'Aiyo, Joseph my G!' he blurts. 'Tell my people what happened to me! Tell them about Armin the Mini Terror. SO for life! Mmmm-mmmm.'

Armin's words turn back into a muffled cry and the sound of his struggling dampens and disappears.

I hit my head against the door, frustrated at not able to help. A burning sensation starts to warm my hands. I look down, straining my eyes in the dark, and see the deep indented lines on my palms move position.

'What the—?!'

I knew I'd felt this when Grey was looking at my palms. I kneel down and — I don't know why — I slowly move my palms over my eyes and begin the count again, slowly: 'One . . . two . . . three . . .' I breathe out, trying to calm myself. 'Four . . . five . . . six . . .' I imagine that the walls around me disappear and that I'm floating in space. 'Seven . . . eight . . . nine . . .' The image of the young blind girl playing peek-a-boo flashes before me. I shift my hands slightly, making more of a pyramid shape with my hands, my index fingers pressing against the middle of my forehead. 'T—'

. . .

. . .

I travel through light and sound and into black.

'Hello?'

Hello?

Hello?

My voice echoes. Where am I?

Joseph . . .

Jossssssseph . . .

'Who said that?'

Who said that?

Who said that?

No response. I can't see a thing; it's pitch-black. What is this place?

Oh God, am I dying?!

Is that what this is?

I think I'm dead.

My body feels like I'm floating in nothingness. I touch my arms to stimulate my senses. There's no reference of up or down, left or right, just sound and touch. This is what I imagine zero-gravity must be like. I need light. Raising my head in the direction I perceive to be up, specks of starlight flicker and gleam, rolling back the dark. It's beautiful. Vibrant colours of purple, emerald-green, red, gold and ocean-blue soar above me like a harmonic painting. Magnificent. It's so peaceful. I fall, drifting slowly down to a standing position . . .

'What is this?' my voice echoes.

I look down in amazement at a carpet of black, crystallised diamond sand; it mounds up like tiny diamonds but feels as fine as dusted powder under my feet.

Then I remember the girl from the hotel. When I saw her die in my dream, her skin looked like this substance. This is wild! My reflection appears on its dark shiny surface, rippling like water as I move across the black diamonds. A colourful, multi-faceted reflection of light shines from above and illuminates my body. The crystallised substance begins to rotate clockwise around my feet. I tread carefully, playing like a child with its movement, watching its texture magnificently evolve: first splashing like water, then scattering and spreading like jewels. Each time I go to grab some it evades me, morphing and moving almost in the same way as the indents on the palms of my hand. The black diamond ocean pulsates like a vein, multiplying as far as my eyes can see. It begins to part into lines, creating pathways. The enchanting colours from the starlight blend the darkness mesmerically into a source of light. I freeze in amazement, as I see pathways appear, surrounding me. Spread out along the pathways, I see what I can only describe as glowing, spirit-like apparitions, formed out of mounds of the black onyx-like stones. They stand motionless as if now crystallised. They fade in and out as they glitch from one path to another. They don't see me. I call out to them, but they drift further away until only one remains. I run towards it, hearing the sound of splashing under my feet. The starlight kaleidoscopes across the sky as if time has sped up. As I get closer, the figure starts to disappear but I manage to make out a small hand holding a spray can. It vanishes back into the lustrous obsidian ocean. My attention turns to what sounds like a child's voice echoing behind me:

'So I'm going to live with you now?'
'Will I ever see them again?'
'I can't sleep, I'm scared.'
Tears roll down my cheeks. That's my voice, memories of my adoption. More voices from my past start to whisper from different pathways, evolving from me as a child into my present voice:
'Hi, I'm Joseph. This is my best friend, Sam; Sam, this is Leiyah.'
'Get off him, leave her alone!'

'We are such stuff as dreams are made on,
love Mum and Dad.'

Screeeeeeeeeeeeeeeeeechhhhhhh!

I cover my ears and collapse into a foetal position. The sound is so piercing that the ground beneath me rumbles. A huge pathway emerges in front of me. The onyx crystals float into the air to form a glistening barrier on both sides. I am contained within its sparkling walls.

'Stop it, stop it! Enough!' I shout.

Voooom!

A force blasts out of me, silencing the screech. I hear only my own breath. I cautiously remove my hands from my ears and look down at the partially lit pathway before me. Slow footsteps walk towards me, getting closer with each step. My vision blurs. I get to my feet, waiting fearfully for the owner of the footsteps to emerge. It appears: a silhouette of a small child.

'Who are you?' I ask.

'You took long enough, Bushy Head,' the small child giggles as they walk closer. I've heard that voice before.

'You!' I say in disbelief. 'But . . . how is this real? Where are we?'

'You're the vigilante, right?! The one who changed me and made the Blackout.'

'I . . . I don't know what you're talking about.'

'I'm Sketch!'

'Sketch!' I mumble under my breath. 'Is that your real name?' I ask. Sketch sticks her tongue out.

'How about you? Is your name actually Ghost, or Vigilante Man, or do you have a real name, Bushy Head?'

'Yes, I have a real name; my name is Joseph! Stop calling me Bushy Head?'

'Why, Bushy Head?' Sketch repeats childishly.

'Hang on . . . you're . . . blind? How do you know my hair's bushy?'

Sketch smiles.

'Look, we don't have much time in here. It won't be long before He and those white shadowy things find us.'

'So you've seen them too?'

'Of course. Who do you think saved your butt from that nightmare you had?'

'That was you?! But how?'

'No time to answer. The grown-ups in here are bad news. They don't know who you are yet. But they will soon if they make contact with those white shadows that are chasing you. We need to escape. You need to do your kick-ass vigilante thingy again.'

'I . . . I can't,' I stammer.

'Why not?'

'I don't know how I did it in the first place.'

Suddenly, a bright, terrible glow appears behind Sketch in the distance. The black diamonds of the walled structure around us begin to glitch.

'They're here! We need to go!'

'No, wait! How do I—?'

The walls around us start to collapse. A terrifying white aura grows. Sketch freezes, turning into a statue of black diamonds, and then crumbles into dust. In the blink of an eye, the light glowing in the distance shoots towards me like a runaway train. Not knowing what to do, I put both hands over my eyes and brace for impact . . .

'—en . . .'

I look down to find myself still kneeling in the position I took when I started counting. I look at my hands, trying to process what I've just seen, trying not to freak out. I take a deep breath.

'Woah!'

CHAPTER 13

3 X Three Eyes

'You've got to be kidding me!'

. . .

'But I have new evidence that could help further the—'

. . .

'This is ridiculous! I need more time!'

'Detective! Get back here!'

Slam!

Kukadia storms out of the room, slamming the door behind him. He grits his teeth and curses under his breath.

'Captain blowing smoke up your chimney?' I ask, leaning against the wall, within earshot of the door.

'He's doing more than that; he's trying to pull me off the case!'

'What?!'

Kukadia signals me to walk with him, away from the captain's office.

'That makes no sense!' I say, which only adds to Kukadia's aggravation. 'If they take you off now, we give the killer space to find more victims. That message left on the last victim's body was an attempt to communicate. It's an invitation.'

'I'm loving your shared concern, Elizabeth, I really am — but we both know that your allegiance is only temporary. I'm your

248

meal ticket to this circus act and I'm expendable when you —
and others — see fit.'

I ingest Kukadia's comment — he's frustrated, which is valid.
But, also, there is truth to what he says. If Kukadia is taken
off this case then I have no access to it, or anyone to feed me
first-hand information. The detective stops in front of a coffee
machine and deliberates over his selection.

'Who are they planning on replacing you with?' I ask.

'That's just it: no one! He thinks there are more immediate
priorities that need attention, which is a load of bollocks!' I look
at Kukadia, waiting for him to elaborate.

'A lot of the prisoners that we locked up from that night
when all hell broke loose in the Industrial are being released.
Some are already out!'

'What?! Why?'

'Someone hired a sweet-talking, three-piece-suit-wearing,
sleazy Loop lawyer, that's why. He's twisted their stories from
criminals to victims, throwing a bunch of legal crap our way,
from false imprisonment to discrimination and unlawful arrest
— the list keeps on going. Either way, we're about to release
some not-so-nice individuals back onto the streets.'

'And there's no way of postponing their release?'

'Nope. The judge has already signed off on it. Everybody's on
edge. There's already a turf war kicking off. A couple of weeks
ago Matthew Nelson died.'

'Kaine Nelson's son?'

'Yeah, "Gecko." Where do they get these names?' the detective
mutters to himself as he finally selects a flat white.

'Was it a hit?' I ask.

'Not sure. If it was, that's worrying, as he was held up in the
criminally insane wing at the TWI.'

I think of Joseph; I haven't been able to contact him. They

told me he needs space whilst readjusting. I just hope Leiyah can give me an update soon. Kukadia grabs his cup and blows on his coffee.

'With the sharp incline of violence,' he continues, taking a sip, 'and gangs battling to fill that Third Loop position after the previous one was knocked off by some made-up vigilante, it wouldn't surprise me if Gecko's death was a move. A message to the Three Heads.'

His comments wash over me as I silently brew over the politics, declining standards, and negligence that have led to dangerous felons being released. The deaths of multiple young women and the elderly victim have been completely overshadowed.

'Elizabeth . . . ?' Kukadia intrudes on my thought process. 'Please tell me *you* don't believe that clickbait nonsense.'

'The Ghost? No, well, I mean, I saw parts of the footage — the picture wasn't great.'

'That's because it was a hoax! End of the day, people will make up all kinds of stuff. The Wretches did something similar — that didn't end so well, did it? We found body parts in bin bags all over the city for weeks, remember? This is just their way of discrediting the crew that actually did bump them off — stop 'em from getting a bigger rep and whatnot.'

Kukadia rotates his injured shoulder, pops a pill, and downs the remains of his coffee with a single gulp. He's most likely right about the footage not being real; it's a push to believe one person could just go down to the Industrial like that and take out over thirty armed and dangerous individuals. But, on the other hand, there are holes in his theory. Putting out footage of them being decimated by one person seems far worse than being overwhelmed by a rival gang. Also, if you had just been toppled, why would you post footage to publicise it? It just doesn't add up.

Kukadia punches his selection of another flat white into the vending machine.

'You want one?' he asks.

'No, thank you. How long have you got till they move you off the case?'

'The prisoners are set to be released imminently and my recall orders will come into effect in forty-eight hours.'

'Okay then, let's get to work.'

I follow Kukadia through the station. Most of the officers look young, inexperienced, nervous.

Kukadia's right: there is an unsettling, tense atmosphere around the place. You could cut it with a knife.

* * *

We enter Kukadia's office. The walls are plastered with mugshots. Out-of-date city maps and blueprints of what looks like the Industrial are also pinned up around the room.

Kukadia removes a bunch of folders from his visitor's chair and plants them on his desk, next to some of the newspaper clippings he's collected from the victim's room and the book from next to the victim's bed.

'Make yourself comfy.'

He pulls his chair out from under his desk and slightly loosens his tie.

'So, you finally got the corner office you were after!'

'After their star officer handed in her shield, they didn't have much of a choice, did they?' The detective rubs the bridge of his nose, as if nursing a migraine.

The filing unit behind him displays two framed pictures: the first one of me and Kukadia as young officers receiving our medal for gallantry and service in the line of duty; the second photo is slightly crumpled and bent. It's a picture of Paul's now-ex-wife and his daughter as a baby.

Kukadia swivels his chair around when he sees me looking. He stares at the image of us.

'Seems like a lifetime ago when we received those medals, eh?'

'I think I still have mine somewhere. You?' I ask.

'No! I got rid of that a long time ago when I realised that bringing down the Dragon just made things worse. And let's not forget his promise of chopping both our heads off when he gets out.'

'Luckily for us he's serving three life sentences.'

Kukadia continues to stare solemnly at the pictures.

'Do you still see your daughter?'

'Nope!' The detective turns his chair back to the desk and logs into his computer. 'She made sure of that, when she took everything I owned.'

He stops typing for a moment. 'Funny really, if I passed her on the street now I don't think she would even recognise me! Probably for the best.'

He resumes typing and I leave that line of conversation there. Some things are best left unspoken.

'Finally!' the detective says, looking at the screen. 'The lab results from your mystery substance just arrived. He mumbles to himself as he scans the documents. While I wait, I pick up the victim's book from the desk. Inside is a collection of old poems and stories. I flick through and it lands on a page which still holds the creased memory of its deceased owner.

'*Kubla Khan* by Samuel Taylor Coleridge?'

The detective breaks away from the screen as I begin to read.

'Yeah, strange book. Definitely not to my taste. I looked through it earlier. I was hoping we might get lucky and pull some DNA from our killer, seeing as how the book was so close to the bed. But nothing. Just some highlighted and circled words from some crazy old writer who was clearly off his face.'

I read the poem, paying attention to the parts that have been circled and highlighted:

> *'And mid these dancing rocks at once and ever*
> *It flung up momently the sacred river.'*

I'm not familiar with the work but the victim clearly found this passage important, circling it multiple times.

An arrow points towards the sentence, under which are the scribbled words: *'THE GATEWAY!'*

I continue to read the poem, trying to envision its abstract yet highly descriptive writing style. Near the end, I hit upon a passage that also stood out to our victim:

> *'And all should cry, Beware! Beware!*
> *His flashing eyes, his floating hair!*
> *Weave circles around him thrice,*
> *And close your eyes with holy dread . . .'*

Next to this section, two words are written in bold capitals: *'THE FIRST!'* Out of the whole book, this poem, this passage was the only section the victim analysed. Why?

'Guess what?! Our test results came back negative. According to this report, everyone in the vicinity at the time the substance was dispersed was infected. It must have settled by the time we arrived, so it wasn't infectious.'

The detective scans the screen for more information.

'A large number of patients and staff had a concentrated amount within their system. Symptoms vary from sudden paralysis, short-term memory loss, hallucination, and narcolepsy. That's why we were feeling tired. Unbelievable. The good news is that it doesn't seem to be fatal. Some of the staff members are already starting to recover.'

'Did they identify the substance?' I ask.

'That's the bad news; they haven't been able to give a definitive answer. At the moment it's just being referred to as Red Sand.'

'Red Sand . . . ?'

Kukadia clicks through the tabs on his browser and I take out my phone to send an encrypted message to my informant, otherwise known as Mr X, who I still have not heard back from.

14:02 — Sent: First was the spark . . .

Now I wait for a response.

* * *

Mr X first made contact with me when I was asked to look into suspected corruption on incoming shipments via the canal system. Since the United Kingdom fell apart, the canal ways in Birmingham have become a reinvested transport option for the city. It made sense; the city boasts more canal passages than Venice, which most Brummies will tell you unprompted. It was a smart move on paper, but unfortunately this gave opportunity to those with a more sinister purpose. As an officer, I was well aware of the so-called 'red zones' that had been carved out by the Dragon. Many of us bluebottles never ventured anywhere near its murky banks; those who did, well . . . They were never seen again. As Kaine Nelson's Loop grew, it didn't take long for the waters to become swamped with illegal activity: weapons, human trafficking, narcotics, back-handed dealings, you name it, it was rife. To this day it's still a lawless labyrinth, which the authorities struggle to contain. The problem is that parts of the waterways run through gang territory and other parts of the Industrial, which makes total control impossible.

While I was attempting to find something tangible to present in my investigation of the canals, I received an anonymous tip. This enabled me to narrow my search down to four officers within the CMPD, who were allegedly deep in the Loop's pockets. After a lengthy process we nailed them; in total, nine officers were arrested and charged. The strange thing was, they never once tried to challenge or defend their actions. All settled for harder sentences, unwilling to cooperate or pinpoint those still in the system. And that burned, knowing that we were missing something. The case closed and we were none the wiser as to what was being shipped into the city. The canal system continues to play its part in supplying Birmingham with the tools it needs for chaos to grow. It's hard to pat yourself on the back for a job half-done, but — luckily for me — that's when my anonymous friend unofficially introduced himself: Mr X.

He said he was a friend of the city and began to direct me down the road of missing individuals, especially those assumed to be suicides, specifically those that had drowned in their bed. It was hard for me to grasp at first but, as more deaths started to pile up, I noticed the stench of cover-ups. It wasn't hard to see that there was something much more insidious going on, right under the gaze of those who had taken an oath to protect and serve. I've been walking the trail with Mr X ever since.

Ping!
1 new message
14:08 — Imādris gave birth.

Finally, a response! I quickly text back the last part of our coded greeting, hoping that Mr X might know something about this substance.

14:09 — Sent: Infinite light formed!

14:09 — How can I help you Elizabeth?

14:09 — Sent: Newly deceased victim, possibly our killer.

Elderly male found in a residential home.

Lacerations across left eye and the word 'guilty' branded onto his chest.

14:10 — Interesting. Cause of death?

14:10 — Sent: Still waiting for official report but looks to be the same — asphyxiation. Found in his bed drenched with water.

14:10 — Was another symbol left behind?

14:11 — Sent: No, but we found something of interest. Think killer may have been using it to drug his victims.

14:11 — ?

14:12 — Sent: Properties and molecular makeup still unknown but oddly looks a bit like red sand.

. . .

I wait eagerly for a response but I don't get one. The three dots disappear from my screen.

14:14 — Sent: ??

Nothing.

'Bingo!' the detective exclaims, clapping his hands together.

'What is it?' I ask, still looking down at my phone.

'Cara — the victim from the hotel. I asked for her final autopsy report to be sent over — and guess what?! Traces of the same red sand substance was also found in her system!'

'That must be what the coroner was rushing to try and tell us before he was killed,' I add.

'Must've been. At least now we have a feasible link between the two deaths. We just need to figure out a connection.'

'What time are we speaking with Charlotte?' I ask.

'She should be here soon. But listen we're going to have to tread lightly, she's been through hell these last couple of weeks with her twin sister's death, identifying the body, she unstable it's only now that she's agreed to talk to us.'

I start to look through some of the newspapers that the victim collected. They all seem to be dated within a specific time frame, going back to around fifteen years ago. I skim through random articles, comparing two or three newspapers at a time. Why did he keep these specific cuttings?

'There you are!' I voice to myself, as I make a discovery.

Kukadia glances up.

'Jill, the woman who came to visit the deceased victim at the old people's home, mentioned that he'd worked at Saint Mordred's before it burnt down, right?' I ask him as I read.

'Yeah. Yeah, she did say that.'

'I think I've found something in this article. Does the name Sarah Barns ring a bell?'

A look of recognition flashes across his face. He furrows his brow. I'm reminded of the last time I saw him make that face, when Jill mentioned the name of the hospital.

'Sarah Barns, Sarah Barns,' Kukadia repeats to himself. He closes his eyes, searching his memory. 'Why do I know that name?'

'You'd heard of Saint Mordred's before, right?'

'Yeah . . . '

'Well?!'

'Ghost stories. My mother used to tell me and my siblings stories about that place to frighten us: asylums, experiments, a labyrinth of cages below the city. Urban myths, that's all; a horror story for a lot of inner-city kids.'

'Take a look at this.'

I hand the newspaper to Kukadia and he begins to read aloud: 'Saint Mordred's burns in inferno! Innocent lives lost and many critically injured . . . The fire reportedly broke out at 3:15 p.m. Firefighters battled all day to combat its blazing fury . . .'

He peers over the newspaper at me and lowers his voice.

'When that place burnt down, a lot of things started to surface about its history. There might've been some truth to the horror stories. I read an article about the mistreatment of the mentally ill in our city, from past to present. It was heavy stuff, even for me, and Saint Mordred's was top of the list. The place was supposedly a deathtrap: experiments, shock therapy, inhumane torture, you name it, a complete hell-hole. After the turn of the century, officials eventually grew a conscience and closed the place down. It was abandoned for ages and was said to have been secretly used by the occultist Aleister Crowley — the self-proclaimed "Son of the Devil."'

I don't say anything but my eyebrow gives me away.

'Just telling you what I read. Crowley was rumoured to have done all sorts of weird and crazy shit down there in those ruins. Séances, sacrifices, and high society orgies. Decades later, the site was restored and reopened, but it never shook its damaged reputation.'

I pull out my phone to try searching for more information as the detective looks at another article.

'The fire resulted in the death of Sarah Barns. She was a patient there,' Kukadia reads. 'A lengthy legal case was due to take place to determine whether or not the fire was deliberately started.'

'Strange,' I say. 'There's no mention of Sarah Barns online, not even the court proceedings. The only information is that the hospital burnt down.'

'"An unfortunate death and the nail in the coffin to what many already believed was a cursed blight on our city . . ." And our victim — John — he worked there?'

'Yeah. Can you pull up some case files on there? This is useless,' I say, discarding my phone on the detective's desk.

Kukadia turns back to his computer and turns the screen so I can see.

'Let me try and widen my search.' He types away, entering specific reference words. 'File locked! What's that about?' He frustratedly types in a passcode but again it fails. 'Their files should not be data protected! Give me a minute . . .'

Kukadia continues typing away, trying to bypass the security; meanwhile, I check my phone again and send another message to Mr X. Very strange that he suddenly went dark.

'We're in!'

Kukadia starts to bring up archived pictures and case files relating to the fire, as well as log books and evidence submitted during the investigation.

'Why has all this information been kept under lock and key?' I ask. 'Can you bring up employment details so we can see when he was there?'

He scrolls down a list of names.

'The victim's name doesn't seem to be here,' the detective says, scanning the screen. 'I can't find a John Mitchell anywhere— Hang on . . . Just found something else.'

'What?'

'A Doctor Emit Barns — associate medical physician and therapist, specialising in advanced treatment, around the same time as the fire.'

'Barns? As in Sarah Barns?'

Kukadia clicks on the name. Files begin to pop open on the screen, as well as a group picture of staff members, their names assigned underneath them.

'Emit Barns, there he is!' the detective says, pointing. A tall, skinny man with jet-black, slicked hair stands out amongst the other employees.

'It says he was employed at Saint Mordred's for six years. Your intuitions were right; he was the older brother of Sarah Barns.'

'Was?'

'Deceased,' Kukadia informs, clicking on another file.

I read over the next file on the screen: a note-form summary of the investigation and court hearing. Five individuals, including Doctor Barns, were suspected of unsanctioned treatments and arson.

'Looks like Barns never got his day in court,' Kukadia announces. 'Suspected suicide; his body was never recovered.'

Kukadia and I look at each other as we spot familiar words in the autopsy report.

'He . . . drowned?'

'Paul . . .'

'Already on it!' Kukadia interjects. He pulls Emit Barns's last known address. 'It's a long shot but it's something at least.'

'Go back to the staff pictures, please.' I ask. The detective obliges and I look more closely at the picture. 'Zoom in there.'

I lean closer to the screen, tilting my head slightly and looking intensely at one of the individuals.

'Who does that look like?'

He looks at the image then zooms in again.

'I'll be damned!' Kukadia exclaims. 'It's John!'

'Now look at the name.'

'Alfred Haultz . . . ?' The detective says in confusion. 'So let me get this straight: our victim, John Mitchell, is Alfred Haultz? He changed his name — why?!'

Suddenly the file disappears from the screen, as do the other documents and files.

'What's happening?' I ask.

'Someone's deleting the files!'

'Can you stop it?'

'Not from here. Someone must be doing it from the central hub. It's the mole!'

At once, Kukadia jumps up out of his chair and darts out of the room. I follow him as he runs in the direction of the central computer room, yelling at officers to move out the way. Kukadia barges through the half-open hub door, out of breath— only to find the room empty.

'Damn it!' He kicks the bin over in frustration. He looks around the computer room. All but one of the desktop screens are off. He goes back outside, looking up and down the corridor.

'Everything alright, detective?' a plain-shirted IT staff member enters holding a hot drink.

Without hesitation, the detective lashes out and grabs the poor man, slapping the coffee out of his hand and slamming him against the wall.

'Paul!' I shout, trying to the calm the situation as onlookers notice the commotion.

'Who else has access to the computers?!' Before the IT guy can get his words out, the detective claws at him again, gripping him tighter. 'Come on, spit it out!'

'N-n-no one — just me and one other maintenance worker but she's not here today.'

'Where is she?!'

'At home; she's ill! She's been at home all week.'

'Paul!' I shout again, trying to get the detective to ease up. Kukadia lets go of the IT guy, who looks pretty shaken up.

'What're you all looking at?!' the detective yells at the group of onlookers that has formed. 'Don't you all have work to do, criminals to catch?!' The small crowd disperses quickly.

'You! In here!' Kukadia says to the IT guy, going back inside the computer room.

'What's this all about?'

'Someone's been blocking and deleting files and that can only be done by one of these computers. Since the others are off, I'm assuming it's this one.'

'Look, detective, I don't—'

'Oi, I don't want any excuses! The one thing I hate more than criminals are dirty cops, so you're going to tell me who last logged in.'

The IT guy nods his head fearfully and cooperates.

'Are those cameras working yet?' Kukadia points above the door.

'No, most of the equipment is still fried from the Blackout. We're working to get everything sorted.'

We both stand waiting, watching the technician work. My mind wanders — who might benefit from deleting and hiding this information?

'Anything?' the detective asks impatiently.

'No, nothing . . . Sorry. Whoever used it covered their tracks well. There's also a high possibility that your hacker switched to a remote device and manipulated the system from elsewhere. The Blackout fried a lot of our security system, we're still playing catch-up. I'm sorry!'

The detective breathes out a sigh of frustration and we leave the room.

'Why does it feel like I'm always one step behind?! That

information has been sitting there and it's only now we make the connection.'

'Nothing good ever comes easily, Paul; you know this,' I say, trying to keep positive. 'It's a stretch but at least we have names and questions that need answers. Something will give, it always does. In the meantime, let's dig into why John Mitchell changed his name — what was he running from? And who was Doctor Emit Barns, and his sister Sarah, and those involved in the fire? We have a last known address — let's follow it!'

'Detective, come quickly!' a voice calls from the far side of the corridor, grabbing our attention. We turn and see Officer Lace beckoning urgently.

'What's going on?' Kukadia asks as we rush over to the officer.

'It's Charlotte— something's happened. This way; she's been held in an interview room.'

The detective stomps in the direction of the interview area. Lace and I follow closely behind.

'Did you manage to find any more leads on the serial killer?' the young officer asks.

'Possibly.'

'Oh, good!' Lace says with a youthful optimism, reminding me of myself as a young bluebottle. 'Hopefully we can nick whoever's behind it soon and put an end to this nightmare.'

'Hopefully. We have a name and an address. It's a long shot but—'

My words fall short, hearing hysterical shouting and Charlotte's muffled cries.

We charge into the room.

Charlotte is being held in place by Officer Scott, who has her handcuffed to the table, pressing his hands on her shoulders to keep her seated.

'Detective, I need to speak with you — I saw it! I need to

talk to you — please, I'm not crazy, I need to talk!' Charlotte blurts, tripping over her words. Her face is drenched with tears, panic, and fear.

'Okay, calm down. I'm here now,' the detective says. He turns his attention to Officer Scott, who is standing like a statue, unmoved by Charlotte's distress. 'Why is she cuffed?!'

'Thought she might hurt herself, sir!'

'Uncuff her now!'

The officer slowly takes Charlotte's handcuffs off, but keeps his eyes fixed on me in a cold stare. Officer Lace, clearly uncomfortable in his presence, looks down at the floor.

'Seems you have a knack for misjudging a situation, officer,' I say, hoping to get a reaction.

Scott looks at me, then at Lace and the detective. Mindful of his surroundings, he doesn't take the bait. He smirks to himself and puts away his handcuffs, seemingly unfazed by my comment.

'We'll take it from here. You can both leave now.'

'Sir, she could be—'

'Did I stutter, officer?! I said leave, now!'

Both officers exit the room and Charlotte rubs her wrists where the handcuffs used to be.

'Sorry about that, Charlotte. I'll be having words with him after we finish. You'll have the opportunity to file a complaint, of course.'

We sit down and I hand her a tissue to wipe away her tears. She calms herself and takes a deep breath, readying herself to speak.

'It's my sister, detective . . .'

'I'm sorry. I understand; we know the last couple of weeks must've been very upsetting seeing a loved one under such circumstances. We'll make sure that we organise a grief councillor for you.'

More tears roll down Charlotte's cheeks. Again, she tries to collect herself before getting her words out.

'My sister — Cara — she knew this would happen to her!'

Kukadia opens his mouth, but I grab his arm under the table to stop him from interrupting.

'She . . . she told me many times that something was chasing her . . . in her . . . in her dreams. I didn't believe her, I think I just didn't want to. We had been through so much; I couldn't lose another family member — first Mum, then Cassey, and now . . .

'Okay, take your time Charlotte,' I say, trying to keep her calm.

'You're saying this has happened before?' Kukadia exclaims.

In my pocket, my phone starts to vibrate, multiple times in succession, but I stay engaged.

Charlotte swallows her tears: 'Cassey started getting the dreams first. It started a couple of years back, just after she . . .' Charlotte hesitates slightly. 'You see, she started to get really fast. And strong. Like, really strong.'

The detective knits his eyebrows, confused — which makes two of us.

'After Cassey had run away, it wasn't long until things started to happen again, just like before. Only this time with Cara. One minute she would be sleeping, then she would disappear in a flash of blue smoke and end up on the roof! Well, at least that's how she explained it. I know it all sounds crazy but I just need you to hear me out.

'Our mother died fifteen years ago. They told us it was suicide — she'd drowned herself. We were only young . . . She used to move us from place to place, house to house. We thought it was a game until . . . it wasn't anymore. She used to tell us that we were from here — Birmingham — but we moved around so much after Mum's work burnt down that we didn't know where to call home.'

The detective looks at me, silently acknowledging the familiar set of words.

'When I saw your announcement on the news, I knew I had to get in contact. I went to visit her one last time to say goodbye, you know, before they ... just then — seeing her just lying there cold, grey, bloated — I knew it was all true. It was like déjà vu; I had seen this happening before. It had tried to drown Cassey, but she escaped. Cara promised she wouldn't do the same thing and leave me alone, but she has. I was so angry at her leaving me — I didn't answer her calls ... And now ... Now she's dead! My family's cursed, detective ... ' Charlotte bawls.

The detective hands her another tissue.

'Your mother ... what did she do for a living?' he asks.

'Some sort of doctor. She never really spoke about it much.'

'And Cassey — she was your older sister?' the detective pries.

'Yes, by seven minutes; we were triplets. And now it's coming for me!' Charlotte's eyes widen in fear.

'What is?' I ask.

'It knows I'm here!'

'Who does?' Kukadia asks.

'It's coming for me, it's going to get me!' Charlotte yells manically.

'Who's coming for you?!' The detective has to raise his voice above her clamouring. Charlotte's eyes close and her hands starts to clutch and scratch at the table. She begins to shake as if she's having a fit.

'EYES RED, HOOVES FOR FEET! A WALKING DEMONIC NIGHTMARE WITH A MASK OF DEATH!' Charlotte wails hysterically, waving her arms.

She repeats the words over and over as if in a trance. Kukadia attempts to calm her, struggling to keep her in her seat, almost an exact recreation of the tableau we walked in on.

My mind races. That description was exactly the same as the lady in the ambulance gave ...

My phone vibrates once more. I gasp as I see the number of urgent messages I've missed:

14:54 — Messages received:
They are on to you!!

The red sand you discovered has put a mark of death on you both.

You're in danger!

Leave the police station IMMEDIATELY!

Leave now!!

Trust no one, they are watching!

Get out!!!

I immediately call over to Kukadia: 'We need to go now!'

'As you can see, Elizabeth, I'm a little occupied!' he says, holding a still very confused Charlotte, who begins to come back to her senses.

'Paul, I really need you to trust me!'

The detective knows me well enough to see the sincerity in my face.

'What the hell is going on, Elizabeth? What have you got me into?'

'Bring Charlotte with us, it will be safer!'

The detective curses under his breath, but looks at me and nods. He quickly but discreetly places a small, thin device under the computer desk. I help him pull Charlotte to her feet and we make a swift exit out the back of the station.

CHAPTER 14

Three Heads

'Zachary Zhao! You're free to go.'

EEEEEEEeeeeeeeeeHHH!!

The barred doors buzz and slide open, jamming half way and clattering to a stop. The pig officer that has come to collect me pulls out his nightstick, places it between the bars and pushes it open forcefully. I limp out of my cell, nodding in acknowledgment. For good measure, I throw up a G3 sign at the incarcerated.

'G3 forever!' I shout.

'Quiet, Red!' the officer says, walking behind me, pushing me and prodding me in the back with his nightstick. My exit down the prison walkway is greeted with a rowdy reception of boos, gun-fingers pointed at me, murderous stares, and middle-fingered goodbyes from multiple ops and rival gangs. I wink ironically and wave back like I'm on the red carpet to show them I don't care. Pricks! They're lucky they're still in here and not breathing through tubes like Trizz or Tin Man. At least in here you're kinda protected: rumours are that it's hell out there now. Blood's been spilt in the water and now unknown crews are coming to claim that third spot. I hear Golden Charley's caught a couple of bodies and carved up a fair few who've been brave enough to try it. But, with Tin Man down and most of our guys out of action too, it won't be long until he's overrun.

'Keep moving, Red!' the bluebottle instructs, prodding me again.

You'd be surprised how fast news travels in here. Word of Gecko getting snuffed spread like wildfire. At first, everyone fingered the Sons of Jack and the Obeah Kings as the obvious culprits — they both famously have no love for the Loop. But I know that, even though their lines run deep, they don't have the kind of connection to get into a secure facility, untraced and unnoticed. Whoever did it wanted to send a clear message to Cerberus. It wouldn't surprise me if it was the Ghost. Truth is, everybody in here is spooked. They talk about 'the Black Ghost' like he's some sort of mythical boogie man. We used to be the ones that gripped the streets with fear but now there's something else, prowling the rooftops and roaming the city streets and grizzly, trash-heaped alleys. The one that walks at a deathly pace, slumped over, is still out there, just waiting to pick us off one by one.

Maybe I shouldn't've taken that video, but I needed proof. Cerberus doesn't allow mistakes; I needed something to show them what we're up against. I'm not sure who or what the Ghost is — he might not abide by the laws of physics, but he's definitely real and if he's real there's gotta be a way to make him bleed.

The escorting rozzer hits his stick against the metal bars to shut the prisoners up. It doesn't work; it only escalates their rowdiness. The prison-block door closes behind me, locking magnetically. I stand in the processing area next to the scum officer, who's wishing for me to give him one reason to crack my head open and lock me back up. What he doesn't get is that leaving this place isn't freedom for me; it's death row. The Loop would rather wipe a whole circle out than have to watch for a blower.

'Get off me, you piece of shit mutton-shunter!' another prisoner yells, as he is ushered past me by two badges. I've been in here for weeks — I got off easy in the long run: a fractured ankle, bruises to the face, not too much of a biggie. At least that burning feeling streaming through my body has calmed down now. When it first happened, I felt as if I was crawling, waking from a dream. I don't know what it was but I've not felt the same since.

'Sign here . . . and here,' the desk officer instructs, as the other uncuffs my wrists.

'Who paid my bail?' I ask.

'How'd I know?! Maybe one of your scum, murdering bosses, in your sewer-infested Industrial,' the desk pawn responds. She walks over to a revolving hatch, retrieves a box of my stuff, and scans my release form. She pulls out my phone and bags it in a plastic evidence holder, then slams my bronze, die-faced lighter down hard onto the counter in front of me.

Clink sslinch!

'Careful with that!'

She eyeballs me.

'Everyone's a tough guy these days,' I scoff. How I would love to Blackbeard her smug face right now, or simply tear her throat out . . . but there'll be another time for that. Now's the time to find out who paid for my release and why.

* * *

Outside the police station, a black-tinted 4x4 skids from across the street and pulls up onto the kerb. For a sec, I thought it was gonna be a drive-by, but the car just waits, humming in neutral. I lower my head and keep walking, keeping the car in view out of the side of my eye, just in case my first instincts were right and this car's out here to bury me with a hit squad.

Skkhhhurchhh, vroom!

The car wheels spin, pumping smoke from its exhaust. It swerves, only inches away from me, almost crushing me with its massive black metal bumper. Pricks!

'What you doin'?!' I blare, picking myself up off the ground. Two well-dressed guys in fitted black suits, long black mobster coats and sunglasses step out of the car. 'Shit!' They look like associates of Mr Vagus. One of them calmly walks over to me while the other opens the back passenger door.

'You've been requested,' the associate calmly says. I look left and then right up and down the street as people go about their normal lives, oblivious to this filthy city. The open door of the 4x4 gapes at me as I look at its inviting light brown plush and leather interior. I pull out my lighter and strum.

Clink sslinch! Clink sslinch! Clink sslinch! Clink sslinch!

Well, that's a shit bit of luck; it doesn't work. Never a good omen for me when that happens. I limp over and get into the back of the vehicle, closely followed by the associate. The driver turns, removing his glasses with a cold frown. The doors slam shut quickly and I am dashed across the seat and sandwiched into the middle, wedged between the two guys. I can barely move my arms. Can't help but think that this is it for me. They're either going to choke me out here and now, or roll up to one of the many backstreets around the scrapheaps of Witton to pop me in the back of the head and dump me in the canals. The burning sensation in my chest resurfaces slightly and the car engine cuts off. The driver restarts it — two, three, four times — and it eventually revs back up. The sensation passes and I can catch my breath and start to feel normal again.

We drive through the city and I watch the streets of Brum slip by, taking it all in, maybe for the last time. For the first time in a long time I look at people's faces and see — really see — the hardship of life, the daily panic and fear ever-present in their minds as they go about their business. I've had my hand in terrorising this place, even caught a couple of bodies too. I know I ain't innocent; I chose my path. What goes around keeps going around. It was, and still is, structured violence.

We drive into the Industrial and through the Southside, passing twenty-four hour gambling joints and neon flashing lights for titty bars. Never thought I'd be seeing this dump again so soon; to be honest, I was hoping I never would. The car trails through the entrance of an old wooden crate factory and pulls up around the back. No one's around, no words are said. I sit and wait for one of these pricks to make their move. The guy to my left reaches into his inside pocket and I ready myself, closing my eyes. This is it, Zach, this is how you go.

'They're waiting,' a voice says calmly. I hear the door unlock and I look to my left at the open door. The guy in the black suit waits for me to get out of the car.

'Where we goin'?' I ask. I get no answer and the other associate pushes me out of the car. I follow the shadow of the mobster in front of me into the rear of the rusted frame of the warehouse. Tall, unopened, wooden crates line the walls and passageways of the clay-tiled hallways. I hear the sound of production and forklifts, reversing and beeping loudly. As we walk into a loading bay, I see these black, shiny cylinder-shaped bed pods with the words '*Sleep Pods*,' stencilled into the their dark glass exteriors. They're placed into the wooden crates and loaded onto trucks by some shady-looking individuals — the criminal-minded-looking types — overseen by more men in black suits and shades sporting Uzis.

'What's those things going in the crates?'

Again, the associate doesn't acknowledge my question. Leaving the truck docking area behind, we climb some metal fire safety stairs that clang and vibrate with every step. Raised voices escape from the room we are moving towards, which is being closely guarded by two more mobsters with autos. Before entering the room, I am stopped and frisked from head to toe.

'Ey, watch it! You almost grabbed my piece!' I say, straightening myself up. Eventually I'm let into the huge open space of the upper warehouse, only to be stopped dead in my tracks by what I see. Large conical metal spotlights hang from the exposed copper-panelled ceiling. At the far end of the room, sitting behind a long table out of the light, making it hard to see facial features, are three heavily guarded individuals.

'Shit!' It's Cerberus, the heads of the Loop. They're all here, gathered together in one place. And there, smack-bang in the middle of the room, directly under the centre light, his blonde dreads shining under the rays and standing tall as if awaiting his sentence, is Golden Charley. Dotted around his feet, with their heads twisted and popped to the side like discarded chickens, are some of my brothers, members of G3.

I'm hauled into the centre of the room and kicked to my knees beside Charley and the wretched corpses of my fallen comrades. Their half-opened lifeless eyes stare at me from their stricken faces like glass marbles. Bastards! Someone's going to pay for this! I look up at Charley, his calm, unshaken physical demeanour morphing into a sadistic, piercing gaze, directed towards the Three Heads at the table. He breathes slowly and deliberately under his surgical mask with wrath and malicious intent, like a ticking time bomb.

A tap squeaks as it's turned off. Looking over, I see the massive, Goliath-like frame of Mr Punch, Vagus's driver and most trusted bodyguard. He treads heavily towards me, stops, and towers above me like Frankenstein's monster, partially blocking out the glare of the spotlight. His knuckles crack as he slowly stretches his fingers, wiping the blood from his shirt, waiting for his next orders, which are most likely for him to snap me in half to join the others on the ground.

'Good of you to join us,' an emotionless female voice says from the direction of the Three Heads behind the table. One by one they lean forwards into the light, highlighting their faces like a multi-headed dog looking to devour its next meal. On the left I see a woman known by two names, the first being Madam Kishi. She sits there, staring sternly. Her hair is thick, long white dreadlocks with black tips. Her chiselled face, brown skin and razor-sharp cheek bones are sculpted to perfection, her hauntingly cold beauty almost transfixing. One side of her face is tattooed with the face of a hyena and under her bottom lip is the sign of an upside-down pitchfork with words running down her neck, which are too far away to read. Word on the streets is that she worked her way up from the workhouses onto the street corners and brothels of the city, before rising to own most of the clubs and real estate on the Southside of the Industrial. Apparently her parents gave her up willingly due to financial hardships. Well, they're now dead and it wasn't natural causes. Some say she laughed and howled as she slashed and tortured them, dancing in their blood with a smile on her face. Others say she ate pieces of their bodies, grinning maniacally while consuming their flesh. From then on, Madam Kishi was also known as Lady Hyena the Dreadful, one of the Three Heads of Cerberus and a leader of the Loop.

'You're the one who filmed the footage of the Black Ghost?' she intones, rolling her long nails against the table, which tap out an unnerving rhythm.

'Yeah, it was me,' I reply, trying to keep the fear out of my voice.

'And this "Ghost",' continues another of the Three Heads, 'who you say wiped you all out and put your pissant silver-toothed overseer in the hospital, he did it alone?'

' . . . Yeah,' I respond, as my brain belatedly acknowledges who I've just addressed: Rav the Six-Handed Raven, one of Kaine Nelson's most loyal henchmen. He used to do all his top-tier dirty work, from takeovers to collections to assassinations. When the Dragon was taken down, Rav felt personally responsible for not being able to protect him. As an act of loyalty and show of failure, he mutilated himself, cutting off his right hand. He now sports a razor-sharp, raven-clawed diamond hand. This intricate weapon he can wield as precisely as any surgeon's blade, sometimes switching between attachments for a more brutal shank, depending on the occasion. He was single-handedly responsible for the Moore Street Massacre that juiced a police chief and six pig uniforms shortly after the Dragon was jailed. The Raven is not to be trifled with. Even though he's now one of the leaders of the Loop, a top dog that doesn't get his hands as dirty as he used to, this guy's still a killer, with a reputation that few will ever obtain.

'Tell me, do you remember what this Ghost looked like?' the Raven persists with his questions.

'I . . . I can't really remember, it was all a blur. It happened so fast and it was dark. One moment he was there and then he wasn't. It was like he was a moving shadow, a ball of rage and horror, hunting us for sport.'

Some of the guards around the room look at each other unsure, then start to laugh under their breath.

'Enough with your bloody excuses and ghost stories!' Karl Vagus says, sitting in the middle of the table, his red glass-eye reflecting the light. Mr Punch keep his eyes firmly on me. The laughter stops and the room quietens.

'Charley, Charley, Charley!' Vagus says, addressing his nephew whilst he lights up a Cuban. 'You and your little red-haired Oriental girlfriend here have already cost us more than a few pennies. Because of your incompetence, people now think they can do what they want, that the Loop is broken! That video sparked a little hope of rebellion and now one of our own — the son of the Dragon — has been clipped, like a common rat!' Vagus blows smoke into the room. 'As I am sure you are well aware, this is bad for business. I'm not into excuses. You don't get the job done, you're dead, as you can both clearly see. It's about restoring the natural balance to the city. Whether or not the rumours are true about this so-called "Ghost" is neither here nor there. Violence has always been part of the place and no made-up ghost story is going to stop us—'

'It's not a ghost story though!' I say. 'He's something el—'

'Don't you ever interrupt me again, boy!' Mr Vagus cuts me off, gritting his teeth in anger. He then nods his head, motioning one of the guards to place a pistol against Charley's head, who doesn't even flinch. A heavy, brick-footed kick from Mr Punch hits me square in the chest. I land on my back next to the guard.

'End them,' says Vagus. The burning feeling I experienced returns and flows through my body, but this time it feels slightly different. Seeing the guard cock his hammer, ready to blow Charley's brains out, I reach out to grab his leg to stop him as he squeezes the trigger . . .

Click click . . . Click click.

His gun jams!

Click click . . . Click.

Bang!

The guard's gun fires but somehow the barrel malfunctions and shoots backwards, punching a hole between his eyes. The guard crashes to the floor, a dead weight. Charley looks down with the slightest flicker of amazement in his glare.

Vagus snaps his fingers and Mr Punch growls and stomps. The floor shakes as he rushes at Charley and me.

Crack! Boof!

Wooden splinters explode from a huge crate, sending Mr Punch flying across the room. The guards all snap to attention, readying their guns. Walking casually from the door, with blaring white eyes, are two bald women — one Black, one White — both in smart, white jumpsuits. The blaring light from their eyes starts to fade and they stroll, confidently, fearlessly into the centre of the room like felines, walking in unison. Who the hell are they? I've never seen this gang before.

I rack my brains, trying to work out who they might be affiliated to, based on any tattoos I can recognise. I spot different zodiac signs imprinted into the skin on their wrists and necks. The White lady has an Aries sign on her; the Black lady has a Sagittarius. All the guns around the room point in their direction, yet, when they reach the centre, they stand there, unfazed and focused.

'What do you want?' the Hyena asks bluntly.

'Something of ours was placed in your possession and you have lost it,' Aries answers.

'And now we want you to retrieve it. You were entrusted to keep them safe and you have failed,' the other bald lady continues.

'How dare you come in here unannounced!' the Raven shouts.

Vagus puts out his cigar and looks over at Mr Punch who is completely out for the count, a picture no one has ever seen before.

'As you can see, ladies, we're currently busy,' Vagus responds, his tone noticeably changed.

'We have not come to ask.'

'We have to come to demand.'

The Raven slams his diamond-clawed spikes into the table. 'Do you know where you are right now?!' he shouts in a threatening tone. The women look at each other and blink simultaneously.

'Your predecessors would never have done this with the Dragon! We do not take orders; we give them!' the Raven continues, switching to Urdu to add insults into the mix.

As he goes on clapping his gums, the femme fatale on the right strides towards the Raven. One of his bodyguards steps into her path and charges at her, his gun pointed. Before he can even get a shot off, Aries springs in the air towards him, presses one thumb onto the area around his arm and the other thumb near his heart, freezing him in agonising pain. Without her even breaking stride, he melts to the floor like paper, dead as a doornail. The other guards bravely raise their guns but Vagus and the Hyena raise their hands to stop them.

'You must have an early death wish,' the Raven says, standing readying his claw.

The Aries lady says nothing in response, but continues her run.

'Go and tell your master at Ava—'

Before the Raven can even finish his word, from three feet away, she rapidly leaps, flipping forwards onto the table. She rips the claw from his hand and embeds it into his skull with such speed that it blurs.

Doof!

The Raven's body drops forwards onto the table. Another guard finds confidence from somewhere and tries to shoot the Aries in the back as she crouches on the table over the Raven's body. He is quickly snapped in two by Sagittarius, who whips around him so fast that nobody sees her. We only hear a *snap* as his body slumps.

Vagus and the Hyena immediately stand to attention. Everyone in the room saw the unnatural speed and strength that these women moved with. The guards holster their weapons. The woman on the table, unscathed, walks up and down its wooden surface like a lioness, marking her dominance as she kicks the

Raven's body off the table like discarded trash.

'What is it you want?' the Hyena asks.

'The red sand, the sample that was placed in your possession, is in the hands of police. The ones who sent us cannot allow that,' the lady on the table says.

'Attention has been diverted in our direction. Our leader is not impressed. Do not forget that the only reason your operation in this city exists is because we allow it. You work for us!' the other reiterates.

'You want us to attack and raid a police station? Do you even know what you're asking? How that will look?! Even with the officers on our payroll, this will get messy,' Vagus says with a frown.

'The detective and the woman will no longer be under the police's protection,' Aries says, still on the table.

'We have made arrangements for the woman and her inform- ant,' they say in unison. 'They shall be judged. Death awaits them both!'

'We will deal with them and you shall be called upon! Be ready!' Sagittarius continues, totally ignoring Vagus's concerns.

'But what about business? The crates and the shipments?' the Hyena asks.

'There is no business without the ones who sent us,' they say simultaneously.

'They are the Watchers,' one says eerily.

'The cogs in the wheel.'

'We see all, we are all,' they utter again in unison.

The Aries lady dismounts from the table and joins the other. They both walk towards me and Golden Charley.

'Tell us what happened,' they say as one. 'Tell us about the Black Ghost!'

CHAPTER 15

CheckMATE!

Boom!

Roarrrrrrrrrrrr!

'Attack!'

A rapturous shout and the fierce cry of hundreds of voices erupts, followed by the sounds of swords clashing, shields splintering, and the hissing whoosh of arrows released from bow strings flying through the air.

I'm in the middle of a great battle, treading through thick mud towards an army of Orcs, whose red eyes glare at me with malicious intent. I advance forward, alongside other knights, to infiltrate the enemy's imposing nightmarish castle.

'Fire!' a loud voice orders.

A trebuchet releases a gigantic boulder through the smoke-filled, fire-scorched sky. The ground shakes with a thunderous crack, as the boulder topples parts of the castle wall, sending enemy infantry hurtling in different directions.

'This way to the princess, Sir Jacobs!'

I break formation from the rest of the army as they continue to battle, holding the enemy at bay. I move towards the battlements, accompanied by a small party of knights. We engage more foes and their beastly goblin companions in battle. I parry, slash, and slice, cutting down more hordes with my Buster Sword as we advance and make our way to the tower.

'We will stand guard here, Sir Jacobs, and await your return,' a knight says.

I enter the tower and begin to make my way up the crooked spiral stairway, passing oil-soaked wooden torches that burn brightly, as the sound of battle rages beyond the walls.

Creeeak!

I push open the huge, spiked wooden gates and enter the throne room. Sitting slouched on the throne, with a crown made of human bones, interwoven with gold and shiny red rubies, is the grotesque Orc King. He slurps from a huge ivory goblet; his other hand grips a metal chain, which shackles the veiled princess beside him.

'Who dares to enter my throne room?!' the Orc King spits in a deep, husky growl.

I edge towards him, slowly raising my sword.

'So, you're the brave knight?!' the Orc King smirks as he stands up, towering above me with monstrous height. The iron chains lift, raising the Princess off the ground like a weightless petal.

The Orc throws his goblet to the ground and grins, revealing sharp, glistening, silver teeth.

He stomps towards me.

'Dark is the night for ghouls and ghosts!' he spews, which causes me to drop my guard. I freeze. The Orc King laughs, a bone-chillingly reminiscent laugh, then rips the veil from the princess to reveal her face. Leiyah.

'Joseph, help!' she shouts, sending shock waves through my body.

Seeing her dangling and in danger, I waste no time. I charge at full speed, clashing steel against iron as our swords collide.

Clang!

Our blades lock and grind against each other; sparks flick in every direction from the friction.

'Ouff!'

I am over powered and lose my sword as I clatter to the floor.

'You were too weak to help her before,' the Orc King says, pulling Leiyah's chains. 'What makes you think you can save her now?!'

'Help me, Joseph! Use your ability to save me. Show us what you did the night of the Blackout!' Leiyah shouts, but I notice a slight change in her voice. Something's not right.

The Orc King throws Leiyah across the room, then swings his huge cleaver-shaped sword above his head to finish me off with a final blow. I close my eyes, awaiting my fate.

'Yes, that's it, Joseph! Show us who you really are! If you love me, you'll save me!' Leiyah shouts aggressively, uncharacteristically. As she does so, her voice completely changes. It sounds like Doctor Roth speaking.

My eyes open and I see everything in purple, as if a filter has been placed over my eyes. Time slows down and I see black smoke emitting from my body.

'Yes, show us! What can you do?' the doctor's voice continues to yell in a warped, slowed-down tone.

Leiyah's face begins to glitch and distort. This is not real, I'm dreaming; they've done it again. It's a trap!

'Wake up!' I say to myself, inches away from the Orc King's sword. 'I said: WAKE UP NOW!'

Beep-beep-beep-beep-beep-beep!

I snap back to reality, restrained to a medical bed. Wires connect me to a rapidly bleeping machine. My face is strapped with an oxygen mask. I shout out and wriggle uncontrollably, in a dazed and discombobulated panic.

Pick!

A sharp scratch stings my left arm and I feel a numb sensation that brings me down to a calm state . . .

'Please note that once again the patient's semi-induced Sub-Con therapy was unsuccessful,' Doctor Roth's voice instructs. 'In our next attempt we will need a more concentrated dose.'

Doctor Roth leans over me and shines a light into my eyes. 'The subject is still responsive,' he notes.

He removes the light from my eyes and takes off his surgical gloves. 'Well, Joseph, we almost had you there, didn't we? Sadly I made the mistake of adding your visitor as a romantic incentive. That was clearly an error on my behalf. Whatever you are hiding, whatever ability you're harbouring, I will find it.'

'You're a monster,' I mumble groggily under the oxygen mask.

'You should be grateful. The lady wanted to dispose of you. She thinks you're more trouble than you're worth. I, on the other hand, convinced her that there *is* something special about you, something worth cultivating. How about we try another scenario but we delve deeper into your dreams?'

'No more, please!'

'Double the dosage!' the doctor orders. His assistant resets the machines.

'Doctor Roth! Come quickly, it's an emergency! There's been a breach!' a security porter announces.

Doctor Roth urgently leaves the room, followed closely by his assistant. In his haste he forgets to tighten the restraint around my left wrist. Left alone, and in a weak and drowsy state, I begin to unfasten the restraints that have confined me to the bed. I slowly but surely pull myself up. I have no idea how they're able to induce dreams as easily as selecting a film or replaying a level on a video game. It's just as Armin said: they've managed to harness the power of dreams, peering into the subconscious mind and using it at will for manipulation and control. Who are these people?!

I take small steps towards the door, trying to keep my balance as I try the handle. No luck, it's locked! The handle won't even turn without the access card and, the way my head is spinning, even if I could get out of this room I wouldn't get far . . . I think over my limited options.

It's a long shot but maybe I could . . . ?

I perch back onto the side of the bed and place my hands over my eyes once again in a pyramid shape, hoping to make contact with Sketch. Right, here goes; you can do it. Just like before — exactly like the professor told you — calm yourself, focus, and count: 'One . . . Two . . .'

Focus, Joseph. You've done this before. C'mon, clear your mind . . .

'One . . . Two . . . Three—'

* * *

A surreal airy feeling behind my eyes unlocks, as invisible walls around my mind fall and disappear. I feel like I'm hovering, floating on air, losing all the physical restraints on my body. I travel through light and sound and, once again, I enter into the darkness that is the beautiful, black, crystallised abyss. As before, multiple spectacles of starlight form above me and they begin to shine and glimmer, kaleidoscopically, magnificently. Different pathways reveal themselves under my feet and structures start to self-create from the black diamond stones. They move and join up with each other as one great big orchestrated construction. I stand there, marvelling at its grandeur.

The pathway beneath my feet glows. With each step I take forward, a soft melodic vocal tone fluctuates and plays, like a child's piano stepping mat.

What is that? I look down at a pulsing display of colour under my feet. I vary my speed as I continue to walk. More of the mysterious vocal melody plays, adding more notes and harmonies to each phrase, enriching the sound.

'It sounds like a lullaby,' I say, stopping in my tracks to listen to the ethereal voice softly singing all around me. 'A lullaby I know . . .'

I close my eyes, listening as the composition repeats. I rack my brain. I hear the gentle rumble of stones shaking. I open my eyes again to see a new structure created on the path in front of me.

'Whoa!'

It's a house. Not just any house; it's my house, my childhood home, the one that haunts my memories as a blazing inferno. The black diamonds have recreated it almost perfectly, except here it's not on fire. It's perfect. The path pulses towards the house and the lullaby projects from the newly built structure as if calling out to me.

As I step towards the patio entrance, I hear voices and the source of the lullaby gently being hummed by someone from within the house. I creep quietly, not knowing what to expect, and reach for the front door handle.

A sudden voice from within startles me: 'What was that?! Did you hear something?'

A male voice. The humming stops.

'Are you sure you are not hearing things again?' replies a soft female voice. I step closer towards the window nearest the front door, crouching to listen. Shadows move behind the closed blinds.

'You can never be too careful, Ayamey,' the male speaker says with caution. 'If they find us they will come for the—'

'Nusho!' she replies. That must be his name. 'Calm yourself! Do not speak things into existence over the child. You know the power of words and thought. Speak only of things as they are: be present, be centred, be one. We are safe. You have made no mistakes and for that he is safe.'

'Tīřuvà-ëd aśūto bà-ëd, sdokhrē-ëd aśūto dokhri-ëd.'

They both then speak in an unusual dialect, which makes no sense to me but, again, sounds comfortingly familiar. Their tone and words vibrate almost melodically, their harmonising tones and inflections complementing each other which send a tingling ripple of energy around my body.

'I suppose you are right, Ayamey. Old habits die hard,' he says.

'By the Seven Infinite Rivers you have got us this far. Now, let us enjoy this new life and the precious joys it brings.' Ayamey starts to hum her soothing lullaby again. 'The Twelve Blue Moons of Imādris shine down on us, my little one. We are all protected.'

'Imādris?' I mouth quietly to myself. It's that word again!

'He is so tiny!' she says, affectionately.

'Yes, but don't forget who he is and his purpose. Do you think in time he will remember?'

'Shh! Not now, Nusho. Let us enjoy this time and pretend for once that we are a normal family,' Ayamey proudly exclaims. 'He is such stuff as dreams are made on, our precious and most beloved **Amātriā**: Joseph!'

I hear the sound of a baby stirring momentarily then, as Ayamey softly hums on her sweet song, it quietens. I sit there listening, with a loving warm feeling as the lullaby fills my heart and mind, and I wipe happy tears from my eyes. Those are my parents: Ayamey and Nusho, my real mother and father. I've been waiting for this moment my whole life.

I jump up, nervous, excited to actually see them both in the flesh.

'Mum! Dad!' I call out, rushing to the front door to let myself in. 'I'm here! It's your Joseph!'

The house shudders as I push the door. It won't open. I push again and the black diamonds begin to unsettle and rumble. One stone falls, then more crumble from the top of the house.

The lullaby continues and I try to shout over it: 'No please, please! Mum! Dad! I'm here!'

I'm so close, let me just see them!

'Please — Mum! Dad! Open up! It's me, Joseph!'

I desperately try again to let myself in, but the crumbling house topples, collapsing backwards like a raging wave, rejoining the now dimmed path.

I fall to my knees. The voices of my parents and lullaby fade and disappear into the dormant, glistening stones and I stare with tear-filled eyes at where the structure used to be, reaching out into the void . . .

'What was even the point?!' I shout, clutching my belly. I lie down on the path where the house was . . . I was so close. I begin to hum the melody of the lullaby to myself for comfort.

The path gently shakes and pulses with colour again and I hear a faint echo in the black distance:

'Hey . . . '

Hey . . .

Hey . . .

'Bushy Head — over here!'

'Huh?!' I wipe my face with my hands and sit up, looking around.

'Over here, Bushy Head!'

'Sketch?' I call to the echo. I get no reply. 'Where are you?' I shout.

'Here!'

I turn around in alarm. Sketch stands there in what I can only describe as an Astro-projected black diamond form, glowing with an indigo aurora around her. She giggles, seeing me startled at her appearance.

'I still haven't got used to this yet,' I say, poking at her hand to see if I can physically touch her.

'Quit doing that, Bushy Head!' she says, sticking a sparkling tongue out at me.

'How did you find me?'

'I've been looking for you for the last couple of days in here. Guess I just got lucky. Where are you?'

'In one of Doctor Roth's rooms, hooked up to a machine.'

'Oh, not good!'

'Yeah, very not good.'

'I've been trying to warn you!'

'Warn me? About what?'

'I heard them talking. They know that there's more to you than meets the eye. Whatever tests they're running on you, it's not working. They want me to "sketch" you!'

'What do you mean?'

'I can create images from the past and future. All I need is someone or something to focus on. If I do, it'll mean they'll know you're the Black Ghost!'

'Can't you just blag it? Make it up?'

'It doesn't work like that, Bushy Head. I don't even know how I do it, but once I'm locked onto a subject it pretty much creates itself. Some can be more difficult than others but, if I don't do it, she's going to put you to sleep permanently! And . . . And . . .' Sketch hesitates fearfully, before speaking her next words: 'Terminate me!'

Suddenly Sketch turns her head, as if she's heard something.

'What's up?' I ask.

'Back in a sec.' Sketch's eyes close and she freezes like a statue.

'Sketch . . . ?' I say, prodding at her diamond form, which crumbles to the floor.

'I'm back!' she exclaims, reappearing behind me again, causing me to jump.

'I really wish you wouldn't do that!'

'Stop being a scaredy-cat, Bushy Head.'

'Where did you go?'

'Something's going on out there, on the other side. Looks serious; staff are rushing around and alarms are going off. We need to get out of this place.'

'I've tried, it's impossible. We can't escape.'

'Can't you just use your powers again?'

'It's not that simple! Like you, I don't know how it works. I don't know how I did what I did that night.'

'Maybe we—'

Before Sketch can finish her sentence, a bright blast of that same terrible, blinding white light appears again in the distance.

'We need to go, now,' Sketch says fretfully.

'What is that thing?' I say, squinting as the light slowly travels down a path towards us, hypnotising me with its blaring gleam.

'Joseph! Snap out of it! Let's go!'

'How do I find you?'

'I'm in area AA, room 23. Find me! You're my only hope.'

Sketch disappears. I take one last look at the engulfing white light drifting towards me and then snap back to reality with a huge gasp for air.

I am greeted by the overwhelming alarm blasting over the Tannoy. I readjust and try to refocus my eyes, but the whole room and beyond it flashes with yellow strobe lights, flickering against the plain white walls and surfaces.

Squinting, I can see that the door is open and, without a second thought, I wobble to my feet and head out of the room.

'Negative! The CI Wing is secure,' a security porter yells into his headset, running past me, accompanied by another guard. Neither pay attention to me as I lean against the wall to keep my balance.

'ETA two minutes!'

They run out of sight.

Sketch was right; something's happened. This could be our chance to escape. I head in the opposite direction to the security guards, slowly regaining some strength in my legs. Right! Area AA, room 23 . . . I follow the signs at the end of each hall.

As I journey through the flashing hallways, trying to navigate my way to Sketch's location, the alarm stops. It is replaced by the rowdy noise of patients roaming the corridors, trashing equipment, smashing windows, vandalising walls, and looting whatever spoils they can get their hands on.

Moving through the madness, I reach corridor AB and I hear static and the tinny voice of someone calling through an unanswered communication device:

'Team Two come in — over. I repeat: Team Two, can you hear me? Have you apprehended the intruder?'

The voice intermittently continues with no reply. Turning the corner towards the sound, my mouth drops. Multiple security porters are laid out unconscious on the floor and slumped against the walls. One of the guards is still clutching his security radio, which is where the voice is coming from. Who or what could have done this? It would have taken quite a force to move through these guys like this and, by the sound of it, the intruder is still on the move.

'Team Two, do you read me? Send backup now! We've spotted the intruder, we're going to engage and . . .
Ahhhh!'

290

Unable to bear hearing the screams of other people in pain, I switch off the radio and cautiously keep moving.

Finally, I spot the sign leading to Area AA. Through one of the room windows, I glimpse a patient still strapped to a bed, their face covered with a gas mask. I go to help him, hearing the monotonous *beep* from his machine as I get closer. I lift his mask.

'Armin!' I say in shock. I stop myself from removing the mask completely, unsure if it will cause further harm. Armin's head is completely shaved. He lies there catatonic, with his eyes wide-open, breathing at a steady, consistent pace but not moving.

'Armin! Can you hear me? It's Joseph.'

I click my fingers over his face. His pupils are dilated, unresponsive to my movements. As I stand there, unsure of what to do, I remember his last words to me: 'Don't let them break you, my G!'

'What have they done to you, my friend?!' I say, looking at Armin's drained, unresponsive body.

'Exactly what we did to you!' a voice says from behind me. I spin around.

'You!' I gasp, backing up and holding up my fists in a defensive stance, ready to protect myself and Armin.

'Violence is not necessary, Joseph,' Doctor Roth says calmly. 'I will not harm you and, if you don't want harm to befall your little friend, you won't do anything . . . irrational either.'

'What have you done to Armin?'

'Dear boy, all I have done is try to help those of you who are troubled.'

'By torturing us and using us as guinea pigs?'

'Come now, you are being unreasonable. I can think of far worse treatments that have been used throughout history to try to heal patients in the medical field.'

Doctor Roth checks over Armin and reaches out to touch him but I grab his hand. He looks at me and snatches his hand back, then removes the mask from Armin's face.

'The subconscious mind is a fascinating wonder — the realm of dreams is an untapped power with many levels and caverns to explore. Some believe it is a doorway fed by another reality. With Sub-Con therapy, I have been able to manipulate the mind, reading brain waves, synthesising and inputting select scenarios and memories to help change our concept of reality.'

'Like torturing me with my own traumatic memories on a loop?!'

The doctor doesn't answer and continues reading Armin's numbers on the screen.

'In time we will be able to fix and unlock the psychological problems that are tearing through this world. We are — all of us — so very sad, all of the time. Our lives can never hope to match up to the movies we watch, the video role-play games we play, even the lives that we pretend to have to impress other people we don't know, to amass likes and followers in a virtual world. Such foolishness. Soon we will be united under one banner through a singular consciousness, which will guide and heal our minds, bringing stability and order.'

'By trying to control our thoughts?!'

'I'm trying to free your thoughts, my friend.'

'You're insane! All I see are lifeless shells of individuals that had their own minds, personalities, voices of their own.'

'In all breakthroughs there are risks and then . . . And then there's you!' the doctor's tone turns more ominous. 'We have used the same techniques and methods on countless others over the years.'

Snap!

Doctor Roth clicks his fingers and I am held by two security porters.

'Get off me!' I try to break free.

'Many that we have worked on don't survive the process,' he says, extracting a clear substance from a glass vial with his needle. 'Others do.'

'What are you doing?' I ask worriedly, as the doctor steps over to Armin, flicking and priming the syringe.

'You don't have to do this, leave him alone!' I desperately plead.

Without a trace of emotion, the doctor plunges the needle into Armin's arm and injects the substance into his veins.

'No!'

Within seconds, Armin's body starts to convulse. The heart monitor to his side rapidly speeds up. Armin violently flails from to side like a fish out of water, then stops, as suddenly as it started. A steady tone beeps and the machine flatlines, showing no heartbeat.

'You killed him!'

The security porters hold me tighter as my legs give way. Doctor Roth pulls the wires from Armin's chest, killing the incessant ringing sound.

'You killed him! You killed him . . .'

'Like I said, dear boy, those that do survive the process are special and show great potential, with the opportunity of joining our ranks.'

I try to swallow my tears to get my words out: 'Who . . . are you people?'

Doctor Roth removes his glasses to rub his nose.

'We are the Watchers, the ones turning the wheels. But then, you have already heard that part, haven't you?'

I lift my head and stare at the doctor as he places his glasses back onto his face.

'Your late friend was weak, normal, unusable; he will not be missed. You, on the other hand, have been difficult to infiltrate but we will hack you soon, or your little blind friend will know pain.'

'If you've hurt her—'

'Nonsense, dear boy. Do not speak idle threats. If you are what we think you are, then we will subject her to the most ghastly treatments we can muster just to get what we want from you. You think you know sorrow and pain? Think again. You are yet to know what nightmares are, son of Imādris!'

* * *

We descend towards the underground laboratory. The last time I was in this lift was the last time I saw Armin alive, as himself. The doors slide open and I see Sketch surrounded by spray cans and paints, standing next to a nurse and the woman in grey. Armed security guards stand close by.

'Sketch!' I call, as I'm ushered into the lab and forcefully placed into one of the medical cubicles.

'Joseph!' Sketch replies. 'I'm okay.'

'Silence!' the lady snaps, hitting Sketch across the face with the back of her hand.

'Don't touch her!' I yell, as I'm pinned down and strapped to another medical table.

The porter wheels me beside Sketch and hoists the bed into an almost upright vertical position.

'You see him now?' the woman asks impatiently.

Sketch doesn't answer.

'I'm warning you, girl: do not try my patience!'

'I won't do it! You can't make me! I won't help you!'

'We'll see about that!' the woman's sadistic tone grows more agitated. She nods her head and before I know it a fist plants itself straight into my stomach, knocking all the air out me.

The woman grabs Sketch by the hair, pulling her thick pig tails, causing her to scream out in pain.

'You hear that, girl? Every defiant decision you make has an effect! Hit him again!'

Whack! Thwack!

'Ouff!'

Two more blows pound into my body: another one into my stomach and one in the rib. Sketch screams out as she hears the blows connect with my body.

'You see what happens when you don't obey?! Again!'

More blows rock me. One cracks me in the jaw, nearly knocking me unconscious.

'Ma'am, I need him to be cognitive before I put him under,' Doctor Roth explains.

'She'll do what I ask if I have to rip him in two! Hit him again!'

'No, stop!' Sketch cries. 'Don't hurt him anymore, I'll do it. I'll "sketch" him, just don't hurt him.'

Writhing with pain, I am rolled back so that Sketch has a clear space. She picks up one of the spray cans. She looks up at me through her bandaged eyes; the bandage is soaked through from her tears.

'I'm sorry!' she says.

Sketch shakes one of the spray cans. With her other hand she picks up a thin paint brush. She starts to spray a base colour onto the ground, then begins to create an image, moving at an unnatural speed, mesmerically, painting and sketching on the floor like a printer printing an image.

'Do what you need to do with him!' the woman instructs, dismissing me to Doctor Roth.

'Thank you, ma'am!' Roth replies.

As I am wheeled back into one of the glass medical cubicles,

I hear the lift behind me activate and start to ascend. Doctor Roth and his accompanying staff members start to wire me up to their machines. I see one of his assistants pull out a set of hair clippers.

The distinctive sound of the woman's heels clack against the tiled surface as she walks towards me. She peers over at me as the doctor places an oxygen mask over my face.

'Did you really think you would escape us? We are the cogs behind the wheels. You will submit or you will die!'

The woman backs away and the doctor puts his gloves on. He brandishes a vial with a red, sand-like substance.

'Will that work, doctor?' the woman asks.

'This is the TR-13 in its purest and most natural form. This, mixed in with my advanced compound, will make it extremely potent. If this doesn't allow us full access to his dreams and memories, nothing will.'

'Please don't do this!' I say under the gas mask.

'Administer phase one now!' the doctor orders, ignoring me.

A hissing sound starts. I feel cold air seep into the oxygen mask and up my nostrils as I breathe it in. My eyes begin to get heavy, closing with each intake of breath. I try my hardest to stay awake but find myself drifting away . . .

* * *

Bang! Bang!
  'Stop him!'
  Ratttatttatattta! Bang! Bang!

Suddenly I am awoken by the sound of gunfire and Sketch's scream.

I lift my head, looking around in confusion, as bodies are tossed in every direction. With foggy vision I look over towards the lift, blacking in and out of consciousness, and see its open doors, unable to shut from the pile of bodies wedging it open.

Crash!

Out of nowhere, the body of a security guard flies through the air, smashing through one of the glass cubicle windows.

My eyes blearily trace his trajectory and I see the fuzzy outline of man single-handedly disarming and dispensing security guards left, right, and centre. He moves as efficiently, fluently, and swiftly as wind blowing through tall blades of grass, but as vicious as a lion. At one point, unless my eyes are playing tricks on me, I swear I see his shadowy outline run across the walls, defying gravity, to dodge incoming gunfire. Amidst the madness, I glimpse Doctor Roth and the woman in grey exit through the secret passageway in the wall that I'd discovered earlier.

The sounds of battle in the room fall to a deathly silence.

I can hear Sketch's voice, which keeps me awake: 'Over here! Quickly, you've got to help him!'

I fade out again, feeling the mask being pulled from my face. Someone lifts me up from the bed with arms that feel as solid as oak. My eyes open momentarily and I see the outline of a familiar face, before everything starts to fade.

'Hold on, Mr Jacobs. I have you!'

'Professor . . . ? Is that . . . ?'

CHAPTER 16

True Beginnings

*'Nekuporesa Kwemadzitateguru aka üye neavo zviroto zvinomupa
simba rekuporesa nechiedza chechokwadi uye kufarirwa.'*

'What's happening to him?'
'His mind is fading into oblivion!'
'You've got to help him, please! Stay with us, Bushy Head!'

I'm sitting at the top of a **smoke-filled staircase**, gripping
onto the **bars of the banister** so tightly that the brown pigmentation in **my hand** begins to turn pale.

'Ayamey! More are coming, we must defend him at all costs!'
'I will, Nusho! By the moons of Imādris, they will go no
further!'

Through the bars, barely visible, I can see bright flashes of
white light, almost like sparks, sporadically illuminating the
destroyed, **fire-engulfed living room.**

'Ahhhhhh!'
'Nusho! Can you stand? Another wave approaches.'

'I will be fine. We just need to hold on until help comes. They will not risk being seen by the unawoken.'

'Here they come!'

Horrific, nightmarish spectres roam the downstairs area. I can hear the **sound of glass breaking**, sporadic pops and crunches through the **thick, suffocating smoke**. I glimpse **scorched furniture and blood** trailing across the floor.

'Ayamey-adə, it has been an honour my love . . . Ready?'

'Yes, my moon, I am ready!'

My eyes momentarily flicker open and I glimpse Sketch and the professor.

'It's not working! He's dying!'

Joseph, hear me: I am with you.

Absorb the words I speak:

'Nipa iwosan awọn baba wa ati awọn ti o ni ireti ti wọn si nfa ireti lati Odo Meje, fun u ni agbara pẹlu ore-ọfẹ, imọlẹ, ati ojurere.

'By the healing of our ancestors and those who dream and draw hope from the Seven Rivers, grant him strength with grace, light, and favour.

Let him live!'

I hear the professor's words; his voice pierces my ears, my broken dream collapses like a cleansing rush of water. I hear the sweet and gentle melodic humming of Ayamey's lullaby . . .

Tick tock!

Tick tock!

Tick tock!

The repetitive sound of a clock calmly wakes me from my dream and removes my connection from the lullaby. Ayamey's voice fizzles out, disappearing into sonic vapour, disintegrating into nothingness. A clock chimes and the smell of incense burns. My hearing, thoughts, sense of smell, vision, and perception of feeling all start to combine into conscious thought as I reawaken to reality. I'm still alive.

The room around me is very old-fashioned. Above the four-poster bed is a crystal chandelier with intricate patterns of stars and moons engraved into its surfaces. Thick, emerald-green curtains embellished with gold trimmings drape down the side of the tall bay windows, allowing the morning sun to shine through. The sun beams against the stained dark wooden floor, giving it a cosy feeling. An open fireplace crackles and burns. All around the room fitted shelves protrude from the walls, filled with old books of all colours and sizes, some covered in weathered leather bindings. I get up to look around. I leave the room and head across a long hallway with dark wooden wall panels that stretch from ceiling to floor. Along the walls are strange symbols and annotations mixed in with patterns and hieroglyphs. They seem to illuminate as I walk past.

I continue down the corridor, the smell of incense getting stronger in my nostrils, and I see an antique grandfather clock next to the door ahead of me. This is where the ticking's been coming from. The clock chimes loudly as the hands hit nine o'clock.

Gong! Gong! Gong! Gong!

I carefully open the door, expecting someone to jump out and confront me at any minute. I walk into an old-fashioned lounge resembling a quaint library or those Victorian drawing rooms that Mom used to take me to see at the Black Country Museum. I'm alone. Like the room I was in before, an open fire blazes, warming the space. Above the fireplace a sage incense stick burns, diffusing its fragrance into the air. I wander around the room and notice lots of portraits and photographs hanging on the green, peacock-patterned wallpaper and displayed alongside pristinely kept antique furniture. I pick up one of the picture frames and notice a black-and-white photo of a Black battalion: soldiers standing tall and strong wearing what looks like World War I uniforms. Respectfully placing the picture back down, another photo catches my eye. This time the picture is of a Black man posing in a top hat and tail coat leaning on a cane. Not gonna lie, the fit's cold. As I go to place the picture back, I double-take. I quickly re-examine the 1800s sepia-coloured photo.

The man in the photo looks like Professor Grey. As I look up, I spot another image on the wall: a painting of two white men shaking hands, who I instantly recognise as Matthew Boulton and James Watt, the inventors and leading figures of the Industrial Revolution. It must have been painted in the mid-1700s. Behind them is a group of people and there, once again, standing amongst others, I spot him: a man resembling Professor Grey. This can't be a coincidence, I think, so I pick the photo of the soldiers back up and look at it with renewed vigour, as my mind races with questions and theories.

'No way!' I repeat, as I spot him amongst the other soldiers. One by one, painting after image, illustration after photo, he appears in different eras of time. I spot him near the funeral carriage procession of Abraham Lincoln; I see him amongst the huddling surveyors at the construction of the Eiffel Tower; I even see his face sculpted into a bronze cast from the ancient Kingdom of Benin, next to a sketch of him with a woman who I believe to be the fierce legendary leader Nanny of the Maroons.

'This is insane!' But, out of all the images that I witness, the one that blows my mind is a slab of sandstone, displayed in an airtight glass box with the image of the professor. Going by my student knowledge, it must be Ancient Egyptian. My eye catches sight of a large frame resting against the wall in the corner, which has been covered by a black velvet sheet. Why is that one covered? I'm too far gone now not to know; my curiosity gets the better of me and I go over and remove the material. To my surprise, I see nothing; it's empty, just a blank frame.

'Grand rising, Mr Jacobs! It is good to see you up and about on this glorious day.' I turn sharply, startled by the low, laid-back Jamaican accent of Professor Grey, who is standing in the doorway.

'P— professor, I . . . I didn't mean to pry. I woke up and didn't know where I was,' I ramble as the professor watches me with his oak tree-coloured eyes.

'Bushy Head!' Sketch announces with glee, jumping out from behind Grey, newly dressed and sporting purple-framed sunglasses.

'Sketch! You're okay?' I say, relieved to see her.

The professor closes the door behind them, then places his bags down beside the tan leather pinned sofa near the fireplace. He walks past me and picks up the sheet I removed from the frame. He carefully places it back, brushing out the creases and folded edges.

'Please take a seat, Mr Jacobs.'

He sits and gestures towards another single-seated leather chair across from the one he currently occupies.

Sketch makes herself comfortable near the fireplace and I sit, unsettled. Grey pours himself a drink from his crystal decanter and takes a sip. I glance over again at the pictures, sizing up their likeness of the man in front of me. It's him; his distinctive eyes pop out from every photo.

'I gather you have a lot of questions that you would like answering.'

I stay silent, wondering where I should begin.

'There is no need to be afraid, Mr Jacobs. This is my house and you are welcome here; it is safe from those who would do you harm. You can rest.' The professor places his empty glass onto a coaster and crosses his legs. 'You may have seen and experienced some strange things on your exploration through my house. The signs, runes, hieroglyphs and voices are not harmful. But then, I believe by now you are no stranger to the supernatural.'

I stay quiet, defensively feigning a false naïveté.

'There is no need to hide anything, Mr Jacobs. I will try my best to give you the answers to the questions you most eagerly require.' Grey pours himself another glass and takes a sip. 'After visiting you in that facility and using the cards — it became very clear to me that you were special . . . You are the one from the footage, are you not? The vigilante that the media so love to report on, the "terror of Birmingham". The one responsible for the so-called Blackout.'

'I don't know what you're talking ab—'

'Mr Jacobs, please do not insult my intelligence! I promise you on all that is good and of a true light that I am here to help you and, when we are finished, you will have more clarity and a decision to make.'

'What are you talking about?'

The professor places his glass back down beside him and leans forwards in his chair. 'Joseph, tell me about your dreams and what happened that night of the Blackout.'

Sketch looks up at me and nods, egging me on to tell him the truth. Here goes.

'You're right . . . I am all those things — it was me, but I don't know how or why it happened. It wasn't until I saw the footage and read articles that I started to stitch together what I'd done ... It's still a blur.'

Grey listens intently.

'I've dreamt about a young woman drowning in a hotel, as if I could see behind her eyes. I've seen a homeless man's eyes blaze with a terrible white light, the same light that appeared as translucent beasts — like the things that clawed and killed a police officer in a mirror, then possessed his body and tried to kill me!'

The professor's eyebrows raise as I continue to rant.

'I've fallen into an abyss of black diamonds; I've dreamt and envisioned the house that my parents ... the house they died in; I've had my memories selected, looped, and used to torture me by people who can see and induce dreams at will. I've met people that can do the impossible and, in doing so, I have lost everything: my relationship with my mom, my friends ...'

I stand up, turning my back on the professor and Sketch.

'Professor, I don't know why this is all happening to me ... Am I cursed?!'

The sound of the wood on the open fire crackles in the silence.

'Joseph, you are a Dreamwalker!' Professor Grey announces, also rising to his feet.

'A ... Dreamwalker?' I repeat.

'Yes! You are descended from an ancient race of supreme beings known as Figments, a child of true dream-light and rightful son of the Kingdom of Imādris. You are the one foretold to awaken those who slumber and restore harmony back to the realm of The Infinite.' Grey's words send shudders to my core and the deepest parts of my being, causing me to sit down again heavily.

'I have something for you.'

The professor reaches into his pocket and pulls out my dreamcatcher necklace, which has been repaired.

'What is it?' Sketch asks.

'It's . . . It's my dreamcatcher necklace.' My voice starts to crack. 'It was a gift . . . But how? How did you find it? I thought it was lost.'

The professor places the necklace safely into the centre of my palm and I marvel over it, examining it as if it were the first time I saw it. It doesn't look as if it was ever damaged.

'How did y—?'

'I simply asked for it back at the police station.'

'Really?' I ask, surprised at how easy it was to get it back.

The professor smiles to himself.

'After you gave me an illustrated diagram of your dream-catcher, I noticed some of the symbols. *Usingizi. Húpnos,*' he quietly recites.

'Professor?' I say, completely confused.

'Swahili and Ancient Greek, Mr Jacobs. It means "to slumber" or "to sleep". It took a while to translate the many symbols and dialects, but I can finally tell you what it means:

'When I sleep I wake, when I dream I walk.

'**Tǐřuvà–ëd aśūto bà–ed, sdokhrē–ëd aśūto dokhri–ëd.**'

A weight drops onto my shoulder and I feel a small buzz of energy tingle through my hands.

'These are no idle words, Joseph, but the language of dreams — a once-lost mantra and a gateway for you to be able to tap into your ability. Whosoever kept this safe and sent it to you sacrificed a lot, in the hope that one day you would receive this precious text.'

Ayamey and Nusho. Mum and Dad, I say to myself, holding the dreamcatcher close to my chest.

'The dreams and abilities you speak of, Joseph, are not a curse. It is you, your subconscious power awakening. You have been chosen from the dawn of time to be Imādris's champion and I have been waiting since the first sunsets for you to Awaken.

I rub my hands through my Afro curls, trying to digest all the information. This is deep; it feels as if an atomic bomb has been dropped into my brain.

'That! Is! Super-dope!' Sketch says, throwing both hands over her mouth when she realises that she spoke out loud.

The professor smiles to himself, picking up his half-full glass and downing the remains. I pick up another picture from the sidetable.

'So, are you a . . .'

'Figment,' the professor intervenes helpfully. 'Yes, Mr Jacobs. I am.'

'And Sketch?'

'That is correct, young Tabitha is one too.'

'Tabitha!' I laugh under my breath.

'Hey! It's Sketch to you both.'

Grey and I share a small smirk. I hold up one of Grey's pictures and ask the question that's been burning in me ever since I came into this room.

'So . . . are you, like, immortal or something?'

'No,' the professor responds with a sense of relief. 'No, I am not. I can die . . . just not of age.' The professor says, with a deep sorrow in his voice.

'So you're kind of like Dorian Gray?'

'Your references never cease to amuse, Mr Jacobs. Mr Wilde was a good friend, actually, and he was fascinated by my life, but his story was quite a great reimagining and highly embellished.'

I stare at the professor in awe.

'And you say there are other Figments?'

'Yes.'

'So there are more like me, Dreamwalkers?'

'No, not like you. We all have different abilities that draw from the realm of The Infinite. It is said that the human brain only uses ten per cent of its full capacity, but Figments are born with the ability to unlock and access a higher level of consciousness, allowing them to tap into another realm: the Dream Realm, two realms of infinite imagination that once intertwined. Only a few have knowledge of our existence, but we have been leaving our mark on society throughout the centuries, puzzling scientists, and pushing the human imagination. From the architecture of ancient civilisations to timeless works of art, from heavenly symphonies to iconic pop culture, we have set the backdrop of the modern world.'

'This is crazy,' I say.

'There are three known types of Figments: Alpha, Beta, and Supreme. Beta Figments can use their imagination and higher consciousness to affect their own physical attributes, sometimes calling upon incredible strength and speed, heightening their senses to physical peak. Betas are still bound by certain laws of physics and, even though they can manipulate their power at will, they cannot sustain their abilities for long periods of time. Alphas are assigned one unique ability. It has been known at times to affect them physically or mentally: some can shape-shift, mind-read, or conjure elements; some can see beyond the past and present. Some are even able to reimagine and manipulate time itself. This ability, to those that possess it, is seen as more of a curse, over time it can detach them from their humanity, for example Dreameaters.'

'Dreameaters?' Sketch responds with trepidation.

'Yes. Modern-day fiction has adapted the idea and you may have heard them referred to nowadays as vampires.'

'Rah! No way! So, which one am I?' Sketch asks excitedly.

'An Alpha! There are fewer Alphas now than there were. Time can be cruel . . .'

The professor stands up and walks over to one of his portraits, which displays him standing next to a young lady in Victorian clothing.

'A story I know so well,' he utters to himself, gently stroking the picture. 'And then there is you, Mr Jacobs, the Supreme Figment, believed only to be a myth: the Last Dreamwalker.'

'I . . . What?'

'The Dreamwalker is said to be able to alter and manifest their dreams into physical reality. You are Beta and Alpha all in one and much more. Your smallest thoughts and biggest dreams are subject to your imagination. When fully trained and in a state of lucidity you will be able to change the very fabric of physical reality, bending it to your will.'

Hearing the professor speak with such knowledge and conviction fills me with hope, as well as a kind of dread.

'Professor, you mentioned that I'm the last Dreamwalker . . . Were there others?'

Grey hesitates, leaning in front of the fire.

'There are good and bad things in this world, Mr Jacobs, as you know. That is true also for the world beyond this reality. War has been raging in the Realm of Dreams. It sounds like you have already heard and seen the nightmarish false-white light of the Knight Terrors.'

' . . . Knight Terrors?'

'Yes, Mr Jacobs. These are malevolent beings that were once Figments.'

'Those translucent beast things? They've got control of that police officer.'

'Never before have they been able to sustain their wretched influence and set foot into this realm. That is a worrying thought. Knight Terrors are from the Realm of Nightmares, Akhubós.

They serve The First, their Master, a corrupted light and the Lord of Fallen Dreams.'

'The . . . First?!' I mumble, feeling a cold shiver run down my spine. Sketch sits there in silence, listening to the professor tell us things that sound like they belong in a fantasy novel.

'Do you trust me, Joseph?' the professor asks, walking towards me.

'Yes,' I nod.

'I want to show you both something.' The professor rolls up his sleeve. 'We must first make a connection, meet me in the place you both refer to as black diamonds.'

The professor forms a pyramid with his hands, his index fingers touching at the top. Sketch and I both copy him.

'Hearing is one thing.' Grey says as his low, warming voice drops to a sub-bass, rumbling, echoey tone. 'But seeing — as they say — is believing.'

I begin to count slowly and, before I know it, the room around us feels like it expands then sucks inwards. It goes quiet and I fall, finding myself back in the place of black diamonds. Sketch appears beside me and we watch as a vibrant green aura comes drifting towards us.

'Make a connection!' the professor's voice echoes.

We both reach out and touch the luscious green light. Instantly, the black diamonds form a shimmering astro-projected likeness of the professor.

'What is this place?' I ask reverently.

'This is an ancient Figmetic way of communication, known as The Seeing. It can be initiated by a technique that we call "Palm Pathways". Here, we can connect to other Figments on our pathways. Through this medium we can navigate and search, seeing things that others cannot. We can even unlock our ancestors' sight, thoughts, and visions, to see parts of the past. The Seeing is a living library. In here I can show you how it all began.'

The glistening, starlit sky begins to rotate, twisting us back through time, recreating ancient structures that once stood magnificently tall as the professor speaks.

'Listen to my words and you will see it all:

'First was the Spark
Imādris gave birth.
Infinite light formed and creation was born.
Creation forged the First and the First fell far,
Tears of despair, everlasting night opened.

The bond was broken. The Void roared deep.

Akhubós grew the night, the night grew mares
One became two, nascent dreams
Sleep woke the dreamers and the dreamers walked the Earth
Lucid they roamed, Veil of Imagination unknown
Sleeping, waking, dreaming, walking.
Guardians of the Gate: Last and the First.'

The Seeing place settles. Sketch and I stand in awe after witnessing the incredible depiction of Grey's words.

'You now know about The First; he was once a Dreamwalker,' Grey says with a grim look on his face. 'After the Great Battle of Dreams, The First was said to have disappeared. Some believed that he had indeed succumbed to the mighty Warriors of Imādris — defeated and left to roam the forgotten deep that is The Void — never to be seen again.'

'So . . . he was destroyed?'

'Some believe so. Unfortunately, there are still those who search for him, none more prevalent than a group known as Avalon. You both have already had the privilege of meeting members of this insidious cult. The TWI is just one of their many facilities and fronts that span the globe. They are the Watchers, the cogs in the wheel and devout followers of the First.

'Avalon have been working in secrecy, manipulating key players in the geopolitical system and others towards their agenda. I, alongside a network of allies which form the Waning Order, have been trying to keep them at bay, losing many Figments in our efforts. Your Awakening will not have not gone unnoticed; through you, new Figments like Sketch here have awoken.

'Avalon have been searching for a weapon that is said to open the gateway of the Veil to the Realm of Dreams, unleashing The First and his hordes of Knight Terrors upon the world. If they really knew who you were, things may have been different.'

'So, what happens to us now? Won't Avalon just come after us?'

'It is still unclear to me what Avalon's next move will be. I must consult with members of the Waning Order. In the meantime I must urge you to both rest. Your training will begin come sunset.'

CHAPTER 17

The House on the Left

Kukadia slams his car boot shut.

'How much longer do you reckon she's going to be?' The detective sounds annoyed as he gets into the car.

'Give her some time, she's just getting herself together. She's been through a lot.'

'And a LOT of chocolates. Have you ever seen someone put away that much chocolate in one sitting? I'm surprised she's got any teeth left!'

'Spoken like a true parent,' I say, trying to lighten the mood. Kukadia goes quiet and starts up the engine.

Eventually, he murmurs: 'She's about the same age as Karena. She's been through a hell of a lot.'

'Have you ever tried reaching out to your daughter?'

Kukadia fidgets, uncomfortable with the question. He winds down the window.

'I tried a couple of years back — didn't go so well, so I just kept on doing my thing. Probably for the best really. This job takes it's toll after a while. You were lucky you got out when you did. You got any updates on your son yet?'

'Nothing, but I'll keep trying.'

Beep! Beep!

'C'mon, hurry up!' the detective honks his horn and shouts impatiently out of the window towards the bed and breakfast room where Charlotte is staying.

'You heard from your informant yet?' Kukadia asks.

'No, not yet. He'll contact us when he has more information.'

'Sounds more trouble than it's worth to me. Call me old school, but I think you can never truly trust someone until you've met them. I'm not into the whole "smoke and mirrors" thing.'

'Well, if it weren't for him you would be being detained and questioned right now.'

The detective rolls his eyes. He knows I'm right.

'It's not every day your whole department puts out a warrant for your arrest. Whoever the mole is, they've done a number on me — guess it didn't help being the last recorded person to log into the central hub before those files got deleted.'

Charlotte walks towards the car.

'Er, just a quick thought: all that touching someone's hand and seeing things in the past that she claims . . . do you think . . . ? That can't all be real, can it? It's just some mumbo-jumbo?'

'I don't know, Paul. I'm trying to keep an open mind. All I know is, the way she described the killer was exactly how the nurse from the residential home did.'

The car door opens and Charlotte jumps into the back seat.

'Sorry 'bout the delay, was just stocking up on some chocolate for our road trip,' Charlotte says. 'You want one?'

'No thanks,' the detective waves the chocolate bar away and gestures to her seatbelt. 'Buckle up. It's time to hit the road.'

We drive through the city. Rain and sleet tap against the windscreen. Today more than ever, the city looks grey, down-beaten, and downtrodden.

'This place we're going . . . Has it got something to do with my sister's killer?' Charlotte asks tentatively.

The detective side-eyes me briefly.

I hesitate. 'Yes . . . It has.'

'Do you think that's a good idea?!' Charlotte says, panic in her voice. 'I thought we were going to lay low, you know, witness protection? It wants me dead! It'll find me.'

'*It* is a person. Just like everybody else. Nothing's going to happen to you!' Kukadia says protectively. 'Besides, we're running out of time. This is the clue that could lead us to the killer and stop them, before more people like your sister are hurt.'

'Well, I don't like it!' Charlotte says, sitting back and pouting.

We drive to the northern part of Birmingham, a place called Beacon Hill. I've heard of the hills before: in the Second World War, they were apparently used to spot enemy planes flying overhead. The hustle and bustle of the cramped streets starts to roll back; we see some greenery and fields as we head higher.

'Charlotte, you mentioned that, when you touched your sister's hand, you saw the killer. And also that both your sisters had some sort of ability. Did you all get them around the same time?'

Detective Kukadia looks at me like I'm crazy.

'No, mine only really started a couple of weeks ago when that Blackout happened. I was in the city that night looking for Cara. It was weird — kinda hard to explain — but that's when I started to be able to feel things, see things when I touch them. Before that I just used to get déjà vu, so strong they were almost like apparitions. I'm not sure how it works, but when I touched my sister's cold hand, I saw it. Our mother would tell us stories of individuals she worked with, people with abilities. We used to laugh, we thought she was just making it up. I never knew — years down the line — that my own story would be so similar.'

'There it is: the farmhouse on the left,' Kukadia says, pulling up the handbrake and switching off the engine.

Kukadia pulls out his revolver and checks the chamber, then re-holsters it back under his rain mac.

'Ready?' Kukadia says to me. He looks in his rear mirror at Charlotte, who bravely nods. 'Let's go then.'

We head towards the detached farmhouse. Charlotte keeps close behind the detective and I follow as we make our way up the damp footpath. A cold wind blows, accompanied by a chilling whistle, bending the surrounding tall grass. The weathered welcome sign, which reads: 'Barns' Farm & Residence', sways back and forth with a metallic creak. We pull up some of the dead vines entangled around the garden gate and unlatch it. It squeaks as it opens. The muddy walkway to the house is littered with fallen leaves.

Scattered among the dying cornfield and rotten pumpkin patches are old, dilapidated stables and empty animal pens, covered in moss.

Rusty cans and broken bottles are cradled among the autumn shrubbery and thick tall grass. Looks like they were dumped there by trespassers some time ago. The closer we get, the more eerie and imposing the house becomes.

'This place feels sick, sorrowful,' Charlotte says quietly, as she surveys the house.

The window frames have started to rot, the discoloured white paint flaking from the wood, and a collage of old, damp newspapers blocks out the windows.

Squawk!

Charlotte screams and we all turn.

'It's just a bird,' I say, stopping Kukadia, who already has his hand on his gun.

Caw! Caw!

'Look, up there — there's loads of 'em!' Charlotte points.

An unkindness of ravens swarms and congregates on one of

the bare trees, peering down at the house.

'Aren't they supposed to be a bad omen?' Charlotte asks.

'Yeah — if you believe those kinda things,' the detective replies.

Clap, clap, clap!

Kukadia claps his hands, scattering the ravens into the rain, their charcoal wings flapping against the grey sky.

We recompose ourselves. Kukadia and I nod to each other to signal that we are ready to continue.

Kukadia presses the doorbell. 'Mercia PD! Is anyone there?!' he shouts. The bell doesn't ring, so he goes to knock on the door, but it creaks partially open at the faintest touch. He leans his head in, checking to see if anyone's behind the door, then he pushes it wide open.

'Mercia PD! Anyone in?' he repeats. Again, there's no response. We let ourselves in.

The house is empty and looks like it's been that way for some time. We make our way through the hallway and empty rooms that have bits of old paper, crockery, and clothing dumped around sporadically. Faded spots on the floor linger where furniture used to reside. Charlotte stops abruptly and places her hand on the wall. She closes her eyes.

'These walls have witnessed much pain and suffering!' she speaks softly, commanding Kukadia's attention. 'They grew up together, feeling like outcasts, but she had him and he had her. He admired how fearless she was. She was his best friend, his confidant, the love of his life. He was her protector — their sacred bond as siblings created a knot that no one could break.' Charlotte's eyes flicker back open. She looks stunned, almost unaware of the words she's just spoken.

'Are you okay?' I ask.

'I'm good.'

'Let's keep going,' Kukadia insists, evidently still dubious about Charlotte's claims of extra-sensory powers.

We walk through the kitchen, which smells of rotting poultry from decaying garbage bags. Kukadia covers his mouth and attempts to flip the light switch. The power's off. Old utility bills and envelopes with red letters warning of foreclosure, addressed to a Doctor Emit Barns, lie scattered on top of dusty worktops.

As we head towards the back of the house, I spot a peculiar fumigation-type tube trailing along the floor. I point it out to Kukadia. Taking no chances, he pulls out three small, conical face masks from his jacket pocket. He hands us one each. If the killer is here, this should at least give us some protection against his red sand.

We follow the long tube to a set of stairs. There's a slightly ajar wooden door, tucked away neatly underneath the staircase. The tube stretches into the sliver of a gap in the doorway. I open it and feel a cold draft. I signal Kukadia for his torch, which he hands over.

Click!

The torch shines, revealing a long descent down to the basement. Disturbed dust particles dance in the torch's beam. Charlotte cautiously looks down towards the partially lit declining stairs and steps back. As I go to take the first step down, the detective stops me.

'Maybe we should check out upstairs first,' Kukadia says cautiously, his words muffled through the face mask, mindful of Charlotte's fearful reaction.

'We cover below first, then we move up — no surprises!'

'No surprises!' Kukadia repeats, unsheathing his revolver in agreement.

'Stay close.'

Kukadia takes point and we follow, in single file, down the bricked stairway, following the tube.

Squilsh, splash!

'Careful! Watch your step; it's flooded down 'ere,' Kukadia shouts up.

Charlotte waits at the bottom of the steps, keeping out of the water. I pass her, stepping in up to my waist to join the detective.

Squilsh splash!

'It's freezing!' I exclaim.

'That explains that horrible damp smell. This tube must be some sort of flood pump.'

Kukadia shines his torch around.

'Elizabeth!'

I turn towards the detective and shine my light in the direction his torch is pointing.

'What is it?' I ask, not able to fully make out what I'm looking at.

'It looks like some sort of cage, at least from this angle. Maybe for one of their farm animals?'

I push through the water to get a closer look at the oversized steel cage, half-eroded and submersed in the water. I shine my light in between the bars, highlighting the top panels. 'I don't think it was for an animal, Detective — look!'

Etched into the panels and bars are a vast number of tally charts and the scribbled initials EB, SB, and the words 'SECRETS KILL.'

Something catches my eye, and I plunge my hand into the water, lifting up a set of chains attached to the cage. At each end are cracked and mouldy leather wrist restraints.

'What in the sadistic hell is all this about?' the detective exhales. 'EB and SB: Emit and Sarah Barns, right?'

'Must be.'

'Is everything alright in there?!' Charlotte calls from the stairs.

'All good, just stay put,' Kukadia responds. 'Elizabeth, twelve o'clock: other side, past the cage . . . Is that a door?'

Behind the steel cage we see a door, like an iron safe.

'Maybe if we can shift the cage slightly, one of us can get round,' the detective instructs, putting the torch in his mouth to free up his hands.

I switch off my phone light and get a sturdy grip on the cage. 'Okay, after three. Ready?'

Kukadia gives me the thumbs up

'One, two . . .'

Gragshshhsssshhhhhhh! Buffff!

I freeze.

'Did you just hear that?!' I ask.

'Yeah, sounded like it came from above.'

We turn simultaneously towards the steps.

'Charlotte? Where's Charlotte?!' I cry in panic.

'Shit! She was just here!'

Gragshshhsssshhhhhhh! Buffff!

'Charlotte!' the detective shouts, hearing the sound again come from the floor above. No response.

We make our way out of the water, back to the ground floor.

Kukadia cocks back the hammer on his handgun and places his torch underneath the gun, ready to fire. He signals with his eyes for us to head to the top floor of the farmhouse.

* * *

We head upstairs, searching from room to room, covering each other's backs, just like the old days. In the middle of one room, a four-poster, metal-framed bed has been flipped onto its side. Lying around the room are a set of porcelain dolls, one in each of the four corners of the room. They sit up and directly face a fifth doll that is lying next to the bed. I shine my light on the dolls. Three of the dolls around the room have had one eye plucked out, with a red line drawn through the opened eye-socket in what looks like red lipstick. The marks are similar to the symbol and the laceration we found on the victim's face at the retirement home.

Kukadia crouches on the floor near the bed and strokes his finger across the wooden slats. He raises his finger towards me. There's no dust on his finger. Everywhere else, light dust has settled except where the bed once stood, meaning it has been recently moved. Maybe that was the noise we heard from downstairs.

Kukadia picks up the middle porcelain doll to examine it: it has a crack running down its face and in its hair is a small butterfly hair clip. He removes something from the crack in the doll's head: a piece of paper. He looks at me in puzzlement, then unfolds it. It is a picture of a young woman in her mid-twenties with long, platinum-blonde hair, sitting on this exact bed frame, wearing a white frilled nightgown, holding the doll in one hand. Her other hand is holding someone else's, but the rest of their body has been ripped out of the photo.

As I stare at the picture, the detective moves ahead into the last room.

'Elizabeth! Elizabeth!' Kukadia whispers urgently. I move as fast as I can to join him in the other room. He holds his light downwards, illuminating a piece of parchment spiked to a wooden stool by a letter opener. He places his torch on the floor. I shine the light in the direction that he's looking. Kukadia puts on disposable gloves to retrieve both objects from the wooden stool.

'What does it say?' I ask.

The detective turns the small paper over from front to back.

'There's nothing on it! It's blank. First Charlotte, then the dolls, now a blank piece of paper. The killer's playing games. Is that what you like to do you sick freak?!' the detective shouts. 'Play games?! Why don't you just show yourself?!'

I shine the light closer. Kukadia holds up the parchment to eye-level and sniffs twice.

'Smells weird,' the detective whispers, sniffing again. 'Almost like baking powder. It's still damp. This has also been recently left here.'

The scent of the paper hits my nose. 'It's sodium.' I think fast and quickly flip the torch to UV mode. 'There! See?' Words start to appear on the parchment in an obscure font, intentionally written to be unmatchable. Kukadia squints and starts to read the written text:

Unliving, undying, it can't walk yet runs
And orbits the Earth in less time than the sun.
At night I draw close, unseen, always heard
I give and take life from those who disturb.
Eight are now two, and two shall be one
Once one is opened, her name shall be gone.

Kukadia finishes reading the passage, looking slightly bewildered. My mind races at a hundred miles an hour, trying to figure out the passage.

'Water?' I mumble to myself, '"unliving, undying, it can't walk yet runs"?' I utter the second half of the message aloud to myself, trying to figure out the numbers.

'Elizabeth . . .'

'Hold on, I've almost got it . . . Eight, two? When one is opened . . . ? The doll's eyes! But . . . what does that mean?'

'Elizabeth!' the detective calls again, derailing my train of thought. I look at him in annoyance but he's gone quiet and is pointing his torch at the ceiling.

I look up too, only now seeing what his torch has revealed. Unmasked by its UV light setting, all around us, signs and symbols are dotted around the walls like Tutankhamun's tomb. I see a huge symbol of the Eye, as well as words like: *DEATH!*

BETRAYAL,

Wrath!!

and *Revenge*

written along the tattered, mouldy wallpaper, alongside other words written in a language I've never seen before.

Slam!

A door bangs shut and Kukadia points his revolver as we turn towards the hallway.

'Mercia PD, who's there?!' Kukadia shouts. Suddenly a rumble starts to rise from below, vibrating the wooden floorboards, like the sound of large brass pipes being warmed up. The noise continues to swell, getting louder like a roaring bulldozer.

'Sounds like a generator or something kicking in,' Kukadia tries to shout over the racket. Out of nowhere, he starts to cough profusely.

I switch the torch back to normal light, only to see a cloud of red dust floating around us, covering the room.

'Oh no! Detective! Drop!'

Kukadia turns and a cloud of red smoke explodes directly into his face. I drop to the floor in a haze of panic, able to dodge the majority of the substance. The detective stumbles about, choking. He wipes his eyes and I desperately fumble to refit the mask over my face. The detective hits the ground, eyes bloodshot red, and we crawl towards the open hallway, trying to keep below the smoke. Kukadia continues to choke and cough as he tries desperately to cover his mouth with the inside of his arm.

'We must be infected!' Kukadia says, trying to speak through his cough.

We secure the masks over our faces and Kukadia radios for backup and medical assistance.

'Listen!' I say suddenly, cutting in on Kukadia's call.

We hear the disconcerting sound of dozens of flapping wings and the piercing caws of ravens from outside, all around the farm house. It resembles a roaring wave:

Tttttt, tap, ttttt, tap, tap, tttttt!

The sounds of sharp beaks tapping and hitting the windows gets louder. It sounds as if the birds are somehow trying to chisel their way into the house.

Kukadia slumps at the top of the stairs, trying to catch his breath, then he begins to scream aggressively at the wall. He cocks his gun and lifts his feet up off the floor as if stepping on hot coals.

'Paul, what's wrong?!'

'No, no! Get off me! They're everywhere!' he shouts manically.

Within a moment of hearing those words, I notice the shredded wallpaper start to peel, as if being flayed off a human body. Hands and fingers press and scratch, tearing at the walls from the other side. Faceless heads push with open mouths through the walls around me, emitting muffled, blood-curdling screams, as if they're suffocating, trying to break through for air.

Bang!

The detective fires a shot at the window.

The bird noises fade and so do the shapes in the walls. A deathly silence falls.

Only the panting of fear and confusion from me and the detective persists.

'What the hell is going on?!' Kukadia yells, turning to cover every direction, his gun tightly clenched in his shaking hand.

Boof! Duff! Duff! Boof!

Suddenly a deep, bass sound echoes from above us, like the

hooves of a large beast stomping above the already-cracked ceiling. Kukadia points his gun upwards, watching pieces of plasterboard flake and fall from the weight of the stomps above.

I shake my head, trying to rationalise what I'm witnessing. I head towards the stairs, next to Kukadia, to try to escape. As I step forwards the room starts to bend at a forty-five degree angle, causing me to lose my balance.

Bang! Bang!

Two shots speed past my head.

'Get away from me, you demon monster!' Kukadia shouts as he backs up, leaning against the far wall, barely able to stand. His eyes glare and blaze with a crazy glint as he points the gun directly at me.

'Detective, don't shoot it's me: Elizabeth!'

'Monster, move again and I'll kill you where you stand!'

'Paul, put the gun down,' I plead.

The wooden floorboards shaking beneath us start to crack and the stairwell banister tears away from its structure. Kukadia monetarily comes to his senses and we both head down the stairs.

The stairs begin to move like an escalator, adding more steps the closer we get to the bottom, like an endless loop. We're trapped.

The walls start to close in around us, crunching and grinding, sounding like an ancient death trap. Horrific, shrill screams of pain pierce the air, as steaming, red magma trickles down the wall, eroding the surface.

'We need to jump!' I shout.

Without thinking twice, we leap blindly off the moving stairs through the red haze.

Splash!

We hit the ground, which is flooded with water. The sound

fades as suddenly as if someone has hit the mute button.

I drag myself to my feet. I help Kukadia up; we're barely able to see two steps in front of us, thanks to the hellish-red cloud that is all around us.

I raise my hands to guide us through the smoke and I hear faint whispers within the red mist.

They grow gradually, distressingly, louder:

'Mom!'

'Where are you?!'

'Help!'

Joseph . . . ? Joseph! I'm here, where are you?!' I shout, leaving Kukadia and rushing into the fog, trying to track his voice.

My heart beats with desperation as, strangely enough, it sounds like Joseph's voice from when he was a child.

'Karena! Daddy's here! Where are you? Call out to me, I'll find you,' I hear the detective call from somewhere within the red fog.

'How could you leave me to die, Mom? I'm burning!

'I thought you loved me.

'You said you wouldn't leave.'

As I run in the direction of Joseph's voice, I smell smoke and feel the singeing heat of a blazing fire. The mist begins to part like a curtain and there I stand, in my old police uniform, outside in the rain in front of the blazing house: the house where I first met Joseph.

'Help me, please!' Joseph yells from inside the house.

The fire growls and spits. I run towards it with urgency. The more I run, the further away the house seems. I watch as the fire continues to wreak havoc and I push harder to reach the burning building.

'Help, please!' Joseph's little voice screams. 'It's hot, I can't breathe!'

'I'm coming, just hold on!' I yell fearfully, running as fast as I can.

Inches away from the house, my legs freeze, stuck to the ground as if weighed down by huge anchors. I fall forward onto my belly, tugging at the grass using all my might to crawl forwards to save him.

Splish!

I hear the windows of the house start to crack and pop from the heat. As I try to lift myself back up to my feet, the house explodes into a ball of flames.

'Nooooo!' I scream, before I am blown backwards through the air by the destructive force.

I bawl uncontrollably as the house crumbles to ash before my eyes.

I cover my face and place my head on my knees in utter despair . . .

'Elizabeth . . . ? Elizabeth? Lilly? Why are you crying?'

Huh! I . . . I know that voice . . .

I look up and see my father, sitting in his worn brown leather chair next to the window in the front room.

'It can't be . . . Dad?'

'Don't cry, Lilly. I know it's scary, but no one lives forever.'

'This can't be real, this is impossible,' I mumble to myself.

'I've taught you well: always listen to your gut, don't be scared to tell the truth, and do the right thing. You're a better person than I've ever been.'

'Dad! No, please!'

My dad pulls out a gun from under his pillow, placing it to his head.

'Stop it! Stop it! Stop it!' I shout, trying to fight the hallucination.

'Come on, Elizabeth: fight it! It's not real.'

'Your mind makes it real,' a voice rumbles from all around me.

My dad presses the gun to his temple.

'Bye, Lilly,' he mouths.

I reach for the gun.

Bang!

I stand there, frozen in time, broken, once again reliving my Dad taking his own life . . .

'Elizabeth, fight back!' the voice continues to shout. 'It's not real, it's not real!'

Tears of exhaustion roll down my face and I let myself silently weep.

'Wahhh wahh waahh!'

I hear the deafening sound of multiple newborn babies crying, as the red mist encroaches and engulfs me, pulling me back into its nightmarish snare . . .

Huh!

Something brushes past me through the red dust, laughing as it trails off out of sight.

'Hello?' I call out. It happens once more but this time I glimpse the back of it. My eyes widen: hooves.

'Show yourself!' I demand.

'Here!'

'Here!'

'Here!'

'YOU HAVE ALSO BEEN KISSED BY DEATH'S STING!' A surreal-sounding, husky voice penetrates the air.

'Who are you? Show yourself.'

'I AM A WAKING NIGHTMARE OF VENGEANCE . . . HER INNOCENT VENGEANCE!' the voice replies, sending tremors through the air and my body.

'THEY TOOK HER FROM ME!'

The red fog gets thicker. I feel a tap on my shoulder, followed by laughter. I quickly turn, feeling disorientated, but I see nothing.

'THEY THINK THEY CAN HIDE BEHIND THEIR SYMBOL OF DEATH BUT I WILL EXPOSE THEM AND BLOT OUT THEIR EYE. THEIR EMPIRE SHALL CRUMBLE BY MY POWER!'

'Who are "they"? Show yourself!'

Another tap and I snap back towards the direction I was facing. There, floating in front of me in a sort of cylindrical glass tank, is the young woman that was posing in the photo with the doll.

'Sarah . . . ? Sarah Barns?' I utter. Half her face is covered with a breathing apparatus. She floats peacefully, her long blonde hair softly rippling and feathering in the water.

'Vitals are stable?'

'Everything is ready.'

'Let us proceed.'

Invisible voices surround me.

'Are you sure there is no other way?'

'Your sister has been chosen. You know the rules. Start the procedure!'

The apparatus starts to power up. The noise is like a turbine engine. Instantly Sarah's hand shoots forward and presses against the glass. She jolts like an electric eel as bubbles escape her mouth, her screams silent.

'Switch it off, please! You're killing her!' a voice pleads.

'The subject must complete the treatment!'

I run towards the tank to try to help but, before I can reach her, the glass shatters. Red mist gushes all around me like a raging river. I turn in every direction, trying to cling on to my sanity and focus my mind.

'NOW YOU SEE HOW I WAS BETRAYED!'

'I'm sorry about your sister. But killing innocent people will not bring Sarah back.'

'YOU STILL DO NOT SEE. NONE ARE INNOCENT! I KILL TO STOP THEM! THE COGS IN THE WHEEL.'

'You're . . . talking about Avalon?'

'MORE WILL DIE! I KILL SO THEY DO NOT GAIN!'

'We will stop you!'

'FIRST GET YOUR OWN HOUSE IN ORDER! THEIR EYES ARE EVERYWHERE.'

Another tap hits my shoulder and I spin around. There, standing face-to-face with me, is Charlotte.

'Charlotte! Wake up! Snap out of it. It's me, Elizabeth!' Her eyes stay closed and I survey her bloated, bluish-grey face as water pours from her eyes, nose, ears and mouth. I shake her profusely, attempting to wake her, but her body feels ice-cold, exactly like her sister's did in the morgue.

Click!

She tilts her head, snapping to one side, then projectile-vomits water from her mouth into my face. The pressure hits me like a firehose, knocking me to the floor. The pressure builds and I feel like I'm suffocating, drowning. Water rapidly rises underneath me, submerging us. I have to kick my legs to keep my head above the water. I try to swim towards the stairs.

As the water rises, Charlotte's body floats lifelessly in front of me. I grab her and tilt her head back above the rising water. Suddenly, someone grabs my hair, and a set of hands forces me under.

'No! Please! Charlotte!' I shout, gargling and choking on the copious amounts of water entering my throat. Charlotte drifts from my hands and sinks out of sight.

I fight with all my strength to get free and come up for air. My lungs burn for precious oxygen. I briefly manage to get some air and see that it's the detective attacking me, standing on the bottom step, glaring at me with dimly warped eyes.

'Where is she, monster? Where's my daughter?!' he angrily spits. He tries to push me back under again. I wrestle his hands, bobbing up and down, trying to stay alive. I'm dunked under again and, through the ripples of the water, I glimpse something else, like glowing red eyes.

My head floats up towards the detective's hands once more but this time I pull him from the stairs into the water beside me. We struggle to and fro as he points his gun at my chest. My oxygen deserts me as I exert the last of my energy, making one last push to fight for my life. I grab the gun.

Bmmm!

A muffled gunshot booms through the water and the detective calmly floats away from me. The water around us starts to evaporate and fades as quickly as it appeared. I cough up liquid from my mouth. I lie on the floor, drenched, panting for precious air, holding the gun firmly above my head, still pointing it in the opposite direction of Kukadia, towards the kitchen door.

'Got ya!' I whisper.

A tall, thin structure of a man wearing a dark beige suit and elongated plague mask grabs his arm in pain. Clenching his wound, he breathes heavily and stares at me through his nightmarish mask.

'Emit!' I cry with exhaustion.

Kukadia regains his senses, grabs the gun out my hand, and pulls the trigger multiple times at Barns, who stumbles out and runs off, until the barrel clicks empty.

We lie there, catching our breath. Words fail us in the moment.

We eventually sit up, dripping with water, and surveying the room. It is now completely unscathed; the walls are in their normal positions, as well as the stairs.

Kukadia is swaying in disbelief. He opens his mouth but says nothing. We both look at each other, then towards the kitchen door, where the masked man was standing.

'That was him,' I say breathily, still trying to clear my throat. 'The serial killer . . . Emit Barns.'

We both silently catch our breath, staring at the empty door where he used to be.

'Oh God, oh no. No,' Kukadia says as he crawls across the room.

Charlotte lies on the floor, lifeless, water trickling from her eyes, ears, and mouth.

The detective tries to resuscitate her, 'C'mon Charlotte breathe, C'mon,' he says pumping her chest. 'C'mon, wake up, breathe, don't die. Not like this, please,' he says hitting her chest one last time, but it fails.

'She's gone . . .' he says, cradling her head in his arms. Before we can even take a moment to acknowledge her passing, sirens blare from the street beyond the house. The detective throws me his keys.

'Get going!'

'Come with me. If you stay, they'll arrest—'

'I know what I'm doing; trust me. If they think you've been assisting me, they'll nick you too. You can't catch Barns if you're behind bars. Now get going!' the detective orders again.

The sirens close in on our position. I pick up the keys and take one final, heart-breaking look at Charlotte before I leave.

'Lizzy, do me a favour: find the bastard.'

I nod and exit the farm house. I'm coming for you, Emit Barns and — if I can't find you — I know who can. I need to meet with Mr X.

CHAPTER 18

The ReTURn

'Again! Repeat after me: When I sleep, I wake.'

'. . . When I sleep, I wake.'

'When I dream, I walk,' the professor instructs.

'When I dream, I walk.'

'Good, Mr Jacobs, but this time say it slower and relax: close your eyes and clear your mind — let go.'

My mind starts to drift and, within seconds, images of Armin's lifeless face blink before me.

'Concentrate, Joseph. Confront your fears. Only then can you heal your mind.'

'I'm trying, professor, but it's just not working.'

I continue to repeat the mantra but the more I do, the more I'm confronted with disturbing mental images: my house burns; Tin Man smiles as he gropes Leiyah; Knight Terrors attack the officer; all my anxieties flash and amalgamate into one, triggering, overpowering my thoughts. I start to feel like I'm back in Doctor Roth's medical lab.

'I can't do it, professor!' I blurt out in frustration. I rub my head, emotionally exhausted and, more than anything, annoyed at myself.

Grey stays seated calmly in his chair, next to the hologram-screen computer. He holds a book in his hands.

'It's just too noisy in here, I've . . . got a lot of baggage. I've seen too much . . . Says the whiny student to the man who's immortal,' I add, rubbing my head in frustration.

'Relax, Mr Jacobs. Maybe I have been too hasty. Direction is more important than speed.'

'It's just . . . I can't control or quieten my thoughts. I'm sorry.'

Professor Grey rests his book on the desk and places his hands together.

'The technique that I am attempting to teach you is called "Dozing". Mastering this will be the first part of your training. Since your powers lie within your subconscious mind — such as when you sleep — we need to be able to get you to a place of serenity and peace, for you to fall into a sleep-like state — like daydreaming: absent but present.'

'But where do our powers come from?' I ask.

'It is believed amongst many Figments that we draw from an infinite stream known as the Seven Rivers, which flow from Imādris. It is creation, matter, thought, and dream in one. We are connected to it and we absorb it like oxygen within our subconscious, ready to be used consciously when we Awaken. It reacts to our will and imagination, binding us, surrounding us. To human eyes it seems supernatural. We Figments can only draw our abilities from one individual stream. The Dreamwalker is said to be able to pull from all seven, mixing both light and dark in perfect harmony and balance.'

I sigh, feeling mentally overloaded.

'I understand this is all new to you but the technique we are practicing now is the first step in a long journey towards you controlling your ability. It is not unlike deep meditation — in fact they are from very similar schools of thought — but, to put it graciously, those that seek enlightenment are just scratching the surface. Their humanity will only allow them to see so far. When you are fully trained you will operate beyond the fourth dimension.'

I listen to the professor describe the task ahead and shake my head in defeat.

'Professor, I wouldn't even do yoga with my mom so this is . . . a stretch.'

'But not impossible. You need to rest. Be patient with yourself; these things take time. That is why we call it training.'

Grey resumes his book and I get up off the chair to stretch my legs. Looking around the professor's underground basement — well, I'm not sure if 'basement' is the right word: it *is* underground but it's more like a high-tech armoury-slash-museum-slash-Batcave. The layout expands over two levels and stretches the breadth of the house. It is lit by dim spotlights, lending a bronze tone to the exposed brick walls and slate floors. Looking over the open balcony to the level below, the dojo — equipped with weights, punching bags, and a wooden sparring dummy — reminds me of pretty much every old-school Shaw Brothers kung fu film I've ever seen.

The first level, where I'm currently standing, has strange artefacts that are meticulously placed in secure glass cabinets along with more old books and trinkets. One of the walls has an impressive assortment of weapons on display, from quarterstaffs to broadswords, katanas, daggers, bows, nunchacku, and spears. Next to the weapons is the most incredible-looking body armour, which has been placed on a mannequin in a cylindrical glass chamber. It looks like its missing parts of the armour around one of the arms and legs, but the breast plate is mesmerically embossed with a centre crest of twelve different moons, accompanied by beautifully detailed, golden-leafed calligraphy.

I spot the black cards and walk over to them; next to them are some tiny, peculiar, iridescent marble balls that are kept within a sealed see-through square case.

'What are these?' I ask the professor, tapping the jar. The glowing balls change colour.

'Those are Morpheus Portals. An old tool of war from another time and realm; very rare. Inside they are said to contain the tears of one of Imādris's mightiest warriors.'

'What do they do?'

'It works very much like a grenade. But, instead of exploding, it pulls your aggressor into a dream portal, capturing and suspending them in an abyss.'

'Nice! Kinda like a Poké Ball?'

'It is an extremely powerful tool, Mr Jacobs, and very rare. I have seen it used once and — believe me — it is enough to bring even the mightiest of foes to their knees.'

The colours within the Morpheus Portals change again, from blue to luminous green.

'Have . . . Have you ever been there, to the Dream Realms?'

'Unfortunately I have never had the privilege of seeing Imādris with my own eyes. Books, poems, visioned inscriptions are what I scour through for reference. The *Kubla Khan* is the most famous description of Imādris amongst Figments but — even then — it is vague. I once met a Figment that had walked amongst its blue grass and gazed upon the Twelve Moons . . .'

The professor hesitates to speak, as if the memory he is revisiting is mixed with both happy and sad emotions, then continues: 'But that was a very long time ago; they have now joined the Seven Infinite Rivers in eternal sleep.'

Grey quietly mutters words to himself in an unusual language, almost like a prayer, then snaps himself out of his feelings. He joins near the black cards.

'The material on the black cards — they look familiar.'

'Very good, Mr Jacobs. They have been forged from the black diamonds from the Seeing.'

'So that place exists outside of Palm Pathways?'

'Yes and no. A very powerful Figment named Mamu-Somnus—'

'Cool name.'

'Indeed. She could manipulate certain materials and substances, seamlessly weld them to her body, and absorb their properties. Mamu managed to pull out some of the stones into our reality but, in doing this, she forfeited her existence. The black diamonds appeared but Mamu became lost, her mind trapped within her own pathways. Very sad. The cards are one of a kind. There must always be balance, Mr Jacobs: cause and reaction.'

I continue to wander around the armoury, looking at the different objects. The stuff that Grey has stored down here is unbelievable but, then, I guess so is this whole situation. Sam and Leiyah would love all this, especially Sam.

'Professor, there are so many questions I'm still burning to ask, but my main one is . . .' I take a second before asking it: 'Did you ever meet or hear of my real parents?'

The professor is about to respond but, fearful of his answer, I jump right back in: 'I mean they must have been Figments, right?! If I'm this so-called Dreamwalker? Their names were Nusho and Ayamey . . .'

The professor takes a seat. He can see how much this information means to me.

'I did not know them, Joseph . . . I am sorry. There have been many Figments that walked the Earth — and still do — without knowing who or what they are. Your parents had a great task and responsibility bestowed upon them from Imādris: you. Because of who you are, they wisely would have kept you away from the prying societies of the Waning Order, Avalon, and others who have knowledge of our existence.'

'Well, their secrecy didn't work, did it?! In the end, they were out-matched and alone. They failed!' I blurt out, feeling oddly resentful of being adopted and having to live in an identity limbo for most of my life.

I head towards the exit.

'Joseph—'

I take a breath.

'I'll be alright, professor. Like you said, I think I just need to rest; all this has been a bit of a mind-smash.'

'Rest well.'

I leave the professor and go into the main house, heading towards the lounge area. I hear a song being played on an instrument that sounds almost like a cross between a music box and a harp. The slow, repetitive, ringing melody calms me. Opening the lounge door, I quietly step inside to see Sketch, legs crossed in front of the blazing fire, plucking a small, wooden, hand-held instrument.

'Everything good, Bushy Head?' she asks without turning round.

'How did you—?'

'I could sense your energy when you left the basement. What's wrong?'

Sketch continues playing the instrument.

'What's that you're playing on?' I ask, avoiding her question. I'm really not about to blurt out my woes to a child.

'Professor Grey said it was called a kalimba. It's pretty neat.'

'I didn't know you were a musician.'

'Neither did I. There's a lot of things I didn't know I could do until . . . well, until you Dreamwalked.'

'Well . . . at least *you* can tap into your ability. What use am I to anyone if I can't control my power? I can't even sleep without my dreams haunting me!'

Sketch stops playing and turns to face me. She reaches her hand towards mine, then pats up my arm and feels around my face, tracing it with her hands.

'Ahhh . . . So that's what you look like — your eyes are waaayyyy bigger than in the Seeing,' Sketch says, giggling to herself. 'I think you need to just chill, Bushy Head. Stop over-thinking things and take things day by day. Do something that you like to do.'

'That's it! Thanks Sketch, you're a legend.'

I jump up and head towards the front door.

'Wait, where are you going?' Sketch asks, following behind me.

'I need to get out of here for a bit, contact my mom and go home. I haven't skated for the longest time. Maybe that will help.'

'But the professor said we should stay here. It could be dangerous.'

'It won't be. I'm not a kid. I won't be long; I just need to pick some stuff up. You said do something I like to do.'

'Yeah but—'

'Cover for me. I won't be long.'

As I open the door to leave, Sketch throws on her coat and follows me out.

'Wait, where do you think *you're* going?'

'I'm coming with.'

'No, you're not. It might be—'

'What, dangerous? You just said it won't be. And anyway, if it is, you'll need someone to watch your back.'

'Sketch, no! Go back inside.'

'I'll scream. Then the professor will find out.'

I bite my tongue, annoyed. How have I gone from being an only child to feeling like I have a little sister? I look back at the house, then at Sketch, who has already zipped up her bubble jacket.

'I'm so gonna regret this.'

'Yesss!' Sketch says, jumping up and down, revelling in her victory.

'C'mon: two hours, then we'll come back. Oh, and if Grey asks, we just needed some fresh air.'

'Got it!' she replies with a cheeky grin on her face.

'Cool. Let's go, Tabitha.'

'Hey! Shut up!'

Beep Beep Beep Beep!

'Hey Zara, switch off the alarm!'

Alarm off!

And I'm back. After two bus rides, a brisk walk, Sketch constantly telling me how hungry she is, and one big fence-leap to break into my own house through the back window, I am finally home.

I open the front door to my house and let Sketch in. Mom's car is on the drive, but there's no sign of her in the house. Sketch grabs my arm and I lead her into the open kitchen.

'So, what do you want to eat?' I ask Sketch, who has already felt out the fruit bowl and is crunching on an apple.

'Anything! And a drink too,' she says with her mouth full.

I sort out a couple of snacks from the cupboard and get Sketch a juice box, hoping that will keep her satisfied for a while.

'Right, Sketch, I'm just gonna grab some things. Hang tight and chill, won't be long.'

'Whatever, Bushy Head.'

I head upstairs and hear Sketch activate Zara. K-pop music

beats through the ceiling speakers and I shake my head, smiling to myself. Well, at least she's happy.

I check Mom's room. Her bed is neatly made up as usual and her curtains have been left open, which either means she was here earlier or she's been away overnight at work.

Stepping back into my room feels strange. I haven't been in here since the morning after I first Dreamwalked. My clothes are still bundled in the corner, caked in mud, along with the red hospital tag and bandages. On my bed I see my phone and other personal effects that must have been confiscated when I was admitted to the TWI. They must have given them to Mom.

I switch on my phone and see a wave of backlogged unread messages from Sam, Leiyah, and others pop up on my screen. I scroll through the alerts and see a message from Harmony . . . I pause. Whatever chance I had of us becoming something is probably now out of the window.

I click on the message.

12:22 — Harmony: Hey you, hope you're okay?
Sam told me that you had to go away on a family
emergency. Hope it's nothing too serious

Harmony x

I place my phone against my forehead and sigh with a smile of relief. Sam, you absolute legend — still looking out for me after all these years. I click on my friends' group chat and type:

17:17 — Sent: Hey both @Leiyah レイヤ 🙈📟 X
@Sam 🕹 I'M BACK!

17:17 — Sam 🕹: Ohhhhh my Dayzzzzz!! 🔥 🏮
No way!!!!!!!!!!!!!! Where you at??

17:18 — Leiyah レイヤ 🙈 🍃 : X OMG!!! 😄
BNE!!!!!! 🖤 🙌🏽

        17:18 — Sent: I'll link you both soon, got 2 keep
        my head down. We'll catch up when we meet!

17:19 — Leiyah レイヤ 🙈 🍃:
Just let us know when and where x

17:20 — Sam ♟ : Good 2 hear from u bro.
The team is bk! 🖖

I'm not sure if it was the wisest thing to contact them both, given everything that's going on but, if there's anything I've learnt from TWI, it's to cherish those around you. Tomorrow is not promised.

With that said, I try ringing Mom. It rings once then goes straight to voicemail. I'll try again later.

'Right, time to go,' I say to myself. I put on my backpack and grab my skateboard from amongst my other decks.

I head downstairs. Sketch is singing at the top of her voice, eating snacks, and dancing in the middle of the room. I think of all the other innocent patients that are still at the TWI.

If my training and my ability can help them get out, like the professor did for us, then that's something I need to do.

'Hey Zara, stop music.'

'Hey! It was getting to the best part,' Sketch says in irritation.

'Sorry to be a killjoy, but we got to get going. The professor's probably wondering where we are already and I don't want to take any more risks.'

Sketch unenthusiastically nods in agreement, grabbing another snack from the kitchen counter before we leave.

* * *

Bleep!

I connect to the travel app on my phone, then scan the QR code of the MW: the Mercia Waterways, one of the many modes of public transport available throughout the city. As we board the vessel, which is a cross between an open-top tourist bus and a speedboat, I can see that Sketch feels uneasy. Maybe she has never travelled on water before.

'Do you want to hear a fun fact?' I say, trying to lift her spirits. 'They say it took around nine million bricks to line this tunnel.'

'Nine million?' she says, unimpressed. 'Seems a lot!'

'But the best fact is that each brick was handmade by women and children.'

'Well, we are the best.'

'Obviously!'

We both laugh as we speak in unison. Sketch holds her arms out over the side-railing and spreads her fingers, waving her hand in the wind. We both sit calmly, feeling the small waves rock the boat and listening to the hum of the engine.

'Sketch, can I ask you a question?'

'Sure.'

'How did you . . . How did you know how to contact me?'

'You mean in your dreams?'

'Yeah, that was . . . you, right? You opened a door and helped me escape from that terrible blazing light and those Knight Terrors that were crawling up towards me.'

'Yeah. I don't know how; I just did. I was looking for you. Looking for . . .' Sketch lowers her voice and whispers secretly, '*The Black Ghost!*'

'Don't call me that.'

'The night when it all went dark, I *saw* you. As clear as the black diamonds. That's how I painted that mural of you: I saw you fly into the air and I knew what you looked like. But I managed to stop myself from finishing the image. I didn't want to give away your identity. I may be ten but I'm not stupid.'

Stunned at her words and innocent confidence, I press to know more: 'How did you learn to control what you do?'

'I can't *really* control it, not yet, but I think I just accepted it. The moment I stopped fighting and stopped worrying, the more I could see. And now I see loads, but it's just different.'

'What happened to you that night?'

'I heard you scream. I felt burning energy go through my body. My eyes went black and I couldn't see anymore. It was a bit like falling into a dream.'

Sketch's words drop a weight of guilt onto my shoulders. I was the cause of her loss of sight.

'Don't feel bad, Bushy Head. I see differently now and I wouldn't change it for the world.'

'What . . . *do* you see?' I ask.

Sketch ponders about how best to explain.

'It's kind of like I see the particles in the air that make things colourful, or light, or dark, if you know what I mean? Sometimes it allows me to see a person for who they are.'

Sketch feels for my face and traces her little cold hands around it, eventually resting on my cheeks.

'You shouldn't worry so much, just accept. That's what I did. You're different. It's not a bad thing, once you stop fighting it, Bushy,' she says, ruffling my Afro and giggling.

The number 4 WMW cruises into Birmingham round the back of the Industrial, and ends up directly in the city centre, which beats travelling through Spaghetti Junction by bus in traffic. I find it a more peaceful way to travel: the open air and the fact we are less likely — on this route, anyway — to meet up with unsavoury characters.

'Another fun fact,' requests Sketch.

'Okay. Well, did you know that the canal systems here in Brum are actually bigger than Venice's?'

'Of course I knew that, Bushy Head! Everyone in the city knows that,' Sketch laughs.

Clang!

I spin round swiftly, only to see a drink can rolling down the empty aisle. A passenger must have dropped it. But no one's there. I could have sworn I saw someone sitting in the seats behind us when we boarded.

'Smells funny, I don't like it!' Sketch grimaces. The expression on her face would lead anyone to believe her nostrils were burning.

'It's just the canals.'

'How long till we get off, Joseph?'

I can see she's getting restless.

'Let's get off at the next stop.'

* * *

Bleep!

We leave the canals and change transport to an e-bike. Sketch jumps on the back and we ride through the busy inner-city streets. The smell of spices, curry, and jerk cuts through the air, as loud Bhangra tunes and heavy bass blast from the cars speeding past.

'Smells delicious. It's making me hungry,' Sketch says.

'Looks like the Festival of Culture has started,' I shout back as we cycle through Handsworth down Soho Road.

Suddenly a police siren yelps and I flinch, which makes the bike swerve.

'You okay?'

'Yeah. My bad,' I say, not wanting to alarm Sketch; she's been through enough trauma already. We continue gliding through the streets and I speed up.

The sounds of the city buzz past us, but then my ears pick up at a distinctive hissing grunt:

'WE SeE yOu!'

I look across the road between moving cars and for a split second to my absolute fear I swear I see Officer Scott.

'Whoa! Slow down!' Sketch screams.

'Huh!'

I pull hard on the brakes and we skid, stopping inches away from crashing into a food stall.

'Bloody kids!' the owner shouts before cussing us out in Punjabi.

'Ever heard of drink-driving?' Sketch says sarcastically as we dismount.

'Sorry, I thought I saw something . . . ' I reply, scanning the road behind us, desperately trying to reassure myself that I didn't just see what I thought I saw.

Suddenly I feel a tap on my shoulder.

'Hey, you!'

I turn, startled.

'Harmony?!' I say surprised. Over her shoulder, I clock a police car in the traffic behind her.

'I thought that was you on the bike. When did you get back?'

'Uhh oh . . . I—'

'Yesterday,' Sketch butts in and holds my hand. 'He was just taking me for a ride through the Festival.'

Sketch nudges me to fix up.

'Oh yeah . . . We got back yesterday. Just thought it would be nice to go for a ride through the city.'

Harmony's infectious smiles lights up her face.

'That's so nice. I didn't know you had a little sister. What's your name?'

'It's Sk—'

'Tabitha,' I interject, 'her name's Tabitha. Tabi for short.'

Sketch pinches my hand hard.

The police car finally drives away and I relax.

'So . . .' Harmony and I say simultaneously.

'You first,' she says.

'I . . . Sorry I never replied to your message. It's been a bit of mad house on this end.'

Sketch sniggers and I realise what I've just said. Harmony smiles politely.

'It's okay, things happen. I hope everything went well.'

'Yeah, it did. We're getting there, but it's nice to be back. So, how are things with you? How's uni?'

'Ehh . . . Busy. I've been helping organise the student Hallowe'en Ball, which should be fun. You should definitely come if you're around.'

'Sounds cool.'

'Apart from that I'm good — better than I have been, with everything that's been going on. It just feels great to be out in the streets amongst the people, celebrating. Between that whole Blackout mess and the whole "Ghost" craze, the whole city just felt . . . I don't know . . . It just felt cloudy, fearful. I get it, people need hope in such times, but I don't agree with idolising a violent vigilante. That's dangerous.'

I nod. As I listen to Harmony speak her mind on the Ghost, I'm kind of happy that my secret identity is safe. Sketch starts to get agitated and pulls at my arm to get my attention.

'I need the toilet really badly,' she says, cutting into the conversation.

'Okay, hang on,' I respond. 'I'll try and make it to the Hallowe'en Ball if I can. It would be cool to catch up more.'

'I'd like that,' Harmony responds.

'Joe, I'm desperate!' Sketch says, pulling at my hand harder.

'Well, I better let you both get going. It was nice meeting you, Tabitha. Hopefully see you soon, Joseph.'

'Yeah, see you soon.'

Harmony walks off into the crowd. I watch her meet her friends, the twins Omanah and Omaru, and they disappear amongst the people.

'Joseph!'

'Right, let's find you a toilet.'

'No! Joseph, look!' Sketch drops her act and points across the road. 'Knight Terror!'

Standing amongst the masses, looking at me with a piercing cold stare, is Officer Scott. We lock eyes.

'It's coming towards us,' Sketch says in a panic.

The officer starts to walk over, pushing through the crowd, unbothered by those around him.

'Sketch, grab onto my hand tight! We need to move now.'

We run into the oncoming crowd and then over the road, in between moving parade trucks blasting music from their speakers.

Sketch's little legs struggle to keep up — I pull her close, almost losing her in the chaos of the ever-growing crowd of people.

'Stop, Joseph! My ankle!' Sketch screams. We stop dead. 'I think I've twisted it.'

Still seeing the officer getting closer by the second, I pick up Sketch in my arms and keep moving.

I take her into one of the many shops along the side of the road.

'Sketch, I need you to hide here and wait for me, okay?'

'Please don't leave me,' she begs.

'Listen, it's me he's after. I need to lose him. I'll be right back. I promise!'

Sketch anxiously nods and crouches behind the shop window. I retrieve my skateboard from my backpack and blast out of the shop door at full speed into the road.

'Mercia PD! Stop!'

I push hard on my board, looking back to see Scott sprinting at full pelt, sliding over car bonnets and barging people out of the way, all the while never taking his emotionless glare off me.

It worked! He's following me.

Now I just need to lose him.

I weave between oncoming cars and people, shredding the pavement, trying my best to grow the distance between me and the officer.

I shoot through a set of red traffic lights. Car horns beep as they swerve to miss me.

'Damn! Just my luck.'

A traffic jam.

I kick-flip my board into my hands and continue running through the traffic, looking for a clean stretch of ground to push off from again. I turn to check behind me.

To my disbelief, I see the officer sprinting, jumping across the rooftops of the gridlocked cars. He jumps down and pulls out his gun.

I jump back on my skateboard and swivel through an open shop door.

Pap! Pap!

Two shots sound out above the mêlée of the streets and I hear the shop owners scream as I blow through the back door.

Skreshhhhh!

I lean back on my board and grind to a stop. Ahead of me are a set of steps which lead down into another road. As I contemplate my next move, I look round to see the officer darting at me through the store — his gun raised. Without a second thought, I push off on my board and land onto the hand railing — grinding all the way down — picking up speed all the time and then, suddenly, as if in slow motion, I see an oncoming car. The second I land on the ground it's going to hit me. The driver has already spotted me and is pumping his brakes, honking his horn . . .

My board hits the pavement and I jump, rolling over the bonnet of the car and — by some miracle — landing perfectly back onto my board which had rolled through under the car, unscathed.

The officer stands at the top of the stairs. He re-holsters his gun and watches me as I glide off.

* * *

Sketch is waiting for me patiently, munching on more snacks.

'You came back!' she says happily, hugging me tightly.

For the first time in a long time, I feel as if I have managed to do something good. And I did it without the use of my abilities.

'C'mon, let's go.'

'Is it gone?'

'Yeah, for the moment.'

'That was close!'

'Too close.'

As we exit the shop, a huge sound explodes in the distance. Smoke rises high into the sky.

'What is it?' Sketch asks.

'I don't know. Let's get out of here.'

I hail down a taxi and we jump in.

'Looks like there was a big traffic accident on the old Spaghetti Junction,' the taxi driver says. 'Where to?'

I give him the address to Grey's house and we drive off.

'By the way, your girlfriend, Harmony—' Sketch begins.

'She's not my girlfriend—'

'Whatevs. She's nice, she has a pure aura. I liked her. Well, I did, until she said she didn't like the Ghost.'

CHAPTER 19

HiGH NOOn

'Get in!'

'How do I know it's really y—?'

'We don't have time for this!'

I look around apprehensively, second-guessing myself. Elizabeth, what have you got yourself into? I take a moment: 'Follow your instincts, you need this,' I whisper to myself, which makes my mind up. I take another look at the silver car's tinted windows and get into the driver's seat. I close the door behind me. *Slam!*

'Don't move! Put your hands on the steering wheel where I can see them . . . slowly.'

I begin to move my hands towards the . . .

'A-ah-ah, slower!'

As I follow the instructions, I hear rummaging in the backseat behind me. I look towards the rear-view mirror to try to see into the back but the mirror's been removed. In fact, all the mirrors — including the side mirrors — are gone. I have no visuals.

Fsssshhhhhhhh! Zzzzzz wiiiiiiiizzzzzz — Cssshhhhhh!

Noise from a radio signal transceiver fuzzes behind me, undulating in different frequencies and tones.

'What is that?' I gasp.

I turn my head to look, only to be suddenly stopped by something pressing, protruding into my back through the cushioned seat. It feels like the muzzle of a gun but I can't be certain. My gut told me I was taking a risk jumping into this car, but this is the only way I have a chance of catching Emit Barns. So when Mr X agreed for us to meet I was relieved, especially after he went dark on me at the police station. Then I received a number of encrypted messages that led me to this deprived area: the forgotten backstreets of Witton.

The gangs around here, the Scraphillz and the B6ix Pirates, are known for unprovoked violence. It's a way of showing those currently occupying the Third Loop that they're a threat.

'First was the Spark.'

'P— Pardon?' I stammer. The continuous white noise of the radio signal in the background makes it difficult to hear.

Chick-click!

Great. I know that sound: the distinctive clicking sound of a hammer being pulled back and primed, ready for use.

'I won't say it again. First was the Spark!'

' . . . Im . . . Ima—'

'Careful, no mistakes; you only get one chance at this,' he growls, pushing the object further into my back.

'Imādris gave birth,' I answer swiftly, with a sudden certainty.

'Infant light formed,' Mr X responds without hesitation.

'And creation was born.'

I sit and wait, listening to the repetitive signal frequencies, wondering what the next move is.

Chick-click!

The pressure eases from my back. I exhale in relief as I hear the weapon revert back to safety mode.

'Now what?' I ask.

Ching!

A single key attached to a full moon key ring is dropped onto my lap.

'Start it up! And remember: keep it slow, no sudden movements.'

His voice sounds muffled; he must be wearing a mask or scarf over his mouth to hide his identity. When we would speak on the phone, I knew he was using a voice modifier and now I've noticed small over-exaggerated nuances in his speech. He's trying to keep his accent as neutral as possible to evade any regional detection. Who is he? He must be experienced, possibly even working within the law at some point, maybe an ex-officer like myself.

'I need to speak to you about Emit Barns and the red—'

'Stop speaking!' he says sharply, sounding slightly panicked and raising his voice enough to break the façade of his accent, which is all I needed to decipher where he's from: Wessex. I place my hand down slowly, grab the steering wheel, and push the key into the ignition.

We drive down the main road. I stop at the red light. I see a young man in his early twenties, slim build, skateboarding past the car. He glides past without a care in the world and I can't help but think about Joseph . . . Ever since meeting Charlotte, I've had this unsettling knot in my stomach about what he said.

Fsssshhhhhhhh! zzzzzz wiiiiiiiizzzzzz — Cssshhhhhh!

I hear Mr X switch his device to another frequency that vibrates and crackles in a lower tone.

'So, are you going to tell me why you called to meet me in person?' Mr X asks.

'I've got to tell you, I've never had a gun pointed at me on a first date,' I say, my sarcasm unable to fully hide how pissed off I am.

'Apologies for the abrasive behaviour Elizabeth, but it was necessary. These are dangerous times.'

The traffic lights flick to amber.

'Dangerous times, huh? Tell me about it,' I mutter under my breath. 'Well, word of advice, if you're planning on pointing your gun . . .'

The lights turn green.

' . . . Aim for the head; it's more intimidating.'

I suddenly shift forcefully into first gear and push down hard on the accelerator, over-revving the engine, and abruptly lift my foot off the clutch pedal and drop the handbrake. The car jolts aggressively, wheels spinning and skidding onto the Queensway, throwing Mr X to the other side of the back seat. That will teach him.

'Now's your chance to speak. Tell me what you know,' I say, getting impatient now. 'I have just been through hell. I watched a young, innocent girl drown in a room, flooded with water that wasn't actually there! Now either that was a hallucination, in which case I am losing my mind because I saw it — felt it — she's dead! *Or* it is something else entirely, and what I thought was impossible is actually possible. So you tell me, "Mr X": what in God's name is going on?!'

Click!

Mr X fastens his seat belt.

'Elizabeth . . . I am being hunted.' His tone is equal parts worry and exhaustion.

'What do you mean? If you're in trouble I can get you into police protection.'

'With all due respect, you can't protect me anymore than you can protect yourself! No one can. There are forces at work that do not adhere to the laws of man or reality.'

'What are you talking about?'

'You must understand that things are now in motion that have been foretold. The so-called "Blackout" was not caused by a storm.'

'What are you talking about? What was it then?' I say in frustration, sick of reading between the lines.

'Not an "it" — a someone—'

Mr X stops abruptly. Out the corner of my eye I see him staring out of the rear window. The collar of his black rain mac is flicked up, partially covering the nape of his neck. The tips of his mousey brown hair protrude under a black baseball cap. Black leather gloves cover his hands and I also note a black strap stretched around the back of his head which looks as if it's connected to some sort of face covering or mask.

'What is it?' I prompt.

'I thought I saw something . . . but I can't be sure.'

Once again I hear him tweaking the frequencies on his device, which starts to crackle.

'We are not the only ones that have an active interest in the serial killer's case.' Mr X hesitates.

'What do you mean?'

'The reason these poor victims' deaths have been impossible to explain, without a supernatural reason, is because that's exactly what it is. What if I were to tell you that the serial killer's symbol — the Eye — is a stolen symbol? That, placed intentionally, it is used to send a message to those who are hidden in plain sight?'

Emit Barns's words resurface in my memory: 'THEY THINK THEY CAN HIDE BEHIND THEIR SYMBOL OF DEATH BUT I WILL EXPOSE THEM AND BLOT OUT THEIR EYE. THEIR EMPIRE SHALL CRUMBLE BY MY POWER!'

'They are the Watchers, Elizabeth,' Mr X continues, 'the visioned ones, turning the cogs inside the wheels. There isn't a part of the system they have not infiltrated and, for that reason, you must leave this alone, before it's too late. Blood already stains my hands.'

'What are you talking about?'

'The young girl at the hotel . . . I thought I could help her, but they were already watching. I could do nothing more. To my shame, I had to let her become a necessary sacrifice in order to expose them.'

'You sick bastard! How could you?!'

'Listen to me! Their desperation to protect their ways will lead to further disaster. You must drop this case immediately or you and the ones you love will suffer.'

'You know I can't do that! These people, or criminals, or whoever they are, are a threat to me, my family, and the city. I cannot have more innocent blood on my conscience.'

'I'm warning you: they are not to be crossed. I myself have received my pips and I'm sure by now my fate is sealed.'

'Well, sorry to burst your bubble, but I don't believe that. Our fate is not written for us, but by us.'

Fsssshhhhhhhh! zzzzzz wiiiiiiiizzzzzz — Cssshhhhhh! Beep, beep, beep, beep!

The static noise distorts and changes into a pulsing beep, almost like a submarine's sonar beacon.

'It's them! They've found me!' Mr X says sliding the barrel of his gun back.

Chick-click!

'Whatever happens, Elizabeth, whatever you see, keep driving!'

'Fine! Tell me what you see.'

'White van, unmarked, no number plates. Moving quickly over into the right-hand lane. Take the next exit and head towards Spaghetti Junction.'

'Okay, I'm on it.'

Vrrrrmmmmm!

I focus, gradually picking up speed, overtaking the car in front of me. I ready myself but keep within the speed limit, so as not to alert our pursuers.

'It would have been a huge help if this car had mirrors. I'm practically driving blind!' I shout back over the beeping, which has started to slow down.

'Mirrors are our enemy! Trust me, in this case they would only make things worse!'

'What's that about mirrors?' I ask, remembering what Joseph told me. The beeping on the frequency device stops.

'What's going on? Where's the "beep?"'

Buuuffffff! Crunch!

Out of nowhere a tremendous force courses through the car. We jerk forwards in our seats. The car swerves from side to side. I grab the steering wheel tighter to hold the car steady as it rocks uncontrollably.

Beeeeeeeeeeeeeeppppppppppppppppppppp!!

The frequency returns, a sustained, continuous note like an ECG monitor signalling a cardiac arrest.

Pap! Pap! Pap! Clink, clunk, clung!

Shots fired! The rear window is peppered and shrapnel clangs against the metal boot of the car.

'Keep driving! The windows are bulletproof.'

I hear the rear passenger door open and feel a sudden gush of wind cascade around the vehicle, followed by the sound of blaring horns and screeching tyres. Mr X draws his gun.

Pap! Pap! Pap!

'They're getting closer!' he gasps, falling back into the car and slamming the door shut. I press down on the accelerator harder and race forwards, overtaking more cars, as we speed onto Spaghetti Junction.

Bang!

'Shit!' They ram us again! The white van spikes us and the back end of our car lifts slightly off the ground from the force.

'Faster!'

'I'm trying!' I shout back. 'Here!' I throw my phone over my shoulder. 'Ask for Officer Lace, tell her it's an emergency!'

'Are you sure we can trust her?'

'Yes! Hurry, call her!'

I hear the screech of wheels getting closer. I beep the horn multiple times to warn the cars ahead.

'Watch your left! They're positioning themselves for another charge.'

I shift into third gear, pushing the car's revs up and swerve around another car. I narrowly avoid clipping its rear bumper as I speed past.

More shots rattle and spit against the passenger side window.

'Have you got through to her yet?'

'No! It keeps cutting out. They must be blocking our signal.'

'Shit! Who are these people?!'

'On your six, closing in fast!' Mr X helpfully informs.

'Okay. Hold on!' I drive over to the opposite side of the junction swiftly, weaving between oncoming cars — each one a near miss. They swerve manically — honk their horn, flash their lights — as more shots rain down across the roof of the car. I flinch with each impact.

My stomach lodges into my throat and I'm pumped with adrenaline. One wrong movement and it's over.

'Not today,' I snarl to myself.

'It's ringing!' Mr X announces with some hope in his voice.

'Great! Put it to my ear.'

Mr X presses the phone to my ear as it continues to ring.

'C'mon, c'mon, pick up . . . !'

'Elizabeth? *Fsssjhh zzzz cssshhh!*'

'Lace, I'm—'

'Elizabeth?! *Fzzzsss* 'Why— *czzsss!*'

'Lace— Damn it! The line's corrupt!'

'*Fsshzzzz.* Hello?! *Czzzhhhssszzz!*'

'Listen, if you can hear me—'

'*Chhzzz* I— *fffzssssh* where are— *Zzzzzsss!*'

'We need immediate assistance. We're eastbound on Spaghetti Junction, taking fire—' The line goes dead.

Crash!

'What was that?!' I ask urgently, not daring to look back at the loud collision behind us.

'They've just T-boned a car, mass pileup. Keep going, they're still on us!' Mr X leans out the door and fires more shots.

Pop! Dddddddddd!

The car starts to shudder and tremor uncontrollably. We veer to the left. 'The tyre's been shot out,' I yell. I recklessly swing back onto the left side of the road, ploughing over the traffic barrier cones, sending them flying into the air. I see an exit up ahead. I can make it, I can . . .

Vrmmmmmm!

'Prepare for impact!' Mr X shouts.

Out of nowhere, like a raging, roaring, runaway train, is the white van. Sparks fly as it grinds against the passenger side, blocking my exit.

They ram us twice in quick succession.

The passenger door crumbles from the car and wedges the vehicles together. We speed furiously up the carriageway — one interlocked mass of metal. Smoke rises from the bottom of the car and the smell of burning rubber penetrates the air.

I twist the steering wheel with all my might, and hit the brakes at the same time. Our vehicles unlatch and the car spins and skids to a halt. The engine dies.

A hundred yards ahead, the white van wheel-spins in a one-eighty, as I desperately try to restart the engine, hoping not to be hit by oncoming cars. A quick glance shows that the oncoming traffic has mostly stopped at a safe distance, drivers getting out and running away from the carnage.

The exit is right in front of us, mocking me.

'Come on, come on. Start up, please,' I urge, as the van picks up speed. A single speeding car careens around us, skims the central reservation, fishtails across three lanes and crashes head-long into the van.

Chick-click!

Mr X locks and reloads his gun.

'Here, take your phone. I'll try and hold them off.'

'Wait, what?! Where are you going?!'

'I've left you details and locations on your device that will give you answers. They will help you uncover the truth about Avalon!'

'Avalon?!'

The van backs up, extricating itself from the other car, and in a cloud of tyre smoke, begins bearing down on us again.

'Start at the Thelema Wellbeing Institute.'

'The Thelema Institute? My God . . . Joseph!'

'Seek out a man called Syre Thorn! He is the head of the Waning Order, my group. Sarah Barns's death was no mistake and will not be the last. Trust no one, Elizabeth. Reality is a blanket for those who slumber. They are watching.'

Before I can get another word out, Mr X kicks the bullet-riddled door off its hinges with ease and walks out onto the carriageway, uttering words in a strange language, as if praying. My phone vibrates in my hand. I see an icon of a folder flashing on my screen. Not now. I look back up and find Mr X is already walking down the road, his coat billowing in the wind as he moves forwards. He stands tall and ready, like a sheriff in those old Western movies. High noon; ready for a quick draw.

The van races towards us; the only thing standing between us is Mr X.

With incredible speed, he draws his pistol and fires two shots accurately into the two front tyres of the rampaging white van.

Pap! Pap!

Crshhhhhhh! Almost in slow motion the van flips and tumbles forwards through the air and, in that moment, I witness something truly unimaginable. With the van flying in mid-air, two women in white suits jump out of the doors — holding onto the doorframes with just one hand — balancing their feet on the side of the rotating vehicle as if surfing a wave.

SMASH! BOOOOOM!

The van crashes onto the floor and explodes into a ball of flames.

Mr X stands looking at the destructive chaos unfurling in front of him. His shoulders relax, almost in a sigh of relief.

Bang! Bang!

Immediately shots fire from the direction of the blaze. One hits the windscreen. I duck on impact and exhale. That one was perfectly levelled at my head.

'Get going!' Mr X shouts as he drops to his knees, spinning and sliding behind cover, before returning shots in the direction of the blaze.

'Start up. Come on, start,' I plead, turning the key in the ignition, but it still refuses to cooperate.

Weuw! Weuw! Weuw!

A police car speeds up to the blaze and screeches to a stop. Finally some help.

'Hey officers! Over here, I'm stuck!' I shout out. Officers jump out of their vehicle and shield themselves behind the doors, their guns trained on Mr X.

'Drop your weapon! Put your hands above your head, now! We won't ask again. Get on the radio and call this in,' I hear the officer closest to Mr X say to his partner. 'It looks like World War Three down here.'

'Radio's down, I'm getting nothing on the other end.'

Bang! Bang bang!

Shots ring out again from the direction of the fire. I scream as both officers crumple to the floor. Blood flows from their bodies into the middle of the road. More bullets thrash against my car. Part of the side window shatters. I am totally exposed. I try to open my door but it's jammed shut.

Mr X turns towards me, and I see now he is wearing a white ice hockey face mask. He signals to me with his arms to stay calm. My hands shake as more bullets fly towards me and the screams and cries of scared pedestrians increase.

'Work, damn it!' I turn the key again, then hit the ignition box in frustration with my hand.

Vrmmmmmm! The engine revs.

My joy at the engine spluttering to life is short-lived as I turn the wheel and look towards the chaos I'm about to leave behind. My jaw drops in disbelief.

The two women, their white jump suits now slightly charred, stand strong like statues, brushing ash from their suits. One is White, the other Black, both bald, almost identical in their demeanour but too far away to make out any facial expression. In fact, the Caucasian one looks almost like the shooter from the morgue, but I can't be sure.

One lets out a mighty, warrior-like roar. They look at each other and begin to charge forwards, running and jumping at a speed that I have never seen or thought humanly possible. One of the women stares directly at me through the shattered glass as she runs. My mouth opens in shock and disbelief.

'Charlotte,' I whisper, as she rushes towards me.

A fear the like of which I have never known grips me.

The other woman jumps from car to car with almost animalistic agility, defying gravity with each leap. The ash falls from her suit as she leaps, but . . . No, not ash: dust. Red dust shimmers around them like an aura, glistening and gleaming like diamonds as it falls and collects on the ground, leaving their suits as impeccable as before.

The women's eyes blaze white as they move swiftly — impossibly — a red trail following their every movement. Mr X dodges as one of the women kicks a car with an inhuman force, sending it barrelling across the road towards him.

'Go!' he shouts, darting into the middle of road, narrowly avoiding the tumbling car.

A deathly, blood-curdling yell splits the air.

I turn towards the sound and scream in horror.

The two officers who had been shot, bleeding out on the floor just moments ago, are now standing — limp — in front of my car, blocking my way. Their eyes blaze as white foam streams and froths from their mouths.

'Oh God, what the—'

'WE . . . SeE . . . yOu,' they say simultaneously, their voices resonating at a weird, deeply disturbing vocal pitch.

They point their pistols towards the windscreen and fire a barrage of bullets at the window until their clips run empty.

'Shit!'

I snap the car into first gear, close my eyes, and drive full-throttle straight into them. I feel their bodies bump and roll off the bonnet. I reverse again, needing more space to drive free.

Through the side window, I glimpse Mr X in a brutal hand-to-hand combat with the two women, who are running rings around him. They punch and kick him, the devastating blows eventually bringing him to his knees. Exhausted and beaten, Mr X looks up at me through his cracked mask as the two women circle him like blood-thirsty hyenas. Exhausted, he signals me to go as he rallies his last strength to tackle one of the aggressors. I honour his wishes, and speed towards the exit . . .

Boom! Crunchhh!

My head snaps forwards and thuds into the air bag. The seatbelt jolts tighter around my torso. The car stops dead, with just the sound of the motor spinning.

'What did I just hit?' My vision is obscured from the air bag, but I can see that parts of the bonnet have been completely crushed.

Clunk . . .clunk . . . clunk!

Footsteps tread slowly across the metal roof. Before I can release my seat belt, two fists suddenly punch through the bullet-proof glass and tear out the steering wheel. The hands grab me and rip me out through the demolished glass. I land on my back on the hard tarmac. My eyes blur from the impact; I black in and out of consciousness, hearing only chaos and sirens in the distance. My eyes get heavy as I fight to remain awake. The last thing I see before they close is the spitting image of Cara and Charlotte's face and the symbol of a Sagittarius, and then . . . Then . . .

CHAPTER 20

Trick or Treat

'Elizabeth, I've called it in. There's nothing we can do! The fire's completely out of control! If we go in, we're going to get ourselves killed. Just hang tight; the fire brigade is on its way.'

'Not good enough, Paul. We can't wait that long. The neighbours said they hadn't seen anyone exit the house. You heard them: the couple has a little boy. He could still be inside!'

'You don't know for sure. They might be already dead.'

'Every second you stop to debate is time we could be helping.'

'It's suicide! You won't survive.'

'I swore an oath to protect and serve and if there's an innocent child—'

'You can't save everyone. If you go in and get trapped then you're going to make this situation worse. We don't need dead heroes.'

'You're . . . right. I can't save everyone. But I can try.'

'Wait! What are you doing?! Elizabeth, don't do this!'

'I'm sorry. I'm going in.'

'Officer Jacobs, stop! Stand down. Elizabeth!'

'ELIZABETH . . . !'

'Elizabeth . . . !'

'We need to act fast!'

        'Heart rate's flatlining.'

'Hand me the defibrillator pads.'

        'Here.'

'Ready!'

        'In three, two, one . . . '

'Clear!'

        '. . . Nothing.'

'Again!'

        'Three, two, one . . . '

'Clear!'

. . .

        'We're getting a rhythm. She's back!'

'She's back . . . '
'. . . Back . . . '

'Elizabeth, what are you doing? Rumour has it you're . . . hanging up your shield?'

'. . . '

'Wow. So it's true then?'

'I . . . I was planning on telling you sooner.'

'No time like the present I guess. Just tell me one thing: why?'

'. . . '

'Please tell me it's not to do with the boy?'

'His name is Joseph.'

'C'mon, Elizabeth, he is not your responsibility. You can't just throw your life away because you feel guilty or because you've got emotionally attached. This is the job! That's what you always say.'

'Paul, they were going to put him in a workhouse. He has no one left!'

'Unfortunately that's just the way things go. If I had a penny for every time this city made a kid an orphan, I'd be a very rich man. But I'm not. We do our job and that helps bring stability to the system.'

'And what if the system is not working?'

'Well, then we would be out of a job, wouldn't we?'

'You weren't in there, Paul. Something changed in me when I went into that house. When I saw him sitting there, helpless, I knew I needed to save him or die trying. I feel a connection to him that's hard to put into words.'

'It's called trauma, Lizzy.'

'Screw you! You would never understand.'

'Yeah, I think I do actually! And the truth is, you think by doing this you're somehow going to repay society for that little kid that caught a bullet meant for you. Newsflash: it wasn't your fault. We caught the bastard, remember? He's doing life behind bars with the rest of his scum brethren. Doing this won't fix you, Elizabeth. I know you. You have no idea how to be a mum. And while you're off playing happy families, who's going to watch my back?'

'That is not fair.'

'Not fair?! It wasn't just you that was targeted after we pulled down the Dragon. I backed your play and now you're hanging me out to dry. Half of the guys in here were on the take; you think they're just going to forget that their wallets have been feeling a little lighter? We're partners and now you're pissing that away because you want to be the blonde-haired, blue-eyed saviour to some little Black orphan kid, who — if statistics are right — is going to end up in prison anyway? What about my life? Huh? What about our friendship? Doesn't that mean anything to you?'

' . . . '

' . . . Well. That's that then. Cheers. And for your information, that bullet was meant for me too.'

'BULLET WAS MEANT FOR ME TOO . . . '

' . . . Bullet was meant for me too . . . '

Bang! Boom! Bap!

The rumbling sound of bass from within CBU's Hallowe'en Ball. I walk towards the entrance, passing students dressed in an array of different costumes from monster, to pop icons, anime get-ups, video game characters; you name it. I'm excited to link up with Sam and Leiyah but oddly nervous too.

When Sketch and I returned to Grey's house, he was still in his underground armoury deep in thought, combing through mounds of scrolls and books, apparently unaware that we had ever left. I was surprised when he mentioned the Hallowe'en Ball and that he thought it might be a good idea for me to attend.

'Yoooo, Joseph!'

It's Sam and Leiyah. They come over to meet me with huge smiles. Leiyah greets me first, squeezing the life out of me, while Sam fist-bumps me over and over again, which turns into a hand grab, also pulling me in for a hug.

'It's so great to see you both!' I say, feeling overwhelmed with joy.

'You too, bro! This is so cool. My boy's back, everyone! He's back!' Sam shouts into the night sky. He's dressed like Wesley Snipes from an old classic: *Demolition Man.*

'You look good,' Leiyah says steadying herself on her skates, which presumably have something to do with the character she's dressed as. 'How've you been?'

'I . . . I'm getting there. To tell you the truth, I'm just happy to be here.'

'Yeah you are,' Sam says, dancing about. 'And the night's just begun! Now the real party can start. Yeahhh, boi! Joe's back! The Three Musketeers are back!'

We laugh as he throws his arms around us and we walk towards the entrance of the ball.

'So, Sam . . . is that hair colour . . . permanent?' I ask.

'Ahhh, yeahhh . . . It's a long story, bro. A lot of things happened whilst you were away. Let's just say things got real weird, real quick. Never do a dare over socials for clout, especially when you're drunk and missing your best friend.'

'Well, I think it suits you,' Leiyah says. 'This is one hair colour stereotype that might actually be right.'

'Ha-ha-ha Leiyah,' Sam replies sarcastically. 'And, by the way, who are you supposed to be? A roller-skating waitress?'

'Rude! Actually — if your basic brain didn't know — I've come as Gum.'

Sam and I look at each other, clueless.

'And you boys both state on your profiles that you're urban geeks and "real retro gamers"? Could've fooled me. Gum! You know, from the game *Jet Set Radio Future*? Maybe it's too retro for you.'

'Ohhhh yeah, of course, yeah,' Sam and I say in unison, wide-eyed, pretending to know what she's on about.

'I'm disappointed, guys,' Leiyah says as she skates around us.

'Whatever,' says Sam. 'At least it's better than Johnny Cash over here. Joe's just dressed up in all black, looking like the black Kurt Cobain. Always have to be cool, huh? You could've at least thrown on a bin bag, bro. I'll find one for you.'

We all burst out laughing and enter the party.

* * *

'Wow, this place looks incredible.'

'Not bad, eh?' responds Leiyah.

'Guys, do I really need to wear this bin bag?'.

'Yes, it's a good look, bro. No cap,' Sam sniggers.

'I'm going to find somewhere to put my coat; stay here.'

I try to take in the full view of the student lounge. An entangled labyrinth of cotton cobwebs, glow-in-the-dark spiders, and bats hang from the ceiling. Red and black curtains drape down to the floor, giving the room a stately, elegant feel. Every so often, a smoke machine that is rigged up somewhere pumps a cloud of purple into the room. In one corner of the room, there's a makeshift stage with a DJ booth and a microphone stand. Tunes bump from an automated playlist of hiphop, grime, R&B, electro and old showtune classics, with the odd spooky witch-cackle sound effect, and ghostly 'oohs' that are triggered randomly.

'Epic!' Sam says, taking it all in at the same time as me. 'This is craz—' he quickly pauses, realising his choice of words. 'Hey bro . . . Look, I'm sorry I never came to visit you.'

'It's okay, S—'

'No, it's not. I should've been there. I just couldn't bring myself to see you like that. Really bro, apologies. And I'm psyched you're back.' He realises his poor word choice again and slaps his head. I laugh.

'It's all cool, Sam, for real. It's not a place that you want to go near. I'm just happy I made it out.'

We stand awkwardly, bobbing our heads to the music.

'Oh and by the way, thanks for covering for me with Harmony.'

'Course, bro, I got your back.'

'Hey, guys,' Leiyah says, skating over to us with drinks. 'You'll never guess who I just bumped into: Miles Brown!'

Sam groans and looks warily over his shoulder.

'No, listen. He's, like, changed. He was really chill. I mean, like, his whole vibe was different.'

'Different how?' I ask.

'No way, I don't believe you,' Sam says defensively, still watching his back.

'It's true. I can't really explain it, it was weird. The whole roadman flex was gone. He was more like a spruced-up, sexy, Black Dracula. Anyway, long story short, everyone was all over him. He was dripping with coolness—'

'Not the last time I saw him,' Sam says smirking, referring to his elaborate urine-based venture.

'Eww, Sam, gross! No, but seriously he looks fine, then the twins walked past — they look fiyah too, as usual — and he went off after them, paying no one else any mind.'

'Wow, what a story Leiyah. Thank you for enlightening my life,' Sam says sarcastically. 'Maybe you can see if M. Night Shyamalan wants to buy the movie rights from you.'

I let out a laugh, as Leiyah shows Sam the middle finger. Their bickering is cut short as the music volume drops. Loud mic feedback sharply swells around the hall.

'One two, one two.'

'Yo, Joe: twelve o'clock,' Sam points. 'It's your girl.'

Leiyah rolls her eyes at Sam.

'Can you all hear me?!' Harmony yells down the mic.

'Yeahhhhh!' the crowded hall of costumed students shouts back.

'Happy Hallowe'en, CBU!'

The throng of students whoops and cheers.

'I'm Harmony May and welcome to the CBU Hallowe'en Ball! We hope you're all having a good time tonight. Just a reminder: if you're free this weekend, please come down to Chamberlain Square and join our protest against the corrupt Lord Mayor and his draconian policies! Let's let them know that we will not be silent!'

The crowd cheers again. The lights dim and a footlight illuminates Harmony from below in a spooky way. The sound of a theremin rises and Harmony clears her throat.

'Trick or Treat?
You decide
Force-fed sweets mixed with lies.
Our defiance is our pride
And our choice is our power.
At this moonlight hour,
WITCH will you devour?
Trick or Treat
Which one's your flavour?
Fighting on social media
Or the lies the papers feed the reader?
Black magic is no stranger
But still you scream "danger, danger"
You'll never dampen my soul
I ignite and burn like ether!
Trick or treat: I can choose both or neither.
I can be:
A villain, a vampire, a virago
A goddess, a monster and even a leader.
CBU, have a great Hallowe'en night
Filled with love, light and a thriller's FRIGHT!'

On Harmony's last word, a glitter cannon explodes behind her, sending gold confetti high into the air. A fresh drum and bass tune plays loudly through the speakers. The crowd goes wild, and Harmony puts the mic back and calmly steps off the stage.

Sam nudges me: 'Better put your tongue back in your head bro, she's coming over.'

Harmony makes her way through the dancing bodies of students. I down the remainder of my drink and approach.

'Well, hello stranger!' she exclaims as I meet her.

'Harmony! Hey . . . That was amazing. Also, well done on, well, all of this. You look incredible by the way. Let me guess . . .'

Harmony twirls around slowly to the beat, smiling, to show off her costume. She's wearing her hair loose. Her curls bounce around her head like a halo. She's wearing a crimson-coloured satin halterneck top that clings tightly to her torso, camouflage gym shorts, and black boots. I struggle not to blush or — worse — look bare thirsty. Not gonna lie, that's difficult.

Pointing to the plastic gun holstered to her thigh, I venture: 'Nadine Ross from the *Uncharted* games?'

'Very good! Gold star for you, Joseph. She's one of my favourite characters.'

'Yeah, she kicks ass. Literally. But also, she's completely ruthless and untrustworthy.'

'Ooh, you've got me down to a tee,' she whispers mischievously. 'I can totally see why that would upset the incel-manchildren who get absorbed in their little video games only to find they can't control women in that world either.' She draws back and winks at me with that irresistible glint of *gotcha* in her eye.

'Oh. No, I . . . I meant . . . Actually, you're right. But . . .' I hesitate, eager to keep the conversation alive but aware that what I am about to say is probably mansplaining. 'Just for accuracy's sake though, Nadine wears long khaki combat trousers, not shorts.'

'Well, I guess you could say I'm one of a kind, maybe even "different"?'

I smile, recognising Harmony's re-quoting of our first real conversation. What else can I say to someone who is more than my intellectual match, someone who makes all the right words die in my mouth and my heart beat so loudly that she can probably hear it from here? It's almost unfair.

'You're the Black Ghost, aren't you? Still not sure about that name.'

My stomach somersaults into my throat. What?! How could she know? How could she possibly know my secret?

'Wh— What?'

'The Ghost,' she says pulling at my bin bag cape. 'I've got to say, it's not the best I've seen tonight. One guy even brought his own smoke machine. You're not going to be winning any fancy dress prizes tonight, I'm afraid.'

I breathe a sigh of relief and smile. 'Yeah, dunno what I was thinking. Bit cliché, really. Can I get you a drink?'

'How about I get you one? We've had signature cocktails commissioned: CBU special Hallowe'en punch and, of course, "the Ghost," with a hint of lime . . .'

Harmony's attention flicks to something over my shoulder. She frowns, as if she's seen something odd.

'Wait . . . Isn't that your little sister?'

I turn around to see Sketch waving me over near the entrance. Professor Grey stands next to her. What are they doing here?

'I'll be right back,' I say to Harmony walking over to them quickly through the crowd.

'Joseph, there you are!' Sketch says.

'Is everything okay? What are you both doing here?'

Sketch looks up at Grey, who has a sorrowful look in his face.

'Wh— What is it?' I ask, 'What's going on?'

'Mr Jacobs . . . There has been an accident.'

'Accident . . . ?'

'Yes, involving your mother.'

My heart hits my throat.

'She's in the city hospital. Young Sketch envisioned her, as well as something else that may have a more sinister meaning behind it but . . . I cannot be sure. We must leave at once. Say goodbye to your friends and meet us outside.'

My legs shake underneath me.

'Is everything okay, bro . . . ? Joseph?'

I hear Sam's voice but I am lost in my own head, disconnected from my surroundings.

'Joe, you good?' Leiyah asks.

'No, it's . . . It's my mom. She's been in some sort of accident.'

They gasp with worry.

'She's in the hospital.'

Leiyah lightly nods to Sam and they both slip away in the direction of the entrance.

'I'm so sorry, Joseph. How awful. Is there anything I can do?' Harmony asks, pulling me close with a hug. I stand in her embrace, feeling empty as the crowd dances around us.

'I've got to go.'

'Go be with your mum,' she whispers softly. 'I'll call you.'

She kisses me on the cheek. Funny really; this is not how I would've imagined our first kiss. Trick or Treat. I leave, looking back at her through the small gap in the crowd we had created, before I lose sight of her as the other students carry on partying. Sam and Leiyah stand outside the hall with their coats, both ready and waiting for me.

'What are you guys doing?' I say, tearing the bin bag off me.

'We're coming with.'

I look at Leiyah, who zips up her jacket defiantly. 'Sam's right. You're not going without us.'

I take a deep breath and shake my head, which turns into a nod of agreement. I feel blessed to have such amazing friends. The three of us leave the Hallowe'en Ball together and meet Professor Grey and Sketch in the cold night air.

CHAPTER 21

WAKEY, WAKEY!

We arrive at the City Hospital, the private patients' wing. Grey walks ahead of me towards the reception area and looks around. Sketch and I follow behind, tailed closely by Sam and Leiyah.

'Yo, Leiyah,' I hear Sam whisper behind us. 'Is it me or is it really, really, I mean really quiet in here? Where is everyone?'

The dimly lit reception area is completely empty.

'How would I know?' Leiyah replies, also keeping her voice down.

'Just saying, it's hella dead! No pun intended.'

Sam is pointing out the obvious, but even so . . . However, my mind is solely focused on seeing my mom.

Suddenly Sketch grabs my hand and stops abruptly. She looks up, like she's scanning the ceiling, and counts to herself.

'What is it?' I quietly ask, not wanting Sam and Leiyah to hear.

'I can see her.'

'Who? Mom? Where?!'

'She's on floor twelve, right at the top.'

I waste no time and head straight for the lift, anxiously pressing the button multiple times, waiting for it to descend.

'She's going to be okay, Joe. She's in the best place,' Leiyah says, trying to reassure me.

I wait impatiently, then press the button again. Grey has finished his inspections and walks over to me. A grave look of concern crosses his face.

'Mr Jacobs, head to the twelfth floor; that is where you will find your mother. I will join you there shortly.'

He nods his head with an unspoken statement of caution, then swiftly disappears around the corner.

'Wonder where he's going?' Sam asks.

He gets no reply. Sketch holds my hand and continues to look up.

'Ready?!' she says to me, in a tone of voice which gives me the feeling that there's more than one meaning behind her word.

Ding!

The lift arrives and we all get in. I immediately press the button to go up to the twelfth floor. We stand in silence as the lift ascends. Leiyah gives me a reassuring look, putting on a brave face and Sam looks at Sketch, who's holding my hand. He waves his hand in front of her face, then attempts to peer over her sunglasses. Leiyah nudges him to stop.

'Soooo . . . How long have you had a little sister, bro?' Sam asks. He must have overheard Harmony.

'Errr . . . It's a long story,' I reply.

'For your information, we met in the place of The Seeing,' Sketch casually blurts out. I immediately glare at her, scolding her with my eyes.

Sam looks at Leiyah with a confused gesture and half-smirk across his face.

'You know — the place with black diamonds where time moves but doesn't?' Sketch adds innocently. 'It's all controlled by your memory.'

'Right,' Sam says, sticking his thumbs up. 'Great story. Think someone got her little hands on the Hallowe'en punch. Kids these days,' Sam side-mouths to Leiyah.

'Ay, I'm not a kid, I'm nearly ten,' Sketch fires back, sticking her tongue out.

Ding!

The lift doors slide open.

'This way,' Sketch leads me out of the lift and down the corridor. Sam's right: it is eerily quiet.

'How far?' I ask Sketch.

'We're nearly there.'

'Pssst! Is she blind?' Sam not-so-quietly asks Leiyah.

'Visually impaired! Yes — I think so.'

'So how does she know where she's going?'

We take a left, then another left. All the while the last words I had with Mom replay in my head like a bad soundbite.

'There!' Sketch points to the dimly lit room. 'The door to the right.'

I rush to open the door but again Sketch stops me by pulling my arm.

'Wait!' she whispers. 'Someone else is in there with her!'

Not caring about the warning I open the door. Before I can even set my foot properly onto the floor, I'm pulled in and thrown to the ground.

'Joseph, look out!' Sketch screams.

Sam and Leiyah charge into the room after me, only to find me looking down the barrel of a gun.

'Woah! Woah! Take it easy!' I say in a panic, lying on my back. My hands shake as they stretch above my head.

'Who sent you?! Who sent you?!'

'Back off!' Sam shouts, before quickly raising his arms as the gun points in his direction.

'Why are you here?!' asks the gunman.

'Stop!' Leiyah yells, holding Sketch closely in a guarded hug. My eyes look past the gun and towards the man holding it.

'Detective . . . ?' I say.

He eases away and relaxes his arm. He turns around and switches on the overhead light.

Bib . . . bib . . . bib . . . bib . . .

The machine noise grabs my attention and Detective Kukadia backs away. I see my mom on the bed behind him.

'I'm sorry, kid. I didn't know it was—'

'Mom!' I blurt out, jumping to my feet and racing towards her bedside.

Sam intercepts me and tries to calm me down as I frantically reach out to her in a frenzied state of disbelief.

'I got you, bro!' he says, hugging me as tears roll from my eyes.

'Mom!'

Wires connected to multiple monitors surround her motionless body. Metal connectors stick in her bandaged neck like pins. An oxygen mask covers her badly bruised and cut face.

'Wha . . . What happened to her?' I ask the detective.

'She was in a car acci—' the detective falters, seeing my look. I've had enough secrets.

'Tell me!' I demand as I walk over to him.

'I think your mother was attacked and left for dead.'

'Attacked?! By who?'

'I . . . don't know!' the detective sighs. 'I managed to intercept a call from a bug I planted at the station and I came here as soon as I could.'

'Why would anyone want her dead? She's not even police anymore.'

The detective looks down at his feet and holsters his firearm.

'Your mother was helping me in an investigation . . . She discovered something that wasn't meant to be uncovered and it's put her life at risk.'

'So where are the rest of the police? Why are you the only one here, why is no one here to protect her?'

'I don't know. I've tried to call it in but it's a dead zone. It's like the signal's being blocked.'

Leiyah quickly tries her phone. 'Sam, Joe: try yours.'

'Nothing!' Sam replies.

'Blocked!' I add. 'But she's still alive, so whoever did this failed,' I say, holding my mom's hand.

'Your mum's a tough one, she always has been. But you can guarantee that they'll be back to finish the job. We need to move her.'

'Is that even safe?!' Leiyah asks.

'The medical notes state that she's been induced into a coma to help her recovery.'

The detective clocks my uncertainty.

'I owe Elizabeth my life. I'll be damned before I let anything happen to her. Quickly, give me a hand.'

I watch nervously as the detective starts to prepare to move Mom with Sam and Leiyah's help. Sketch pulls me to the side.

'Maybe you can contact her?' She puts her hands together in front of her to signal what she means: Palm Pathways.

'I don't think it'll work, Sketch. The professor said that can only be used by Figments, and even then, not all Figments can use it.'

'But you're not just any Figment are you, Bushy Head? You're the **Amātriā**! Our last hope, the Son of Imādris — The Dreamwalker! If she's in a dream-like state, maybe you can talk to her and find out what's coming.'

Clang!

Our conversation cuts short.

'Get down, all of you!' the detective orders under his breath.

He moves towards the door, his firearm at the ready.

We all crouch beside Mom's bed, looking at each other. We strain our ears against the silence, trying to pick up the slightest sound.

The handle begins to turn and the door opens sightly. The detective readies himself to pounce.

'Wait!' Sketch shouts as the door opens.

The detective jumps out, gun drawn, to get the drop on the intruder. In a flash he is disarmed and flipped onto the floor.

'Professor,' I breathe out in relief.

'Owww!' the detective grumbles, holding his arm, looking slightly embarrassed and annoyed at being so easily disarmed. 'You know this guy?'

'Yeah, he's with us; it's my lecturer.'

'Apologies,' Professor Grey says, finger-twirling the gun and giving it back to the detective.

'No way! The professor's a bad-ass,' Sam whispers loudly from behind me.

'You're a lecturer?' the detective asks, unconvinced. He grabs Grey's extended hand to haul himself back to his feet.

'Professor Grey, this is Detective Kukadia; detective, professor.'

The detective fixes himself up. Looking as if he's nursing a bruised ego, he nods in acknowledgment.

Grey walks over to Mom and checks her stats.

'You medically trained?' the detective asks him as he pops a pill.

'I have had my fair share of training and experience over the years.'

'Good! We need to move her before another attempt is made on her life,' the detective insists.

'That, I think, would be wise,' Grey responds. 'She will live, but we must leave at once! This place has been abandoned for a reason.' Grey looks at me, then back at Mom. 'Great lengths have been made to isolate her — or maybe all of us,' he mutters softly to himself, deep in thought.

'Sam, Leiyah, you guys should go before it gets too dangerous.'

'We're not leaving you, bro! No way!' Sam says.

'We're in this together,' adds Leiyah. 'Now stop being corny and let's get your mom to safety.'

'Ummm, guys!' Sam calls as he looks out the window. Everyone's heads turn to him. 'Can't believe I'm the "we've got company" guy, but . . .'

'What do you see?' Grey asks sharply.

He quickly dims the lights and Detective Kukadia peeks through the blinds to check.

'Four black SUVs blocking the road and entrance. They've come for her.'

'Joseph, I'm scared,' Sketch says huddling near my arm. Grey instructs the others which wires to unhook.

'It'll be alright. Just stay close to me,' I say, even though I have no idea what's about to happen. Grey walks over to me and hands me a black backpack with a hood attached to the brim.

'Keep this with you; you may need it before the night's out,' he says with all seriousness. His oak-brown eyes pierce through the low-lit room. I place it on my back.

'Let's go!' the detective barks.

We leave the room. The detective takes point; Grey and Sam wheel the bed; Sketch walks in between me and Leiyah. We move slowly, keeping our eyes fixed on the detective and his hand gestures as he signals to us when to walk and when to stop.

The detective balls his fist into the air which stops the convoy. He checks around the corner by himself. We wait anxiously until he reappears again to give us the all-clear.

'There's a service elevator at the end of this corridor. We should be able to use it to get to the ambulance loading bay,' Grey whispers ahead to the detective.

Sketch squeezes my hand to stop me and Leiyah. She is looking in the direction that the detective is about to take with a panicked look over her face.

'What's wrong?' Leiyah asks.

'Someone's coming.'

I whistle to signal Grey, who turns and sees Sketch. He warns the detective and we shuffle into the next available room, closing the blinds and crouching down.

I lock eyes with Sam and Leiyah, who are looking at me with fear written across their faces.

We wait.

Ding!

The lift arrives, followed by the sound of multiple footsteps.

Clink sslinch, clink sslinch! Click.

Grey looks over at Sketch, who uses her fingers to indicate there's seven of them.

The sound of doors being kicked open travels up the hallway like a Mexican wave. Kukadia crouches besides our doorway and primes his gun. Sketch covers her ears as the aggressive slamming noises get ever closer.

Clink sslinch, clink sslinch! Click.

'Oi!' a voice shouts, 'You're wasting time checking those rooms. She's straight down near the end — where they said she'd be. Let's get this done! We don't want another visit from those two bald-headed women, do we? Keep moving.'

The convoy of footsteps moves past us and I breathe out, a sigh of anger that surges up and boils inside me, hearing the voices of those who have come to kill my mom.

Kukadia carefully slides open the door and checks to see if

it's safe. He pauses, which puts us on all edge . . .

He gives the all-clear and we continue towards the service elevator. We move cautiously, pinned against the wall, watching our surroundings, yet picking up the pace now that the very real threat of danger has increased.

Kukadia silently mouths 'lift' over his shoulder towards us and points around the corner. He moves into the open.

Ding!

'Look out!' Sketch shouts.

Bang! Bang! Bang!

Flashes of gunfire spit from the direction of the lift. The detective dives back around the corner, narrowly escaping being hit. Without stopping to catch his breath, he returns fire.

'Get down!' he shouts.

I grab Sketch and we take cover. Sam hits the floor; Grey swiftly moves Mom's bed to safety against the wall; Leiyah grabs my hand, squeezing tighter as shots blare back and forth. Grey looks over at us, sees us all huddled together helplessly, and frowns.

'I'll be right back!' he says.

'Wait, where are you—?'

Before Leiyah can finish, Grey runs around the corner towards the action.

Gunshots rattle in quick succession but then become less and less. Grunts and groans of pain echo down the corridor. Kukadia's mouth drops in astonishment. Eventually the only thing to be heard are the chimes of empty shells as Kukadia reloads his gun. Grey walks back around the corner, straightening his tweed blazer, his eyes lighter than before, almost fluorescent.

'How did you—?' the detective mumbles in shock. 'Lecturer, my arse . . .'

'Is everybody okay?' Grey asks, rejoining us. 'The others would have heard that racket, we must carry on.'

Click!

'Just great!' Kukadia says.

We all turn to see him with his hands up. A guy, barely able to stand, face covered in ink with the inscription G3, points a gun to the detective's head.

Grey steps forward like a prowling lion.

'Nobody move!' the gunman shouts in a shaky voice.

'Take it easy, mate. You don't want to do this,' the detective implores.

'Shut up!' he yells, hitting the detective in the head with the butt of his gun. 'We want the woman! She ain't leaving here alive.'

Grey continues to walk forwards.

'I said don't move!' he shouts, panicking now. 'I'll blow his brains out! Don't try me, old man.' Grey stops as the thug pulls the hammer and presses the pistol forcefully against the detective's head.

Bang!

The gunman falls to the floor.

'You're all clear, detective!'

The owner of the voice walks into sight from the direction of the lift, their gun still smoking.

'Lace!' the detective exclaims in relief, holding the back of his head where he was hit.

'Looks like I arrived just in time,' she greets him.

'Actually, you're late,' he responds sardonically. 'Is the rest of the force on the way?'

'No . . . It's just me,' she answers. 'I tried to call it in after I heard the shots but the signal's down.'

'Wait a minute . . . How did you find us?'

'After you vanished from the farmhouse, I got a distorted

phone call from Elizabeth. I saw the aftermath of a mass pile-up at Spaghetti Junction and put two and two together. I would have been here earlier but I needed to make sure I wasn't being followed. Chief's really pissed off; they're all out for your arrest and now they're trying to finger you for the body at the farmhouse.'

We all look at the detective, unsure of what the officer is talking about.

'I didn't do any of it, I've been stitched up! And I guarantee it's by the people behind all of this.'

The officer looks at the detective, contemplating his words and her next decision.

'What do you need me to do, Detective?'

'We need to get Elizabeth to safety. She has vital information. Also, she's the only one that can prove my innocence.'

'Okay, this way! It should be clear to get to the lift now. We can get out this—'

Bang bang bang!

Shots fire from down the corridor, scattering our group in several directions. The detective and the new officer fire back as Sketch, Leiyah and I pile into the nearest room for cover, leaving behind Professor Grey and Sam, who push Mom towards the lift.

'Mom!' I yell, fearing for her life.

'Joe, Leiyah!' Sam shouts back as gunshots echo from all sides. Broken glass spits everywhere and I lose sight of the others. My heart races as I try to focus and make a decision.

'Joe!' Leiyah points to a door on the other side of the room. Wasting no time, I clutch Sketch's hand tightly and we dart out of the firing line.

We run, not looking back.

A powerful voice commands the shooters to kill us all.

We sprint as fast as we can, keeping Sketch close. We make it to a stairway and travel down three floors, jumping several steps at a time to keep our pursuers at a distance.

'Wait!' Sketch interjects. 'They're coming up from below.'

Voices travel up the stairway.

'Find them!' a voice yells.

We exit onto the nearest floor and scramble forwards, keeping low, following the sign to the service elevators on the other side of the building.

We flinch as sporadic shots pop from the floors above.

'There!' Leiyah calls out and points. 'Dumb waiters!'

We run towards the service lifts. Suddenly, Sketch stops dead, her feet skidding against the polished hospital floors. She releases her hand from my grip.

'Sketch? What is it?' I frantically ask, looking behind us for the incoming danger. She backs away slowly from the elevator and points.

'What do you see?'

'It's here!' she mouths with dread.

Ding!

The lift doors begin to grind open. An uneasy feeling plagues me and I feel my heart beating in my throat. I turn my head, almost as if in slow motion and I gasp, feeling the air expel from my lungs. There, walking towards me, eyes blazing white, is Officer Scott.

Sketch screams and places her hands over her shades. My eyes widen at the sight of him standing there, grinning.

'WE . . . SeE . . . yOu!'

'Run!' I shout.

'TheRe . . . Is . . . No . . . EscAPE!'

Leiyah grabs Sketch's hand and runs in the opposite direction. I turn to run too, but a solid grip digs into my shoulder. Before

I know it, I am tossed against one of the medical ward windows. Glass shards fly everywhere.

Leiyah stops running and turns to see me on the floor, at the feet of the officer. 'Joseph!' she cries.

'Get out of here!' I yell back. The officer claws at me, hoisting me up from the floor and raising me in a chokehold to eye-level.

'I . . . can't breathe!' I gasp for air, trying to break his hold. He looks me dead in the eyes. His soulless, glowing glare shines into my eyes, causing me to squint.

He examines my face and growls:

'We . . . Have . . . SeArChed . . . The ReAlms . . . For You!'

'Get off me!' I shout, continuing to squirm.

'sHOw . . . YouR . . . TRuE . . . SeLF, Son of Imādris!'

'What do you want from me?'

'wE MusT ThANk YoU fOr MoMenTaRilY oPeNing The VeiL AnD LeTting uS through.'

'No!'

His grip tightens.

'ProVE . . . tHAT . . . YOu . . . ArE . . . THe SpARK . . . ThAT . . . wAs . . . FiRsT . . . GiVEn.

'PRoVE . . . ThAt . . . YoU . . . ArE . . . ThE . . . DREAM-WALKER!'

He extends his finger and presses it into the centre of my forehead. A sharp, burning pain courses through my brain.

'Aarrghh!' I scream in agony then, suddenly, my vision flashes white and . . . I leave my body. I am transported to another plane. I float once again above that bottomless void; the voices from beyond cry out amidst the sound of a great battle, echoing across the abyss.

'No! No! Stay away from me,' I yell, as I see that terrible bright form of light reappear. 'What do you want? Why are you hunting me?'

It speeds towards me like a lightning bolt. I have nowhere to run. I close my eyes, readying myself for the crash . . .

'I said: get off him!'

That's Leiyah's voice. My eyes jolt back to normal, just in time to see objects hurtling through the air.

'Yeah, pick on someone your own size!' Sketch yells, also throwing whatever objects she can from a nearby medical trolley.

Leiyah hurls a reflex hammer, which strikes the officer in the face. He releases me from his grip.

I hit the ground, panting, desperately trying to crawl away. The officer lets out a beastly roar, gnashing his teeth, and turns towards Sketch and Leiyah.

'I think we got his attention,' Leiyah says, slowly backing away. 'Now what?'

'How would I know? I'm only ten.'

The officer runs at them.

'Hit the decks!' I shout.

Bang bang bang!

Sketch and Leiyah drop to the ground. A slew of bullets whizz above their heads and pierce the officer's body. He is knocked to the ground. We all freeze.

The incoming shooters jeer and chant from the far side of the corridor.

'Another badge bites the dust!' one shouts.

They resemble more of a street gang than organised assassins.

I hear movement and quickly revert my attention to the officer, whose hand starts twitching. He grabs a handful of the broken glass from the floor. His body starts to convulse then, like something out of a zombie film, he springs to his feet, growling, eyes blazing, as he pushes the broken glass into his mouth.

'What the—?!' one of the shooters yells.

'Roaaaaaaarrrrrrrrrrr!!'

'Shit! Shoot him!'

'Kill the pig!'

'Light 'im up!'

The officer continues to roar like a demonic beast and he leaps — twisting upside down onto the celling — then sprints towards the hostiles, spitting the broken glass from his mouth like bullets.

I drag myself to my feet and pull up Sketch and Leiyah, who are both lying down flat, screaming at the sound of the chaos and violence.

Bang! Bang! Ratttttttaatttttat!

We run, stop, pause, duck, trying everything to get away from the stray bullets that leave puncture holes in the walls all around. We stumble across a storage closet and scramble to get in. We lock the door from the inside and use anything we can to create a barricade.

'Aarrghh!'

'Dieeeeeeeeee!'

'Oh, shi—!'

Outside the door, grotesque shrieks and blood-curdling yelps accompany the sound of crashes and inhuman growls.

'Oh my God, oh my God!' Leiyah mumbles to herself in a state of shock. 'He was shot dead then he was on the ceiling! Wha— What was—?'

'Leiyah, calm down. Listen, I know, I know — but right now, you've got to stay calm, okay?' I say, trying to keep her quiet.

Leiyah shudders and nods with fear. She crumbles to the floor, shaking, trying her hardest to control her nerves.

'Listen!' Sketch whispers. 'The fighting's . . . stopped.' She moves her head from left to right as if tracking something. 'It's searching for us. We don't have long.' She looks up at me. 'Joseph, it's time.'

At this, Leiyah looks up at me too.

'You're our only hope,' Sketch continues.

'No! Sketch, I can't!'

'You can! You've done it before. I believe in you, you can do it,' she pleads.

'That was a fluke, okay?! I . . . I don't know how to and, even if I could, I can't control it. It's dangerous! The professor tried, remember? My mind's too loud, it's all messed up in there!'

'But you don't need to control it; you need to unleash it!' Sketch insists.

'I'm sorry, I can't! It's too dangerous.'

Sketch huffs with frustration. She walks around behind me and reaches into my backpack.

'Hey, what are you doing?' I ask.

Sketch retrieves the kalimba and starts to slowly play.

'Stop it! Sketch! He'll hear you. We need to be quiet.'

I try to snatch the instrument but she quickly dodges behind Leiyah, who is now calm and standing up.

Sketch continues playing.

'Leiyah, tell her to stop.'

'Is . . . she telling the truth? Can you help us?'

'It's not that simple,' I say looking down at my feet. 'I . . . don't know how to . . . I can't, I— I . . . '

Another growl roars in the distance. I glance up at Leiyah and Sketch. They both stare back at me.

'What do you guys want from me?!'

'Just try, Bushy Head!' Sketch pleads.

'I— I can't.'

'Why not?!'

'I'm afraid, okay?! I can't save you, I can't even save myself. I'm not some sort of superhero. This isn't a game! You guys followed me here and . . . look what happened. I'm damaged goods.'

Leiyah steps closer to me.

'Joseph, ever since we've been friends, you've been running. Afraid. You may not see it but you're bigger than your fears. Every other person would have crumbled, even given up after everything you've been through, but you're still here.'

Leiyah lifts my head up and looks me in the eyes.

'You're stronger than you think. Don't be afraid. Be free.'

'Leiyah . . . I . . .'

Leiyah grabs my hand.

'I know . . . Secretly, I think I always knew.'

Doof, doof, doof!

We flinch as the door shakes from the powerful blows from the other side.

'It's here!' Sketch whimpers.

I look at Leiyah, who comforts Sketch. She puts on a brave face and smiles at me, the same caring smile of encouragement that she gave me in the TWI, that gave me hope when I had none.

Doof, doof, doof!

The door starts to splinter around the hinges.

'WaKEY . . . WAkEy . . . LiTtle DrEamWalKEr!'

I watch the door as it dents and caves in, getting weaker with each hit.

I make my choice.

'Let's do this!'

'You got this,' Leiyah mouths.

I sit on the floor and fold my legs in a sort of meditative position.

'Sketch, play it again, but louder! Let him hear it!'

'On it, Bushy Head.'

Sketch begins to play. I pull the black hood attached to the backpack over my the top half of my face. I close my eyes, attempting to zone in on Sketch's melody.

I start to focus, clearing my mind, moving past my heartache, my trauma, all the troubled memories that try to jostle for space in my mind, that try to become loud when I need quiet.

I begin to recite the mantra, speaking the words that were given to me from birth:

'When I sleep I wake, when I dream I walk.'

Doof, doof, doof!

Concentrate, you can do this.

I block out the incoming threat and imagine myself as the threat.

I take all my fear and pain and breathe it in as I go deeper within myself.

Sketch's melody echoes inside me and I feel myself drifting,

becoming weightless,

pure light,

pulsing

a thousand rushing waves coursing through my veins . . .

'When I sleep . . .'

'There iS No eSCApe!'

Doof, Doof, Doof!

'I wake!'

'WE wILl KiLl YoU'

Doof, Doof!

'When I dream . . .'

'And FeASt on YoUr FrIENDS!'

Doof!

'I WALK!'

. . .

. . .

CHAPTER 22
EYES WIDE CLOSED!

. . .

. . .

. . .

I feel **both** present

and absent,

physical

and ethereal,

with a sensation of fully charged energy flowing through me, as if I'm plugged into an overwhelming source of infinite power.

What a strange feeling . . . There's no more pain, no more sadness running through my body. It's . . . beautiful.

To dream without dreaming, to see without seeing, but granted true vision.

To be able to look beyond what reality blankets its physical form with.

Time has no relevance.

It's incredible. My words could never really articulate it fully. It's like asking Heaven what it sees.

My mind's eye
is seeing both
dream and reality
merged into one.

It is both ordered and chaotic: bright, blurring, colours vibrate, shift, and blend, like wet paint on canvas.

I see beyond the physical body of the officer as he bursts through the door, seeing the thing that occupies him — its full, abominable form. Its beastly shape could almost pass for human, except for its four white, blazing eyes, its razor-sharp, spiky teeth, and its elongated arms with three dagger-like claws for hands. It pulses with a dim, translucent fake-white aura, vibrating at a low frequency.

Out of the corner of my eye, I glimpse the aura of another, this time darker, blue. I see his face and I recognise him from the police line-up. The light refracts and glows around the red-haired gang member as he lies on the ground, writhing with pain and attempting to pull something out of his pocket. He's a Figment too! As I watch, his aura lightens, now a fiery patch of red light mingles with it and bursts through— No, not light, actual fire! Flames erupt from the thug's mouth as he spits petrol or some flammable liquid through his lighter, aimed in the direction of the nightmarish creature.

The blast is so hot, so powerful that it knocks us all back, triggering the smoke alarm, and causing me to lose my bearings for a second.

Bee bee bee bee beep!

When I look back, the thug has used the confusion to escape.

'Joseph! Fire! Help us!'

Sketch! Oh no! No! Not now! My focus distorts, becoming violently chaotic. My vision shatters as the smell of smoke and fire floods my nostrils, corrupting my flow of energy and triggering my memory.

'No!'

I'm sitting at the top of a smoke-filled staircase, gripping onto the bars of the banister.

I can feel the heat from the fire.

           'Joseph, do something, we can't breathe!'

I'm losing control! I can't focus.

Gripping onto the bars of the banister.

I can't hold on! The flames torment me . . .

As my control falters and fades into confusion, my actions and vision become a vague blur. I try to place the image of the Knight Terror in my mind's eye, hoping to . . .

      'BuRN . . . LiTtle DreAmEr . . . BuRN!'

I'm sitting at the top of a smoke-filled staircase, gripping onto the bars of the banister.

No!

Sccccccreeeeeeeeeeeeeeeeeeeeeeeeeeeeechhhhhhhhhhhhhhhh!!

I awaken with a burning fury. I evaporate into black smoke, dive through the door, and tackle the Knight Terror, sending it crashing backwards through walls. It claws itself to its feet, standing in the dusty rubble across the hallway.

     'ThErE . . . YoU . . . aRe, SOn . . . oF . . . IMādRIs!'

It roars and charges towards me, revealing skeletal wings on its back. Its jarring movement disrupts the physical imagery it is projecting around itself. Within my dream-like state, my sight is corrupted, blurring between two states of consciousness; the walls seem to bend and warp in a kaleidoscopic manner. I can't tell what's real.

The Knight Terror swipes at me with vicious blows. I block, dodge, and counter.

With each connection it makes to my body I feel its other-worldly strength. Nightmarish, tortured screams from my loved ones echo around me, which begin to suffocate my imagination and thoughts. My vision clouds, I feel drained . . .

'YoU . . . Are . . . WeAk!'

My powers start to wane and I begin to wake up. Fear engulfs me; visions of my mother and friends lying in coffins flash before my eyes.

'YEsss . . . I . . . cAN . . . TaStE . . . YoUR . . . FeAR!'

The Knight Terror opens its mouth, displaying its many rows of teeth. It begins to inhale, absorbing my energy like a leech. It glows brighter and stronger.

'ThErE . . . iS . . . No . . . hOpE!'

I snap back to reality. I am being pinned hopelessly to the floor by the officer. In the corridor lies a trail of carnage and destruction. Water sprinklers in the ceiling douse the remaining embers of fire.

'YoU . . . Are . . . DeAfEtED!'

'Aaaarrrghhhh!'

A sharp pain pierces my skull as the officer presses the centre of my forehead again. Suddenly my vision is transported and shifted, as I envision a great army of Knight Terrors — countless in number — amassing in the distance. They chant, exultant, as they move across a toxic fallen wasteland of steaming, white-hot coal towards a huge monolithic gate.

'yOU . . . SeE tHEm . . . Don'T . . .YoU?

'ThE DeSTruCtiOn Of AlL!

'wHeN . . . I . . . Am . . . doNE . . . WiTh . . . YoU . . .

False . . . IdoL

'I . . . WiLl . . . StArT . . . On . . . tHEm!'

The bestial officer forcefully twists my head towards Sketch and Leiyah.

'No!'

           'Bushy Head! Remember who you are!'

'Sketch!'

           'Fight past your fears!'

'Leiyah . . .'

Adrenaline courses through my veins. I turn my head to look back at the abducted face of Officer Scott. He leans closer, growling, exhaling his putrid, stale breath into my face.

'ThEY . . . WiLl . . . DiE . . . SloWlY! ThEY . . . WiLl KnOw

. . . PAIN! ThEY WIIL . . . TAsTe . . . DEATH!'

I repetitively mutter the mantra silently under my breath envisioning the Gate and imagining the horrors that await beyond it . . .

Scccccreeeeeeeeeeeeeeeeeeeeeeeeechhhhhhhhhhhhhhhh!!

I reawaken.

A surge of uncontrollable power knocks the Knight Terror off its feet.

'. . . No! . . .'

The officer quickly gets back on his feet and charges at me, eyes blazing and frothing at the mouth.

Boom!

A huge cluster of blinding iridescent colours explodes, as bright as the sun, throwing me against the wall.

The Knight Terror is instantly sucked out of the officer's body like an exorcism, fraying, spitting, clawing.

It lets out an almighty roar:

'AlL . . . HalL . . . ThE . . . FIRST!'

then disintegrates, dispersing into red vapour.

I stand,

       taking in the sight

of both reality

and dreams . . .

'It worked, Bushy Head. I may have accidentally borrowed one of Professor Grey's Morpheus ball thingies,' Sketch says sheepishly. 'Bushy Head . . . ?'

I sense a nervous, uncertain energy approaching.

'Joe . . . ? Can you . . . Can you hear me?' Leiyah steps cautiously towards me.

'. . . YES.'

The voice that comes out of me is my own but somehow different.

Something else pulls my attention; I hear shadows and feel disturbing, nightmarish frequencies gathering below.

DANGER!'

'I see them too, big bro.'

'Where?' Leiyah asks us.

'. . . ELIZABETH . . . '

'Then let's go!' Sketch yells.

NO!'

'But I wanna help—'

LEAVE!'

I feel Sketch run up and hug me tightly.

'Please be careful, Bushy Head; you're the only family I've got . . . '

Bang!

'You've got nowhere to go! Send the woman out and we'll make it quick!'

Gunshots prick my ears, startling me as I regain consciousness. I lie flat on a gurney in what looks to be the back of an ambulance. The sound of bullets ricochet, missing me by an inch as they pierce through the metal panels.

'Ugh! Wh . . . What's—?'

'Easy, Ms Jacobs. Don't make any sudden movements,' whispers a deep warm voice with a slight Caribbean accent. The owner of the voice looms over me, deep mystical oak-brown irises reflecting like a cat's eyes in the dark.

'Who—?'

'I am a friend: Professor Grey.'

'Joseph's lecturer?' I whisper, completely discombobulated.

'Correct, Ms Jacobs.'

'And Joseph?'

'We were separated in our attempt to get you to safety.'

'Why was—?'

'I must ask you to trust me. I am sure Joseph and his friends are okay, but right now we have our own matter to deal with. Down!'

Another wave of bullets barrages the side of the ambulance. I raise my arms to protect my face from shrapnel and notice small black pebbles embedded along the pressure points on my forearms.

'What are these?' I ask, attempting to remove one.

'For your own good, leave them be. They are a temporary fix to help get you mobile and back on your feet.'

'How did you—?'

'Shhh! Quiet now,' the professor hisses, placing his finger against his lips.

'You can't stay in there forever!' a bloodthirsty voice yells. Professor Grey calmly removes his tweed jacket, revealing black diamond wrist cuffs. He slides them off and wraps them tightly around his knuckles, moving steadily towards the double doors of the ambulance.'

'What are you doing?'

'"He will win who knows how to handle both superior and inferior forces."'

The professor steps out of the ambulance and closes the doors calmly behind him.

I listen for more movement but hear nothing, just the sound of guns reloading.

'Cut him down!' the same bloodthirsty voice commands.

The silence splits suddenly. All hell breaks loose from the crackling of shots fired. I roll off the bed and crouch down for cover. More bullets penetrate the vehicle; the holes in the frame become wider. I crawl towards the door, fighting the throbbing pain in my body. Through the gaping punctured metal I catch sight of the professor.

'How is he . . . ?' I mumble to myself. I see flashes of movement from the restricted viewing hole; the professor engages multiple individuals, disarming them at an almost supernatural speed . . . Is he like Mr X? And those women that attacked me on the Spaghetti Junction?

Before I can even process the thought, one of the ambulance doors flies open. A hand appears, pointing a pistol at me. Forgetting about my injuries, I jump up and grab at the arm, twisting the attacker's wrist quickly and forcefully down at an angle. The attacker's grip loosens. As I disarm them, my legs turn to jelly and I lose my balance. I fall backwards, juggling the weapon.

'Bitch!' The masked attacker lunges towards me.

My finger squeezes the trigger and the gun recoils. Immediately the attacker drops face-first onto the vehicle floor. A distinctive burning smell trails from the smoking muzzle. I aim the gun at the open door, still panting from the altercation, listening to the chaos beyond it. I remove the attacker's mask and check for a pulse. G3 and Loop tattoos envelop his lifeless face. Why would a Loop gang risk an all-out assault at a hospital just to take me out?

C'mon, Elizabeth, get up. Move! The professor needs your help. Joseph needs you. Without a second thought I exit the ambulance onto the bullet-casing-strewn floor, using the open ambulance door as a shield. I scan round the door, looking for a better vantage point. I count eight armed individuals in total. Alright Elizabeth, stick and move — just like you were trained.

I limp across the loading bay. Shots spit and spiral in my direction clattering against steel bonnets and shattering wind-screens.

I lean against the side of a car for cover while I eject the magazine from the gun. Great; four bullets left.

More guttural noises ensue from the conflict and I peer from around the shattered headlight to see Grey leaping acrobatically backwards off a bullet-riddled car into the midst of three hostiles. He dodges the gunfire with quick, shifting movements, before releasing a swift flurry of blows rendering the gang members unconscious.

Across the far side of the loading bay two more thugs take aim at Grey. I fire three shots, hitting one of them in the shoulder. The other takes cover behind one of the huge stone pillars.

'Don't move!' a voice says from behind me. Cold metal presses firmly against my temple. 'Drop the gun.' I raise my hands, drop the gun, and slowly get to my feet.

'Say your prayers!' I close my eyes in dreaded anticipation.

A shot goes off.

'Amen!'

Huh! I know that voice.

I hear the unmistakable sound of a body thudding to the floor behind me. I slowly turn around to see young Officer Lace standing there, quivering, her gun still raised.

'It's okay, officer,' I say, seeing the shock written across her face. 'You can lower your weapon now, it's okay.' Officer Lace slowly lowers her gun and stares at the body.

Grey rejoins us after dealing with the goon behind the pillar.

'I think that was the last of them,' Grey says brushing himself off.

'I hope so,' I reply.

'Officer, where are the detective and the students?' Grey asks.

'I . . . um . . . I'm not sure. We got ambushed and split up. I was hoping they were here, with you,' the officer replies, holstering her sidearm.

'I will circle back and look for the others. You must get Ms Jacobs to safety.'

Officer Lace helps me back to my feet and walks me through the mass of unconscious criminals towards the closed exit gate.

'Some professor, huh?' the officer says.

'Tell me about it. Have you called for backup?'

'I can't, something is blocking the signal in this whole area.'

'Someone's really gone to a lot of trouble to take me out.'

'Wait here. I'm just going to look to see if I can open the gate.'

The officer searches behind me in the dimly lit bay.

'Tell me, how did you manage to find us?'

'I knew something was off after the way the media and first responders reported the Spaghetti Junction incident. They said the explosion that caused the pile-up was due to an oil spill, but I knew that was a lie. I was the one who gave Kukadia a way to escape the Barns' residence after you left. I believed he was innocent. I tailed him, hoping to find out the truth. And look now — when everyone realises that you discovered the identity of the serial killer, they'll have to clear his name.'

'I hope so, officer. We can only hope that they believe us and help us find the people that Emit Barns is trying to expose.'

'All those innocent victims just to expose Avalon?'

'Exactly . . . Wait, what did you just say?'

'You and the detective were right; you discovered his motive.'

'But, officer, the detective doesn't know about Avalon.'

Click!

I turn to see Officer Lace pointing her gun at me.

'You're the mole!' I say, raising my hands behind my head.

'One of many. But then, you can't really be a mole if the whole system is already full of holes, can you?'

Emit Barns's final words replay in my head: 'Get your own house in order. Their eyes are everywhere.' He was trying to warn me. I shuffle to try to put some distance between me and the officer.

'Don't move, Elizabeth! Don't make this harder than it already is.'

'Why save me, if you were just planning to kill me all along?'

'The order changed. They want to know who else you've mentioned them to before they pass judgment.'

'No one! Like I said, Kukadia doesn't know about them.'

'You don't need to worry about the detective, he won't be speaking to anybody anymore.'

The officer presses the button on the wall to open the exit gates. She pulls out a personal radio: 'I have her.'

'You traitor! You are not worth the uniform you're wearing.'

Officer Lace glares at me with a slight look of shame and remorse.

'I . . . I never wanted this. They got to me early during training. I tried not to bite, but I have loved ones too. Who was going to protect them?! Who could I tell?! Who was there to protect me?! I really wanted to be clean-cut and help this city, like you did . . . But when you're surrounded by mud, eventually you're going to get dirty.'

In the distance, an engine roars towards us. The officer gulps nervously.

'Elizabeth, just tell them what you know and they might go easy on you. Barns is as good as dead for going against these people, there's no point you joining him.'

'Officer Lace, I am sorry no one was there to protect you, but you have a chance to make this right. It's never too late. When you put on that uniform and badge, you are responsible for its values — YOU! No one else. Your choices define you, no matter how tough things get. I still believe one person *can* make a difference.'

'We're not all you, Elizabeth: the *Great Officer Jacobs*, the star officer that single-handedly took down Kaine Nelson. Yeah, they know all about you. You were a legend in so many people's eyes. Look at you now: battered and bruised, no badge, no hope, and now the city you fought so hard to protect is about to be swallowed up by its own filth. There's nothing you can do. You'll be forgotten like the rest of us.'

Headlights begin to appear and I shuffle slowly to the side, hoping the officer keeps her eyes pinned on me.

'Stop, Elizabeth! Please don't make me shoot you. I will if I have to. I will. They'll kill me if I don't give them what they want.'

The sound of the vehicle gets closer to the sloping exit ramp behind me.

'I'm so sorry Elizabeth.'

Suddenly, Officer Lace's gun is snapped out of her hand and she is thrown head-over-heels to the floor.

'Thanks!' I gasp.

'You are welcome, Ms Jacobs.'

Grey hands me Officer Lace's firearm. The vehicle is now visible and seconds away from the exit gate: it's another white van with tinted windows, similar to the one that attacked me and Mr X.

Officer Lace groggily tries to sit up and recover the wind that's been knocked out of her.

'You need to run, Elizabeth, before it's too late!'

The officer coughs. 'They're here!'

Grey's face knits with concern as the approaching vehicle's lights beam directly at us, illuminating the dim loading bay. We step back slowly as the van draws to a halt, blocking the exit tunnel.

The stationary vehicle seems to stare at us, as the engine continues to hum.

The doors open.

I gulp silently. My hand grips the gun a little tighter.

From beyond the gate, high-heeled footsteps tap sharply against the cold concrete floor. Two silhouetted figures emerge from the darkness. The professor straightens his back, holding his ground, as they walk purposefully and regimentally — almost robotically — towards us.

'Stay behind me,' the professor says intensely. 'Whatever happens, keep back. You are not equipped for this.'

'Who . . . Who are they, professor?'

'*Agentium Zodiaci.* Zodiac Enforcers: Agents of Avalon!'

In unison they step into the dimly lit underground area: the same two bald women who attacked me and Mr X, both wearing white jumpsuits. One of them is the identical triplet of Cara and Charlotte: Cassey! The gentle features that Charlotte wore are lost to her stone-cold face, void of emotion, soulless.

'It is him,' the two women say in unison. 'The excommunicated Luna.'

Grey stands there in silence.

'Your skill is well known amongst our kind, Karnak the Ageless,' Cassey says.

'Step aside,' the other demands. 'We have come for the woman. She has seen too much, heard too much, and must be judged!'

Suddenly their eyes blaze white and they sprint towards us, leaving a faint trail of red vapour behind them.

I fire my gun, emptying the clip, but it fails to stop them — they mesmerically dodge every bullet with great speed.

Grey pushes me out of the way. They attack him with devastating blows, moving at a superhuman rate. He battles back fearlessly, almost on autopilot, blocking and countering, dishing out roundhouse kicks and precision blows with the flat of his palm, which send them to the ground. Each time they fall, their eyes reignite and they spring right back to their feet.

The injured Officer Lace's mouth drops in disbelief as Professor Grey runs halfway up one of the support pillars, defying the laws of gravity, before pushing off, propelling himself into a backwards somersault to re-engage his two adversaries. As they circle the professor, I glimpse the Zodiac signs on the back of their necks: Cassey, Sagittarius and the other, Aries.

They battle back and forth with the professor, each trying to outmanoeuvre Grey to gain the upper hand. I grab one of them in an attempt to help but I am swiftly sent flying backwards.

I crash onto the ground.

Grey glances at me in concern, which causes him to lose his footing and his attackers finally get the upper hand.

They circle him like hungry felines, ready to pounce and kill.

Aries jumps behind the professor and coils herself around his body, gripping his neck in a reverse chokehold.

'Professor!' I shout. Again, I desperately try to help, but I am hit so hard that I almost black out.

Sagittarius places her sharp heel in my back, pinning me to the floor.

Her heel digs deeper into my spine and I scream out in pain. 'Get off her!'

In my peripheral vision I see Officer Lace dive forwards towards the enforcer, but, before she can connect she is struck brutally and sent sprawling.

'Cassey! I don't know what they've done to you, but your sisters — Cara and Charlotte — are dead because of Avalon!'

The heel withdraws from my back and I look up into Cassey's face. Her eyes blink as if waking up from a nightmare.

'Charlotte said she missed you when you went away.'

'Charlotte . . .' Cassey mumbles as if momentarily remembering. She looks down at me and I see Charlotte's gentleness flow through her. Then suddenly her eyes blaze white again.

'Foolish worm,' she says, crouching on top of me, crushing my arms with her knees. I squirm. 'You have no idea what pain is. We have already dealt with your informant, Mr X,' she whispers. 'Did you really think you could compete with the might of Avalon?'

'They are the Watchers,' Aries adds.

'The cogs in the wheel.'

'We see all, we are all,' they utter in unison.

'Judgment has been passed,' Aries says, her finger to her inner-ear device. 'Eliminate her.'

Professor Grey tries to break free from Aries's grip as Sagittarius readies her hand for the killing blow. I shut my eyes and prepare for the inevitable, taking one final breath . . .

Sccccccreeeeeeeeeeeeeeeeeeeeeeeeeechhhhhhhhhhhhhhhh!!

A terrifying, high-pitched screaming violently ruptures around the underground loading bay. The ground vibrates and the support pillars shake. Cassey falls off me, grabbing her ears, as does everyone else. The professor is able to wriggle free. The sound is unbearably deafening, full of anger and wrath. A thick black-purplish smoke covers the room, as thick as thunder clouds as the screeching stops. The only thing I can see are shadows and silhouettes of the partially incapacitated Avalon agents through the beams of light still streaming from the white van.

Slow, sluggish footsteps scratch and drag against the ground. I squint, batting away the mist to try to see. My breath quickens as the steps get closer. I see something moving towards me in the shadowy mist. At first it's just a faint outline, and then . . . My eyes widen as if waking from a dream in recognition of the distinctive figure in front of me.

'Joseph!' I shout, trying to crawl over to him, but my body gives up on me. 'Joseph!'

I get no response; he just keeps on walking sluggishly towards me, his face shrouded by the mist.

His black boots stop in front of me and I look up at him. 'Joseph?'

He stands still as a statue, breathing slowly, his head slightly hanging down. I pull myself to his eye level.

'Joseph, are you okay? Are you hurt? You shouldn't be here.' Still no response. I raise his head. His eyes are closed.

'Joseph, what's wrong with you? It's me, Mom!' I say, shaking him. 'Wake up! Open your eyes.'

I reach to check his pupils. Suddenly a hand grabs my wrist.

'No, Ms Jacobs! Do not do that,' Professor Grey orders. 'You must not disrupt his dream.' He releases my hand.

'Wha— What are you taking about!? What's going on?! What wrong with my son?'

'He is in a sub-state of restful consciousness.'

'What do you mean?! He's . . . sleeping?'

'Yes, dreaming-walking.'

'But how is that—? Why is he—?'

'Nōmesì!'

Joseph says in a dialect I have never heard him use before. What was that? He speaks calmly and sombrely. It is both his voice and it isn't, different to the son I know. His eyes start to flicker rapidly underneath his eyelids. Immediately, black smoke emits from his body, cloaking him. Grey pulls me back.

'No, wait! Joseph!'

I Awaken!

My mind's eye sees the red, fallen auras of the Zodiac Enforcers in the haze.

With an appetite for vengeance, I engulf the room in more thick black mist, sensing the danger, wanting to separate the Enforcers from Elizabeth. I dream huge shadow-like hands that form out of my mist and snatch the aggressors away.

My body starts to feel light and I raise my head upwards, dreaming of the sky. My physical form pulses and I cry out, a loud siren that rings from my core, and I begin to ascend. Out of the gate and upwards I fly, rising and shooting higher, faster, towards the night sky. Several streams of light flow upwards like a river. Distorted phantoms and spectres float over the city, invisible to the rest of the world. Colours flash and blur past me; sounds collide and clash as one harmonic explosion; the very air around me ripples as if I were a torpedo gliding through deep water.

I reform my face, feeling each part reconfigure in my imagination. The cold wind and rain refresh me as they hit my face. The barriers of light and sound bend and I push onwards, wanting to get them away from Elizabeth, dreaming of going faster than the speed of light.

All the rage inside me bubbles.

I feel limitless, painless, God-like. An immeasurable, incomprehensible power . . .

I scream, unable to control the surge of energy rupturing my body. An intense pressure builds behind my eyes and they snap open. Light beams shoot from them towards the sky as I fall like a comet. I crash onto the hospital roof helipad. The Enforcers drop out of my black mist, choking, gasping for air as they also hit the roof of the hospital.

'Bushy Head!'

That's Sketch's voice.

The rooftop rumbles as a thunderclap booms around us. The sky twists and alters fantastically, morphing to my own distorted imagination. I see Sketch, Grey and mom on the roof, gripping the ground, holding on for their life, trying not to be blown away by the expanding sonic force pulsating from me. Parts of the roof begin to crumble and crack.

'Close your eyes, Bushy Head!'

I begin to levitate, now slave to the overwhelming power that consumes me, restricting every inch of my body as the world falls around me.

'Joseph! You must stop!'

Professor . . . Help me!

'If you can hear me, focus on my voice!'

I see the professor and Sketch's vibrant auras. I see my mom too, fighting to stay on her feet. She is looking at me with a mixture of disbelief, amazement, worry, and fear.

'MAKE IT STOP!' I beg, but I can't manifest my words into reality.

The sky crackles and cries; a huge cloud slices in two, as if cut by a blade. A powerful gust of wind twists and twirls like a vortex, punching a gateway in the sky. Through it I see thousands of floating mirrors looking down. Beams of light project from my body in every direction, completely engulfing me . . .

Then I see it again, like a faint mirage: the Gate! The same gate that I envisioned when Officer Scott touched my forehead! Horrific chants from the Knight Terrors roar from behind it. The Gate shakes and swells, cracking slightly, through which falling specks of light escape, descending from the night sky and vanishing into the distance.

'Joseph, try and place your hands over your eyes!' the professor yells.

I listen to his instruction and begin to fight against the unyielding tension in my body. I slowly turn my arms and wrists so that the palms of my hands are facing towards me. The sheer force that permeates my body inhibits my movement; every inch gained is an excruciating struggle. I try with all my might to raise my hands. The beams of energy blasting from my eyes push my palms away.

'That's it, Bushy head!'
'Fight it, son! Don't give up. You can do this!'

Mom!

With one final scream of determination, I push through the anguish, forcing my palms over my eyes . . .

It all goes black . . .

* * *

A melody hums faintly in my ear. I listen to the familiar voice vibrate and soothe my mind and I am back in the place of black diamonds: The Seeing.

'Sketch? Where are you? Professor?'

The atmosphere all around me shudders like the aftershock of an earthquake. The usually kaleidoscopic and colourful starlight blinks and falls like melting ice shards, shattering on the black diamond ground.

'What's happening?'

'Your powers have become unstable and your mind is breaking!'

I turn to see the astro-projected versions of Grey and Sketch appear behind me. Sketch hums Ayamey's lullaby.

'Professor, I'm sorry. I didn't mean for all of this to happen. I was just trying to help!'

'I know, Mr Jacobs, but right now the reality of all we know is in great peril. You need to reconnect to your physical mind and body and take control.'

Stronger rumbles part the black diamond sands into waves of raging chaos. Grey looks around in worry.

'We do not have much time. We must hurry. Take my hand, Mr Jacobs.'

As Grey extends his hand, a blinding flash of light explodes above us. I look up to see a terrifying ball of light: the entity that has chased me so many times before has returned once again. This time it begins to form the ghostly outline of a human body. It descends slowly towards us.

'Time's up, Joseph! Hurry!' Grey shouts.

'What is that thing?!' I say in fear.

'Concentrate, Joseph!'

We link hands and I focus on Grey. The ground beneath us starts to sink. I feel the entity's chilling presence grow closer.

'Focus, Joseph. Focus on the melody.'

I close my eyes and zone in to Sketch's song; it gets louder. Everything around me is drowned out. My mind begins to drift, reconnecting to my physical self.

My powers begin to slip away. Everything around me begins to blur . . .

I see Sketch near the broken edge of the hospital roof, her hands over her face.

'Sketch! Watch out!'

As if in slow motion the two Enforcers reach over and snatch Sketch off the ground.

My eyes
begin to darken
and I start
to lose
consciousness.

'Sketch! Professor, help her!'

Sketch's voice in my head begins to softly fade, as she is dragged away by the Enforcers.

My eyes
soften.

'What are you doing, professor?! Please! Stop them!'
They

close

'*It's okay, Bushy Head.*'
Her voice echoes softly in my mind.
And I

fall

back

'Easy does it, Mr Jacobs. I have you.'

To reality . . .

'Mr Jacobs . . . ? Joseph? Are you awake?'

A cold breeze blows and I stir. I feel the swaying sensation of water gently rock underneath me. Her face flashes before me and I flinch.

'Sketch!' I cry, jumping to my feet.

'Steady, Joseph!'

The professor grabs hold of me to reassure me. I look around to see that we're travelling down a canal on a narrowboat, floating further away from the sirens in the distance.

'No! Where are we!? We need to help—'

'They have her,' the professor murmurs, steering the boat through the dusky water towards an abandoned-looking tunnel.

'Why didn't you stop them?! We have to find her. You should've protected her, not me.'

Through tear-filled eyes I see him calmly surveying me.

'It's my fault. Isn't it? It's my fault! I was supposed to protect her. She saved me and I failed her.'

The professor looks sternly at me. His eyes illuminate and glow in the dark tunnel.

'Sketch's journey, like yours, is part of a bigger plan.'

'But she's just a child! What use is all this power if I can't control it or protect the ones I love?'

The boat bobs in place as the professor cuts off the engine.

'The phoenix must first burn before it re-emerges, Mr Jacobs.' The professor hands me a sealed enveloped, titled: To Bushyhead.

'What's this?'

'Young Tabitha entrusted me to deliver this to you in the event of something happening.' I hold onto the letter tightly.

'We are here.' The professor strikes a flare and ties up the boat. We disembark onto a thin, moss-covered cobbled path.

'The Netherton Tunnel?' I mumble, looking at a decaying mould-eaten plaque. 'Where are we going?' I ask, following behind the professor.

'Somewhere safe.'

'What about my mom? My friends?'

'They are safe . . . For now.'

' . . . Professor?'

'Yes, Mr Jacobs?'

'When I was . . . When my eyes opened I saw something. A huge army of Knight Terrors at some sort of gate.'

The professor suddenly stops. He turns, illuminated by the spitting red flames of the flare, grievous concern etched across his face.

'So the prophecy is true,' he whispers to himself. "And the Gate will tremble and cry out at *his* return when the blood moon rises."

'P— Pardon?'

Grey walks on and we arrive at an old rusty iron door embedded into the rock.

'What— What happens next?'

'Next?' The professor pulls out an old iron key and inserts it into the lock. 'It has already begun.'

With great force he opens the door.

'This way, Mr Jacobs.'

I walk into what looks like an old mine shaft lift. The iron doors grind shut, echoing down the shaft. The professor pulls the lever. Rickety chains rattle and plunge us down into the depths of the earth. The flare extinguishes and I hear the sound of rushing water.

The lift screeches to an abrupt stop, and the doors rattle open, reverberating into the dark cavernous space ahead. Through cracks in the ceiling above, faint rays of moonlight shine through.

'Smells . . . old,' I say nervously.

Grey pulls another lever. It snaps and sparks and an electrical buzz travels through the cavern as rows of lights above us snap on, revealing a huge underground facility carved into the inside of a rocky hill. Amazed, I see a small indoor waterfall pouring into a spring; beside it an abandoned nineteenth century steam train. Old armour lines the walls; cobwebbed furniture stands covered in scrolls of blueprint designs and books. And there, hanging on the main wall, lit by a moonbeam, is a huge shimmering symbol depicting the eight phases of the moon's luna cycle.

'Welcome to the Luna Cove,' the professor announces.

I stand there in awe at the path laid before me.

'Here is where it begins. Here is where we shall make our stand. Here is where your training must begin if we are to liberate young Sketch. War is coming, Mr Jacobs, and we must be ready.'

We Are
Such Stuff
As Dreams
Are Made On

Step into the world
of
LUCID

Acknowledgements

My parents once told me that when I was two years old, I asked them if there was a door out of this world. Encouraged by this inquisitive spark, they nurtured my interests and opened the door, allowing me to begin my journey as a creative. So, first and foremost, I want to thank them both for their unwavering support, constant encouragement, faith, and love.

To my inner circle – my team, my 'day ones'. My rock and heartbeat'– Princess Johnson, thank you for walking this dream with me, holding down the fort and never allowing me to give up. Big sis and creative force of nature – Tonia Daley-Campbell, thank you for having my back; you did what you said you would do and here we are. Language extraordinaire – Matthew Lim, thank you for your time, and effort and for being my second eyes. The visionary – K.Francis, thank you for your words of knowledge, guidance and friendship.

I would also like to thank my incredible Agent Davinia Andrew- Lynch. Thank you for all your hard work, support, transparency and for seeing my vision. You are the best. May this be the first of many great adventures.

Special thank you to Emad Akhtar for seeing my potential and being a great guide and mentor. Your support, patience and knowledge have been priceless. I'm looking forward to switching on the bat signal once more. Also, a massive thank you to Millie Prestidge, Corinne Jean-Jacques and Jenna Petts for your fierce passion and support for *Lucid*, making sure no stone was unturned. Your commitment to this project always reignites my spark and reminds me of why I love to do what I do.

Finally, a huge heartfelt shout out and thank you to all the creatives who have contributed their time, talent, and effort to my journey over the years, from the early conception to this moment. I genuinely appreciate you all. Orique Johnson, Hayden Thomas, Elliot Martin, Pamela Cole-Hudson, Nick Toon, Victoria Tew, Mark Small, Joshua Bronks, Sole-Jo, Estelle South, James South, Rob Wilkinson and Alexandra Machinist.

God bless you all, peace x

Credits

Oraine Johnson and Gollancz would like to thank everyone at Orion who worked on the publication of *Lucid*.

Agent
Davinia Andrew-Lynch

Editorial
Emad Akhtar
Millie Prestidge

Copyeditor
Jamie Fox

Proofreader
Andy Ryan

Editorial Management
Jane Hughes
Charlie Panayiotou
Lucy Bilton
Patrice Nelson

Audio
Paul Stark
Louise Richardson
Georgina Cutler-Ross

Contracts
Rachel Monte
Ellie Bowker
Tabitha Gresty

Design
Tomás Almeida
Nick Shah
Deborah Francois
Helen Ewing

Photo Shoots & Image
Research
Natalie Dawkins

Finance
Nick Gibson
Jasdip Nandra
Sue Baker
Tom Costello

Inventory
Jo Jacobs
Dan Stevens

Production
Paul Hussey
Katie Horrocks

Marketing
Corinne Jean-Jacques
Louis Patel

Publicity
Jenna Petts

Sales
Dave Murphy
Victoria Laws
Esther Waters
Group Sales teams across Digital, Field, International and Non-Trade

Operations
Group Sales Operations team

BRINGING NEWS FROM OUR WORLDS TO YOURS . . .

Want hot-off-the-press info about the latest and greatest SFF releases?

Look no further than the Gollancz newsletter! Your one-stop shop for news, updates, discounts and exclusive giveaways.

Sign up now:

@gollancz